The

Replacement

A NOVEL

JASON PELLEGRINI

THE REPLACEMENT

This book is a work of fiction. Names, characters, places, and incidents are either products of the author's imagination or used fictitiously. Any references to real people, or real places are used fictitiously. Any resemblance to actual events, places, or persons, living or dead, is entirely coincidental.

First Edition January 2015
Printed in the United States of America.

Story by Jason Pellegrini

Cover Design by Natasha Fishman
www.tashatoons.com

Author Photograph by Lisa Bianco
www.lisabiancophotography.com

ISBN-13: 978-1503244405
ISBN-10: 1503244407

To my Godson, Bennett, who was born ten weeks early; weighing 1lb, 15oz, and underwent open-heart surgery at 9 weeks.

If you can go through all that, and come out the other end, there's no reason I should be afraid to give this a try.

PART I

CHAPTER 1

It was an average New York City day.

The usual congestion of traffic swamped the streets, and the sounds of horn blasts dominated the afternoon air. The sidewalks swelled with people of every race, color, and religion. Each coming and going; minding their own business, not talking to one another. Just trying to get where they need to be with minimal hassle. Still, somehow the streets boomed with the deafening sounds of activity. From below, sounds and vibrations of the constant running subway systems (along with the not-so-faint odor of urine) drifted up through the sewer grates as they pounded along from one stop to the next. There were street performers of all kinds, here and there. Hot dog vendors and McDonalds almost everywhere. Nothing—maybe except the traffic, which could only be described as sluggish, at best—moved slowly. Everything and everyone moved at a million miles an hour.

All in all, it was an average New York City day.

Patrick Sullivan sat in his police cruiser, enjoying the few precious moments of his ass-busting day where he could sit back, drown out the rest of the world, and enjoy a single cup of coffee.

Patrick had been a member of the New York City Police Department for six years. Every day, since his first day out of the academy, when he was placed in the dingiest and poorest parts of the five boroughs—where he often wondered if he was even going to make it through the day alive—he managed to find those few important minutes where he could, in peace, drink his coffee.

He took his daily Cup of Joe the same way every day; black as the devil's soul. He never added a single drop of milk or sugar, and he certainly never added any of that flavored creamer crap people were always pouring into their coffees these days. He simply drank it black.

As if the grimace look etched upon his face each time he took a sip wasn't enough, Patrick often admitted the taste of black coffee was vile.

"I don't think I'll ever get used to the taste of this crap," he often said.

He joked with friends and colleagues that it put hair on his chest and kept him more alert than that coffee diluted with milk, sugars and creamers. The truth was, Patrick had no idea why he drank his coffee that way. It had simply become habitual, and he was in too deep to break it now.

The familiar Manhattan sounds and smells (mostly unpleasant) filled his cruiser, but Patrick was completely oblivious to them all. At that moment, he and his black mistress were the only two things that existed in the universe.

He brought the cup to his lips, blew down on the steaming surface, and took a long sip. He cringed at the familiar detestable taste, and just like every sip that came before it, it was perfection.

Patrick Sullivan had only made it to his third sip before some moron on a bike crashed onto the hood of his cruiser.

Patrick was viciously ripped from his safe haven; dragged back to harsh reality, like an angel being expelled from heaven and thrown back to the plain of humanity, where it would be forced to walk among such ugliness after knowing such divine beauty.

To say he was not pleased by this sudden inconvenience would have been an understatement. This, like his distaste for black coffee, was obvious by the look on his face. With a stony stare, Patrick bore a hole through the young man. The bicyclist looked utterly petrified, and who could blame him? Not only did he crash his bike into a police cruiser, but the officer inside was obviously not very pleased about it.

"S-S-Sorry, sir," the young man managed to say in a broken, nervous voice. The actual words were drowned out by the loud city sounds—not to mention the screaming rage inside Patrick's head—but Patrick was able to read his lips just fine.

"It's fine," Patrick shouted through his cracked window. "Just move along."

Relieved that he hadn't gotten into any trouble, the bicyclist thanked Patrick with a wave and a smile, then rode away. Patrick watched him through the rearview mirror as he disappeared; sinking into the monstrous sea of Manhattan life.

Patrick tried to return to his cup of coffee and a few more moments of peace, but it was too late.

The moment had passed, and now he was really annoyed. He had told the poor young man, who obviously lost control of his bike trying to weave in and out of traffic (like every other bicyclist in the city) that his accident was fine, but it certainly, most definitely, without a shadow of a doubt, was *not* fine.

Not even a little bit.

That punk ass on his stupid bike had to crash into Patrick's car. Of all the cars in the city, it had to be Patrick's, and it had to be during the few minutes in the day where he was escaping the chaos that was reality. Accident or not, Patrick was pissed off.

Really pissed the fuck off.

What Patrick really wanted to do while that guy was leaning over the hood of the cruiser, his bike tangled between his legs, was get out of the car, get in the idiot's face, and tell him to watch where the fuck he was going. He wanted to tell the cretin that if he ever crashed into his car again—or into any car in the entire city of New York, for that matter—he was going to take out his gun, and bash his skull into pieces with the butt of it.

He wouldn't though. He needed to stay composed. Patrick could not allow his emotions to get the best of him.

Knowing it would be a lost cause, but still hanging onto that last shred of false hope, Patrick brought the cup back to his lips for one last effort to sink back into that familiar peace. Like he had expected, all the heavenly feelings that swig of coffee usually brought him were gone. It was nothing more than a cup of disgusting black mud.

The sudden sound of a long, drawn out horn blast from the car behind him caused Patrick to jump in his seat. This resulted in the remaining contents of his cup to spill all over his lap; staining his uniform and, more importantly, burning his legs.

That is it! Patrick screamed in his head. *Somebody is definitely getting pistol whipped.*

He unbuckled his seatbelt, and grabbed hold of the door handle.

"Temper, Temper, Patrick. You have to control that temper."

Patrick looked over to the passenger side of his car, and sitting there comfortably was Wallace Freewaters, better known to the community, as Baby Tooth.

Baby Tooth was the ringleader of a circus of drug dealers throughout all five boroughs. He was a tower of a

4

man. His hair was tied back in cornrows, and he was wearing a suit that easily cost two thousand dollars. He frequently lived by the motto 'Just because a nigga lives amongst the poor, doesn't mean that he can't dress with a 'lil class'.

The truth was, Wallace Freewaters didn't need to live in one of the worst neighborhoods in New York City. It was common knowledge that Baby Tooth had made quite the fortune for himself thanks to his not-so-legal business. The choice to live in the same rundown neighborhood he had grown up in, was his own. He always said with pride that it was a constant reminder of where he came from, and what he overcame.

That didn't mean that Baby Tooth didn't live like a man of class.

He spent most of his nights in some of New York City's finest clubs. He was there usually on business, supplying a celebrity in town with a weekend fix, or some hot shot business man with a sea of cocaine. However, sometimes he would go for entertainment purposes; never indulging in his own product, though. Baby Tooth may have been dumb enough to sell that shit, but he certainly wasn't dumb enough to snort it up his nose and rot the brains his dear 'ol mamma gave him, was another frequently cited line of his.

When he was home, which was mostly during the day to sleep, shower and get ready for a night of business, Baby Tooth's life was certainly not anything to complain about, despite the location in which he lived.

In addition to his closet full of suits that cost a minimum of two grand a pop, Wallace's what-should-have-been-a rat hole two room apartment was completely decked out with the most expensive, state-of-the-art home accessories; ranging from his flat screen LED HD television—complete with Blu-ray DVD player and angelic surround sound system—to his six hundred dollar blender that he had never once used.

Owning such elegant and expensive stuff didn't worry him, either. His belongings were as safe as a baby in its mother's warm embrace. No matter how desperate people in his neighborhood were for food or money, no one was stupid enough to steal from Baby Tooth.

"We all know what happens when you let your temper get the best of you, Patty Boy," Baby Tooth said, looking out the windshield at the bustling city life.

"No," Patrick argued. "*You* know what happens when I let my temper get the best of me."

"Very true," Baby Tooth's lips parted into a small smile. Patrick could see Wallace's baby tooth as his grin expanded.

After everything that happened to him that god damn baby tooth still didn't fall out. Patrick thought.

When Wallace Freewaters was a child, his upper lateral incisor on the left side of his mouth was impacted into his gums. As a result, it never descended, therefore his baby tooth never got pushed out. His parents, who were not blessed with the same fortune their son would one day have, did not have any dental coverage, nor could they afford (or cared enough) to have the problem fixed. He would go on into his teens and then his twenties with his incisor stuck up in his gums.

Over the years the tooth slowly loosened, but never fell out. When he had become wealthy enough to finally see a dentist, Wallace politely declined surgery to remove it, and have his adult tooth pulled down to take its rightful place amongst the rest of his teeth.

In truth, his baby tooth was Wallace Freewaters' trade mark.

In his teens, when he was just getting started in the business of drug dealing, serving as a mule, Wallace

THE REPLACEMENT

Freewaters had adopted the nickname 'Baby Tooth' from his higher-ups. When he reached his twenties, and started to make his way up the ranks, it became more than a simple nickname. It would become his modus operandi.

When a client of Baby Tooth had the misfortune of being short or late in payments, Wallace had a unique and torturous way of making sure this client never forgot his mistake.

After being beaten down, bloodied, and bruised for not being able to pay, Baby Tooth would then proceed to take a pair of pliers, and shove them into his clients' mouth. He would then proceed to latch onto the upper lateral incisor of the left side of their mouth, and rip it right out with one hard, fierce pull. From that point on, whenever they looked into the mirror and saw the empty space where a tooth once resided, they would always remember to pay Baby Tooth in full, and always remember to pay him on time.

In Patrick's head, the second horn blast sounded more like a nuclear explosion, and he once again gripped the handle to his car door; ready to get out and give this horn honking asshole a piece of his mind (maybe even a piece of the butt of his gun). He quickly regained his composure. He did not want Baby Tooth to see his temper get the best of him. He wouldn't give him the satisfaction.

It, however, was a little too obvious that Patrick was ready to unleash his fury at any moment. Even though he sat there, staring out the car window (he hadn't made any eye contact with Patrick since their little chat began), Baby Tooth knew that Patrick was moments away from flying off the hinge. Anger seemed to be seeping from his pores. Or maybe it was because Baby Tooth knew Patrick so well.

"Why you letting this dumb-ass nigga get to you so much?" Baby Tooth asked.

As he asked this considerably reasonable question, Wallace Freewaters continued to stare out into the street ahead. Patrick was glad they weren't making any eye contact. What he was even more grateful for was that Baby Tooth hadn't turned towards him. He knew what the other side of that face looked like. He had seen it plenty of times before; in pictures, in the paper, and in his head whenever he closed his eyes. He did not need to see it again.

"You act like this is the first dumb-ass mother fucker who ever got horn happy in Manhattan," Baby Tooth continued. "People act like this every God damn day. Shit, nigga, there's no reason to get yourself all worked up."

Despite his attempts to just ignore it, when the third horn blast came, Patrick could feel his grip on the car door handle tightening; digging in and making impressions in his palm.

"It just pisses me off that people think they can get away with being assholes, that's all," Patrick finally managed to say. He really wanted to tell Baby Tooth to fuck off and mind his business, but he was attempting (poorly, but still attempting) to practice control to the best of his abilities. "He can go around me, but he chooses to sit there and blast his horn."

To this, Baby Tooth responded with another toothy grin, and once again Patrick saw that baby tooth hanging there, long overstaying its welcome, between the central incisor and canine tooth.

"Very true," he eventually said. Patrick knew he had waited a few seconds before responding just so he could smile, and taunt Patrick with that freaking baby tooth. "But you can't go letting your temper get the best of you anymore. Like I said, we both know what happens when that temper of yours gets out of control. You got too many people relying on you now to let it happen again. You wouldn't want to let anyone down… not again."

Unfortunately, Baby Tooth was right. It was the last thing Patrick ever wanted to admit, but it was the simple truth of the matter. Patrick couldn't let history repeat itself. Not with this once-in-a-lifetime opportunity.

With the fourth ear shattering horn blast, however, everything Baby Tooth had said was erased and forgotten. Patrick pulled the handle, and gave the door a push. As his one foot hit the pavement outside, he felt Baby Tooth's hand grip his leg. It was ice cold.

So this is what death's cold touch feels like. Patrick thought, as the door sat ajar; resting on his leg.

"Don't do it, Patty Boy."

Patrick turned back towards Baby Tooth. He was still facing forward, but his eyes were now locked on Patrick. He really wished that Baby Tooth wouldn't look at him. As he made eye contact with NYC's biggest drug lord, he felt a mixture of emotions; ranging from anger, to sadness, to guilt. He tried (wished) to look away, but couldn't. Baby Tooth had Patrick paralyzed; trapped in his stare.

BEEEEEEEEEEEP!

Before Patrick could react, Baby Tooth tightened his grip, and Patrick felt a shiver rocket up his spinal cord; penetrating the depths his brain.

"You don't want to do this, Patrick. You know the consequences. Do you really think you can live with them again?"

"I did after that first time!" Patrick fired back. "I can do it again!"

"Do you really believe that? Shit, nigga, you're barely dealing with the first time. I mean, that's why I'm here, isn't it?"

"I don't know why you're here! I don't fucking want you here. So why don't you leave, God Dammit!"

BEEEEEEEEEEEP!

"Do I need to show you?" Baby Tooth asked. "Do you need to see it again, so you remember why you shouldn't to lose your temper?"

"I don't need to see anything!" Patrick shot back without a moment's hesitation. Of all the things in life he had become uncertain of, the one thing he knew for sure was that he did not want to see what Baby Tooth was about to show him.

BEEEEEEEEEEEP!

"I think you do."

"I see it every fucking day when I close my eyes. It haunts me when I sleep! Fuck, it haunts me when I'm awake. I can't escape it! So don't act like I've forgotten."

BEEEEEEEEEEEP!

"I am going to shoot this motherfucker in the face!" Patrick screamed.

"See what I mean, Patrick. Clearly you've left me with no choice."

"NO! DO NOT LOOK AT ME, WALLACE!"

It was too late, though. Baby Tooth, for the first time during their little chat, turned his head. Patrick tried to look away—he tried with every fiber of his very being—but he was locked into that stare.

The right side of Wallace 'Baby Tooth' Freewaters' face barely resembled that of a human being's. His temple was caved into his head, and his eye was swollen to the size of a golf ball—which was nothing compared to his broken cheek bone, which had blown up to the size of a baseball. The bridge of his nose was badly fractured, and a dark trickle of blood ran down from his right nostril. His jaw hung slacked on one side after being dislocated (not broken, but did it really matter at this point?). His bottom lip had ballooned up to about ten times its normal size, and his upper lip was split completely up the middle to his nose. When he smiled, most of the teeth on the right side of his mouth—excluding his lateral incisor and first molar—were knocked out or broken. There was a noticeable indentation at the top of his head where his skull had been crushed in, and blood stained and matted his cornrows.

The site of what was now Wallace 'Baby Tooth' Freewaters' face made Patrick sick. He felt his stomach contract, and he thought he was going to heave right there. Looking at Baby Tooth made him want to run away and hide. Like a dog hiding from a thunderstorm, Patrick wanted to curl up in a corner and whimper.

Unfortunately, the site of Baby Tooth's face wasn't enough to keep Patrick's anger at bay. Obviously, Baby Tooth thought it would—even Patrick thought the site of that mangled face would be enough to get him to gain control of himself—but with another blast of the horn from the car behind him, Patrick went ballistic.

He kicked the door open, and grabbed his gun from its holster.

"Patrick," Baby Tooth gripped Patrick's shoulder in attempt to restrain him.

BEEEEEEEEEEEP!

"Shut up, Baby Tooth."

BEEEEEEEEEEEP!

"Don't do it, Patrick. Let this mother fucker go. Just let it be."

BEEEEEEEEEEEP!

"You can't handle another one on your conscious. Isn't it bad enough you always have to sit in this car with me? Imagine what it would be like with someone else along for the ride."

"I told you to shut up"

BEEEEEEEEEEEP!

"FUCK YOU, ASSHOLE!!!!!!!!"

Patrick freed himself from Baby Tooth's chilling grasp, and shot out of his seat. He drew his gun, and pointed it at the skull of the person sitting in the car behind him.

There, sitting behind the wheel, a huge grin painted on his face, was Wallace 'Baby Tooth' Freewaters. His face was completely fine; exactly the way God had created it. The light of the afternoon sun seemed to be bouncing off his pearly white baby tooth. It was taunting Patrick. With an obnoxious grin painted on his face, Baby Tooth waved, and then, with both hands, slammed down on the horn.

BEEEEEEEEEEEEEEEEEEEEEEEEEP!!!!!!

Patrick released a deafening scream filled with rage, and he pulled the trigger.

The explosive sound of the bullet leaving the chamber was the last thing Patrick heard before shooting up out of bed; sweating profusely and breathing frantically. At first, he had no idea where he was. He then slowly became aware of his surroundings, and realized that he was home; in the comfort of his own bed.

The sounds of a car horn had transformed into the buzzing of an alarm clock. He reached over and grabbed the clock, which was sitting atop his nightstand. He fumbled blindly in the dark for the 'off' button. When he finally found it, the buzzing sound instantly ceased. Now, with the exception of his breathing, which was tapering towards calm and controlled, there were no other sounds in the room. He reminded himself that he was in his bed, which was in his room, which was located in his home. He was not sitting in an NYPD squad car with Wallace 'Baby Tooth' Freewaters. For that fact, Patrick couldn't be more grateful. It was all only a dream. He kept repeating that line over in his head. As if he dared to stop, it would become a reality.

He looked over at the alarm clock. It was time for Patrick to wake up.

CHAPTER 2

Patrick Sullivan sat up in his bed; cold beads of sweat pooling on his forehead and dripping down his back. He was as still as the dead; staring down into his lap.

To the average bystander, Patrick would seem as if his stare was one of complete emptiness; as if he was trapped within the depths of boundless reverie. His face was void of all emotion. He resembled a person who was in a state of shock. An explosion could have occurred in the same room—in the same bed—and he wouldn't have flinched or even heard it. It was as if the lights were on but nobody was home. This, however, was not the case.

In fact, it was the complete opposite.

The reason for Patrick's blank stare was that he was trying to expel, from his brain, the events of the dream he just awoken from. He wanted so badly for it to turn out like most other dreams; the ones you have already forgotten by the time you've climbed out of bed. This dream, however, remained stubbornly stagnant. Patrick had been sitting in his bed for five long minutes, which seemed equivalent to a single eternity, and he still remembered every detail. Turns out, only the superb dreams where he was having sex with Jennifer Lawrence were the ones he ended up forgetting completely.

This hadn't been the first time he dreamt about Baby Tooth, but it had been the first dream in quite a while—four months; maybe more.

Patrick finally gave up, and unwillingly welcomed defeat. The dream wasn't going to bury itself in his unconscious, and he wondered why he even had tried. Baby Tooth dreams had always had an unsavory knack for sticking around for weeks, even months. He let out a sigh—his first movement since sitting up—flicked on the lamp, and threw the blanket off of him.

That's when Patrick noticed the beautiful woman lying on the opposing side of the bed; peacefully sleeping next to him. How he could have possibly forgotten about her presence, he had no clue. His nightmare must have really irked him if he was able to forget that there was a woman so perfect, she could only exist in the words of a love song, sleeping next to him.

He stared down at her for a few moments before getting out of bed. He was infatuated with her beauty. Even as she lay there, asleep on her side, Patrick couldn't recall anything more exquisite. She wore a tiny pair of red boy shorts that exposed the bottom of her shapely back side, and a tight white tank top that clung to her flat stomach and perfect breasts. Her brunette hair rested on her cheek; hiding most of her face, but it did not mask its sublimity. He couldn't remember, not once in his entire life, seeing something so incredible. He brushed the hair away from her face, and kissed her softly on the cheek. She gave a faint smile at the feel of his lips upon her gentle skin, but did not wake. He covered her with the blanket over her, and got out of bed.

He stood at the foot of his bed, taking in the suburban sounds that flowed in from outside his window. Four-thirty in the morning here was, on all counts, completely different from where he had lived in the city. Instead of the sounds of young teenagers staying out much too late; causing havoc, getting high, or something equally distasteful, he heard birds chirping in the bushes below his window. They were singing their songs; welcoming the impending sun. Patrick could hear the sounds of a train traveling through the silent morning air as it pulled into the Wantagh station a few miles away. It replaced the unwelcoming sounds of cars backfiring and horns blasting. When he would wake up in his old apartment, Patrick knew there were already thousands of people in the city who were already up and living their busy lives. Now, as he stood in the master bedroom of his new house, he felt like he was the only person in the world.

He had gone from living in a one bedroom apartment in a horrifically poor neighborhood to living the American dream. His life was good now, but it hadn't always been. For the longest time, it seemed like he was trapped in a deep hole (more like a bottomless pit) that there was no escape from. Everything in his life had spiraled out of control all at once. He had believed that he truly wrecked everything beyond reconstruction, and would never be happy again. Sometimes miracles happen, though, and things changed. That part of his life was over, and buried in the past.

At least, he had hoped.

As Patrick donned a pair of basketball shorts and a white t-shirt, and left the room, the dream of Baby Tooth lingered in the back of his mind; tainting the pleasant thoughts of his new life.

He grabbed his iPod from the kitchen counter, where it had been charging, and made his way down to the basement. There, he would pop in his earbuds and press play. He would stretch thoroughly before putting on his running shoes and heading out for his morning run. Working out was something Patrick tried very hard to keep up with on a daily basis. Every morning, he would get up before the sun did, drown out the rest of the world through his music (mostly 90s alternative and grunge), and do a solid hour of cardio. In the evenings, he would do a plethora of weight training.

As Patrick was stretching the muscles in his legs to physically prepare himself for his morning jog, he was also mentally preparing himself for the day ahead of him. He had once considered that part of his life—law enforcement—to be over, but as it turned out, fate had other plans for Patrick Sullivan. He had gone through the academy once before—with New York City—so he knew what to expect, and it had been smooth sailing, so far. Yet, he still found himself getting nervous each morning.

Once he felt that all his muscles had all been sufficiently stretched, Patrick headed back upstairs, where he would set out for his morning jog.

It was still dark when Patrick stepped outside, but there was a strong sense of the oncoming morning in the air. He jogged along the streets, listening to bands he had grown up on (Nirvana, Alice in Chains, Bush and Pearl Jam), admiring the beautiful suburban houses of Levittown. At one point in time, each house looking exactly alike; all sitting on small plots of land right next to one another. Now, they all looked uniquely different from each other with all the renovations done since the town was first established after the Second World War. There were now only a few original Levitt houses left, which he would spontaneously spot while driving or jogging around town. His own home wasn't an original Levitt house. Patrick didn't think he could live without a basement, which was something all Levittown houses lacked. His house had originally been a farm house from back when this suburban town was nothing but potato fields.

THE REPLACEMENT

He kept a steady pace; controlling his breath, as he ran down the winding streets. Still, after a month and a half, he found himself getting lost in the crazy, curving Levittown roads. He would turn down one street, thinking it would lead him one place, and find himself somewhere completely different. He sometimes wondered if the people who built the town were drunk when they plotted the streets. He knew that even after living there for twenty years, he would *not* surprisingly find himself on streets he didn't even know existed.

When he had finished running the route he had mapped out for himself so not to get lost in the morning hours, he stood at the foot of his walkway; staring in awe at his beautiful new home. It really was a dream come true. Patrick Sullivan never thought he'd be where he was at that exact moment in his life.

He allowed himself a few minutes to soak it all up. Not just his new home, but the simple things he had never appreciated before; the dew on his front lawn that should have been frozen over if not for the abnormally warm weather they were having, the fall breeze that hit his sweaty skin; sending goose bumps up and down his arms. It was hardly believable that the man standing in front of his home now was the same man who woke up terrified only two hours prior.

It was not long after six in the morning when Patrick walked back inside his house. The sky over Long Island began to lighten, and over the course of the next half hour, a brand new day would dawn. Soon, the sun would be completely up, and daylight would stake its claim over the Eastern Coast. Parents all over would be attempting—likely failing miserably—to wake up their adolescent teenagers; making sure they were up and getting ready for school. Uneager sons and daughters would try their hardest to ignore their parents pestering demands in order to catch a few more moments of precious sleep. Some would fake sick, some would swear before almighty God that they were awake, only to face-plant their pillows moments later. Some people would be getting ready for work, while others would already be there. Morning traffic on the Long Island parkways would start to become more congested as the minutes crept towards nine o'clock.

Patrick sat in his kitchen eating a carb filled bowl of oatmeal with flax seed. As he ate, his thoughts couldn't help from traveling back to his good pal, Baby Tooth. He thought he was done beating himself up over the infamous New York City drug lord and all that had gone down almost one year ago.

Apparently Patrick was wrong, because, here he was, having dreams about him again, and thinking about him over his morning cereal.

Would Baby Tooth ever truly let him be? He had promised Patrick a few months back that he would, but that turned out to be a lie.

Regardless, Patrick wanted him gone. He didn't want to go the rest of his life seeing that disfigured face whenever he slept.

He couldn't sit there anymore; fixating on the subconscious that he couldn't control. He had to wash the sweat and stink off of him, and get his day going. He slid his chair out from under the table, walked over to the sink, and washed his bowl before heading towards the bathroom.

He plugged his iPod into the little radio he had in his bathroom, and turned up the volume. Patrick hoped the sounds of nineties grunge and metal would drive away the thoughts of his least favorite person.

As shuffle switched from Soundgarden to Metallica's rendition of Bob Seger's *Turn the Page*, Patrick reached through the shower door, and turned the volume to its max.

THE REPLACEMENT

By the time the drums and bass had joined the guitars at the top of the second verse, Patrick was singing along with James Hetfield as he shampooed his hair. He was completely unaware to the bathroom door slowly easing open.

Circumstances couldn't have been more perfect. The sound of running water over Patrick's ears combined with the blaring music completely drowned out the sound of his shower door carefully being slid open. With his eyes squeezed shut as he rinsed the suds from his hair, he was completely blind to the hand creeping into the steamy shower; reaching for his shoulder.

As he ran his fingers through his hair for one final rinse, Patrick felt smooth fingertips on his skin.

He jumped at the completely unexpected touch of another person's fingertips on his shoulder. For a fraction of a second his fears took hold of him, and Patrick thought it was Baby Tooth grabbing at him. Basic rationalization quickly ruled that out though. This was reality; not a dream, and Baby Tooth could not get to him here in the real world.

Except that wasn't entirely true.

Even though he could not physically take hold of him, Baby Tooth certainly had quite the grip on Patrick's mind.

Knowing he wouldn't see the pummeled face of Wallace Freewaters, Patrick opened his eyes to the pleasant sight of his wife, Claire.

The brown hair that had covered her face as she slept was now resting on her shoulders. She was no longer wearing a pair of shorts or the tight tank she had been sleeping in. Claire was wearing absolutely nothing.

Patrick stood there, staring in awe at his naked wife—her perfectly sized breasts, her soft skin, and her flat stomach, which he loved to kiss before they made love. The very site of her expelled all negative thoughts he had

19

been having that morning. He now only had one thought racing through his mind as he felt his penis hardening.

"See something you like, Mr. Sullivan?" Claire asked as she, flirtingly, ran her hands down her side. She had a seductive smile on her face that made him want to jump out of the shower, and have her right there on the bathroom floor. However, before Patrick could act on his primal instincts, Claire climbed into the shower to join him. "You're looking a little stressed, baby. Is there anything I can do to help out with that?"

"Uh-huh," was all Patrick could articulate as a response. He was finding it very hard to find words at the moment.

"Well," Claire said; kissing her husband's neck; knowing full well it drove him crazy. "Let's see if I can guess how."

She moved away from his neck, and kissed her way past his chest and down to his stomach. She looked up at him with those beautiful eyes before slowly making her way down to her knees.

Patrick had frequently heard, from one source or the other, once you got married, the sex becomes mundane. Even on the night of his bachelor party, friends of his who had been married for years joked that after his and Claire's honeymoon, the blowjobs were over, and there was nothing left for him but the missionary position until the day his dick decided to just give up.

He and Claire, however, proved this theory to be very wrong. They were married now for three years, and the sex had become anything but boring. On the contrary, as their relationship evolved, the sex intensified and only got better.

For one thing, the blowjobs never stopped, and neither did Patrick's reciprocation of the favor. They were constantly finding new, exciting places to have at each other, whether on their new couch, the kitchen counters and table, and both, washer and dryer. They had even done it in the backyard in broad daylight; not even considering (or caring) that someone could possibly see them. The sex was always sporadic, and always mind-blowing.

Now, as Claire so excellently disproved the theory that blowjobs ended after marriage, Patrick felt his penis begin to throb as orgasm grew nearer. He gripped the bar on the shower door, and let out a pleasurable moan as he reached climax.

"Stress free now, baby?" Claire asked as she got to her feet.

"I definitely am," Patrick assured his wife.

"Good. I'm glad." She gave him a quick peck on the cheek. "Now get out of here, stud. I need to shower."

"Oh, I see how it is," Patrick rebutted. "No cuddle time afterwards. You must be the all business type?"

"You bet your butt. Just leave the money on the kitchen counter before you leave, or I'll have to send my pimp after you."

"Yes, ma'am."

Patrick stepped out of the shower, and dried himself off. He headed back to the bedroom to get dressed.

He now stood in a room with walls painted powder blue. Large fluffy clouds crowded the ceiling; mimicking the sky of a gentle spring day. Scattered along the four walls were tall trees with luscious red apples dangling from their thick branches; creating the scene of an enchanted forest. Birds flew over the green blades of grass where a deer had stopped to nibble upon an apple that had fallen from one of the grand trees. Above a tiny bed placed in the far corner of the room that Patrick now stood over, were the letters A, B, and C. They were made from a blue and white gingham patterned fabric, and stuffed with white cotton. Claire had made them as one of her projects when she was so pregnant that she refused to move unless it was absolutely necessary. It was indeed a very nice room for a toddler, and he was proud of himself and Claire for putting it together.

At this particular moment, the world ceased to exist. There were no such things as disfigured drug lords with silly nicknames. No such thing as new job jitters. There was only him and his two year old son, Connor.

Patrick stared at his son; completely content. Connor lay on his stomach; his legs sprawled out. His thumb rested on his bottom lip from when it had fallen out of his mouth while he slept. He had the softest skin and finest blonde hair, which he had inherited from Patrick's mother. Under those closed lids were big blue eyes, which he got from Claire. Like his mother's eyes, they were the kind you couldn't resist falling in love with once they had you locked into a stare. When he was awake, he had a personality that matched his physical beauty. Again, he took after his mother in that perspective. Once Connor warmed up to someone, which didn't take long, he was the most lively and entertaining child to be around. Everyone loved him within minutes of knowing him. Just like Claire.

He heard Claire enter the room, but did not turn to acknowledge her presence. He didn't want to stop looking at his son. Just like he was on the day Connor had been born, Patrick was hypnotized by his perfection. He had held this brand new human being, who was completely void of flaw and knew nothing of wickedness, and was overcome by a feeling of intense adulation. Connor was made up of nothing but pure innocence, and as Patrick held his newborn son for the first time, he knew right then that nothing else mattered. His sole purpose on this Earth was to keep his family safe.

Claire slipped her arms around Patrick's waist. He felt her warm cheek pressed against his back as she hugged him. He locked his fingers with hers, and squeezed gently.

The moment was perfect. It was the kind of moment you never wanted to end.

"He's beautiful," Claire said.

"He sure is."

He took one last long look at his son; letting the love that seemed to be resonating off his little body seep in, and turned to Claire. She was wearing her robe and a towel around her head. Even then, she was the most attractive woman in the world. It was no contest. He leaned in, and gave her a long kiss on the lips.

Now, four years after their first kiss, Patrick still got the feeling of butterflies in his stomach when their lips met. Some people went their whole lives without ever knowing that feeling (true love), but he was fortunate enough to experience it every day.

"I love you, Claire Sullivan," he said once their lips parted.

"I love you, too, Patrick Sullivan," she said; smiling. "Or should I say Officer Sullivan? Oops! I mean Detective Sullivan!"

"Not just yet. I'll be detective in a few months—once I go through the academy again—but I have to admit; it definitely has a nice ring to it."

And it did.

As much as Patrick had wanted to bury his career in law enforcement in the past, his pending new job title gave him a sense of honor and prestige. He could do some real good with this job, and make an amends for the mistakes of his past.

Claire took two steps back, and looked her husband up and down.

"You're definitely one handsome man," she said; adding a nod of approval.

"Why, thank you, ma'am. You're not too bad yourself."

He leaned over Connor's bed, and kissed his little forehead. He put his arm around Claire, gave her one to match. Arm in arm; the happy couple walked out of the room.

The two ate breakfast in their newly renovated kitchen. They had moved into a house that probably hadn't had any major upgrades since Reagan was shot. The carpets were old and worn down. The whole house needed a good paint job. Both, kitchen and bathroom looked incredibly tacky, and that was just the inside. On the outside, the house needed to be sided, and the gutters should have been replaced at least a decade ago.

The couple had moved into a fixer-upper. With the help of some old cop friends, Patrick had taken it upon himself to do all the necessary repairs. The end result was nothing short of gratifying.

Patrick leaned against the counter, eating a piece of dry toast with his usual morning cup of [black] coffee. He was reading the sports section, enjoying the recent streak the New York Jets had been on. Claire was sitting at the kitchen table. She was eating the same breakfast that she ate every morning; a grapefruit, followed by a yogurt (today it was blueberry). She was skimming the penny saver for some deals and coupons.

"So, seriously; Patrick, are you nervous at all?" she asked.

"You know… I was, but not so much anymore," he replied before taking a sip from his mug.

This statement was the truth. Maybe it was their moment in the nursery, maybe it was the blowjob in the shower— probably a little bit of both—but the fear and worries that had been weighing down on him ever since he decided to return to his former career seemed to have drifted away.

"Good, because I know you are going to be an excellent detective."

"Yeah... because I made such an excellent police officer." His sarcasm was apparent.

Claire stopped looking through the paper. She got up from her seat, walked over to Patrick, and looked him dead in the eyes, which he knew meant to pay attention.

"Patrick, you were an excellent police officer. Don't you dare think, otherwise!"

"Sometimes I can't help it. Things didn't exactly end well the last time"

"You can't let isolated incidents, like Wallace Freewaters,"—Claire never referred to him as Baby Tooth—"define you as a whole. Not as a police officer, and certainly not as a human being."

"It's a pretty big isolated incident, Claire."

She placed her palm on the apple of his cheeks. "You are a good person, Patrick. The greatest person I have ever known—that goes without question—and you are going to be a great cop, and an even better homicide detective. I know you are going to do a lot of good."

She leaned in and kissed him. He loved her so much in that moment. Truth was, he loved her in every moment; each one a different reason than the last. He knew she would never just say something simply because she felt obligated to as his wife. Claire spoke what she believed. She always had. Even on the day they met. If she told Patrick she thought he was going to be a great detective, it was because she truly believed it.

"Thank you, babe. That really means a lot."

He glimpsed over at the clock. He needed to finish getting ready, and Claire needed to leave to drop Connor off at daycare before heading to work, herself.

As he was dumping what remained of his coffee down the drain, the house phone rang. Claire walked over, and answered. After greeting the person on the other end and asking who was calling, she covered the mouth piece, and told Patrick, in a low voice, an Officer Summers from the 8th precinct was on the phone.

"Gimme," he mouthed; taking the phone from her. "Hello, this is Patrick Sullivan."

"Hello, Detective Sullivan, this is Officer Summers calling from the 8th precinct. How are you this morning?"

Patrick told her he was good, and asked how she was; exchanging all the appropriate pleasantries. What he really wanted was to get past those as quickly as possible, and get down to real meaning of this sudden phone call.

"I know you've been going through the academy; preparing for your new position with us here," she said; finally getting down to business. "but there's been a sudden change in plans, and you are unofficially being pushed through the academy. You are to report directly to the field; starting today."

Change in plans? Pushed through the academy? Reporting directly to the field?

Patrick had so many questions, he didn't know which one he should ask first. This was absolutely unheard of.

"I'm sorry," Patrick said; finally able to somewhat gather his thoughts. "I'm just a bit confused to what exactly is going on. I'm to report to the field? I haven't even made it half way through the academy."

"I know it's a lot all at once, and I apologize for that. We don't usually do this, but there's been a murder, and you've been requested by the onsite detectives. It's been approved by the captain, and you're to report directly to the scene."

This whole thing was just bizarre. In his six years on the force, Patrick had never heard of anything remotely like it. That was because it simply was not allowed. People just don't skip the academy. It didn't matter if he had police background, and had already gone through it before with New York City. It was just something that did not happen.

He knew what he had heard, though. He wondered what type of murder could merit this strange occurrence. As exciting as getting out of repeating the academy sounded, Patrick found himself suddenly petrified of being thrown right into action.

"What address am I to report to?" he asked; pushing aside the other hundred things now racing through his mind. He signaled to Claire for a pen and pad.

"96 Merry Way Drive in Seaford. Do you know where that is, detective?"

"I have a GPS. I'll have no problem finding it," he assured Officer Summers; jotting down the address.

"Okay, when you get there identify yourself to an officer, and request to see Detective Murphy. He will have your gun and credentials with him, and he will brief you on the situation so far."

"Okay, thank you, officer."

"You are welcome. When you return from the field, you are to report to me immediately. There's some paperwork I'm going to need you to fill out.

When he hung up, Claire inquired about the nature of the phone call. Her reaction was the same as Patrick's; confusion.

"Well, be careful, Patrick."

"I will," he promised Claire.

He kissed her goodbye—she and Connor would already be gone by the time he was ready to leave the house—and ran up the stairs to get dressed.

He dressed quickly in clothes he didn't think he'd be wearing for at least another few months, and left the house. In his car, he typed the address Officer Summers had given him into the GPS, and backed out of his driveway.

The chain of events that would change the life of Patrick Sullivan forever were about to begin.

CHAPTER 3

"Make your next left, and destination will be on the left," the voice on Patrick's GPS told him.

On the car ride over to 96 Merry Way Drive, nervousness continued to creep up on Patrick. As his destination drew nearer, he began to think that perhaps he was about to get himself in too deep with something he wasn't fully prepared for. He had been pulled from the academy months before he was supposed to, and now he was about to become part of an active murder investigation. He found himself feeling underprepared and a bit overwhelmed, and it hadn't even started.

But maybe he was just being too hard on himself.

After all, Claire believed in him. She had told him so. She thought Patrick would be a great detective, and here was his chance to prove her right. Claire was always right. She always was; ever since the first day they met on the roof top of her Brooklyn apartment building.

Once he put his mind to ease on the matter of law enforcement competency, Patrick's thoughts drifted to memories of the past year of his life. In the few minutes that remained of his drive, he recalled the intense rollercoaster ride he and his family had endured.

Nine months ago (almost to the day) Patrick Sullivan decided to resign from the New York City Police

Department to pursue his interest in architecture. That was at least what he and Claire had told everybody.

Truth was, Patrick had no interest in designing buildings, but there was no way people could know the truth behind his leaving the NYPD. Only he, Claire and his father—who if hadn't been informed by Patrick, would have found out from his department connections, anyway—were the only people who knew the truth.

It was hard leaving the force. True, the only reason he had become a cop was because his father had expected it of him, but Patrick had grown to love the job, and like all things in this world we fall in love with, it hurts when we are forced to let them go. Patrick didn't have a choice, though. He couldn't stay on. Not after what had happened.

Breaking the news to his father was no walk in the park, but telling Claire broke his heart. She was having a hard enough time as it was finding a teaching job, but now Patrick, who was their only source of income, was also without a job.

She had been upset about Patrick having to leave the force, but what really devastated her were the circumstances surrounding his departure. Still, despite the shock that her husband was capable of doing such things, Claire vowed to stick it out, and stand by her husband.

"For richer or for poorer," she said; quoting the infamous line often uttered during wedding vows.

Once they both decided that nothing could tear their loving family unit apart, the terrifying reality that they were both unemployed and had little in the form of savings quickly sank in. They desperately needed money to get by.

As if admitting the truth to his father wasn't hard enough, Patrick now had to swallow his pride, and ask his parents for a loan to keep his family afloat until he found employment. That was something he did not want to do, but there was no choice in the matter. He and Claire had an eighteen month old to provide for, and turning to Claire's parents for financial aid was not an option. He wouldn't allow it. On that matter, he remained stern. Claire's father was never fond of Patrick—hate would be a more suitable adjective to describe his feelings towards his son-in-law—and Patrick refused to admit to his father-in-law that he was in any sort of financial peril. He would not take a single cent from the hand of that miserable man, and risk having to listen to a long drawn out speech on how Patrick had failed his wife and son.

So Patrick would suck it up, and ask his father for the money he needed. Not for himself, but for Claire and Connor. He would throw himself at the mercy of Edward Sullivan for them.

Patrick received the money he requested—enough to hold them over for a year—and vowed to pay back every last cent borrowed.

Despite promising himself he would be back on his feet and have the remainder of the loan returned to his father by the six month mark, Patrick found himself four months later still without a job. He had applied for every position he could possibly think of, and couldn't land one. He couldn't even land himself a gig doing security, and they were always looking to employ former cops. It seemed as if there was absolutely nothing out there for Patrick Sullivan.

As if his terrible luck finding employment wasn't enough to quell his spirits, Patrick's nightmares had begun. Every night he would see the brutalized face of Wallace 'Baby Tooth' Freewaters. Like a small child, Patrick would wake up petrified; afraid that Baby Tooth would jump out of his closet or spring through his window like some creature of the night; seeking his revenge for what Patrick had done.

THE REPLACEMENT

The dreams had gotten so bad that Patrick had found himself panic-stricken in the middle of the day. Every time he passed a dark alleyway, he braced himself; expecting Baby Tooth to jump out, and snatch him up into the darkness.

In late June of that year, their financial situation took an upward turn when Claire secured a job with the Bellmore school district (a few towns over from where the Sullivan's currently resided) as a kindergarten teacher, and would be starting that September. It was only half a solution, but it unquestionably lifted a significant weight off both of their shoulders.

While attending a Fourth of July barbeque with his family, Patrick was approached by his friend and former colleague, Joey Vanzetti. He and Joey had grown up together, had joined the force, and gone through the academy together, and when Joey learned that his lifelong friend had fallen on hard times, he decided he needed to do what he could to help.

He came to Patrick with some inside information on a job offer that was immediately deemed too good to be true.

Over on Long Island, an opening in the Nassau County Police Department's homicide unit had recently become available. One of their finest, most respected detectives was retiring at the end of the year, and they were interviewing for his replacement.

Joey told Patrick he could have his father, who was a captain with the NYPD, place a phone call to Nassau County, and make sure Patrick got in for an interview.

Despite his less than slim chances of actually getting the job, Patrick couldn't pass up this once-in-a-lifetime opportunity. He told his friend to place the call to his father, and Joey did just that. The very next morning, Patrick received a phone call from the Nassau County

Police Department to schedule a meeting between him and their captain.

The night before his big interview, Patrick dreamt of Baby Tooth yet again. It would be the last time Baby Tooth visited him. That was, until the morning Patrick would become Detective Sullivan.

In the dream, they were sitting on a bench in Central Park. It was a clear summer day. Kids were playing with one another on the playground. Couples were having afternoon picnics, and enjoying quaint carriage rides together. Dogs chased Frisbees; catching them, and bringing them back to their impressed masters.

The two watched, in silence, this picture perfect scene unfold before them. When Baby Tooth finally decided to speak, he reminded Patrick of how important this meeting was to the survival of his family. He let Patrick know how proud he would be if he got the job. Patrick responded by informing Baby Tooth, quite bluntly, he didn't give two shits if he made Baby Tooth proud or not. The only person he wanted to make proud was Claire. He wanted his wife to swell with pride; knowing her husband had done right by his family, despite what he had done to let them down.

He then did something he had never been able to do in life or any of his dreams. He put his anger and all-encompassing hatred for Baby Tooth aside, and confided in him about how scared he was that he would fail his family. He didn't mean to, but it came pouring out, like flesh torn open by a carving knife.

That was when Baby Tooth struck a deal with Patrick.

If Patrick went into that interview and walked out the other end with a new job, Baby Tooth would leave him alone. He would never again be visited by that mangled drug lord. He would never be forced to stare at that God forsaken baby tooth, and have an unnamable enmity boil up inside of him. Patrick Sullivan would be ridden of

Wallace Freewaters once and for all, and that was a deal too good to pass up.

The next day, he walked into that interview a man with a mission. One where he would be the husband and father that he was destined to be, and just as importantly, it was a mission to rid himself of the man who had ruined his entire life up until that point.

When the meeting had concluded, Patrick's adrenaline was pumping so hard, he couldn't recall a single word exchanged in the entire hour he was there. Still, he left feeling confident. More confident than he had felt in months.

Not even two weeks later, Patrick received a phone call informing him he would be the new homicide detective for the Nassau County Police Department. His training would begin that September.

That night he told Claire the good news over a surprise candlelit dinner that had taken him all afternoon and two attempts to prepare.

The reality that their dire financial peril was now ending brought tears of joy and relief to both their eyes.

Later on, while lying in bed together after making love, the happily married couple decided it would be best to move out of their crappy Burroughs apartment, and into a suburban house on Long Island. After all, they now had steady jobs out there. They fell in love with the very first house they saw, and with his blessing; they used what remained of Patrick's father's loan for the down payment on their brand new home.

Patrick turned onto Merry Way Drive, and parked across the street from the house Officer Summers had given him the address to.

It was a quaint little white house with green shutters, a peaceful lawn, and a cute picket fence. From where Patrick was sitting, it looked like a typical suburban home; picture perfect. Then he took notice of the small group of people that had gathered on the sidewalk. They stood on one side of yellow police tape that read: '**CRIME SCENE: DO NOT CROSS**'. On the opposite side of the tape, stood a handful of uniformed Nassau County police officers. Parked at the curb were two patrol vehicles, and an unmarked black Lincoln Townscar. An ambulance was parked in the driveway.

The sense of pleasant suburbia had now withered away. Patrick was looking at a crime scene.

"Here we go," he told himself before opening the car door.

He was nervous. No question there. His heart was pumping hard against his chest, and he could feel his pulse throbbing in his neck. Even though he had seen numerous crime scenes while with the NYPD, Patrick was about to enter his first as a Homicide Detective. There was a monumental difference between the two. He had spent months attempting to mentally prepare himself for this job, but now he found himself completely unprepared to enter the unknown.

Regardless, he took a deep breath, opened the car door, and crossed the street.

"I'm Detective Sullivan," Patrick told the officer standing opposite him, once he made his way through the small crowd. "I was told to ask for Detective Murphy."

"May I see some identification, sir?"

"I wasn't issued any credentials. I was told I would receive them when I arrived."

For a moment, Patrick feared no one had informed the officers standing the perimeter that he would be coming, and that he wouldn't have the proper identification. This officer probably thought he was some crazy person; dumb enough to try and impersonate a detective to sneak a peek at a murder scene.

"Your license will do just fine."

Patrick produced his driver's license, and handed it to the officer. He examined the license then looked at Patrick. He proceeded to repeat the process until he felt certain Patrick was who he claimed to be.

"My apologies, detective," the officer finally said; handing Patrick back his I.D. "I'm sure you understand. If you could hold on for just a moment, I will get Detective Murphy."

"No problem" Patrick said; stepping under the yellow tape to the opposite side. There, he stood; patiently waiting. A few minutes later, the officer returned; followed by who Patrick could only assume was Detective Murphy.

Detective Murphy was a man nearing the age of retirement, and it showed. He was short in height, and greater in weight; putting on those unwanted pounds that comes with the crashing of one's metabolism as they age. He was balding, and what was left of his hair had gone almost completely grey. He had little neck, and it looked to Patrick as if his head was merely resting upon his shoulders.

"Detective Sullivan," he greeted Patrick; extending his hand. "I'm Detective Murphy."

When he was younger, Patrick's late grandfather had always said you could size up any man's confidence based only on his handshake. By Detective Murphy's shake, he was a confident man.

"It's nice to meet you, Detective Murphy," Patrick said. "I just wish they could be under better circumstances."

"You and me, both," Detective Murphy said; breaking their handshake. "You ready to get right down to business?"

"I hope so," Patrick answered. The tone he used may had been one of half joking, but the words that passed his lips were dead serious.

"You better be. Here are your credentials, and service pistol." Detective Murphy handed Patrick his badge and gun (a police issue Glock .19). "This way, please, detective."

Patrick walked side-by-side with Detective Murphy towards the house. As they walked, he noticed the garden in the front yard; running along the foundation of the house. Most of it had withered away due to the time of year, but he could tell that it was well tended and cared for in the spring and summer months. Sticking out of the dirt was a little white sign that had a pink and yellow flowers painted along the border. It read, in cursive *Estelle's Garden*.

Patrick knew that murder victims were supposed to remain just that; murder victims. It was a big no-no for an investigating officer to get emotionally attached to their victims or case, but, already, he could see how hard that would be when you looked around a person's home, and saw the many things—like a garden that would never be tended to again—that made them more than just a lifeless body, or a nameless face.

"Our victims are an elderly couple," Murphy told Patrick; briefing him as they walked to the house. "Their names are Arthur and Estelle Ramsey. They were discovered this morning by seventeen year old Samantha Melina. She's in the ambulance right now being looked at by paramedics." He pointed to the ambulance parked in the driveway. The doors were closed but Patrick could see people inside. "The onsite therapist is in there with her. The girl seems pretty shook up, and, quite frankly, I don't blame her after what she saw. We couldn't get much out of her except for her name, and the names of the victims. She's said a few things here and there, but nothing very coherent. She might as well have been speaking gibberish."

"What was she doing here?" Patrick asked.

"We're assuming she was dropping off some groceries. She hasn't been able to tell us that much, but there was a bag on the kitchen table filled with fresh milk, eggs, a canister filled with coffee grains, and three days' worth of Newsday's."

"And what about the victims?"

To this question, Detective Murphy raised his eyebrows, as if saying 'You aren't going to believe this…'

"I think you better come in and see for yourself, Detective Sullivan. But I warn you… it is like nothing you could possibly begin to imagine."

Detective Murphy said no more. He pulled open the door; allowing Patrick to enter the house.

The kitchen, where they stood upon entering the home, was dimly lit. The shades were drawn, and the only sunlight that entered was whatever had managed to sneak around the edges. The bag of groceries Murphy had mentioned was on the kitchen table; its contents emptied out onto the table. There was a distinct odor in the air. It was an odor that Patrick had never been able to mistake for anything else since the first time it hit his nose. It was the smell of death and decay.

In his first year out of the academy, Patrick was dispatched to an abandoned building. There had been numerous phone calls from neighbors about the unbearable smell coming from the boarded up building. What he found when he arrived were two bodies deep within the stages of decomposition. The smell of muscle and skin deterioration mixed with the release of bodily gases and fluids was so putrid that Patrick had to fight the continuous urge to throw up with everything he could muster. From that day on that smell stayed with him. If he had lived to see a hundred and twenty years on this planet, and had gone completely senile; he still would remember that fetid stink of death.

"The victims are in the den," Murphy said. "If you would follow me, please, detective."

Patrick followed Detective Murphy down a small hallway into a living/dining room. The same dismal lighting that lit the kitchen lit this room, as well. The furniture was very old. It looked as if someone in this household liked to buy antique furniture, and restore it. This sight only brought the victims even more to life. If what he had already seen wasn't enough to make him feel terrible about the abrupt ending to the lives of the two victims, what he saw next sealed that deal.

The far wall of the room was covered with portraits. They descended by generation; forming a family tree of photos. At the top, closest to the ceiling, was a black and white photograph. The couple in the picture was a very young, very happy couple on their wedding day. Patrick assumed this picture to be the two victims; Arthur and Estelle, Detective Murphy had said their names were. Below the wedding picture were high school graduation photographs of the victims' three children—all daughters. Next to those were photos of each daughter dressed in white wedding gowns alongside their husbands on the day of their respective weddings. Below the children were many photographs of the grandchildren. They were all smiling in their school pictures; ranging from kindergarten to high school seniors (possibly in college now).

The photos ate away at Patrick. Like the garden outside and the restored furniture, the photos told a story, and brought the house to life. A happy couple had lived here. They had raised a family here. They had grandchildren who came to visit, and ran through the house; possibly playing in their grandma and grandpa's garden.

Now they were dead. He hadn't even seen the victims yet, and, already, Patrick was carrying the weight of their deaths on his shoulders.

The smell of death grew stronger as they made their way through the living room. When they made their way into another hallway that came off the living room, the smell hit Patrick full on, and he found himself glad he hadn't eaten a big breakfast that morning.

The doorway to the room at the end of the hall was blocked off with more yellow tape. He could see the forensic team inside; photographing the scene, dusting for print, and looking for fibers or anything else that could aid them in their upcoming investigation.

The bodies are in there, Patrick thought. *It's go time. Get over whatever fears you may have left inside of you. Let go of them, so that you can catch the bastard sick enough to murder an innocent elderly couple who had grandchildren. Grandchildren, who probably loved their grandma and grandpa more than anything in the world.*

"Ah, Carl," a voice called from inside the room. "I was beginning to think you may have gotten lost."

A man stepped from the room; ducking under the police tape. Patrick guess that he was about Detective Murphy's age; only he was six inches taller, and in far better shape.

"Just bringing the new guy up to date," Murphy answered. "Patrick Sullivan; meet Detective Jonathan Hawkins."

Detective Hawkins was a dominating presence, even at first glance. He still had a full head of hair that had only begun to grey on the sides. The skin on his face was rugged, yet showed minimal signs of aging. He would have made an excellent television drill sergeant, Patrick noted to himself. He wore a pair of slacks and a button up shirt, just like Patrick and Detective Murphy, but unlike the two, who more than likely shopped at the same Kohl's for the best bargains on work acceptable clothing, Hawkins' clothes looked quite expensive. This man refused to look like anything but a top of the line Nassau County Police Detective.

"So... this is the replacement, huh?" Hawkins said; looking Patrick up and down, as if checking if he was adequate enough to even be breathing near a murder scene.

"Excuse me, sir?" Patrick asked.

"Detective Hawkins is only kidding around," Murphy cut in. "He will be retiring at the end of the year. You were hired to relieve him."

"Replace me," Hawkins corrected.

Right as Patrick was beginning to feel a little uncomfortable (not mention unwelcomed), Hawkins emotionless face turned into a friendly smile.

"I'm just playing hard-ass, kid," he said.

Kid? Did he really just call me 'kid'? Patrick asked himself.

He was thirty years old and had been a hard working member of the police department for six long years, and he was being referred to as *kid*. He definitely didn't like that, but he would hold his tongue. Hawkins meant no harm by it, Patrick didn't want to leave the impression of being 'too sensitive' on his first day.

Like Detective Murphy minutes before, Hawkins extended his hand in welcome, and Patrick shook it.

If there was any truth to what Patrick's grandfather had told him, Detective Jonathan Hawkins was the most confident son-of-a-bitch in all existence. He never thought he would say this about a handshake, but it was flawless. Patrick could feel the pride and confidence radiating off of Hawkins' warm palm.

In that single moment that they shared shaking hands, Patrick was able to size up Jonathan Hawkins perfectly. He was a man who was defined by his job. A man who gave his livelihood to it. No words needed to be exchanged on the matter. In one handshake, Patrick understood the man opposite of him completely.

"Sorry to hear that you are leaving the force," Patrick said as they broke their shake.

"Me, too," Hawkins responded. "I have to though. Doctor says it's my damn ticker." He banged his fist against his chest twice. "Apparently, it's not what it used to be."

This news shocked Patrick. He had known the man for less than a minute, but he already believed that nothing could be wrong with him, despite his age. He had an aura of invincibility to him. Still, Patrick guessed, no matter how hard you tried to outrun it; time is going to catch up with you, eventually.

"Truth is," Hawkins continued. "I'd stick around for another twenty years if they'd let me, but if the old blood pump is having problems, then they can't risk keeping me on board."

"It's a damn shame, too," Detective Murphy added. "Detective Hawkins here is the best homicide detective in not only the department, but in the whole damn state of New York."

"I wouldn't go that far, Carl. I'm no better than anyone else doing right by the law."

"Whatever, Hawkins; you're just being modest. You know, they don't call you *Ace* for nothing."

Ace? Patrick wondered. It was an interesting nickname. It sounded like a nickname that a cop in a good mystery novel or detective movie would have.

"Why do they call you *Ace*?" Patrick asked.

Before Detective Murphy could answer for his partner, Detective Hawkins cut him off.

"That is a story for a different time and place, kid. Right now, we have a double homicide to investigate."

"Of course," Patrick said; feeling a bit embarrassed that he had been shooting the shit with his new coworkers, instead of giving his undivided attention to the recently deceased. "My apologies."

"No apology needed. It's perfectly acceptable, and under normal circumstances, you'd be able to hear all about my fascinating nickname, but, unfortunately, these aren't normal circumstances, and here, when you're working alongside me, we steer the course. Those two people in there are our number one priority." He pointed to the room behind him "When we nail the son-of-a-bitch who took them away from their family and friends; that's when we'll all sit down to a nice cold beer, and bullshit with each other."

Patrick respected Jonathan Hawkins' words, because everything he had just said was exactly how he felt, himself. It was probably how any police officer standing near Detective Hawkins felt after hearing him speak. This veteran officer of the law was a natural leader. People looked to him for guidance and for confidence, and when they looked, they found.

"You ready to make sure that the dead don't go unheard?" Hawkins asked Patrick.

"Yes, I am, detective."

"Okay, then let's go in there, and take a look at the bodies."

Hawkins headed back into the den. Detective Murphy followed suit, and then Patrick. When his eyes locked on to the two bodies on the couch, Patrick couldn't believe what he saw. He had been expecting a lot of things walking in to a murder scene, but nothing like what he was looking at now.

CHAPTER 4

It is like nothing you could possibly begin to imagine.

That is what Detective Murphy had said. Now, after seeing the victims for the first time, Patrick realized that had been the understatement of the past millennia.

The bodies of Arthur and Estelle Ramsey were propped up on a blood saturated couch like two mannequins in some grotesque window display. The elderly couple, who probably spent many nights over the course of their long marriage sitting on that very couch; watching television, enjoying conversation, or, perhaps, simply sitting in silence; relishing each other's company, were skinned.

That's right; at first, the voice inside his head was Baby Tooth's, but he would only haunt Patrick momentarily. The voice quickly shifted back to the one Patrick was accustomed to hearing inside his head on a daily basis. *Skinned!*

The two bodies on the couch barely looked like human beings. They faintly resembled pictures that one would see in a biology textbook of the human muscular system. Only difference being that this was a whole lot bloodier, and a hell of a lot scarier.

"Holy shit," Patrick said aloud; staring wide eyed at the two bodies that used to be the Ramsey's. He had meant to say it to himself, but the words just fell out of his mouth as they ran through his head.

"You can say that again," Hawkins said. He was standing on one side of Patrick while Detective Murphy stood on the other; all three staring at what remained of Arthur and Estelle Ramsey.

"I told you," Detective Murphy reminded Patrick. "Like nothing you could even begin to imagine."

The more he fixated on that statement, the more Patrick realized how true it was. Heading into his first murder scene, he had prepared himself to see a lot of disturbing things—some of which he had already been exposed to in his previous years on the job—but none of those things even came close to what he was looking down on now. Every inch of skin that had once covered the bodies of Arthur and Estelle Ramsey was now completely stripped away from their bodies.

Patrick then noticed something that struck him as odd.

Along with being propped up in the sitting position, the Ramsey's hands were conjoined. Not in the simple right hand in left hand sort of way, though. Arthurs' skinned hand was stretched across his gory lap, and was joined with Estelle's left hand. The symbolism of this gesture wasn't lost on Patrick. The handholding represented unity, just like marriage. Arthur and Estelle Ramsey had lived most of their life together, and now they had died together. To their killer, it would only be fitting if they were found linked together by their hands. Whoever did this had a mind for the theatrics.

He stared; fixated on those hands. Patrick knew there was something else. He just had to concentrate, and find it. Then he saw what he was looking for. It was the frosting on this extremely unappetizing cake.

He wasn't positive if he was looking at what he thought he was. He couldn't see them clearly, because they were covered in blood. Maybe his mind was just playing tricks on him, and he was seeing what he wanted to be seeing. Those two bodies were such a mess that what he was looking at could have been almost anything. Patrick would need to get a closer look to confirm.

"Have the bodies been photographed, Detectives?"

"They have," Hawkins answered. He could see the wheels turning in Patrick's head. He had probably already seen what Patrick saw, because he was that good. What he wanted was to see if Patrick could figure it out.

Hawkins was feeling his replacement out.

"May I approach the bodies?"

"You may…"

Patrick donned a pair of latex gloves, and knelt in front of Arthur and Estelle Ramsey. With his thumb, he wiped away the blood from both Ramsey's wedding rings.

"What the hell…?" Detective Murphy asked. He and Hawkins were now beside Patrick; examining his find.

"He put their wedding bands back on them after he killed and skinned them," Patrick answered.

"This just keeps getting more disturbing by the minute." Detective Murphy shook his head in disbelief.

"Wow," Hawkins was all said. The tone of his voice was neutral. He wasn't going to let any of this phase him. No matter how out of the ordinary it was. "Good find, kid. I'm impressed."

"Thank you," Patrick said; trying to absorb the compliment, and ignore being called *kid*.

However, Patrick wasn't sure how impressed Hawkins really was. He had noticed the hands, and he likely noticed the wedding rings, even while they were covered in blood. So finding something that he had already known wasn't going to impress a guy like Hawkins. He, undoubtedly, expected no less from the man who was to replace him in a month's time. Patrick was going to have to make a discovery in this case that no one else was able to pick up on. Then he would truly impress Jonathan Hawkins.

A man then knocked on the den door. He turned out to be the onsite psychologist, and informed the detectives that Samantha Melina—the young girl who had found the Ramsey's bodies earlier that morning—had been checked out by both medics and himself, and was ready to be questioned.

Hawkins thanked the psychologist. He told the forensics team to make sure they photographed the hands, as if they were inept at the job they were trained to do. The three detectives then left the room to go handle another fragile part of their investigation.

"Okay, here's the game plan," Hawkins said once they were halfway down the driveway; taking his natural role as leader. "The replacement over here will talk to the girl. Carl, you and I will talk to neighbors.

"Sounds like a good plan to me," Detective Murphy agreed. Patrick doubted Detective Murphy ever questioned his partner's decisions. He didn't think there were many who did.

"You going to be okay doing this on your own, kid?"

"Yeah, I should be okay."

Patrick hoped that was at least half true. He had never questioned someone before, nor had he ever observed an interrogation, unless what he saw on *Law & Order* and *Bone*s counted towards anything, but he doubted that.

"I have a feeling that you'll do fine," Hawkins said. He gave Patrick one last look up and down; making sure he was adequate enough to handle such a task. He seemed confident in his decision. "Most newbies are barely competent at questioning—they're all nervous and shit— but I'm willing to give you a try to see what you've got."

"Thank you, detective."

"Well, good luck."

With that being said, Hawkins and Murphy took off down the driveway.

Patrick gave himself a few moments to prepare. He took a deep breath, and let it out. It helped calm his nerves a little. He then headed down the driveway towards the ambulance.

Samantha Melina sat at the rear of the ambulance. On one side of her stood a medic, the other a police officer. They both seemed pretty bored, being that all the action was going on inside, and *their* job was to babysit a teenage girl. Samantha, herself, was staring down at the cracks in the Ramsey's driveway. Her face was void of emotion; a lot like Patrick's face had looked like minutes after he had awoken from his nightmare earlier that morning. Only difference was that Samantha actually was in a state of shock.

The freshly turned seventeen year old now looked twice her age. Patrick guessed that she hadn't looked so aged before seeing two human beings propped up in the sitting position on a couch drenched through with blood; their skin no longer attached to their bodies. She wore glasses and her mess of frizzy hair was pulled back with a hair tie. Sitting there, not weighing an ounce over a hundred and five pounds, she looked so fragile; as if made of porcelain.

If this girl wasn't already delicate enough..., Patrick thought as he approached to introduce himself.

"Samantha," he said in the most comforting, not intimidating voice he could muster. "My name is Detective Sullivan. I just need to ask you a few questions. Is that okay?"

Samantha gave no answer. She hadn't even flinched. She gave zero indication that she was even aware there was a stranger standing in front of her; attempting to talk with her. She simply continued to stare down at the cement driveway. He slowly took two steps towards her and

47

repeated her name; only this time, he put his hand on her shoulder to get her attention.

And get her attention, he did.

At the exact moment of contact, Samantha jumped like a skittish cat.

"I'm sorry," Patrick said. "I didn't mean to startle you. I was just trying to get your attention, Samantha. I'm Detective Sullivan. I'm a police officer... with the homicide department."

She just stared at him, like she was questioning whether or not she should believe the man standing in front of her. Her eyes were red and wet. She was on the verge of tears. Patrick was shocked that the little start he had given her hadn't sent her right over the edge.

"Would it be okay if I asked you a few questions?"

After some more silence, he began to believe that getting this poor girl to talk right then would be impossible. She was in such shock and so fragile, Patrick was almost certain she might never speak again. Still, he would try once more, because he had no other choice. He needed the details of that traumatizing morning while they were still fresh in her mind. He had to grab hold of them before Samantha Melina could bury them deep in her subconscious, because one of those details—even the smallest, seemingly insignificant—might be the key to finding the murderous beast who did all this. So he would push one more time. Not for himself, and not to prove his competency to Detectives Hawkins or Murphy. He would push this girl, who didn't deserve to be after all she had seen, because he needed to find justice for the Ramsey's, who now sat on a couch in the house behind him; lifeless.

"Samantha, I know it's hard to talk about this right now, but it is very important that you at least try. I really need you to be strong, and do this for—"

"'You shouldn't worry yourself so much over boys, Samantha,'" she finally said in what was barely a whisper.

"Excuse me?"

The one line might be the only thing he'd get out of her, and it was about as useful as her saying nothing at all.

"That was the last thing he ever said to me—Mr. Ramsey," she explained. "He told me not to worry so much about boys. That I was too young and too pretty to let myself fret over such silly things." She then paused; recollecting her last moments with Arthur Ramsey while he was alive. "Mr. Ramsey was always really nice like that… Positive, you know? He was always calling me pretty—not in a creepy old guy kind of way, but the way that made you feel good about yourself. He was so genuine and honest. Everyone liked him so much."

"Samantha, I know talking about this morning is going to be really hard, but you have to try. The longer we wait, the more prone you are to forget things… things that might be important to finding the person who did this."

"I understand. I'm okay to talk… I think."

"Thank you, Samantha. Just take your time, okay? I don't want to make this any harder for you than it has to be. If you feel like you can't talk anymore, and you have to stop, you just tell me and we will take a break. Okay?"

"Okay."

Now that he had finally gotten her to a point where she was willing to try and talk about what she saw, Patrick realized that he had not the slightest idea of what to ask young Samantha Melina first. Yes, he had about two dozen questions running through his head, but he just had no idea which ones to deem important enough to cover first.

And not to mention safe enough.

Questioning Samantha Melina was as delicate as disarming a bomb. You snip one wrong wire, and it detonates. He was lucky enough to have been able to get her to this point, and at any moment she could revert right back to step one. This was all foreign territory to Patrick, and he was in it alone. Still, Hawkins deemed him competent enough to get through this on his own. Not to mention there was the Ramsey's to think about. One by one, he ciphered through the different questions he had; seeing which ones he could hold off on asking. After a quick deliberation, he decided to go with the simplest, yet one of the most important questions.

"Samantha, what were you doing here at the Ramsey's residence this morning?"

Arthur Ramsey was a usual at the deli Samantha Melina worked at, she explained in a voice desperately trying to remain calm. She had worked there since she was fifteen, and every day, just after six in the morning, Arthur Ramsey would come in, and buy himself a large coffee and an issue of Newsday.

"I would always ask him why he didn't just make his coffee at home, or get the paper delivered," she reminisced with a small smile on her face. "He would always say something along the lines of he enjoyed the little human contact he got each day, or that a walk down the block probably did someone his age some good."

The weak dam that held back the waterworks almost burst as Samantha remembered the kind old man that she saw every day. Miraculously, she managed to regain some resemblance of composure instead of breaking down.

"When was the last time Mr. Ramsey had come into your job, Samantha?" Patrick was aware that his first question had yet to be answered, but he followed his gut and asked another; knowing they'd be able to come full circle back to his original inquiry.

"Friday morning." She explained that she had been distraught about boyfriend issues that entire week, and the last day she had seen Arthur Ramsey alive was the day he told her that she was too pretty to be worrying so much. "I acted like my stupid fight with my boyfriend was the worst thing in the world. Meanwhile, it doesn't even compare to what happened to Mr. Ramsey and his poor wife. I feel like such a childish idiot."

"Don't beat yourself up over that, Samantha. We all have our own problems."

"I guess."

"You say he was there every morning, every day, yet the last time you saw him was on Friday. That was two days ago."

"Yeah, he didn't come in either yesterday or Saturday."

"Did anyone point out that he hadn't been in? He was a regular customer, so his absence must have stuck out."

Everyone working at the deli had taken notice to Arthur Ramsey's absence that weekend. This wasn't the first time this had happened though, Samantha explained to Patrick.

"Mrs. Ramsey has—had—a heart condition, and times when she felt weak, he stayed home with her to watch over her, instead of coming in. He really loved her. He carried a picture of her in his wallet. He loved to show it off. Anyways, when he didn't show up Saturday or Sunday, we figured that was likely why. That's the reason I came here this morning."

Samantha's boss had called her that morning, and asked if she could come in for a couple of minutes to bring a bag he had put together for the Ramsey's over to their house. It was his little way of showing his appreciation for their continuous business over the years. With the promise of a few extra bucks for a few minutes of work, Samantha said okay. This explained the bag of groceries on the kitchen table.

The question Patrick had to ask next was one he didn't want to. He could piece together the sequence of events that followed Samantha Melina's arrival at the Ramsey's house that morning, but he still had to ask her to relive it. He had no doubt that this would be the hardest part for the frail girl, and there was a chance he might lose her after she had come along so far.

Still he asked, and Samantha explained.

When she arrived at the Ramsey's home, she knocked on the back door, and got no answer. After a few tries with no response, she opened the door and went inside; calling Arthur Ramsey's name.

She nearly broke down a few times as she spoke, and had to take small breaks to regain herself. She spoke of the smell, and how it made her want to throw up. Patrick wondered if the smell of death would follow Samantha around for the rest of her life, like it did his. She placed the bag on the kitchen table, and made her way through the house. Hysterics hadn't yet come, but tears began to stream down her face as she began to remember what she had seen when she pushed that den door open.

"The smell was so strong that I wanted to turn around and leave, but I opened the door, anyway. When I did, I saw them there; looking the way they did, I couldn't take it. I ran as fast as I could from the house." She had remained calm as long as she could, but now she was full blown crying; forcing her words out. "I collapsed in the grass in the backyard, and vomited. I waited there... I couldn't move. I just stared at the puddle I had made. Then I forced myself to call the police."

"Thank you, Samantha." Right now, that was all Patrick needed to know, and he had zero intentions of making this poor girl go through more than she had to. "You've been a tremendous help."

"Really?"

"Absolutely, Samantha. You were great."

Patrick saw Detectives Hawkins and Murphy coming back up the driveway. He thanked Samantha for all her help, and excused himself.

"It's not fair," she said as Patrick was walking away.

"Excuse me?" he asked; turning back to the girl.

"It's not fair that they had to die. I mean, like the way they did. Everybody dies, but no one should ever have to die like that."

"I know, Samantha."

He turned his attention to Hawkins and Murphy, who were now standing next to him, and got them up to speed with everything Samantha Melina had told him.

"Poor kid," Hawkins said in a low voice when Patrick had finished. "No girl should have to see that. I hope she's able to get over it."

"Me, too," Patrick said; although he doubted she would. He knew from firsthand experience that it was the bad things in your life that had a tendency to not go away.

"How'd you make out, Carl?" Hawkins asked Murphy.

"Not so good."

Detective Murphy told his two partners that the house next door was rented out by a few college students. Three out five were home when he went over, and none of them had much to say. The relationship they had with the victims was a simple one. It consisted of seeing them in passing, and exchanged pleasantries. None of them had noticed the victims missing, nor did they hear anything over the weekend coming from the Ramsey house that would merit them calling the police.

"Okay, that's good, I guess. Doesn't really help us much, but who knows," Hawkins said at the conclusion of the update.

"How'd you make out, Ace?" Murphy asked.

"Not much better." Hawkins told them. "No one was home."

"That's because Mr. and Mrs. McKensey live there…"

All three detectives turned towards Samantha Melina, who was staring at them.

"Excuse me, ma'am?" Hawkins asked.

"Mister and Misses McKensey live next door. Mr. McKensey always comes in to the deli with Mr. Ramsey. They're all like best friends. They've probably lived next door to each other longer than I have even been alive."

"Mr. McKensey didn't mention anything to you, or anyone you work with, about why Mister Ramsey wasn't around?" Hawkins asked. "Or, if the two always go to the deli together, then how come this McKensey didn't find the bodies?"

The latter question was likely meant to be directed at Patrick and Murphy, but Hawkins' gazed stayed remained on Samantha.

"Because the McKensey's always fly to Georgia to visit their children this time each year. They haven't been home."

That response hit Patrick like a ton of bricks. Actually, it felt more like an entire building collapsing on top of him. This new information changed everything. As if the crime itself wasn't bad enough, this made it worse.

He looked to Hawkins, who bore an expression on his face that told him, like two people who answer a question in unison, they were thinking the exact same thought.

It was Patrick who spoke, and said exactly what they were all thinking

"He knew…"

CHAPTER 5

The air in the 8th precinct, located on North Wantagh Avenue, felt thick and stale to Detective Patrick Sullivan. One could attribute this to the unseasonably warm November weather, but Patrick might argue it was due to the fact that his first case as a homicide detective was an extremely disturbing one, which was becoming more unsettling as new, unpleasant details came to light.

He sat at Detective Murphy's desk, which sat opposite the desk that belonged to Jonathan Hawkins. The desk that would become his upon Hawkins' forced retirement. Until then, Murphy had offered up the use of his own desk to the new guy. He assumed Murphy felt his partner deserved to keep his own desk until his last day.

The two desks mirrored each other in that they were the same exact desk, just purchased twice, and each had the same model desktop computer on it, but that was where all similarities ended.

On Detective Murphy's desk were pictures of his family; his wife, Annette, whom he had been married to for thirty-one years, his two sons, who were now cops in the city, and his one daughter, who was in her senior year of high school. He spoke highly of his family to Patrick as he went from picture to picture. He loved them, and he was proud to have them displayed on his desk for anyone to see.

Hawkins desk, on the other hand, had no pictures. There were no indications what-so-ever that he had any kids or was even married. Patrick couldn't even tell if the man had a single friend or hobby outside of work. This was the desk of a man who was strictly business. No time to decorate with reminders of happy thoughts when there were murders to be solved. The desolate feel of where Jonathan Hawkins worked didn't surprise Patrick. He had already learned enough about the man to expect nothing less.

Currently, Hawkins was in another room; trying to find a contact for one of the Ramsey's daughters. He had volunteered to carry the burden of delivering the awful news of their parents' untimely demise.

Patrick was assigned the task of retaking Samantha Melina's statement of the morning events. At the request of Detective Hawkins, his meeting with Officer Summers had been put off until the following morning. The paperwork could wait.

The retelling had been just as difficult for Samantha as it had been in the driveway just a few hours before. When they concluded, the young girl was sent home with her parents to live out whatever permanent trauma this experience would have on her psyche, and the rest of her life.

After some minutes of just looking around; taking in the new scenery that was his job, Hawkins entered the room. He was carrying three manila envelopes. He plopped two of them down on the desk in front of Patrick and Murphy.

"What's this?" Murphy asked.

"These," Hawkins answered. "We will get to these in just a moment. First, let's go over what we've got so far." He turned his attention to Patrick. "Kid, you go first."

"Well," Patrick said; trying to simply ignore the fact he was in his thirties, and being called *kid* for what seemed like the sixteen-hundredth time that morning. "Our perp knew what he wanted to do to the victims, and he knew it would take some time—maybe a few days. He knew things about them, like Arthur Ramsey's daily trip to the deli, and his wife's heart condition. He also knew, given the information he acquired, that if he wasn't seen around, people would just assume his wife had fallen ill, and he was staying at home to take care of her; like he had done in the past."

"Okay, good. What else? Carl, don't think just because there's a new guy here that you get to sit out, and not participate."

"Damn, and here I was; hoping you wouldn't notice," Detective Murphy joked. "The perpetrator also knew that the next door neighbors, the McKensey's, who were good friends with the victims, would be out of the state; visiting their family. This meant they wouldn't be stopping by for any surprise visits. This gave the perp privacy, and time to kill and skin the victims."

"That is correct. Now, what does that lead us to believe? This question is open to anyone to answer, by the way," Hawkins added; waving his envelope from Patrick to Murphy.

"That the perp could have chosen the victims' months before committing the actual murders," Patrick spoke up. "He studied their daily routines; learning everything about them in order to plan his murder perfectly."

This scenario, Patrick knew, was a bit of a stretch. There was one that was far more logical that he could have said, but his gut told him to suggest the more unlikely of the two.

"That is certainly a possibility," Hawkins said nodding in approval. Clearly, this unlikely scenario had crossed his mind as well. "There is, however, a more feasible explanation. Do you care to venture what that might be?"

"The other scenario—the more likely one, like you said—is that somebody who knew the victims had committed the crime. A crime of passion."

"Bingo," Hawkins said, slapping his folder down against the edge of the table. "A crime of passion, which brings us to the contents of this."

He waved his folder back and forth for his two partners to see.

He explained that he had managed to get in touch with the Ramsey's physician in hopes of getting the numbers for their emergency contacts. He also made an inquisition about anyone calling in the previous weeks; attempting to get any information about Estelle Ramsey's medical history. The doctor's answer was no, and that if someone had called asking such a thing, they would never get it due to doctor/patient confidentiality.

"So I thanked him for the contact information, and his valuable time," Hawkins went on. "And right as we were about to hang up, he said something I found to be rather interesting. He said that it was a shame that Arthur Ramsey had died without making peace with his son."

Hawkins' words hit Patrick's ears, and at that moment, he was no longer in the squad room of the 8th precinct. He was standing in the living room of the Ramsey's household; staring at a wall of framed photographs. He could see each picture hanging perfectly from their hooks, as if he was actually physically there, instead of within a memory from earlier that morning. Not one of them were one of a son.

"Arthur and Estelle Ramsey didn't have a son," Patrick pointed out. He explained the wall of photos he had seen earlier that morning.

"Exactly," Hawkins said. "So you could see how the mention of a son got my attention."

When he was asked about the Ramsey's son, the doctor told Hawkins all he had known on the matter, which wasn't much: Arthur and Estelle Ramsey had a son, who they no longer spoke to. The reasons for this estrangement, Arthur Ramsey decided to keep to himself; kindly explaining that some issues stayed strictly between families.

"Have we contacted any of the Ramsey's daughters yet?" Murphy asked. "I'm sure they could provide us with an insight into why their parents and their brother no longer talked."

"I didn't have to," Hawkins explained. "I ran Stephen Ramsey's name through the system, and he popped right up. Now, if you two would so kindly open your folders, we can learn all about him."

Stephen Ramsey had been arrested six years earlier in front of a trailer park off Route 110 for picking up a hooker, and receiving a blowjob in his car. The hooker was a male. He was arrested, again, four years later. This time, for beating a male hooker bloody in a motel room.

"Stephen Ramsey is gay?" Patrick asked.

"Yes, he is," Hawkins answered.

Hawkins didn't need to go on. Patrick already could see where all this was going. All the pieces were coming together, but he wasn't convinced he believed it.

"You think Stephen Ramsey murdered his parents?" He asked Hawkins.

"I don't know nearly enough to think anyone killed the Ramsey's yet, but, if I was to go on the facts we currently have in front of us, then, yes; I would look into Stephen Ramsey. We have enough to at least bring him in to question."

Hawkins then laid out his theory for Patrick and Murphy.

Stephen Ramsey had publically come out of the closet, and his parents (Arthur more than Estelle, Hawkins guessed) did not approve of their only son's lifestyle preference. This caused a rift in the family, which eventually led to a full blown falling out. Over the years that followed this, Stephen Ramsey had grown to resent his parents for exiling him from their lives, when they should've supported him. He developed an unhealthy obsession with his hatred. He let it eat away at him until, finally, he couldn't take it anymore. He snapped, and brutally murder his parents.

The hypothesis was perfect. Yet, Patrick still couldn't believe it was true.

"The type of crime that you are describing usually is spontaneous, and definitely messier," Patrick argued. "The murderer would have left behind something for forensics to pick up. This murder was so well planned out, and the cleanup was impeccable. Forensics hasn't picked up a single fiber or print. I don't see Stephen Ramsey as your guy. He doesn't fit the profile."

"I'm aware of that, kid," Hawkins fired back. "I've been in this line of work long enough to know what profile fits what murder, but sometimes we get a murderer who doesn't fit any profile."

"I know that, but why, after all these years, does Stephen Ramsey finally decide to kill his parents? And not just kill them, but completely strip them of their identities by skinning them? It just doesn't make sense."

"Carl, you care to put your two cents in?" Hawkins asked; hoping to get a little backup from his partner.

"I don't know, Ace… the son being our guy certainly makes sense, but Detective Sullivan is right about it not fitting the profile. Then again, this isn't an ordinary case."

"Do you think it merits bringing him in for questioning?"

"I don't see how it could do any harm."

"You don't see how it could do any harm?" Patrick snapped at them. "The guy just lost both his parents. Whether he was on speaking terms with them or not, he still lost them, and lost them in the most violent of ways. I don't think he should be brought in, and have to endure a traumatizing ordeal on a simple hunch."

"I'm sorry you feel that way, but it's a pretty sufficient hunch, and it's all we have right now, kid."

"You do know that I'm thirty years old," Patrick snapped back. He didn't mean to, but Hawkins and Murphy were heading in the opposite direction that they should have been, and his temper was getting the best of him.

"Listen, *kid*," Hawkins rudely fired back. Patrick found himself wanting to hit the man he had been admiring only a few hours ago. "I was putting on my first police uniform when your mama was putting you in your first diaper. To me, you're still a kid."

There was no rebuttal. Patrick was speechless.

"I know you're new to this," Hawkins continued. "So I'm going to cut you some slack. If you don't want to believe Stephen Ramsey could have done that to his parents, then fine; you don't have to. Hell, I don't want to believe it, either. It's fucked up beyond all human comprehension, but guess what; it still happens. As sad as it is to say, sometimes children kill their parents. So we're bringing him in to question. End of story. We won't push him hard, unless we have to. That guy is our only lead right now, and either he did it or he didn't. So we either need to nail his ass to the wall for this, or we need to clear him, and continue on with this investigation."

The rage inside Patrick began to subside. He didn't side with Hawkins' theory, and he still thought he was wrong, but he knew this wasn't an argument he was going to win. Hawkins had a strong enough theory that, no matter what type of fight Patrick put up, Stephen Ramsey was going to end up in that interrogation room.

"Fine," he finally said with an obvious reluctance. "Let's bring him in."

"Glad you are seeing things my way, kid. You'll learn soon enough that it is usually the right way," Hawkins said; smugly, then turned his attention to Detective Murphy. "Carl, could you contact Stephen Ramsey? Inform him of his parents' death, in case his sisters haven't told him yet. Tell him we need him to come down, because we have some questions for him."

"You act like I don't know the procedure," Carl joked; getting up from his seat. "I've only been doing this as long as you, if you remember."

"My apologies, friend," Hawkins said; giving his partner an encouraging slap on the back as he headed off to make the phone call. He then turned his attention to Patrick. "Hope you're ready, kid."

"Ready for what?" Patrick asked.

"You're going to be the one who questions Stephen Ramsey."

CHAPTER 6

Patrick was sure he was going to get an irate earful for questioning Jonathan Hawkins' expertise on the subject of murder investigation. To do such a thing would be blasphemy. He had waited; mentally preparing himself for some sort of verbal lashing, but there was no such tirade. There was not even a peep from Hawkins' end on the matter.

Patrick began to think Hawkins hadn't minded him speaking up, and defending his own opinion. The notion that Hawkins may have even been impressed by it began to creep into his mind. Maybe this veteran even admired the fact that the new blood (*The Replacement* or *New Kid* would have been Hawkins' choice of names for Patrick) had some guts to be an individual. Perhaps, after all these years, he was glad to see someone actually question his calls. After all; he was only human, and despite what most people around him thought; he was going to be wrong every now and then.

Now, while looking in through the one-sided mirror at Stephen Ramsey, who sat waiting to be questioned, Patrick realized he was tremendously wrong on all fronts.

This was his punishment. This is what you got for standing up for your individual beliefs against the ones of Jonathan Hawkins. You got to question a man you thought was completely innocent. This was Hawkins' way of letting his replacement know not to challenge him, because he will always win.

That admiration and respect he found himself having for Hawkins only minutes after meeting the man had slipped away. It was slowly being replaced with loathing. Hawkins was playing a twisted game, but Patrick wouldn't give him the satisfaction of knowing that he was getting under his skin. He would ask Stephen Ramsey the questions that needed to be asked, no matter how tough they were, or how much he believed them to be unnecessary. Then, once Stephen Ramsey's name was wiped clean of all suspicion, he would walk out of that interview with his chest swelled with pride. He would bask in the fact he was absolutely right, and Hawkins was wrong. It would be known that no petty little games would have an effect on Patrick Sullivan.

He entered the interrogation room a man determined.

Patrick had heard throughout his life that some homosexuals couldn't help being gay. They were just born that way, and it was who they were. Stephen Ramsey was one of those homosexuals, although his unkempt hair, patchy beard, and outfit that looked as if it had been purchased at a low-end thrift store tried to show, otherwise. Still, he possessed the look that is often associated with some homosexual males.

It was very clear that Arthur and Estelle Ramsey's only son was trying very hard to cover up the obvious, and failing at it.

"Mister Ramsey," Patrick said upon entering the room. Stephen Ramsey's eyes were bloodshot, and his cheeks were stained by tears. Patrick couldn't believe he was about to put this poor man through such an unnecessary ordeal. He was going to get this over with as quickly as possible. "My name is Detective Sullivan. I just have a few questions concerning your relationship with your parents."

"Is it true?" Stephen Ramsey asked; completely ignoring Patrick's statement.

"Is what true, Mister Ramsey?"

Patrick sensed that this would not be an easy interview, no matter how hard he tried, otherwise.

"That they were found... found..." He began to stumble over his words as he fought desperately to fend off more tears "...found without their skin?"

"Yes, I'm afraid so. As Detective Murphy told you when you arrived, your parents were found this morning in their home. They were murdered, and their skin had been removed."

"Oh my g-god," Stephen Ramsey managed through the sounds of his own gagging.

Patrick instinctively grabbed a nearby wastebasket, and got it in the hands of Stephen Ramsey just in time for him to throw up the contents of his stomach. Once he was through vomiting, Patrick allowed a few moments for Stephen Ramsey to regain some resemblance of composure. He then tried again with his interview.

"Mister Ramsey, I know the details of your parent's murder are very disturbing, and I have no doubt they're not something you want to think about right now, but there are a few questions that I need to ask you."

"You're going to ask me if I murdered my parents, and the reason you are going to ask that is because I am gay, and my parents and I do not talk anymore."

Stephen Ramsey had known the entire time why he was being brought in to be questioned. It wasn't exactly difficult to figure out.

"Well, did you?" Patrick asked; straight up.

He had originally intended to approach the question more subtly, but there had been no point in pleasantries, any longer. Stephen Ramsey had put it out there, so Patrick planned to roll with it.

"No, I did not," he answered; starring Patrick stonily in the eyes. "Why would I murder the only two people who accepted me when I couldn't even accept myself?"

"Mister Ramsey, with all due respect, you and your parents had an estranged relationship. From what your sister told another detective on the phone earlier, you have not spoken to either of them in almost eight years."

"That had nothing to do with my parents, detective," Stephen Ramsey fired back; beginning to get defensive. It was obvious he took exception to Patrick's insinuation that his parents had disowned him for being gay. "The decision to cut ties with my parents was my own."

"I'm sorry, but I'm a little confused. Would you care to elaborate, Mister Ramsey?"

In the latter years of his twenties, Stephen Ramsey came out of the closet, and told the world that he was gay. It was something he had always known deep down inside, and chose to fight as long as he was able to.

Unfortunately, publically admitting that he was a homosexual did not come easy for Stephen Ramsey. The people who Stephen Ramsey called his friends throughout his life suddenly stopped calling him to go out, and eventually stopped speaking to him all together. The same people who had patted him on the back and commended him for making such a brave decision did a disappearing act, and completely vanished from his life. Coworkers began to distance themselves so much that it became nearly impossible for him to function properly at his job; forcing him to eventually resign.

Everyone had always guessed that Stephen Ramsey was gay, but apparently there was a huge difference between guessing and knowing.

Once he was out of the closet, the world had become a much colder place. Stephen Ramsey slowly began to hate himself for the person he couldn't help being, and this explained his peculiar not-your-average-gay-male appearance. He admitted he hated his homosexuality so much that he often tried to appear as heterosexual as possible. Still, as it had been before he officially came out, it was obvious what Stephen Ramsey's sexual preference was. Only now, his careless demeanor made him easily undesirable to other men. There was no one who wanted to surround themselves with the company of Stephen Ramsey; gay or straight. This inevitably led to the male prostitute altercations.

Of all the people who had turned their backs on him, the two people who stood proudly by his side were his parents. They had accepted their son for who he was, and proudly declared to the world they loved him unconditionally; no matter what his lifestyle choices were.

"I don't understand," Patrick interrupted. "If your parents were so supportive of you, then why the rift?"

"Like I told you, detective, that was my decision, and my decision, alone. I hated myself so much for being gay, and no matter how many times my parents told me that they and my sisters still loved me, and that there were other people in the world who had gone through exactly what I was going through, I still believed that I didn't deserve to be loved by anyone; not even my own parents.

"My hatred and absolute detest for myself became so overpowering, I tore a rift right between us. I would constantly lash out at them anytime they attempted to be supportive. I tried so hard to get them to hate me just because I felt they should. I mean, everyone else hated me—I hated me—why not them? Still, they refused. No matter what I did, or what hurtful things I said to either of them, they fought back.

"When my attempts to drive them away failed, I simply stopped talking to them. Just like that, I cut them out of my life. They tried numerous times to get me to talk to them, but I wouldn't. My father had even showed up at my apartment once; pleading outside my door to let him in, but I never answered it. Eventually, they reluctantly gave up."

"But I stood in their living room; looking at their wall of family pictures. There were no pictures of you. It was like you didn't exist."

"I heard about that the last time I talked to my sister. From what she told me, my mother had taken me leaving extremely hard. My father, being afraid of what the stress was doing to my mother's health—she had always had heart issues that had progressively gotten worse since her mid-forties—so he took down all my pictures. He figured it was best to remove a daily reminder of what my mother had lost. From what I understand, he had put together a scrap book of all the pictures they had of me."

Patrick had no doubt that Hawkins was on the other side of the window at that moment; ordering for the Ramsey's house to be searched for the supposed photo album.

"Listen," Stephen Ramsey went on; trying hard to fight back the tears that were resurfacing. "My mother and father are dead; murdered by some monster in a way I could never imagine somebody being murdered. I refuse to have their memories tarnished by letting anyone doubt they were anything other than extraordinary people, who were caring, loving, and accepting. I won't let them be seen otherwise! Do you understand? It was my own stupidity that we didn't talk, and I would give anything just to be able to speak to them one last time, and tell them I'm sorry."

The heartache and realization of never being able to make an amends with his parents finally overwhelmed Stephen Ramsey, and tears began to stream down the boney cheeks into his beard. In that moment, Patrick found himself feeling sorry for this man sitting across from him.

There was now no way he would ever be at peace with himself.

"If you want to peg me as a suspect in their murder; go ahead, but don't you dare insinuate that my parents were bad people. I won't let you."

"No one is insinuating that, Mister Ramsey," Patrick tried to explain, but he knew it was pointless. Stephen Ramsey hated Patrick. He could feel it; pungent in the air. Meanwhile, the whole time, he had believed Stephen Ramsey was completely guiltless. It was Hawkins who had brought this on this fragile man, yet it was Patrick who was set up to be the bad guy. No matter how this ended, he was going to walk out of it looking like a villain in the eyes of the man he thought was innocent. "We just needed to clarify the specifics of your relationship with your parents."

"Well, Detective," Stephen's Ramsey's voice was thick with acrimony. "Has everything been clarified? Or are there anymore accusations you would like to make about my parents?"

"No, Mr. Ramsey, that is all." Patrick tried to hide the shame in his voice. "Thank you for your time and cooperation."

"I would like a few moments to myself, please."

"That's fine, Mister Ramsey. You may take your time."

Stephen Ramsey burst into uncontrollable sobs. He lowered his face into his palms, and wept deeply. He wept for his parents, and wept for himself. He wept over the fact that his parents were gone from this world, and he was now truly alone. Patrick retreated quietly through the door in which he entered.

On the other side stood Hawkins. He was silent. He did not congratulate Patrick on a job well done, nor did he apologize for doubting him. He just stood there staring, and Patrick stared right back.

Patrick had hoped, as their eyes locked in a silent embrace, Hawkins could read his mind right then, because it was screaming *FUCK YOU!!*

Hawkins had made him feel less than human. He made him feel dirty, as if making someone go through that kind of pain made him evil; just like Baby Tooth, and the monster who had killed the Ramsey's. For what he did to Stephen Ramsey, Patrick felt like he was right there on their level.

Hawkins must not have picked up on any *fuck you* vibe that Patrick was trying to get across, because he simply nodded his head, as if he was giving his stamp of approval, which Patrick couldn't give two shits about, then walked out of the room.

Patrick wondered, as he stood there alone; hearing the sounds of Stephen Ramsey's wails of despair coming from the opposite side of the door, if this is what he had to do to be a good homicide detective. Did he have to stop being compassionate? Did he have to become detached from people and their feelings? Did he have to become numb?

Numb like Jonathan Hawkins.

CHAPTER 7

It had taken Stephen Ramsey nearly forty-five minutes to finally regain any resemblance of composure once he and Patrick's interview had concluded. Once he was calm enough to articulate, he gave the police his whereabouts over the last few days. All three detectives had no doubt his alibi would check out. As far as the investigation was concerned, Stephen Ramsey's name was now completely liberated from the any inkling of suspicion.

Once they had gotten everything they needed from him, Stephen Ramsey was sent home; looking miserable and defeated. There was no fight left in that man. Now that the only people who ever accepted and supported him were laying on cold metal trays at the Nassau County Medical Center morgue; nothing left of their identity but a tag bearing their names, it was clear Stephen Ramsey found no reason to even attempt to find any happiness within himself.

Patrick spent the three hours since Ramsey's dismissal not speaking to anyone. He was too tied up with harping on what he had just done to that delicate man. Conversation, work related or not, did not exactly seem appetizing to him.

Even though questioning the Ramsey's homosexual son had been Hawkins' plan, it was Patrick who had to do his bidding. He was the one left feeling like he had done something cruel, while Hawkins felt nothing at all on the matter. It was becoming quite clear this job had more depth to it than just simply catching the bad guys. He had never thought it'd be *that* easy, but he didn't sign on to this job to put innocent, grieving people through turmoil in an attempt to get the answers. It was an idea Patrick Sullivan did not like, nor did he respect, at all.

He was sitting at Murphy's desk, coming to grips with a few harsh realizations about his new job when Detective Hawkins took the seat next to him.

"Listen, kid," he said in a neutral voice. "I know it sucks accusing someone of murdering their parents—especially one you think didn't do it—but, unfortunately, that comes with the job. There's nothing else to it. It's simply just part of the job. What you need to see is, now, we've eliminated him as a suspect. We can move on with this investigation. You know as well as I do that it is imperative we waste little time eliminating people who look like they may have done it, and didn't. On paper, Stephen Ramsey was a perfect suspect for this murder, and I had every right to bring him in for questioning. Now that we know he's innocent, we move on. We're one step closer to finding the scumbag who did this."

"Okay," was Patrick's cold response. He wondered if Hawkins had that little speech planned from the get-go, or perhaps he was that good at making his case on the fly.

In truth, Patrick wasn't even mad at Hawkins anymore; at least not for having Stephen Ramsey brought in for questioning. He had been in the right there; it made perfect sense. What bothered him was the idea of the man he would have to become in order to be a good homicide detective. Both, Hawkins and Murphy were good detectives, and neither even flinched at the idea of ruining all that was left of Stephen Ramsey. The idea of that numbness engulfing him and taking control, made Patrick feel like he, himself, was a monster.

Baby Tooth was a monster. He had put innocent people through hell, and ruined lives without even feeling a hint of compassion or guilt. To Patrick, that was exactly what he had done to Stephen Ramsey. Only he had felt remorse, but would he next time, or the time after that? Undoubtedly, it was something he would have to do again. Would he feel equally as bad as he had with Stephen Ramsey, or would those feelings eventually abate? Would he be able to put someone else through that ordeal again, and not even flinch at the thought just because they 'looked good on paper'?

"Listen, Carl's checking what is left of Stephen Ramsey's alibis," Hawkins explained to Patrick. "We still have a few more hours here, but after that, unless there's some evidence or a new suspect to question, we're pretty much done here for the day. We won't hear anything from the Medical Examiner until tomorrow afternoon at the earliest, so there's no point in just sitting around here. We're all starving. No one has eaten all day."

At the mention of eating, Patrick suddenly became aware his stomach was yearning for something delicious, not to mention greasy. After the day he had, he deserved a juicy burger; loaded up with bacon, cheddar cheese, fried onions, and pickles with a huge side of loaded fries.

"There's a place we all like to go to after shitty days like this," Hawkins continued. "They have some damn good food, and even better beers. It's a nice atmosphere to unravel, and let the stress roll off of you. Why don't you come along? You can grab some grub, and chase it with a beer or two. After all, you're part of this family now, and we'd all love to get to know you."

"Thanks for the offer, but my wife usually cooks dinner. She's been on this whole family dinner kick ever since we've moved here."

"Why don't you call, and find out?" Hawkins insisted; picking up the nearby phone from its cradle, and handing it over to Patrick. "If she's cooking, you go home, and enjoy a nice family dinner—Hell, I would. If not, you come out with the guys, and have a good time. What's the harm in asking? Either way, it's a win for you."

The man had a point. Patrick could use a night out to get to know the men he'd be calling his colleagues. Claire would think that it was important and a good idea. Not to mention, life had been so hectic for her (for both of them) that she deserved a single night off from cooking. She could relax with a soothing bath once Connor was asleep, and let the stresses of work and life wash off of her.

He dialed his wife's cell, and ran the idea past her. The proposition had barely passed his lips when Claire gave him an ecstatic yes; she thought Patrick should go out.

They concluded their conversation with him letting Claire know he wouldn't be home too late. He passed the phone back to Hawkins for him to hang up, and let him know that he'd be joining the guys tonight.

"Perfect," Hawkins exclaimed; slapping Patrick on the back. "I'll let the guys know, and once Carl finishes up, we'll get freshened up, and head out."

As he watched Hawkins walk away, Patrick began to remember the little game the man had just played with him a few hours earlier. The game that ended with Patrick walking away; looking like a bad guy. Were the games over, or only getting started? Was this invitation genuine, or did Hawkins still have more in store for his replacement?

CHAPTER 8

O'Reilly's Pub was located in Bethpage; a neighboring town of Levittown. Compared to some of the other rank bars in the area, it was a nice set up. For starters, it had an actual dining area and kitchen. Decorating the wall behind the bar were old New York State and police squad car license plates, dating back decades. There was a small stage, where an Irish folk band was playing *Whiskey in the Jar*. The crowd that frequented was an older crowd. Patrick guessed that maybe, every now and then, a group of younger guys would wander in; hoping to pick up a cougar. Right now, however, Patrick Sullivan was the youngest person in the establishment.

They had put a few smaller tables together to form one large one. There were fifteen of them; all Nassau County police officers, and all laughing and having a great time. Together, they enjoyed food, beer and, most importantly, each other's company. This was their escape from the stresses of their jobs and lives.

Patrick was three quarters of the way through his second beer, and definitely feeling the effects.

He was the furthest thing from a drinker. He barely even drank socially. Truth was, he could probably count every time he had been drunk since the age of fifteen on his two hands. Maybe it was because he didn't like seeing his father drink nightly when he was growing up, or maybe he just didn't like the way alcohol took his control away from him (his temper seemed to be doing that well enough). Whatever the reason, Patrick wasn't a fan.

Now, however, he decided he would indulge a bit. It was a celebration of his new job. Only he wasn't too sure if he wanted to be celebrating it after some of his recent realizations.

Hawkins sat at the head of the table. Patrick watched as the other officers all greeted him with handshakes of the utmost respect. They refilled his glass when it was drained, they joked with him, and they all praised him, like he was their mighty king who had led them through many great wars.

It wasn't just the officers either. The moment that man stepped foot into the bar, everyone knew who he was, and greeted him with warm welcomes. He would greet the patrons with a single wave, and shouted to the bartender for a round of beers. When the beer arrived, the waitress told him the first round was on the house. That garnered a roar of appreciation from all those around the table. Everyone knew it was Hawkins' presence that had gotten them their free booze. Patrick wondered how great of a cop someone must truly be to be able to demand—and get—such respect from, not only his peers, but everyone he came in contact with.

Even Patrick, who had admired then despised Hawkins all in the span of a few hours, found himself, once again, respecting the man who had spent his years earning the reputation that he had.

Everyone at the table had been polite to Patrick; greeting him, and welcoming him to the force. He was well aware, however, he was the enemy among these men, and would not be so easily accepted as one of their own. After all, he was, as Hawkins had referred to him as, the replacement.

He was the man replacing the person who just so happened to be a messiah to these men.

"So, kid," Hawkins called across the table. "You got any new thoughts on the Ramsey murders that you'd care to share?"

At the mention of the topic of the case, there was a sudden uproar from everyone at the table. They all burst out in laughter, and started banging their near empty glasses on the table.

"Oh, come on, guys," Hawkins argued. "I was just making conversation with the kid. It's his first day, and I don't want him to feel like the outcast"

"Doesn't matter, Ace," Detective Murphy laughed. "The rules are the rules."

"Fine," Hawkins said; throwing his arms up in defeat. He got up from his chair, and pulled out his wallet. "You're just lucky I don't carry my gun outside of work, Carl."

"Yeah, yeah," Carl responded; brushing off Hawkins friendly threats. "Just get me my beer, tough guy"

Hawkins left the table, and made his way through the crowd to the bar.

"What was that about?" Patrick asked.

"We have one single rule at this bar," an officer sitting next to him, whose name, Patrick believed, was Mitch Henderson, explained. "And that rule is there is absolutely no talking about cases, or anything else work related while in this establishment. If you break the rule, you buy the whole table a round."

"That seems like a pretty good rule."

"Oh, it is…" Detective Murphy added. "For us. Not so much for Ace."

"Why's that?"

"Because," another officer answered. "Detective Hawkins is always the one who has to buy a round for the entire table… every… single… time."

Another fit of laughter from the table filled the room. He knew it was just light-hearted running joke amongst these cops, but Patrick also saw it as proof Jonathan Hawkins could not just leave his work behind when his day was over. It followed him wherever he went, because his job was an extension of who he was.

"Yeah, but that's just how Ace functions," Murphy explained. "There's no off time for him. In all the years I've known and worked with the stubborn son-of-a-bitch, he's never taken a single vacation, and to be honest, if he tried, he wouldn't be able to make it through a single day. I'm convinced that not being at work would drive him clinically insane. It's what makes him such a damn good cop, though."

"Detective Murphy, why do you call him 'Ace'?" Patrick asked. He had wondered that earlier in the day, but didn't get his answer, because it wasn't the time or place. Now, however, was.

"Because that's the best way to describe him," Detective Murphy answered. "And, please, call me Carl. Outside of work, I'm Carl; not detective."

Carl could tell by the confused look on Patrick's face that the simplicity of his answer would not suffice, and he was going to have to explain.

"You ever play Texas Hold 'Em, Patrick?" he asked.

"Yeah, I love poker."

"Well, imagine this: You've spent the night playing through a long grueling tournament. You're exhausted and it's finally come down to you, and one other person. The final two! The whole game, you and this guy across from you have smoked the competition. You've been neck-and-neck for the position of chip leader the entire time, and now it's down to the two of you.

"The cards get dealt, and you land a jack and a king; off suit. Not stupendous, but certainly playable. I'd say it was something you'd call, even raise on; just to feel out the other guy. Instead of doing this, you decide it's time to end the game, once and for all. You've managed to get ahead just slightly, so you're going to push this guy all in. You let it all ride on this one hand, and if you lose, you're not out, but you certainly don't have enough to survive much longer. This one hand is do-or-die.

"So, now this guy calls, and you each throw down your cards. You, with your Jack and King, and what does this son-of-a-bitch throw down? BAM!" Carl slammed his hand on the table. "Pocket tens! Right there and then, all hope seems to be lost, but you're still going to hang on. You just pray the flop does you some good.

"Then the Flop comes, and what gets thrown down? Two garbage cards, and another freaking *ten*! Now this guy's got three-of-a-goddamn-kind! And you have shit. Sure, the ten helps you out a little bit—your chances of getting a straight are still alive—but we all know an inevitable doom is in store for you.

"Next, comes the Turn, and with it, comes a Queen. You're still alive in this! You know the chances of actually taking it all home are still slim, but you start to feel Lady Luck riding on your back. All you need is that Ace to beat this guy, and you win it all. You plead with whatever higher power is choosing to listen to you to see that Ace come out, and guess what… before the River card even gets thrown down, you see it. You can see that last card getting flipped over in your mind, and you see that beautiful Ace laying there on the table.

"Finally, after what seems like an eternity, the River is thrown down, and BAM!" Murphy then slammed both fists down to add emphasis to his point. "It's the mother fucking Ace of Spades! You've just won it all!"

The guys at the table, who have, undoubtedly, heard this story a million times over, burst into a cheer, as if this hand Carl was describing was being played out right in front of them!

"The point is," Murphy continues. "If you can't figure it out on your own, Patrick; Jonathan Hawkins is the Ace you so desperately need to win it all."

He stared at Detective Murphy; taking in this analogy. It made perfect sense. Patrick had known Hawkins for less than a day—barely twelve hours!—but he knew it was the absolute perfect way to describe what the man meant to the homicide squad of the Nassau County Police Department.

He was their Ace on the River.

"That really happened, didn't it?" Patrick asked as a smirk stretched across his face. "Detective Hawkins really played that hand in a game of poker."

The table again burst out into a thunderous roar of amusement.

"Why do you think Reilly over here hasn't retired yet?" one officer joked; pointing to a detective who was around Hawkins and Murphy's age. "Hawkins pretty much took his entire pension in that hand of poker!"

"What's so funny?" Hawkins asked; returning to the table with three pitchers of fresh beer.

"Oh, nothing," Murphy answered nonchalantly. "We were just talking about getting a game of poker together soon."

"Why?" Hawkins asked. "Does Reilly want to have to work another ten years before he can retire?"

The wave rushed over the table yet again. A few of the guys were actually keeling over from laughing so hard. Everyone except Detective Reilly, who was still obviously bitter over his loss to Hawkins.

"Oh, Jim; get over it. I'll buy you something pretty next time we're out." Hawkins said as he poured beer into his friend's cup.

Detective Reilly tried to suppress his smile, but eventually broke, and joined in on the laughter.

"Okay, boys," Hawkins announced; putting the pitchers down on the table. "Drink up!"

As soon as he put them down, the pitchers were emptied.

"I'd like to make a toast." Hawkins announced to his colleagues as he stood at the end of the table with his glass already raised.

"Yeah, lets toast how fucking awesome you are, Hawkins!" yelled one of the officers, who clearly had the following day off, based on the amount of alcohol he was taking in.

"No, no," Hawkins said, even though it was obvious he would truly never get enough of the praise everyone gave him. "There will be plenty of time for that at my retirement party. Right now, I'd like to toast the newest member of our precinct, and my replacement."

To this comment the fun and laughter turned to jeers and boos. Patrick knew all of which were in good humor—it was just the boys hazing him—but he couldn't help picking up on a sense of seriousness from the sneers. It was a cold realization for these men. Hawkins, the man who clearly mentored most of these men, was soon leaving them, and Patrick was his replacement. He knew that no matter how much he proved himself adequate to his peers, he would never be Jonathan Hawkins.

Jonathan Hawkins was a legend. He was an icon. He was forever.

"Now, come on, guys," Hawkins continued; calming everyone. "Don't blame the replacement for me leaving. Blame the son-of-a-bitch cardiologist who said I had to hang it up. The kid over here is good peoples. Believe me;

I wouldn't be saying it unless I knew for sure. He's been on the job just one day, and he's already seen more than some homicide detectives see in their entire career. What's even more impressive is that he held it together, and he's still here. You can always tell when somebody is going to be good at the job and when they aren't going to make it. He's going to be one of the guys who are good at the job. I don't say this often, but today you impressed the hell out of me, kid. You made some good calls. You're a natural at this, and you're going to be just fine. So here's to the replacement. He's going to be a phenomenal detective."

Everyone sitting and standing around the table raised their glasses, and toasted the newest member of their police department. In that moment, simply due of the words Hawkins spoke to these men, Patrick felt accepted into their brotherhood. Once Hawkins told them it was okay to accept his replacement with open arms, they did. He had seen it numerous times throughout the day, but Patrick was truly in awe by the pull that Jonathan Hawkins had over people with just his words.

Patrick, too, raised his glass, which had been topped off by somebody when the pitchers were drained. He sent Hawkins a nod of thanks and appreciation, and Hawkins returned it. He brought the glass to his lips, and drank in his own honor.

CHAPTER 9

That last beer Patrick had during the toast in his honor was enough to send him over the edge of mildly buzzed, and into the land of a little bit tipsy. He left the bar that night feeling good. The moment he got home, he removed his shirt and pants. His mind may have been hazy, but his intentions were clear. He crawled quietly into bed, slid over to Claire's side, and started to softly kiss the nape of her neck.

"Oh, my," Claire said; waking up to her husband's seductive kisses. He was now running his hand over her stomach. "Somebody's had a little more to drink than he probably should have."

"You may be right," he answered; moving his lips to the front of Claire's neck.

"I'm thinking I kind of like you like this."

"I'm thinking you're about to like me a lot more."

Patrick got between Claire's legs, and started kissing her passionately. His hand began to roam south of her stomach.

After they had made love, Patrick slipped into slumber, easily. There was no such thing as stresses of first days, murder cases, and fragile lives he had ruined. They had all slipped away with orgasm. It made finding sleep simple. Unfortunately, his dreams were not as pleasant as his descent into twilight had been.

He was walking through the woods. A light mist rose steadily off the ground, and the browning leaves beneath his bare feet were moistened with the morning dew. In the distance, through the meshing sounds of the forest, Patrick could hear the sounds of laughter. It was a familiar sound. It was the laughter of his own child, he realized. He followed the sound of Connor, and, as Patrick drew nearer, the excitement in his son's voice grew.

As he raced through the foliage in search of his baby boy, he began to hear the faint sound of music as well. The two were intertwined—the laughter and the music. The music had been the source of Connor's hilarity. Patrick hastened his pace, so not to miss out on what Connor was so ecstatic over. He had already missed so many moments in his son's precious life, and he was determined to not miss this.

He stealthily weaved in and out of trees until he came to a large clearing. There, also standing at the edge of the tree line, was his son. Connor was jumping up and down in a spell of excitement; pointing.

"Look, da!" Connor yelled. "LOOK!" He then took off as fast as his tiny legs would allow him into the clearing.

Patrick took chase to catch up, but Connor had now disappeared into a mass of people who were entering an enormous circus tent. The music he had heard earlier was coming from within the thick canvas walls.

As he reached the tent, Patrick saw his firstborn, now holding hands with Claire, enter into the tent. He tried to push forward in order to catch up with his family, but was stopped by the people who had been waiting patiently. He was forced to the end of the line to wait like everyone else.

As he neared the entrance, Patrick saw a man standing on a stack of wooden milk crates. A small crowd had gathered around him; all of them staring up in awe and amazement. He was telling the spectators all about the spectacle inside.

That man was Wallace 'Baby Tooth' Freewaters.

Baby Tooth wore a bright red tailed ringmaster jacket. He had a top hat that he waved more in his hands than he wore on his head. To top off his picture-perfect ringmaster ensemble, he wore a monocle in his crushed eye socket.

"Come one, come all!" he exclaimed; waving his arms, and gesturing the crowd into the tent. "Who says love is only skin deep? Please, I implore you all to come inside, and see what love looks like completely stripped down!"

As Patrick reached the front of the line, he presented his ticket to be ripped. He tried to avoid all eye contact, but he knew Baby Tooth was staring right at him.

"I'm glad you could make it in time, Patty Boy. You wouldn't want to miss the main attraction." Baby Tooth gave a mischievous wink, which sent an unsettling feeling rushing through Patrick.

He began to forcefully push forward in an attempt to enter the tent. In that moment, he wanted nothing more than to create as much space as humanly possible between him and Baby Tooth. As he was about to step foot into the enormous tent, he heard his name one last time.

Not wanting to, but still doing so against his will, Patrick turned back, and saw Baby Tooth with his arms up in the air, and a huge toothless grin—except his damn baby tooth—stretched across his half demolished face.

"Enjoy the show!!!"

Once he was finally in the tent, Patrick could not spot Connor or Claire anywhere among the massive crowd of onlookers. All the seats had been taken, and there was now standing room only.

Suddenly, the lights were killed, and he was in complete darkness.

A spot light snapped on, and standing there, in the center of the tent, completely naked, were Arthur and Estelle Ramsey. Their aged sagging bodies were exposed to all those looking on to see.

At first, they did not move. They only stared at each other. Patrick could feel the love these two shared emanating from each other's stare. It was that unnamable love he felt for Claire. Arthur took his wife by the hands, and drew her nearer. Estelle ran her wrinkled hands up her husband's deflated arms. She halted at his chest, and waited there for a few staggering moments—letting the crowd's anticipation grow a bit. She then sank her long nails into her husband's chest, and ripped the skin clear off his sternum with one swift yank.

Patrick screamed out in protest, but his voice was muted by the overwhelming eruption of the crowd's cheers.

Estelle, with a huge beautiful smile upon her face, threw her arms into the air; her husband's skin dangling from her hands. His blood was trickling down her arms. The crowd's cheers thickened as she showed them what she had done. She took the blood-soaked skin, and tossed it into the crowd for someone to catch, and take home as a piece of disturbing memorabilia.

Arthur then took his wife by the hand, and slowly spun her under his arm; looking her up and down. He then methodically made his way around her; making the crowd yearn for his next move. He stopped behind Estelle, grabbed onto the skin of her back, and gave it one hard pull. There was a sick tearing sound of skin and nerves being wrenched away from muscle as Arthur yanked the skin right off his wife's back. The crowd ate it all up, and began to cheer louder; begging for more.

Patrick couldn't sit by idly, and watch this. He started to push his way through the other bystanders, so that he could put a stop to this madness. When he reached the front of the crowd, he felt two sets of hands slam hard into his chest; preventing him from moving any further. In front of him stood Carl Murphy and Jonathan Hawkins.

"End of the line, kid," Hawkins said, but Patrick ignored him, and tried to push forward.

Again, he was pushed back, and when he tried a third time to break through Hawkins and Murphy, they grabbed him by the arms. He thrashed back and forth violently, as he tried to free himself, but he couldn't overpower his two partners.

"I have to stop them!" Patrick yelled as he was being escorted from the tent, but it was to no avail.

He watched, as he was being dragged from the tent, Arthur and Estelle Ramsey lock lips in a long passionate kiss. As their lips met, they grabbed at each other's face, and began to slowly pull the other's skin away.

"STOP!" Patrick yelled, but his pleas went unheard, and the last thing he saw as he was heaved from the tent were the Ramsey's holding up the skin from each other's face for the crowd to ogle at and admire.

As he hit the ground, Patrick was woken up from his slumber, but thanks to a combination of exhaustion and alcohol, he fell right back into the depths of sleep, where his dream would remain; forgotten.

CHAPTER 10

Sleep had finally released Patrick Sullivan from its tight grip early the following morning. Upon opening his heavy eyelids, he felt two immediate sensations; neither of them were pleasant.

The first being the unforgiving pounding of his head. It felt like a steel toed boot kicking him in his temples; back and forth to the brutal tempo of a metronome. The second sensation was extreme nausea. Patrick was convinced the chances he would not upchuck last night's dinner (not to mention beverages) before he could make it to the bathroom were slim. His body always responded poorly to any amount of alcohol; even when he was younger. One thing was certain: there would be no exercising that morning.

Instead, he chose to lie down in a steaming hot shower for almost an hour, and let the near scolding water bounce off his skin, and help sooth his ailing stomach. He had not the tiniest inkling of recollection of his frightening nightmare.

When he arrived at the police station, Patrick was immediately directed to see Officer Summers. He found it impossible to concentrate on whatever it was she was talking about. His headache, combined with the Ramsey's murder case, and the fact that he simply didn't care about whatever mind-numbingly boring information was being fired his way made for the perfect cocktail of complete loss of attention.

About an hour into the orientation—and absolutely zero information absorbed—Detective Hawkins busted into the room without even a courteous knock.

"Excuse me, Detective Hawkins, but we are in the middle of an orientation!" Officer Summers said firmly.

"I know, I know," Hawkins shot back. "But we really need to get over to the hospital to speak to the coroner. She just called about our victims, and needs to speak to us right away. I thought, being that Detective Sullivan is an active investigator on this case, it would be of the utmost importance that he came along to hear what the lovely coroner has to say."

"Well, unfortunately, we aren't finished here."

"Oh, come on, Sue; we all know the deal; great benefits, great retirement plan, blah, blah, blah. I'm sure the kid knows all about this crap from when he worked for the city. We really need to see the coroner. Can you please let him go?"

Officer Summers stared at Detective Hawkins for a few moments; seemingly standing her ground. Patrick was shocked she hadn't given into the request right away, but he knew what the end result would be, and he guessed Officer Summers knew as well.

"Fine," she finally said; giving in. "He just needs to sign a few things. Give us ten more minutes."

"Ten minutes is perfect. You are a doll, Sue." With that said, Hawkins was out the door.

"Never a dull moment with Detective Hawkins, huh?" Patrick asked.

"Nope," Officer Summers said; laying out the proper paperwork to be signed. "I'm shocked the man even finds time to sleep. To him, sleep is just a pesky interference to solving a case."

The three detectives were escorted to the coroner's office once they arrived at the Nassau County Medical Center. Patrick stood in the rear of the small office, looking obviously anxious. Eagerness was crawling all over his skin, as he was itching to learn any new details that could help them along in this case.

Detective Hawkins and Murphy, on the other hand, looked calm and collected as they occupied the two chairs in the office. They sat there silently with their hands in their laps, as if they were doing something as casual as waiting for the bus on a warm spring day. Patrick wanted to scream just so he could get some sort of reaction out of either of them.

When the coroner, Doctor Margareta Wilkensis, entered her office, she was greeted by Hawkins and Murphy with a warm welcoming smile. Despite the unfortunate circumstance which brought them together, they were genuinely happy to see each other; like three childhood friends reuniting at their high school reunion. When they were finished with their pleasantries, Hawkins introduced Patrick to the doctor.

"Tense," the doctor stated; pointing out the obvious as the two shook hands.

"Well, you know how they are on their first case," Hawkins joked. "They're like teenage boys about to lose their virginity. They're so anxious and worked up that they have absolutely no idea how to just play it cool."

A quick laugh at Patrick's expense was exchanged as the three took their seats again, but the moment their butts hit their seats, the mood in the room did a complete one-eighty. It had changed from light-hearted to all business.

"I don't like this one, guys," she said. "I mean, I've seen some grotesque stuff in this line of work, but this one… this one takes the cake."

"I know, Margareta," Hawkins responded.

"No, Ace… you have no idea," she answered with a face made of stone.

"What do you have for us?"

"Well, first off, this guy knew what he was doing. He was by no means a professional, but he wasn't slicing away blindly at these victims. He managed to skin them both right down to their dermises, but his cuts weren't perfect. They weren't anywhere near the kind of cuts a surgeon would make."

"So this guy's done his research?" Detective Murphy asked.

"He is certainly well-versed in anatomy. I can tell you that," Doctor Wilkensis answered.

"So, maybe we're looking for a medical school drop out?" Patrick asked.

"It's a possibility that he—*or she*—had once attended medical school, but if I had to guess, I would say you should look more into your perp being a nurse or an orderly at a hospital."

"Why's that?" Hawkins asked.

"I was up all damn night with this, John; calling in favors to have the blood work rushed. So you three better be grateful."

Doctor Wilkensis produced three manila folders, and passed them across the desk to Hawkins, who passed them to Patrick and Murphy. Inside, were photocopies of the official autopsy report on the Ramsey's.

"I found significant amounts of Pancuronium Bromide in their systems," Doctor Wilkensis explained as the three looked over her report.

Pancuronium Bromide, she told them, was a paralytic drug used during surgery, alongside anesthesia. What it did was completely paralyze the patient so that there was no involuntary muscle movement during complicated operations while they were under.

"There was no trace of anesthesia in either of their systems," the coroner continued. "Without proper anesthesia the patient is completely conscious, and aware of what is going on around them. They can feel every single thing that is happening to them, but they are incapable of doing anything about it."

Patrick felt from inside him, a hatred detonating within the depths of his soul. It had been there, ever since he laid eyes on those two skinned bodies for the first time, lying dormant. It was an aneurism; ready to burst at any moment.

And it just had.

"Are you telling me Arthur and Estelle Ramsey were alive and conscious while they were being skinned?" Hawkins asked in a neutral, professional tone that Patrick couldn't believe. Not even the news of this couple suffering through an unfeasible amount of pain warranted any sort of reaction from him.

"That's exactly what I'm telling you, Ace. The female got off lucky—if lucky is what you want to call it. It's your male victim that I truly feel sorry for."

His name is Arthur Ramsey! Patrick screamed in his head. *And her name was Estelle! They were people who were tortured to death, and you are all talking about them like they are just two cadavers you just studied in med school.*

"Pancuronium Bromide," Doctor Wilkensis went on. "Can cause some serious complications for someone who already suffers from lingering heart conditions…"

"Estelle Ramsey had a heart condition," Detective Murphy pointed out.

"Yeah, she did. Now, I opened her up, and I can tell you that the cause of death for your female victim was myocardial infarction."

"So, she had a heart attack?" Hawkins clarified.

"Yes, between the combination of the paralytic, and the stress of what was happening to her, she died within minutes of the first cut. Physically, she barely suffered."

"Well, that's good news... I guess," Detective Murphy said; attempting to put everyone's hearts somewhat at ease.

No, Patrick thought. He was fighting the temptation to spew his inner dialogue out on everyone in the room. *Good would be Estelle Ramsey dying peacefully in her sleep from old age. Good is not being paralyzed, and dying from congestive heart failure, because her heart can't handle the stress of her skin being torn from her body.*

"Unfortunately, your male victim is a different story..."

Arthur Ramsey, Doctor Wilkensis explained, had a much larger amount of Pancuronium Bromide in his system than Estelle Ramsey did; implying he had lived significantly longer than his wife. The doctor had put the time of death of each victim at least twelve hours apart.

This, by no means, was the worst of the coroner's news.

She went on to explain to the detectives that Estelle Ramsey had been continuously injected, post mortem, with the paralytic drug.

"Couldn't he have been unaware that Estelle Ramsey had died?" Detective Murphy asked.

"I don't think so," Doctor Wilkensis responded.

She explained that their perp had drastically decreased the dosage that he (or she) was injecting Estelle Ramsey with after she had died. The amount she was being injected with, post mortem, wasn't enough to keep someone fully paralyzed if they had been alive, even someone as weak as Estelle Ramsey.

"He wanted Arthur Ramsey to think his wife was still alive and suffering," Patrick said.

It explained why the perp needed a few days of privacy to commit his crime. This was way more than a get in, get skin, and get out sort of crime. This was methodical and evil.

"Seems that way," the coroner clarified. "From what I was able to conclude from my findings, that is more than likely the case."

Patrick couldn't contain himself any longer. He began to pace from one end of the small room to the next; biting the knuckle of his thumb.

He felt Hawkins hand grip his elbow.

"Hey, kid; you need to cool off."

Patrick didn't want to cool off, though. He imagined having to sit there, utterly defenseless, while Claire was ripped to shreds before his eyes. He tried to envision what it would feel like fighting with every fiber of his being to help his wife, but being incapable, because he was turned to stone by paralysis. No, cooling off was definitely not an option right now.

He hated this son-of-a-bitch for what he did to Arthur and Estelle Ramsey. There was only one person he had ever felt anything close to this sort of putrid hatred for. He had felt the full wrath of Patrick's fury, and, now, he was no longer around to tell the tale.

Patrick found himself wanting to inflict that same fury onto the Ramsey's killer. He wanted to tear the flesh off their murderer's bones with his own bare hands. He wanted to hear him scream and plead for the end, and Patrick would end him, but not until he felt the same suffering the Ramsey's felt before they died.

"I know all this sucks," Hawkins continued. "But we're going to nail this bastard, and he's going to get the needle; just like he deserves. Until then, you need to stay calm."

Hawkins words did nothing to calm Patrick. He still fumed ferociously, but he would put on a mask for everyone else to see. He would take that deep breath he used to compose himself, even though he was sure he'd need more than just one for this, and he would focus on the case. Then, once they caught the beast who killed those two people, Patrick would take justice into his own hands.

Like he had done once before.

CHAPTER 11

Patrick had managed to get his anger under control, or so he hoped that's how it was coming across. He planned to cage his ire until the perfect opportunity for him to unleash it came along.

He suspected Hawkins wasn't buying into his front. His veteran instincts were likely fully aware Patrick hadn't heeded his advice to gain his composure. He made no mention of it though. For now, he seemed content with the charade.

Once the meeting with the coroner concluded, they decided the best course of action in their investigation would be to contact local hospitals, and find out if any units of Pancuronium Bromide had gone missing from their inventories. Hawkins had gone by himself to meet the Nassau County District Attorney, so that they could acquire court ordered subpoenas for the hospitals' records.

Patrick felt completely useless sitting around; just waiting for Hawkins while the Ramsey's murderer was out there; breathing precious oxygen he or she had no right breathing.

The unbearable waiting wouldn't end there, either. Once Hawkins returned, they'd have to contact multiple hospitals, and then wait for them to respond; hoping one supplied them with a viable lead.

THE REPLACEMENT

Around two thirty in the afternoon, Patrick took notice of his stomach. It was starting to growl. He was getting quite hungry. He had woken up feeling too ill to eat, and once they met with the coroner and learned the new facts surrounding the investigation, food had become the last thing on his mind. Now, however, after being back at the station for a few hours, his empty stomach began to call out, and plead for some substance. Claire had made him lunch that morning—a fantastic turkey and Swiss cheese sandwich—but he had been too out of it to remember to grab it on his way out the door. He was currently cursing himself out for that mistake.

Forty minutes later, when his hunger pains made him want to scream, Claire showed up; carrying the brown paper bag that contained her husband's forgotten lunch.

"Hungry?" she asked; walking up to his desk.

"Yes! Thank God you came with that. I'm starving."

Patrick stood up, kissed his wife, and snatched the bag away from her. He removed the contents of the paper bag, and tore into them like a rabid animal.

"I think we just figured out where Connor gets his messy eating habits from," Claire joked as Patrick devoured his sandwich within seconds.

"Kid, didn't anyone ever tell you to eat with your mouth closed?" Hawkins said as he and Murphy made the way across the station room. He had finally returned with the much needed subpoenas. "Also, eat your food one bite at a time. You're an animal."

Patrick barely heard the man. He was completely preoccupied.

"Who's the pretty lady, kid?" Hawkins asked once Patrick had swallowed his last bite of food.

"Sorry," Patrick said; pulling an apple from the bag. "This is my wife, Claire... Claire, this is Detectives Jonathan Hawkins and Carl Murphy."

"Nice to meet you," Claire said with a smile; shaking Hawkins and Murphy's hands. "You'll have to excuse him. I'm still trying to teach him all his manners."

"Pretty, and funny," Hawkins astutely pointed out. "Those are two great qualities. How did a stick-in-the-mud like you end up with such a good catch?"

"Believe me, I ask myself that question every day," Patrick joked.

"As do I," Claire added with a teasing grin. "I wish I could stay for a bit, and get to know the wonderful people Patrick will be working with, but I have to get going. Connor's still at daycare. I told them I'd be a little late."

Patrick gave his wife a kiss; thanking her again for bringing him his lunch.

"Do you have any idea when you'll be home tonight?" Claire asked. "I know you're super busy, but I'm cooking dinner and I just need to know if I should set a plate at the table for you."

He had no answer for his wife. They were both used to the strain that long hours put on their family life while he was with the NYPD. Now, with the new job and an investigation right off the bat, Patrick knew he was in for some long, home-cooked-dinnerless nights that he would be spending at the 8th precinct, instead of home with his family.

"Don't worry; he'll be home in time for dinner," Hawkins answered before Patrick could get an answer past his lips. "He just has to fax these subpoenas over to some hospitals. We probably won't hear back from them until tomorrow morning, the earliest, and if we do, Carl or I can handle it. There's no reason for him to be stuck here all night."

Patrick had his doubts about Hawkins. He had wondered if the man was human or robot, based on his lack of emotional response to some situations, but he couldn't help but be moved by this gesture. Hawkins didn't want to see Claire disappointed by the idea of her husband not being home to spend time with his family.

"Thanks," Patrick said.

"Don't mention it, kid. Enjoy it, too. Home cooked dinners become a rarity in this line of work. I haven't had a hot home cooked dinner in… well, I can't even remember how long."

"Well, why not?" Claire asked; surprised. Patrick guessed she hadn't been able to pick up on that *work is the only thing that matters in life; nothing else; just work* vibe Hawkins usually gave off.

"I haven't exactly been able to get around to cooking in a good long while. It's usually TV dinners for me after a long day."

"That's ridiculous," Claire stated. "Why don't you come join us tonight for dinner?"

Say what? Patrick asked in his head.

Sure, he was touched by Hawkins' kindness, but he still wasn't sure if he admired or despised the guy. Now, Claire was inviting him to dinner!

Patrick definitely was not keen on the idea.

"I couldn't," Hawkins answered, "I wouldn't want to intrude on a family's evening together."

"Detective Hawkins, I insist you come over tonight for dinner. I cook a mean chicken, and there will be plenty to go around.

And there goes my leftovers tomorrow, Patrick complained to himself.

"Well, a home cooked meal certainly sounds delicious."

"Then it's settled; you'll join us."

"Doesn't look like you're leaving me with much of a choice now, does it?"

"Nope; I'm sorry. I refuse to take *no* for an answer."

I really wish you would. Patrick thought.

"I can't refuse a pretty lady… never could. I'll see you tonight then, Claire."

"Yes, you will."

Claire extended an invitation to Detective Murphy, who politely declined; saying dinner would be ready for him when he got home. She then checked her watch, excused herself because she really had to pick up Connor, and told Hawkins to come by around seven that evening.

"You see, kid," Hawkins said once Claire was gone. "That's how you get something you want from someone while making them think it was their idea. It's a great tool to use in interrogation."

Everyone around the desk burst into laughter at Hawkins' jape. Even Patrick couldn't help but laugh. Still, as laughter passed through his lips, he remained indecisive over how he felt about Jonathan Hawkins breaching the barrier between work life and home. He guessed he would find out for sure in a few hours.

CHAPTER 12

Patrick returned home to the smell of food cooking, and the sound of the vacuum running. Claire had always kept a tidy home. She devoted Sundays to cleaning the entire house from top to bottom; even the parts that didn't seem to be dirty to begin with. Yet, whenever the Sullivan's were having guests over, the house just never seemed to be clean enough for Claire's expectations. Patrick would repeatedly find his wife vacuuming, dusting, wiping, or scrubbing something that she had just gone over twenty minutes earlier. Given that you couldn't clean something that was already clean, he found this whole process counterproductive and, at times, annoying. He never argued this point, though. He knew his battles to pick, and this was not one of them.

Upon entering his home, Patrick removed his shoes—he wouldn't dare walk across the carpet in anything other than socks!—walked over to Claire, and took the vacuum from her hands. He promised he would finish vacuuming the room from wall to wall, corner to corner, even though he knew she had already done that—while she concentrated on cooking. She reluctantly gave over the reins; not trusting Patrick's ability to vacuum to perfection, and headed to the kitchen to finish up with dinner.

At seven o'clock on the dot the Sullivan's doorbell rang. Patrick opened the door, and standing there on the adjacent side, bottle of wine in hand, was Detective Jonathan Hawkins. He had changed from one ridiculously overpriced button-down shirt into another ridiculously overpriced button-down shirt. Apparently, there was some kind of difference between pricey work clothes and dinnerware that Patrick wasn't aware of, and, quite frankly, couldn't tell the difference.

"Kid," Hawkins said with a friendly nod.

"Detective Hawkins, please come in."

When he entered the Sullivan's household, Hawkins did a quick once over of the living room; sizing it up. Patrick knew exactly what was going on. Hawkins was attempting to gain some insight into his replacement's home life based on his surroundings. Just like he would do at a crime scene.

He's probably not even aware he's doing it, Patrick thought as he watched Hawkins. *After thirty years, it's become his natural response when entering someplace new. Well, I hope he's noticing how squeaky clean this room is!*

"Detective Hawkins, I'm so glad to see you," Claire said; entering the room.

"Claire, it's so good seeing you again!" Hawkins responded.

He had a friendly smile stretched across his face. Patrick couldn't recall seeing him smile once in the two day span he had spent working side-by-side with the man.

"This is for you." He handed the bottle of wine to Claire. "It's not much, but I couldn't come empty handed."

"It's perfect. Thank you."

"It's the least I could do for being welcomed into your gorgeous home, Claire."

How it is my wife gets to be called by her first name before I do?? Patrick complained to himself.

102

THE REPLACEMENT

"And who might this little man be?" Hawkins asked; looking down at the two year old standing behind his mother's legs. He attempted to stay well hidden, so that he could do some recon on this unfamiliar face in his house. Once he was made, Connor took tight hold of Claire's leg, and tried to hide his face in the back of her knee.

"This is our son, Connor. He has no qualms about running up to complete strangers in the mall, and striking a conversation with them," Claire joked. "But he turns into a big 'ol scaredy cat when somebody he doesn't know comes into his home. Don't you, honey?"

She picked up Connor, and he immediately buried his face in her shoulder.

"Well, hi there, Connor," Hawkins said with a foreign tone to match that warm smile. "My name is John. It's very nice to meet you."

Connor lifted his head from the safety of his mom's shoulder, and stared at Hawkins; doing a little sizing up of his own.

"Hi," he said, then quickly buried his face back in Claire's shoulder. The cuteness of the whole thing got a laugh out of everybody.

"He'll get used to me. Kids love me," Hawkins promised. "We'll be best buds before the night is through."

Patrick couldn't believe the man he was standing with right now. If he was a betting man, he would've guessed Hawkins was the same with kids as he was with adults; a wise cracking hard-ass. Turned out that it was not the case at all.

"Dinner will be ready in just a few minutes," Claire announced, and headed back to the kitchen with Connor.

That evening, they ate Lemon and Garlic Chicken over brown rice with a side of roasted vegetables at the dining room table. The kitchen was the usual room they ate their family meals, but not when they were entertaining. When they were having company over, Claire chose to eat in the more spacious dining area. She even went so far as to take out the 'good china' for their current guest. To Patrick, this was all a bit much.

"This is absolutely delicious, Claire," Hawkins raved; taking another bite. "Do you like your mommy's cooking, Connor."

"Yeah," Connor answered; now completely won over by Hawkins.

"What's your favorite food your mommy makes?"

"Spespetti," Connor answered; matter-of-factly.

"Spaghetti?!" Hawkins asked; ecstatically. "I hear that is a very fine dish."

"Yeah, it's his favorite, because he had it for dinner last night. Tomorrow night his favorite food will be chicken," Claire joked. "The night before last, his favorite food was cut up hotdogs in mac and cheese."

"Nuh-uh," Connor informed his mother.

"Uh-huh." Claire leaned over, and blew a raspberry on her son's cheek; causing a burst of hilarity.

"Well, Claire; again, I must say: this is absolutely remarkable," Hawkins praised. "It has been too long since I had something so good. Not since Maryanne."

"Is Maryanne your wife?" Claire asked; wiping off Connor's mouth.

"She was… she passed away almost ten years ago, now."

"Oh…" Claire was obviously embarrassed for bringing up what could only be a sensitive subject. "I'm sorry."

"Don't be. I like talking about her. She was really quite lovely."

Jonathan Hawkins and his late wife, Maryanne, had been high school sweethearts. They ran away together after their senior year, and traveled the country for an entire summer. When the two returned home that fall, they were married.

Patrick couldn't imagine that guy. The Jonathan Hawkins who would just pack up, and travel the United States on a whim; with a girl he was completely over the moon in love with, none-the-less. Honestly, it was shocking that Hawkins had even once been married. Patrick figured the man's one true love had been, and always would be, the job.

Hawkins reminisced with overwhelming fondness as he spoke of how his late wife was the most beautiful woman he had ever seen. She was a woman who could command an entire room with just the faintest upward curvature of her lips. In their years together, Maryanne would wait up for her husband each and every night he worked long shifts. There was always a warm, home-cooked dinner waiting for him, no matter what time he got home.

"Then she got the cancer," Hawkins told them. He tried to mask it as he stared down at his plate, but there was a sadness now in his voice. Some subject matters brought out emotions in people that just couldn't be covered up, no matter how hard they wished they could. For Jonathan Hawkins, this was that subject "She never smoked a day in her life, my Maryanne, yet she still got lung cancer."

"I'm sorry." This time it was Patrick who offered his condolences. He tried to imagine Hawkins' pain, but he knew he was only treading the waters of a vast ocean of emotions he knew nothing about. If it was Claire who Patrick lost so early on in life, he couldn't begin to imagine the emptiness that would consume him.

"Don't worry about it, kid. I cherished every moment I spent with her when she was alive. Some people lose the ones they love, and then realize they never truly appreciated what they had. I wasn't one of them. I loved her every day we were together, and I cherish every memory we built together. Those are what keep her alive, even though she's gone" Hawkins told the married couple sitting across the table from him; patting his hand over his heart. "She's the reason I do what I do so well."

He explained about the day of her funeral, and how he had promised his late wife, as he watched her casket being lowered into the ground, that Jonathan Hawkins would devote what remained of his life to preventing others' lives from being cut short. For those who were taken away before their time, much like Maryanne had been, he would make sure he caught, and brought to justice those responsible. He couldn't cure cancer, but he was a damn good detective. That was how Jonathan Hawkins honored the memory of his wife.

"That's beautiful. I'm sure she would be so proud of you," Claire said; obviously moved by Hawkins' story.

"I'd like to think that she would be."

"Did you two have any children, Detective Hawkins?" Claire asked; attempting to sway the subject to the more uplifting side.

Unfortunately, she had no such luck doing so. Hawkins told them that he and his late wife did not have any children, because they were unable to conceive.

"We never got checked out," he told them. "Not that the doctors back then knew nearly as much as they do now, but we weren't interested in knowing where and with who the problems were. We thought it better to not know whose parts weren't working properly. That way, there would be no resentment. We were always happy with the other's company, so we didn't need to have children to fill a void, like some people do. Still, it would have been nice. I know she would've been such an amazing mother."

Patrick looked over at his son, who was not very interested in the current conversation. He was more thankful now for Connor than he ever thought possible.

The topic of conversation may not have been the happiest of subjects, but Patrick felt a warmth fill his heart as he stared at that beautiful two year old.

"Jeez... I'm just asking all the wrong questions tonight." Claire said in a half joking tone of voice. Her face had gone red from embarrassment.

"Don't worry about it," Hawkins assured her. "Besides, as you two know, it can be quite hard on a family when one of the members is in law enforcement. The hours are definitely brutal when they need to be, and I'm not saying that to be negative, or put you two down—you seem to have a lovely family unit set up here—but sometimes I'm glad it was just the two of us. I worked a lot of hours back then—not that I still don't—and I just don't think it would have been fair."

"I can relate," Claire said. "I've never had a problem with Patrick's long hours—I knew what I was getting myself into when I agreed to marry him—but I have to say, it feels nice knowing this Thanksgiving is the first one he's had off since we started dating. He would always rack up the overtime hours with the Macy's Day Parade when with the NYPD."

Patrick was also grateful for the opportunity he had to spend this particular holiday with his family, and he was glad that Claire felt the same joy. She had always been patient and understanding, and she deserved the moments when they all could be together. They both did.

"So, enough about me, and my depressing stories," Hawkins said; taking a second helping of chicken. "Tell me how you two met."

"Oh, nothing as interesting as your story," Patrick answered, "We just met through a friend on the force. We went on a few dates, and we just clicked."

This, however, much like the reason they told everyone Patrick had resigned from the NYPD, was a bold faced lie.

One that the two of them had mastered, and told so many times to so many people over the years, it almost seemed true. The truth was the two first met on the rooftop of Claire's Brooklyn apartment building, while Patrick was standing on the ledge; ready to end his own life.

One week before his one year anniversary of graduating the academy, Patrick was assigned to a Narcotics sting operation. The objective of this operation was to seize a sizeable quantity of drugs that the NYPD, along with the FBI, needed in their long battle against the trafficking of drugs in and out of New York City.

Narcotics had received word from one of their undercover officers of a precise date and location to where these drugs would be. The plan was simple: move in, obtain the drugs, and hopefully arrest some extremely important players in their ongoing war.

Plans, however, went terribly awry, even before the operation could begin.

Maybe the whole thing was thrown together too quickly and they had been spotted before they could move in, maybe there was a mole in Narcotics close to the operation, or maybe it was some other factor. Whatever it was, the targets had become aware of the presence of local and federal law enforcement.

Before any command to move in could be given, the abandoned warehouse where the drugs were being stored was ablaze. Once aware that the building was on fire, Patrick and the other officers assigned to this operation were told to immediately move in. This proved to be a very bad and very embarrassing call by Narcotics, who, later on, would have the blame dumped on them by the FBI. Between the civilians fleeing the surrounding area, and the fire department arriving on scene only minutes after the fire was set, chaos had erupted. This made it impossible to properly move in to secure the building, and prevent anyone from escaping.

Patrick made his way down a narrow alley towards the back of the building to secure any rear exits. When he turned the corner, he was greeted by a woman who had a gun pointed right at him. Before she could put one in his chest, Patrick took refuge behind a dumpster, and drew his own weapon. He ordered the woman to drop her firearm, but instead of complying with his orders, the woman told him, rather bluntly, to fuck off. That was when he heard the explosive shot from her gun, followed by the deafening sound of bullet meeting metal.

What happened next was a combination of training, mixed with raw survival instinct.

When the second shot was fired and he heard it bounce off the dumpster, Patrick turned towards the woman, and pulled the trigger of his own gun. The bullet entered the woman's stomach, and she immediately collapsed to the ground. She clutched her stomach; desperately trying to stop the flow of blood from the entry wound the bullet had made. This was useless. It wasn't the blood leaving her body that was the issue, but the blood that was pouring into her stomach that was killing her.

Patrick radioed for assistance as he knelt over this dying woman; telling her to hang in there. A few tears streamed down her face, and then she slipped from the fragile plane of mortality into the fearful unknown.

The events of that day were a complete failure. The drugs that the NYPD and FBI hoped to obtain were destroyed by the fire, and all the major players they hoped to arrest had slipped away undetected during the chaos. If they had even been there to begin with.

Throughout the days that followed, Patrick was forced to reprise his story for numerous people. The NYPD needed to know exactly what led him to opening fire on this woman, whose name was Vivian Chambers, and was pronounced dead on arrival at the hospital. After all inquiries were finished, he was ordered to see the department psychologist. It was there he learned that Vivian Chambers had been five months pregnant.

This had come as a devastating blow. Not only had he killed another human being—self-defense or not, it was still something that weighed heavily on his conscious—but Patrick had ended another's life before it even had a chance to start. He robbed a completely innocent and precious life of its opportunity to exist. It didn't deserve that. It had absolutely zero control over its circumstances. It didn't choose to be involved in the lifestyle its mother had chosen to participate in. Patrick hated Vivian Chambers for not getting out once she became aware she was pregnant.

But he hated himself more.

As often as he told himself there was no way he could have known Vivian Chambers was pregnant, or that he had no other choice but to shoot her, Patrick Sullivan still found himself up nights; riddled with guilt. The few hours he did manage to sleep, solely because his body couldn't physically stay awake any longer, he dreamt of Vivian Chambers, and her child.

In his recurring nightmare, Patrick walked into a hospital room where Vivian was sitting in a rocking chair; cradling her newborn child in her motherly embrace.

He'd stand over the smiling mother as she hummed a nameless tune to her child. Vivian would look up, and stare into his cold eyes. The smile on her face would disintegrate; leaving behind fear and sadness. She would ask Patrick if he had to, and each time, he would answer with only a cold nod.

Vivian Chambers would kiss her baby softly on its smooth forehead, and say she would love it for always.

Patrick would then draw his weapon, and proceed to shoot the newborn in his tiny chest. He'd then watch as it turned to ash. His weapon would then be directed at Vivian Chamber's stomach, and fired. A single tear falling from her dying eye would be the last thing Patrick saw before waking up; screaming.

Unable to come to grips with what he had done to that baby and his continuous torturous nightmares, Patrick had made the decision that he could no longer live with the guilt.

That was how he ended up on Claire's rooftop.

Standing there on the building ledge; waiting for the courage to step off and face whatever came after this, Patrick heard the roof door swing open. He whipped around to see who was joining him, and nearly lost his footing. As he regained his balance, he asked himself why he had bothered doing that; given the reason he was there in the first place was to throw himself off the roof.

A woman, with a cigarette pressed between her lips, stepped out onto the roof. She was unaware of the man standing twenty feet away from her; on the ledge of her apartment building. Her hair up in a ponytail, and she was wearing sweatpants and an old Led Zeppelin tee-shirt. Patrick thought she looked positively beautiful.

At least this woman will be the last thing I see before I die, he joked with himself as he watched her light her cigarette.

That's when the woman turned around, and became aware she was not the only one out for some nighttime air.

Don't come any closer, were the first words that came to Patrick's mind, but he refused to let them pass his lips. He wasn't about to have such a cliché line be the last thing he ever spoke.

Instead, they just stood there in silence; accessing the situation. It was she who finally spoke, and uttered a simple *Hey*. A friendly greeting was the last thing Patrick had anticipated. She could have said about a dozen different things to him, or she could have freaked out, and gone into complete panic mode. Instead, she simply went with *Hey*. Patrick, had no response for that, so he returned her greeting with a plain *Hi*.

"How's it going?" she asked, as if catching up with a friend she hadn't spoken to for few weeks, and not talking to a complete stranger, who was clearly standing on the ledge of her building with the intention of committing suicide.

"Eh, not so great," Patrick answered.

Was he really doing this? Was he really having a conversation with someone he didn't even know when, moments ago, he was gathering up the courage to plunge to his messy death?

"I can tell," she pointed out, and then, without knowing the man she was talking to at all, his current state of mind, or how he would take it, she cracked a joke. "I mean, I wouldn't be so great either if I chose *this* roof to stand on the ledge of. There are far nicer ones with far more pleasant views to stand on than this dump."

Patrick should have been offended by this woman making light of his situation. He had every right to be irate that she had the audacity to even joke in this obvious low point of his life.

However, instead of anger, he felt laughter building up in his chest. He wanted to mask the fact he was fighting off a smile, but it was too late. His lips curled upwards against his will, and he was smiling.

She smiled back at him, and when he saw it, Patrick thought maybe he had already died and gone to Heaven. As he looked back years later, he was convinced that was the exact moment he had fallen in love with Claire. Perhaps it was the reason she was able to talk him off the ledge that night. Patrick Sullivan didn't know it just yet, but he found what he needed to survive.

"May I just say one thing about your current…um, situation?" she asked politely; pointing to his feet, which were half on the concrete ledge, and half in the vast nothingness that lay between him and the street below.

He didn't have to say yes. Who cares what she had to say? What did she know about Patrick's current situation?

Still, he agreed to hear what she had to say.

"Whatever it is in your life that has you thinking you can't escape… whatever it is that has you on this ledge… It isn't worth dying for. Whatever's got you in its ugly grasp, you can break free of it, and walk away."

Of course she was going to say that. Was she going to tell Patrick that he should jump, because clearly he can't handle the shit going on inside his head?

"Not this," was his answer.

If he didn't end it now, Patrick would be haunted by the woman he killed, and the child who never even received a name. They'd never free him of their vice-like grip. If only he had known then that Vivian Chambers would be the very least of his problems in regards to his past coming back to haunt him.

"Just let me give you an example of what I mean from my own experience" she said. "Six months ago, I was in a relationship with someone I did not want to be with…"

"This is a little different than that," Patrick shot back; cutting her off. This was a little ruder than he had intended, but who could blame him? This woman—this complete stranger—was trying to make him see reason with an example that wasn't even close to the same level as his own.

"I'm not saying it is," she said; trying to calm the situation. "Clearly there is something really colossal eating

113

away at you. If there wasn't, you wouldn't be up on this ledge. Can you at least just hear me out?"

Patrick did. He listened to the story of the relationship she had been in for the last two years with a guy she never felt any real connection with. She had only agreed to go out with him on a few dates because her father—a man she had always strived to make happy—thought so highly of him. One thing led to another, and because she wanted to appease her father, the two eventually ended up dating.

She explained to Patrick the claustrophobic feeling that she felt whenever she was with this boyfriend; the slow suffocating feeling she constantly felt when in his arms. It was a feeling she desperately longed to be rid of.

Eventually, she took action. Once the talks of an engagement had begun, she found herself at an important crossroads in life. She would have to choose between something that would ultimately consume and destroy her, just to make dad happy, or she could walk away from it, and start living life on her own terms.

"Now, I don't know what your own personal demons are," she continued once she concluded her own story. "But if you walk off that ledge, you are letting them win. This ledge is your crossroads. You can jump off and let those demons win, or you can fight back and free yourself of them. I suggest the latter, because living your life on your own terms is quite liberating"

Patrick felt something pulling him back towards the safety of the roof. It was the part of him that still wanted to live; the part that was still willing to fight, because it wasn't ready to give up yet. If this woman could escape her own personal chains, there was no reason why he couldn't. All he needed to do was have a little faith that he could leave Vivian Chambers behind where she belonged; in his past. This young, beautiful woman renewed that faith.

Without even realizing, he had stepped back onto the roof.

She may not have known it, but she let out a sigh of relief once she saw Patrick step off that ledge. She took a seat on a milk crate, and offered him the one next to her. He took it; realizing his legs were putty, and his knees were going to fail him at any moment.

"You know," Patrick said to her; watching her light another cigarette. "You should really quit. Those things will kill you."

"Says the guy who was just going to jump off my roof," she joked. This time Patrick didn't attempt to hold back his smile.

"My name's Patrick Sullivan."

"Claire Johnston."

"It's nice to meet you, Claire. I'm glad you decided to come up here for a smoke tonight."

"So am I, Patrick."

He knew the question he was about to ask her was absolutely absurd; given the circumstances in which they just met. There was no possibility of getting any other answer from her other than no, but he was going to ask her anyways. The words were leaving his mouth, whether he wanted them to or not.

"If you aren't busy, would you like to go grab some coffee?" Even as the request passed his lips he could hear how ridiculous it sounded. "You know, as a thank you." He quickly tacked on.

"See, the thing is… I don't usually go on dates with guys I talk off roofs."

"Get those a lot, huh?" he asked; trying to make light of the fact he was clearly getting rejected.

"At least once a week." she joked.

Patrick then noticed a look on Claire's face. It was a look he'd become very familiar with over the years that followed. She was weighing her options, and choosing which road she wanted to take.

"I usually wait about a week before I even consider seeing them again," she finally said. "Tell you what; you take my number, and in a week, if you still want to thank me with that cup of coffee, you can call me."

"That sounds fair."

She wrote down her number in a matchbook, and they said their goodbyes. He had thanked her, and she said it was her pleasure to not only help him out, but to meet him.

"Oh, Patrick," she said before exiting the roof. "If you don't call, and I never see you again, just remember; don't get trapped."

"I won't," he promised, and watched as Claire left the roof.

The week that followed, Patrick still dreamt of executing Vivian Chambers and her child. He didn't think they would just simply cease, because he had chosen life over the escape of death. However, the toll they had taken on him began to lessen. The idea of hope that had been instilled in him made those nightmares a little more bearable.

Exactly seven days after he was staring down eight stories at an unforgiving Brooklyn street, Patrick called Claire, and asked if he could take her out for that cup of coffee. This time, she agreed, and that evening they met up. She drank Green Tea, and Patrick had himself a steaming cup of black coffee. They talked and they laughed, and it was as if they hadn't met under the most uncomfortable of circumstances only a week earlier. It was a pleasant outing, to say the least. That was the first date, and that was all they needed. They both knew after that afternoon that they'd end up spending the rest of their lives together.

CHAPTER 13

They stood outside—Patrick and Hawkins—under a cloudless November night sky. Even with the sun now hours gone, the air was still uncommonly warm for the time of year.

Claire stayed inside to put Connor down for the night, and to clean off the dining room table. Hawkins, being the gentleman he is—Patrick thought charmer would have been better word to describe him—offered his and Patrick's services to clean up the messy table while she put her son to sleep. She, of course, refused such help, while thanking him for his kindness.

Now, the two colleagues stood outside the Sullivan's home. The air was filled with the rich scent of the cigar Hawkins had been puffing away at.

"You know, I really shouldn't be smoking these things," Hawkins pointed out; blowing ash and embers off the cigar's tip. "Maryanne never approved, but they help me unwind after a long day."

"I like the smell," Patrick responded. He found it a tad bit disrespectful for Hawkins to be indulging in an activity that could result in the same ill-fated ending as the man's late wife, but he wouldn't dare to say that out loud.

"So, tell me, kid; what made you become a cop?"

117

"Well, my dad and granddad were both cops with the NYPD."

"Oh, shut up," Hawkins snapped; cutting Patrick off before he could say anymore. "Don't give me that 'my daddy and granddaddy were cops, so now I'm a cop' story. It's complete bullshit. You can spot those guys from a mile away. The job's filled with them. I'm not saying that's bad thing—I'm sure these men and women make fine police officers—but they're still lacking something... a fire inside them, I guess you could say.

"*You,* on the other hand, kid... You're the exception; the rarity. Sure, your dad and granddad were cops, but that's certainly *not* the reason you became a cop. You did it, because you have the fiery passion burning up inside you. What I want to know is what happened to ignite that fire."

Those words were like a key, and they unlocked a door to Patrick's past that had been closed tight for decades now. Sure, he remembered the incident and everything that followed it, but he never saw the correlation. He never realized that the true reason he became a cop was because of a single event; buried in the memories from his childhood.

When Patrick was twelve years old, a group of his close relatives took a trip to Maine for a weeklong camping trip. It was something the family had done every year as far back as he could remember, and it was something he had absolutely loved.

That particular year, Patrick's family did not attend the trip, because his father had been scheduled to work, and could not get off. Patrick found himself irate with his father for this. He was still young, and he didn't care about the importance of providing for your family. All he had cared about was going away, and having the time of his life with his cousins. Especially his cousin, Michael.

118

THE REPLACEMENT

Patrick and Michael were only four months apart in age, and had grown up on the same street together in Brooklyn. They had a strong bond with each other that went beyond that usual cousin relationship. The two boys were best friends.

While away that week, Michael had wandered off into the woods in the middle of a clear day, and never returned. For a month straight, search teams, local and state law enforcement scaled the woods, but there was no trace of Patrick's cousin. Eventually, the search was called off, and Michael was presumed dead.

This was a blow that devastated the entire family, but to Patrick, it was something completely different. His entire world changed once he was forced to come to grips with the reality that he would never see his cousin, a person who was more like a brother to him, ever again. There wouldn't even be a funeral for him to say his final goodbye. He found himself lost, and not at all prepared to cope with the loss of someone so close to him. To deal with his despair, Patrick found a very peculiar—and probably unhealthy—outlet.

Back when he was a child, there was no internet to provide people with various news stories from all over the country and the world. So in the months that followed Michael's memorial service, Patrick found himself writing to libraries throughout the state of Maine; asking for copies of their archived newspapers to be sent to him. To avoid questioning from his parents, he had his packages delivered to his aunt and uncle's, who both worked late hours, and wouldn't be home when the mail arrived. This left him ample time to swoop in, and retrieve his requested articles undetected.

He would sit for hours, locked away in his room; studying those old newspaper articles. At first, he focused on disappearances, but his search quickly expanded into

119

murder, which eventually transitioned into plain bizarre and unexplainable incidents. One thing he noticed was that there had been a high number of strange occurrences happening in the state of Maine; especially since the early 1970's.

Soon, his obsession began to evolve, and Patrick found himself looking beyond the borders of Maine. As his search area and curiosity grew, so did the list of topics of inquiry. Rape, assault, domestic disputes were all added to the list.

Once his mail deliveries were halted due to his yearlong savings of allowance running dry, he took his obsession home. He fed his curiosity by asking his father about his line of work. He would constantly overwhelm his father, who, at that time, had just been promoted to detective, with questions of the crimes he saw, and the steps they took to go about solving them. His inquiries had gotten so frequent, that his father had forbidden his son from asking anymore questions about his work.

With sources scarce, Patrick's obsession dwindled, and eventually fizzled out. It was replaced by the more normal interests that teenage boys took on, like girls. His unhealthy fascination with the horrible, and sometimes strange, things that went on in this world got locked away. That was until Hawkins pried that door wide open.

"Sorry to disappoint," Patrick lied. "But there is no other reason. Maybe it's just in the genes, or something. My father was a great cop, and so was his father. It was just something that was expected of me."

"Uh-huh," was the response Hawkins chose to give. He knew Patrick was lying.

Patrick had no idea why he had lied to Hawkins. This sudden revelation was certainly an answer to a lot of questions he had been asking himself over the long year;

like why he let things nest so deeply under his skin when it came to the job.

Yes, there were some people, like Jonathan Hawkins, who had a greater passion (fire, was how it was described moments earlier) about the job than others, but they were able to control their emotions. Over the past year, once the fallout from the Baby Tooth incident had cleared, Patrick found himself harping on why he had such difficulty doing this. Maybe the subject that served as the catalyst to why he had this fire burning inside him was the source of his anger.

After a few moments of awkward silence (at least for Patrick), Claire joined the two in the front yard.

"Would you like some coffee or something to drink, Detective Hawkins?"

"Thank you, Claire, but I'm going to pass. You have been far too kind to this grumpy old man," Hawkins answered; again, turning up that charm everyone loved so much. "Plus, it's time to lay these creaking bones to rest. It is way past my bed time."

"Jeez! Mine, too," Claire joked; looking at her watch. It was half past nine. "I'm not even up this late on the weekends."

Claire then did something that Patrick immediately wished she hadn't. She invited Jonathan Hawkins over for Thanksgiving dinner.

Patrick understood why she had extended the invite, but he really wished she had consulted him first. That way he could flat out tell her no. Despite his charming personality throughout the night, it was still yet to be determined how Patrick felt about the man standing opposite of him and his wife right now. The whole Stephen Ramsey incident was still too fresh in his mind, and he knew the other side of Jonathan Hawkins

It was too late, though. The invitation had already been extended, and he was now helpless against the inevitable. Of course, being the noble man he was, or at least liked to come off to be, Hawkins would decline; not wanting to encroach their family event, but Claire, being the persistent gal she was, would not stand for taking no for an answer.

And that was exactly how it went down.

They went back and forth, until Hawkins finally agreed to join them; just so long as they were positive he wouldn't be a burden. Claire assured him he wouldn't be, even though Patrick didn't exactly share that same belief. So, in the end, it was decided; Jonathan Hawkins would be joining the Sullivan family for Thanksgiving dinner.

CHAPTER 14

Patrick Sullivan woke up that following morning feeling more refreshed than he had expected. He had been anticipating a miserable morning, as sleep had not come easy to him the night before. In addition to the Ramsey case running laps through his head, he now had his new Thanksgiving Dinner guest to worry about. It was bad enough he would have to try to remain calm with his own father there—something that wasn't always possible when that father/son combination got together—but now, Jonathan Hawkins was joining in on the festivities. He could only begin to imagine the possibilities for disaster when those two got together.

On the plus side, he had no dreams involving Baby Tooth. That was something worth celebrating, and likely played an important role in Patrick's lack of exhaustion.

He did his usual cardio, followed by an additional sweat session with Claire beneath the sheets. He left his house in a good mood; feeling optimistic as he drove to work. Unfortunately, that feeling would take a pessimistic turn once he arrived at the station.

Hospitals and medical centers throughout Nassau County started getting back to them as early as six thirty that morning. By the time Patrick stepped into the 8th precinct on North Wantagh Avenue, all the major hospitals in the county had responded to their subpoena. Each hospital delivered the same disheartening news; all inventories had been checked, and none were missing any units of Pancuronium Bromide.

As the day rolled on, more hospitals began to get back to them with the same results. By six thirty that night—twelve hours after the first report had come in—the last hospital they subpoenaed had gotten back to them; all units of the paralytic drug were accounted for.

With this vital lead in their investigation hitting a pretty big bump in the road, Hawkins, once again, met with the district attorney to, hopefully, acquire warrants for hospitals in the neighboring Suffolk County, and even the Five Burroughs. This was a little more difficult, now that their investigation was crossing lines of jurisdiction, but it needed to be done.

To add to the bad news they had been receiving that day, forensics had spent the two days searching the Ramsey's house from top to bottom for any evidence that might help in with the case, and the end result was that they had absolutely nothing. The team couldn't find a single finger print, hair fiber, clothing fiber, blood sample, or anything else. The Ramsey's murderer had cleaned up after himself perfectly; leaving himself a phantom.

This didn't set well with Hawkins, who convinced their captain to order forensics to return to the house for yet another sweep. Everyone knew the chances of them returning with something useful was grim. The Ramsey's house was squeaky clean.

The only shred of good news that day was that the Ramsey's neighbor, Robert McKensey, had flown back from visiting his children in Georgia to speak to the police.

The elderly man was visibly distraught over the loss of his dear friends, who he had known for almost forty years.

THE REPLACEMENT

Arthur and Estelle Ramsey had moved into their house six days before the McKensey's moved into theirs. Both families watched as the other's kids grew up, graduated high school, went off to college, got married and started families of their own together. He was the only person who knew the entire truth of the circumstances surrounding the Ramsey's estrangement from their son, Stephen. As Patrick interviewed Robert McKensey, he saw a man struggling with the truth that his friends were really dead.

Some of the information he got from McKensey was stuff they had already learned from Samantha Melina on the morning she found the bodies, like their daily trips to the deli, Estelle Ramsey's heart problem, and Arthur sometimes staying home to take care of his wife. What he was able to do that Samantha couldn't was provide Patrick with a window of time in which the Ramsey's could have been abducted by their perp.

The Ramsey's never locked their back door throughout the day. From the morning, when the two friends would leave for their daily walk to the deli, until about ten o'clock at night, when Arthur Ramsey was about to head to bed, the door would remain unlocked. This meant the perp likely entered the home on the Friday Arthur Ramsey was last seen at the deli between the hours of seven in the morning and ten at night.

This new information was helpful, but it still wasn't enough to provide a strong enough lead for their investigation. With forensics coming back for a third time with nothing that evening, finding the hospital or medical facility the Pancuronium Bromide had come from was their biggest lead, and that had been an absolute bust so far. He could only hope they'd have better luck with their inquiries at the hospitals their search had expanded to.

That night, he sat up in bed; attempting to read the Ian McEwan novel Claire had recommended earlier that month to, hopefully, get his mind off of things. His attempts to distract himself from his own thoughts proved futile, in the end. He had read eight pages of the novel, and couldn't recall a single word.

Claire was busy doing lesson plans for when class resumed following Thanksgiving Break, so Patrick wasn't about to bother her just so his racing mind could be put to rest. He tried to read another page of the book, but his eyes were heavy from exhaustion. He was mentally drained from the day, and before he could even decide to give up on the book for the night, Patrick was asleep.

Unfortunately, once he descended in twilight, he was greeted by an old familiar, disfigured face.

He sat in a grand dining hall with stone walls, and towering pillars. Sunlight stretched across the vast floor; painting it in an array of colors as it shined through the stained glass windows. Patrick sat at the head of a table that seemed to go on forever. Upon it, was a feast fit to serve royalty. A golden brown turkey that was more than triple the size of any Thanksgiving bird he had ever seen served as the centerpiece of the extravagant feast. Next to it, and almost as large in size, was a ham; topped with pineapple, and drenched in a rich glaze. There was a multitude of stuffing, potatoes of every combination, cranberry sauces, string beans, and corn still half-wrapped within their stalks; melted butter dripping down the kernels into their leafy blankets.

To Patrick, it looked like the scene out of Charles Dickens' *A Christmas Carol* when Ebenezer Scrooge has his meeting with the Ghost of Christmas Present.

Unfortunately, the ghost sitting at the opposite end of the seemingly endless table was no jolly giant, and even though Wallace Freewaters had a joyous grin fitting of the festive holidays painted upon his half-mangled face, Patrick found nothing pleasant about his company.

THE REPLACEMENT

From his filled plate, Baby Tooth picked up a turkey leg the size of a human limb, and bit down into it. Patrick watched; gritting his teeth, as that cursed baby tooth pierced the skin of the cooked bird, and sank into its tender meat. He wanted to step up onto the table, grab one of the many heavy golden candle labrets that served as decoration, and proceed to bash Baby Tooth in the mouth. He wouldn't let up; not until that damn tooth, that should have been left under his pillow to be exchanged for fifty cents decades ago, finally fell from his wretched mouth.

Patrick couldn't give into his desires, though. He had to remain composed, and even though the thought of thrashing Baby Tooth repeatedly in the mouth gave him great pleasure, he would never let himself cross that line ever again. He would sit there; looking as calm as he possibly could, and watch, as Wallace Freewaters devoured his Thanksgiving feast.

"What's the matter, Patty boy?" Baby Tooth asked through a mouth full of turkey. "You haven't touched your food."

"I'm not hungry," Patrick answered.

He looked down at his plate, and saw it filled with his favorite holiday foods. The site of which now made him feel ill.

"That's a damn shame," Baby Tooth responded; waving the turkey legs in front of him; using it to point out all the delicacies upon the table. "All this food for a nigga, and he's not even going to try any of it. I'm insulted."

"Well, God forbid I ever insult you, Baby Tooth."

Patrick continued to stare down at his plate; afraid to look up from it. He knew if he looked across that table one more time, his emotional restraints would snap, and he and Baby Tooth would find themselves on the floor; Baby Tooth being beaten within an inch of his life.

127

Patrick noticed, as he stared down into his plate, that the succulent juices that seeped from the moist turkey had turned a hint of a red. The meat looked as if it was beginning to bleed.

"Well you have to eat something, Patty Boy. There's still dessert coming, and you have to make room on your plate for some warm apple pie."

"I already have enough on my plate, Baby Tooth."

Baby Tooth laughed at this response, as if the man he loved to torment had said something extremely silly.

"Patrick, my dear friend… You don't nearly have as much on your plate as you're about to."

Patrick knew Baby Tooth wasn't speaking literally, anymore.

"You know," Baby Tooth pointed out; taking a bite out of his turkey. "This broken face and jaw makes it extremely difficult to eat."

"It sure doesn't seem to prevent you from speaking," Patrick said through gritted. "Because you never seem to shut the fuck up!"

His fist reigned down furiously upon the table, causing the silverware in front of him to bounce in place. As the hatred inside him began to boil, the red liquid seeping from the turkey began to darken. Only now, the meat wasn't the only thing in Patrick's plate that was bleeding. Blood dripped down the cob; between the kernels of corn, and pooled in the leafy silks. The gravy that had poured down the mountain of mash potatoes was now a crimson pool. The entire plate was filling up with blood.

"Why are you doing this?" Patrick asked. He forced himself to look into the ugly face of Wallace Freewaters. "Why do you always do this?"

"Do what?" Baby Tooth actually sounded genuine; as if he had not the slightest clue to what Patrick was talking about.

128

THE REPLACEMENT

It was then that he meant to let loose upon Baby Tooth. Emotional restraints be damned. He was going to do every violent thing he had ever fantasized about doing over the course of the past year, and then some, but as Patrick finally let his resistance waver, he found that anger had taken a back seat to defeat.

"Torture me…" he said; overtaken by forfeit. "Why do you have to torture me like this?"

"Torture you? Is that what you think I am doing, nigga;?" Baby Tooth's tone, with a facial expression to match, was one of dead seriousness. "You got it all wrong, Patty Boy. I'm not here to torture you… I'm here to help you. I always have been."

Patrick couldn't withhold his laughter. The claim was absolutely absurd. There was a long list of things he could have called what Baby Tooth had been doing to him over the past year, but help was not one of them.

"You promised you'd leave me alone." His voice quivered with weakness. Patrick sounded as if he was on the verge of tears. "You said if I did what you wanted—if I did what I needed to do—than you'd leave me alone. I did it, but you're still here. You're still fucking here!!"

"Patrick," Baby Tooth said; throwing down what remained of the bird leg onto his plate, and wiped the grease from his hands. He placed the silk napkin back on his lap, so not to risk staining his expensive suit. "You think I care about what you did to me? You think I've been harboring all these bad feelings over it, and I've come back here to make your life hell?"

"*Yes!*" Patrick answered. "That's exactly what I think is going on."

"You're wrong… I couldn't care less about what happened. I know why you did it, I even respect you for it. You're a man of your own beliefs, and you didn't stand down when someone challenged them. Shit happens, nigga. It's the way of the world. I'm over it. I'm here because you need me here, and Patty Boy; I'm only here because you want me here. You need me, because, if you didn't, we wouldn't be enjoying this lovely dinner together."

Before this outlandish claim could be addressed, there were three deafening knocks at the door. They echoed throughout the hall; sounding like war drums through an open field on the eve of battle.

"Oh, wow," Baby Tooth exclaimed. "We have a guest, and just in time for dessert! Maybe it's Vivian, Patrick! It's been so long since we've seen her, and I know she just loves a homemade apple pie! I got one in the oven right now; kind of like how she had something baking in her oven when you put one in her belly"

Baby Tooth pantomimed shooting a gun with his fingers.

"I don't want to see Vivian, Baby Tooth."

Patrick could feel that familiar anger coming back to him, and coming back strong.

"But we have apple pie, nigga! You can't deny a woman some mother fucking pie!"

"Patrick…" The voice calling his name through the thick wooden door was not Vivian Chamber's. It was Claire's.

"Oh, my…" Baby Tooth said; his good eye widening with excitement. "Claire is here! That makes things far more interesting than Vivian! You wait here, Patty Boy. I'll get the door."

"NO!!" Patrick yelled from across the long table. His anger blew through him at the idea of Baby Tooth answering the door for his wife, and having her have to look upon that frightening face. He reached to his side for his gun, but it wasn't there. "Do *NOT* answer the door, Baby Tooth!"

THE REPLACEMENT

"Of course," Baby Tooth said; throwing his hands to let Patrick know he was backing off. "I'm quite sorry. She's is your wife, after all. You should be the one to answer the door. Please…" He gestured with his hands. "Be my guest."

Patrick remained frozen in his seat. He had no desire to let Claire know that he was there, having Thanksgiving dinner with Baby Tooth. He chose not to tell his wife about New York City's biggest drug lord's surprising return to his dream. He and Claire had barely discussed them when they had first occurred. He saw no reason to tell her that they had started up again. It would only worry her, and she had done enough worrying already that year.

"Patrick…" Claire called again. "You need to answer the door."

"Well go open it, Patrick. This apple pie that I have spent all day baking is best served warm right out of the oven, and now, because of you, it is getting cold!"

"Patrick…"

"Oh, Jesus Christ; if you aren't going to answer the door, nigga, then I am!" Baby Tooth threw his napkin down on the table, and got up from his chair!"

"NO!" Patrick called again from across the table. "Don't let her in."

It was too late. Baby Tooth was already making his way across the enormous room to answer the door. Patrick got up from his own chair, and made haste to catch up before Baby Tooth could let Claire in. As he crossed the table, he grabbed the carving knife that sat next to the turkey. With his fingers wrapped securely around it, he resumed his b-line towards Baby Tooth.

He caught up, right as Baby Tooth was reaching for the knob. He grabbed Wallace Freewaters by his bloody cornrows. He could feel the dent in Baby Tooth's skull

131

where the top of his head had caved in. He quickly let go; not wanting to touch any of that broken head.

"What?!" Baby Tooth asked; turning around. He seemed annoyed. "I'm just letting Claire in."

"Patrick…" Again, his wife called through the door.

"See," Baby Tooth said. "She's waiting. I don't know why you are being so fucking weird, Patty Boy."

As he went to turn around again, Patrick grabbed Baby Tooth—this time by his collar—and dug the carving knife into his stomach. He could feel the knife forcing its way through Baby Tooth's muscular abdomen, and he could feel the blood poured out onto his hands, like it had poured from the food on his plate moments earlier.

He tried to pull the knife from Baby Tooth's stomach, but the drug lord gripped his wrist hard.

"All I wanted was to help," Baby Tooth said; looking at Patrick with his one good dying eye. "Leave room on that plate of yours, Patty Boy, because shit's about to get heavy, nigga."

Once he got the last word in, Baby Tooth released Patrick from his grasp, and fell to the floor.

Again, there were three loud bangs at the door. They were so loud that they propelled Patrick from his dream, and sent him cascading back to reality.

When his eyes shot opened, Claire was leaning over him from her side of the bed.

"Patrick…" she asked. "Are you awake? Someone is here; knocking at the front door."

He sat up, and forced away the heaviness of sleep. It was then that the knocks from the door echoed throughout the house, again. He looked at the clock, and became enraged when he saw it was ten after five in the morning. Normally, he would be up by now, but it was Thanksgiving, and he didn't have work. He planned on actually sleeping in.

132

THE REPLACEMENT

He threw the blanket off of him, and stormed out from the room. He made his way down the stairs, and opened the front door; ready to verbally (Not physically; never physically!) tear into this idiot, who had the audacity to knock repeatedly at his door, and wake his entire family up so damn early. When he swung his front door open though, he did no such thing.

Patrick just stared in silence at Detective Hawkins.

CHAPTER 15

"Nice legs, kid," was the greeting Hawkins gave Patrick, who stood in the doorway in his boxer-briefs.

That would be the extent of the jokes that morning. Hawkins wasn't at the Sullivan's home at five-fifteen in the morning to exchange japes. He was there on business.

Patrick hoped that there had finally been a break in the Ramsey murder investigation, but that was news of the call-until-you-got-finally-get-through variety. It wouldn't merit Hawkins showing up at Patrick's home hours before sunrise. There had to be another reason why he was staring through his screen door at the man he was hired to relieve of his duties come the year's end. He had an idea what that reason was, but he immediately pushed it away as soon as it came to the forefront of his mind. He prayed that it wasn't what he was thinking.

But it was.

"There's been a murder," Hawkins said; confirming Patrick's fears. "From the preliminary reports we've gotten from the officers who first responded to the 911 call, it's pretty bad."

We barely have evidence to make any real progress with our current investigation, Patrick thought. *Now we have another one?*

THE REPLACEMENT

"I just need a few minutes," he said; knowing he had no time to start worrying about things that were out of his control. "Please, come in."

Hawkins entered, and immediately his attention went to the staircase. Patrick turned around, and saw Claire standing halfway up the stairs. That's when it hit him. He'd be missing yet another Thanksgiving because of work.

"Claire, I am so sorry," Hawkins said; before Patrick could open his own mouth to usher an apology. "I know you were expecting your husband home today, but, unfortunately, there's a new case, and he's needed right away. I promise you, though; I'm going to try my damn hardest to get him back here for dinner."

That was a lie. Patrick knew it, Hawkins knew it, and he was fairly certain the Claire knew it, as well. There was no way Patrick was getting home in time for Thanksgiving dinner or dessert, which he really hoped didn't involve apple pie.

"Thank you, Detective Hawkins," Claire said as sincerely as possible. She'd be understanding, just as she always had been, but Patrick knew his wife had gotten her hopes up on having their first full-family Thanksgiving dinner, and now that it had been ripped out from under her, she was disappointed. "I'll make sure to save both of you a plate."

"That would be amazing, Claire. Thank you very much." Hawkins turned to Patrick, and gestured for him to get ready.

"I'm so sorry," Patrick whispered to Claire as he passed her going up the stairs.

"It's okay," she said; kissing him on the forehead. "Go, and be a great detective."

When he came back down the stairs, wearing work clothes that seemed like rags compared to the fine stitch Hawkins wore day in and day out, Claire and Hawkins were sitting on the couch; laughing over something that had been said.

"You ready, kid?" Hawkins asked as Patrick entered the living room.

Hawkins got to his feet, and wished Claire a happy Thanksgiving. Patrick kissed his wife goodbye, promised that he'd be home as soon as he could, and headed out the front door.

On the ride over, Hawkins briefed Patrick on all he knew so far. The victim was female. She was discovered in her Levittown apartment by her mother. It was the landlord who made the call to the police.

"Carl's there now," he told Patrick as they drove down the streets of Levittown. "He'll fill us in on what he's learned once we get there."

After a few minutes, they were pulling into a 7-11 parking lot, where Hawkins threw the car into park, and killed the engine. Patrick made the safe assumption that their victim did not live at a 7-11 convenience store. They were stopping to get coffee.

A poor woman is dead, and we're stopping off for coffee? he thought as he watched Hawkins throw his car door open.

This was the same guy, who only three days ago, told Patrick they needed to steer the course. Their victims needed to be their number one priority, and he was now stopping off for a Cup-of-Joe.

"Don't worry, kid," Hawkins said; as if he could read the exact thoughts passing through Patrick's head. "This will only be a minute, and you'll be thanking me in a little bit. The God damn sun hasn't even come up yet, and we are both exhausted—you look like actual hell—and we are going to need some serious caffeine in our systems if we're going to survive this day."

THE REPLACEMENT

The man had a point. On any given day, Patrick needed that steaming cup of coffee before he did any real functioning. If he was going to work at his full potential, he needed his morning fix of caffeine. He threw open his door, and followed Hawkins into the convenience store.

"Hey, Kenny," Hawkins said; greeting the man at the register as he and Patrick entered the 7-11. "My partner and I are in a real rush this morning. Do you mind if I get you back for two cups of coffee tomorrow morning?"

"Don't worry about it, Ace," the cashier said. Apparently, he had earned the privilege of calling Hawkins *Ace*, when Patrick had not. "Today, it's on the house. Happy Thanksgiving!"

"Happy Thanksgiving to you, too, Ken," Hawkins said, then turned his attention back to Patrick. "Told ya, kid… in and out."

At the coffee station, Hawkins watched as Patrick filled his large cup. Like always, he filled his cup to the brim, and applied the cover without adding a single drop of milk or sugar.

"Damn, kid; I'll give you credit. I can't tolerate the taste of straight up coffee."

"Neither can I," Patrick joked, but as he took a sip, and that revolting taste hit his tongue, he remembered how true that was.

Hawkins pulled out a bottle of hazelnut creamer, and poured it into the last quarter of his own cup. If it was something Patrick had to make an educated guess on, he would've figured Hawkins was, at least, a milk and sugar kind of guy. He never would have expected him to be the kind of guy who spent his mornings loading up their coffee with that flavored creamer crap.

As the two walked out of the 7-11—Patrick with his straight black coffee, and Hawkins with his sissified Hazelnut one—Hawkins, again, thanked Kenny for the

JASON PELLEGRINI

two freebies. They got in the car, and no more than five minutes later, as Patrick was finishing off the last sip of his size large coffee, they were pulling up in front of a house that was in the process of being sealed off with yellow police tape.

Patrick took notice of the group of people forming in front of their victim's residence. These were likely neighbors who had been woken up by the commotion and flashing lights of police cars outside their window. Being it was so early, and most people on the block were still asleep, the crowd was small, and not nearly the size of the one that stood outside of the Ramsey's home on the day their bodies had been discovered.

They crossed the barrier, and made their way up the driveway to the rear of the house, where the entrance to the second floor apartment was. Standing at the bottom of the staircase that ran up the back of the house was Detective Murphy.

"Carl," Hawkins called out as he walked towards his longtime partner and friend "What the hell are you doing standing around?"

Detective Murphy didn't answer. He wouldn't even acknowledge the presence of Hawkins or Patrick. He just stared right past them; into absolute nothingness.

As they got closer, Patrick noticed the color had drained from Murphy's face. The paleness of his complexion made him look older, somehow. Not just older; more fragile, like Samantha Melina had looked in that morning in the Ramsey's driveway, not long after she discovered their skinless bodies.

"Detective Murphy," Patrick asked; not bothering at an attempt to cover up the concern in his voice "What's the matter?"

"Carl," Hawkins said; putting his hand on his partner's shoulder. "Talk to me, buddy."

138

THE REPLACEMENT

"I can't..." Detective Murphy said; finally finding the ability to articulate. "I can't go back in there, John"

This was the first time Patrick had heard Detective Murphy refer to Hawkins by his actual name, instead of his popular nickname. It was the smallest change, but it brought the severity of what they were about to walk into up to a whole new level. Detective Murphy had an entire career's worth of exposure behind him. What could possibly be up those stairs, in that apartment, that would bring a veteran cop to the state Carl Murphy was now in?

"Carl, what's in there?" Hawkins asked.

"Just go up without me," Murphy said; refusing to answer Hawkins question. "I'll be up in a little bit. I just need a few minutes."

"Okay, Carl. Take your time. We'll be up there whenever you're ready."

They climbed the stairs—Patrick and Hawkins—to the second floor apartment. Sitting outside the entrance in two white lawn chairs was a middle-aged couple. They looked as pale, and as in shock as Detective Murphy had. They were the home owners, and they had been the ones who had placed the call to 911 that morning.

"Where is the victim's mother?" Hawkins asked the officer standing with the landlords. "She was the one who found the body, correct?"

"Correct, sir," the officer answered. "Detective Murphy had her sent to the hospital to be checked out. She was in a state of hysteria after what she saw, and completely nonresponsive to us, or Detective Murphy."

"The victim's in the bedroom?" Hawkins asked.

"Yes, sir," the officer responded. The color left his cheeks, and his skin turned pallid at mention of the victim. "In the bedroom, sir."

With every person they came in contact with, Patrick found himself becoming more and more uneasy about

139

what they were walking into. There was something bad in there, and not just the everyday kind of bad. It was something that no human being, whether it's part of their profession or not, should ever have to see.

When they entered the apartment, they were standing in a small kitchen. Like he had at the Ramsey's, the first thing Patrick took notice of was the kitchen table. Only there was no emptied bag of groceries atop it this time. Instead, there was a variety of wedding themed magazines sprawled all across the table. Already, he could feel a pit forming in his stomach.

He then took notice of the refrigerator. He walked over to it, and examined the contents hung up on the door by magnets. There were a few Save the Dates for weddings in the spring, an old New York Mets season schedule magnet from the season that had ended that past September, a picture of a couple standing on a hotel balcony; overlooking a tropical beach, and a print of a sonogram.

"My God…" he heard Hawkins say from the bedroom. "Kid, get in here… now."

Patrick made his way across the living room, and entered the bedroom. His eyes went directly to the body on the bed.

Laying there, lifeless, perched up by two pillows, was a young woman. It was obvious she had been pregnant based on the size of her belly. Her legs were spread apart, and bent at the knees; propped up and covered in blood. The bottom half of the bed was a disaster. The once white sheets were now the deep crimson color. Patrick thought there had been a lot of blood soaked into the couch they had found the Ramsey's on, but that was nothing compared to this.

He looked away; not being able to look at that poor, mutilated girl, anymore. Instead, he looked over at Hawkins, whose eyes were fixated on the lifeless body on the bed. Only he wasn't staring at the bloody lower half of the bed. Patrick followed his gaze, and when he saw what Hawkins had been staring at, he wanted to die. That way, his brain wouldn't be functioning, and he wouldn't be able to process what he was seeing.

Patrick was alive, though, and his brain worked just fine. He was fully aware that he was staring at the tiny body of a lifeless infant. The exact infant this young woman had been carrying in her womb just before she had died. Only now, it was placed carefully in her dead arms; arranged as if it were being lovingly cradled.

CHAPTER 16

Patrick stood at the edge of his property; thinking about his life. He had a perfect suburban home, a high paying job, a gorgeous wife, an adorable son, and it was nothing more than a smokescreen. All of it, and not just Patrick's life—everyone's life—was a well put together mask to hide the ugliness that existed in the world. He realized that we all wrap ourselves tight in a protective sheet to shield us from the things we fear. That, maybe, if we don't acknowledge them, then they won't exist.

That morning, the sheet had been pulled away from Patrick Sullivan's eyes, and he saw life's real face. It was hideous.

It was just past midnight. Thanksgiving—a joyous holiday that was reserved to bring families together—was now over. He felt no joy, though. Instead, he stood there, thinking about Evangeline Carpenter; the young woman who had been cut open, and had her unborn child ripped out of her.

Eighteen hours had passed since Patrick was woken up from his dream of Baby Tooth by Hawkins' unexpected knocks at his door. He had awoken from one nightmare, only to be dragged out of his bed to witness another. The lurid images of what they had seen in that bedroom stained his mind, and he knew they'd never wash away.

n, and her infant boy, who had been

her dead arms; his stone white skin,

ng through his small blood stained

hear her baby boy cry. She would

She would never read to him,

him when he needed to be fed.

from her, and her child, who

rld wailing away in a hospital

Island, never even got to

ir.

to whoever was listening

bility to produce words.

d him or not, he turned

om photographed," he heard Hawkins

the forensics team. "And you turn this place upside down until you find something. Do you understand me?"

Patrick, not wanting to go back in that room and see the bodies, was put in charge of speaking with the landlords. They told him the young girl's name, and that she and her fiancé rented the apartment from them.

"She was a very nice young woman," said Nicole Levenberg; one of Evangeline's landlords. "She was always kind and courteous when we would see her—same with her fiancé—but that was the extent of the relationship we had. They were private people, and kept to themselves, mostly."

The Levenberg's had been awoken that morning by a sudden unimaginable scream coming from the apartment above them. They rushed up to respond; fearing that something terrible had happen to their tenant, and they were right. Only their thoughts were that something had gone wrong with her pregnancy. What they walked into was beyond anything they could comprehend.

JASON PELLEGRINI

Evangeline's mother, Eileen, was collapsed on the living room floor; screaming. It was her screams that had awoken the Levenberg's. She was curled up; hugging her knees, which were buried in her chest, rocking back and forth; repeating the same singular line through her hysterics.

'My baby girl... my baby girl'.

Missus Levenberg had told Patrick that Eileen Carpenter looked like a mental patient locked up in one of those padded rooms in the movies. She attempted to calm Eileen, even if just enough to find out what was wrong, but failed in her attempts.

It was David Levenberg, Nicole's husband, who found out the answer to their questions. He walked into Evangeline's bedroom, and saw the body of his young tenant; her thighs and pubic region covered in blood. His wife crept up behind him to see what her husband had discovered, but he slammed the door, and told Nicole to call 911. When she asked why, he told her they needed to report a murder.

That was all the information they had to go on for the first few hours of that Thanksgiving morning. Eileen Carpenter, the mother—and grandmother; depending on how you looked at it—of the deceased had been given a sedative to knock her out once she had reached the hospital. Her screaming had subsided in the ambulance, but she was in an intense state of shock, and completely non-responsive. She was given Ativan by the attending physician, and the detectives had no other choice but to wait for her to finally wake up from drug-induced slumber.

It was around noon when they were finally told Eileen Carpenter had woken up, and the doctor felt comfortable enough with her being questioned by the police. It was decided that Detective Murphy would be the one to handle this delicate deed, while Hawkins and Patrick waited

144

outside. Throughout the years, Murphy had always been considered the compassionate one, while Hawkins, not so much. The current situation called for Carl Murphy's expertise.

"Listen, kid," Hawkins said as Detective Murphy spoke with a semi drugged-up Eileen Carpenter. "I know the other day you and I didn't exactly see eye-to-eye when it came to Stephen Ramsey. You pushed for what you believed in, and I pushed for what I thought was right. In the end, you were right, and I should've taken you a little more seriously. Being as thick headed as I am, I dismissed your opinion, and I'll admit, partially because I couldn't take you seriously because you were just the new guy. That was wrong of me, and I just want you to know that I'm sorry."

"Why are you saying all this now?"

It had been days since their very first disagreement over Stephen Ramsey's possible involvement in his parents' murder, and Hawkins hadn't shown the slightest interest in issuing any sort of apology. He had sat with Patrick, and explained his reasoning for it to justify his stance on the matter, but that was the closest thing Patrick had gotten to an apology.

"Because..." Hawkins said; staring through the window at the man, who in just a month's time would be his ex-partner, interview a poor woman who would never get to see her grandson smile. "Either tomorrow or the next day, we are going to get a phone call from Doctor Wilkensis. We're going to take the drive over to see her once she's finished with her autopsy on our victim, and she is going to tell us that she found the same exact drug inside that poor girl's system that she found inside of Arthur and Estelle Ramsey. After that, all this becomes a whole new ball game."

Once again, Patrick and Hawkins' minds seemed to be in sync with one another. This time, Patrick had been the one thinking it, and Hawkins had said it out loud.

Ever since he laid eyes on that odious second scene, Patrick knew there would be a link found between the two murders. Both murders were so disturbing and unfathomable, it was impossible for them to be isolated incidents.

"You and I have to be on the same page, kid," Hawkins continued. "We can't be butting heads, and going against one another. I just want you to know that I will respect whatever it is you have to say, and I will take it into serious consideration. I won't brush you off, kid. You have proven already that you are a good detective, who knows his shit."

"Thank you," Patrick answered. "That means a lot"

And it did. Patrick was certainly caught off guard by all this. He thought he had Jonathan Hawkins all figured out, but apparently he was wrong. Hawkins had manned up, and cleared the air between the two of them. He made sure he and his replacement were on the same wavelength, so they could coexist during this investigation, which was on the brink of escalation.

Detective Murphy exited the room once he had concluded his interview with Eileen Carpenter, and took a seat. Patrick wondered, as Carl Murphy buried his face in his palms and let out an exhausted exhale, if the same grim conclusion had been reached by Detective Murphy that had been reached by his two partners earlier.

After a few moments to let everything sink in, Murphy told Patrick and Hawkins the story he had just heard from Evangeline Carpenter's mother.

Eileen Carpenter had arrived at her daughter's apartment just after four that morning. They were scheduled to take a seven hour car ride upstate to visit Evangeline's cousin's home for the holiday. With hopes of defeating the threat of the usual holiday congestion, they decided to leave extra early. Eileen, knowing her daughter's lifelong refusal to get up early, decided it would be best to arrive a half hour before their agreed upon departure time to make sure her now pregnant daughter was up, out of bed, and ready to go once the time came to hit the road.

When she arrived, she let herself in; using the key she had demanded, just in case of an emergency, and the last thing she remembered before waking up in a hospital bed was seeing her daughter's face.

"She kept going on about how she could see her daughter's fear; frozen in her eyes. She made sure I got that point down," Murphy told them.

That's because he made her watch, Patrick thought in disgust. *He paralyzed her with that damn drug, and he made her watch as he sliced her open, and stole her child right from her own womb.*

Life's most beautiful experience had been taken, twisted and turned it into hell for that young woman. Patrick remembered Claire when she was pregnant with Connor. With the exception of the occasional hormonal mood swing in the beginning, she was so full of joy and excitement throughout her entire pregnancy. He had fallen in love with Connor the second he laid eyes on him, but he knew Claire had loved him the second she found out she was pregnant. Evangeline Carpenter probably had that same love for the child she carried inside her for all those months. Patrick couldn't imagine any other thought passing through that woman's mind as she passed on from this world, other than a plea to God to not let this monster bring harm to her baby.

Unfortunately, God didn't answer.

"What about the fiancé?" Hawkins asked. "Where was he through all this?"

"Away on business," Detective Murphy answered.

Evangeline had been engaged to her fiancé, Brian Mulley; for almost a year, Detective Murphy went on to tell them. They had begun the celebration of their matrimony a tad bit early, as Evangeline's mother delicately put it, and Evangeline had gotten pregnant. Instead of having a traditional Shotgun Wedding, the two decided to put the wedding on hold until after Evangeline delivered. That way she could fit into her dream dress, she could still have the wedding she had been fantasizing about ever since she was young.

"He's flying back as soon as he can get a flight out of Chicago," Murphy told them

"So we can rule him out as a suspect," Hawkins said.

We don't need to rule out anyone as suspects, Patrick thought; wanting to say it out loud. *We know exactly who did this. We just can't do anything about it yet.*

But they did choose to do something about it… Just not officially.

When they returned to the station, they decided the next best course of action was to find a common link between the Ramsey's and Evangeline Carpenter. Unfortunately, after hours of reviewing information they had gathered that afternoon from various sources, they came to a harsh realization that no such link existed.

The Ramsey's and Evangeline Carpenter lived in different towns. They did not shop at any of the same stores. They even went as far to inquire about which college the Ramsey's youngest daughter, who was close in age to Evangeline Carpenter, had gone to; hoping she had possibly known the victim. Unfortunately, no such link was discovered. As far as they could tell, the Ramsey's, or anyone close to them, had never come in contact with Evangeline Carpenter. This could only mean, assuming a link didn't suddenly appear as they trudged on, their perp was choosing his victims at random.

To make matters worse, forensics had turned over Evangeline Carpenter's apartment, and the end result was as disheartening the Ramsey's house had been; not a single print, fiber, or fluid was found. This was their first official link between the two murders.

Doctor Wilkensis would soon confirm their next one, and then it would be official.

Patrick walked through his front door at ten past midnight. His house was silent. He threw his keys down, and headed to the kitchen.

He grabbed a glass from the cabinet, and poured himself some water from the refrigerator. He had seen his father sitting at the kitchen table through the corner of his eye, but refused to acknowledge him. He would wait for Edward Sullivan to engage him in conversation. The sound of his father's glass coming down on the wood table was his way of alerting his son of his presence. Patrick took a long sip of water, and finally spoke.

"You're up late," he said; staring at his half-filled cup.

"I couldn't sleep," his father replied, and then brought his own glass to his lips.

"I thought only the girls got your special treatment."

Patrick had been the second eldest of five Sullivan children, and the only male. He could remember, starting from his oldest sister all the way down to his youngest, his father waiting up for them to return home each night they went out from the moment they turned sixteen until the day they moved out of their parents' house. Edward Sullivan would sit at the kitchen table in the dark—much like he was now—nursing a drink—also, much like he was doing now—and when one of his daughters returned home and questioned him about why he was up so late, he would give them the same exact response, every time. He couldn't sleep.

"Back then, I didn't have to worry about you. Your sisters were the ones I was concerned about."

"And now you have to worry about me?" Patrick grabbed the bottle of Jack Daniels from the counter, and made his way over to the kitchen table. He topped off his father's drink, and took a seat.

"I don't know, son. Do I?"

"No, you don't." Patrick knew his answer would not be enough. His father would call bullshit on him, and he had every right to.

"You know, Patrick," Edward Sullivan continued as if his only son hadn't just said everything was okay. He also never called Patrick by his given name. He always referred to him as *son*. He reserved using his actual name for the times he was about to say something of extreme importance. "I've seen some horrendous stuff during my tenure with the department…"

"Oh, give me a fucking break, dad," Patrick shouted; cutting his father off. He wasn't going to let his father go any further into his lecture. He shot up from his seat, which he didn't even know why he had taken in the first place. The conversation had been doomed to escalate to shouts from the beginning. "I don't need to hear about all the bad things you saw while serving."

While working for the great city of Manhattan, Edward Sullivan served as a detective in the Missing Children's Unit. He never brought his work home with him; at least not in the form of verbal discussion. There were some things about his line of duty that he never wished to expose his family to.

"Yes, you do, Patrick."

"No, I don't, *dad*." The volume of his voice managed to come down to an enraged whisper. He was not about to wake an entire household filled with family members. "I'm sorry that you've seen children dead; washed up on the banks of the Hudson River, or buried in shallow graves."

"Or how about stuffed in garbage cans after being dead for days in some random closest."

"Fine; that really sucks, dad, but don't you dare sit there, and act like you've seen the worst things imaginable. I saw a lifeless baby, dad—an *infant*—that wasn't even supposed to be born yet, propped in its dead mother's arms, like it was some God damn doll. It didn't even have a chance to breathe, dad. Its life was just snuffed out like that." Patrick snapped his fingers in his father's face for emphasis. "He was so tiny and so helpless, and he's just gone. Don't get me wrong, I feel for you, dad; I really do, but you have no idea what it's like to see something like that. So, whatever it is that you feel you need to say, I don't want to hear it."

"I'm sorry, son." Switching back to *son* from *Patrick* was Edward Sullivan's attempt to try and diffuse an argument that wasn't going his way. "I just don't want there to be another repeat of Wallace Freewaters... For your sake."

His composure failed him, and Patrick brought his half-filled glass down upon the table. The bottom cracked and separated; spilling what was left of his water all over his kitchen table.

"This will be nothing like Baby Tooth," Patrick yelled; not really caring who he woke up. "Do you understand me, dad? NOTHING!"

He couldn't stay in the same room with his father any longer. His anger was getting the best of him, and he wouldn't let his father see that happen. Without saying another word, Patrick turned away and stormed out of the kitchen.

"Where are you going, Patrick?" Edward Sullivan asked as his son was walking out of the kitchen.

"To bed," Patrick answered. "Make sure you clean up that mess before you go to bed." He added, and then ascended the stairs.

When he stripped down and crawled into bed, his head was still racing. The moment his head hit the pillow, he realized sleep would be nowhere near. His anger had chased twilight away, and he would be up all night with his thoughts for company.

He felt Claire's soft hand slide across his chest. She wrapped her arm around him, and hugged him tight.

"I love you," she said, and kissed the back of Patrick's head. After that, she said no more. She didn't need to.

Patrick locked his fingers with his wife's, and felt the floods of anger rapidly recede. Once they had washed away completely, all that remained was sleep.

CHAPTER 17

Patrick treated himself to a deserving extra hour of sleep the following morning. Claire, along with her mother-in-law were already gone from the house. They were up early for the Black Friday Door-Buster sales at the mall. He gave himself a few peaceful moments to wake up, and then slipped out bed. He gathered together his wardrobe for the day, folded it nicely, and placed them carefully in a duffle bag. He then threw on his basketball shorts, white t-shirt and running shoes. He planned on leaving the house before his father could wake up, and continue their conversation from the night before.

When he got to the station, Patrick threw his duffle bag in his locker, and set out on his morning jog. The 8th precinct was located on and surrounded by main roads that he was now familiar with, so he did not have to worry about getting lost in unfamiliar territory. He jogged for an hour and a half; listening to The Smashing Pumpkins, Nirvana, and other of his favorite 90's bands. Patrick had some unneeded stresses about the argument with his father that he needed to sweat out before he got going with his day. When he returned, he cleaned up in one of the locker room showers. He did not expect to see Jonathan Hawkins sitting there, next to his locker, when he came out.

"Trouble at home?" Hawkins asked.

"Yeah," Patrick responded; drying his hair. "But not the trouble you're thinking of."

"I never said what trouble I was thinking of." Hawkins smartly fired back. "Never assume, kid. It's a terrible thing to do in this line of work."

"Thanks for the tip." Patrick said dryly. "Why are you here so early?"

"Are you kidding me, kid? I was here before you. I saw you walk in, but you were too distracted by that music—nonsensical noise, as I like to refer to it as—coming from your headphones, not to mention whatever else you have going on inside that head of yours, to even notice."

"Do you find yourself more at home here than you do at your actual home, or something?"

"Or something," Hawkins answered in a non-sarcastic tone that wasn't fitting of his normal self. "I haven't enjoyed being at home much over these last few years. Not since my Maryanne died. It's just not the same as it used to be when she was there. She brought that house to life. Now, it's just a place to eat and sleep."

Patrick found himself feeling sorry for Hawkins. He had only known the man for a few days now, but it was hard to remember the fact he once had a life outside of his work. He had a wife that he loved, and then lost to cancer.

"I'm sorry."

"Don't worry about it, kid. I was just making sure everything was okay at home. You wouldn't be the first guy to come in early, because they want to escape the chaos of their home life."

"My parents are over, and, this morning, my father isn't exactly the person I want to see, and have a cup of coffee with."

"I hear you loud and clear, kid. Anyways, I'll get out of your way. You're probably embarrassed of what you have under that towel, so I'll leave you to your insecurities."

"He has jokes." Patrick said; light-heartedly. Sarcasm was painted thick on his voice. "What a surprise!"

The two partners shared a laugh. Partners… Patrick had never thought of Hawkins as that up until then. It was what they were, wasn't it? At least they would be until the turn of the year, and Hawkins retired from active duty.

For the first time since meeting Jonathan Hawkins, Patrick felt like an equal, and not just the guy who was coming in to replace him.

"I'll see you up there in a few." Hawkins said; leaving Patrick to finish getting ready.

They got the call from the coroner's office at noon. Twenty minutes later, they were walking down the long corridor of the Nassau County Medical Center, towards the office of Doctor Margareta Wilkensis.

When Doctor Wilkensis entered the room, there was no welcoming smile upon her face like there had been last time. There was also no friendly exchange or lighthearted jokes between her and the detectives. The mood had done a complete one-eighty since their last meeting.

Doctor Wilkensis' did not need to speak. Her face said it all. The answers that they were looking for—the ones they had known since the morning before—were etched on her face.

"You know," She finally started. "Sometimes I've wondered why I got into this field. This happens to be one of those days."

"Believe me; I know what you mean, Margareta." Hawkins answered.

Patrick doubted Hawkins ever questioned his line of work.

"Your victim died from severe loss of blood." She informed them. This, of course, was obvious by the bed they had found their victim in the morning before. "The one small light in all this, and believe me, it's a very dim light, is that your victim did not physically suffer at all. The keyword I'm using here is physically. Mentally, this might have been the most torturous murder any expecting women could go through."

Like she had done during their last meeting, Doctor Wilkensis produced three manila envelopes for the detectives with copies of her official coroner's report tucked inside. However, unlike the Ramsey's file, Evangeline Carpenter's had a picture in it. It was the small of her back. A portion of her skin had been stained an orangey-yellow color, which Doctor Wilkensis informed the detectives was iodine. In the center of it, between two bumps of her spine, was a single red dot. Patrick knew, as he was sure Hawkins and Murphy also knew, the tiny dot was a puncture wound.

Evangeline Carpenter's murderer had injected her with something.

"Your perpetrator gave your victim an epidural." Doctor Wilkensis informed the three detectives.

An epidural, she told them, is a form of regional analgesia. In simple terms, it prevents pain impulses from travelling through nerves. Rendering the person receiving it incapable of feeling pain. This would make for the perfect addition to a twisted murder, if you didn't want your victim to pass out from the extreme pain they'd be feeling.

Pain, like getting your vagina cut up, and ripped open enough to have an infant pulled through it.

The sick fucking bastard wanted her to watch him, Patrick thought. *It wasn't about her feeling the physical pain. That didn't matter to him. What mattered was Evangeline Carpenter going through the mental torture of the whole thing.*

"Jesus," Hawkins said; obviously figuring out the exact conclusion Patrick was. "What about the infant, Margareta? Please tell me that that baby didn't suffer."

"It didn't," Doctor Wilkensis said to ease the minds of everyone in the room. "It never even drew a single breath. Once the umbilical cord was cut between your victim and her son, and he no longer able to receive oxygen from her, he drowned in the fluids that were in his lungs."

It looked as if Hawkins wanted to say something along the lines of at least that was some good news, but he didn't. He was speechless for what Patrick assumed was the first time in his life. No matter how you tried to paint it, there was no good news here. An innocent child still had its life stolen from it, even before it could begin.

"It's not the worst of it, either." The coroner informed the detectives.

"Really?" Detective Murphy asked. "Because it seems to be pretty bad at the moment."

"Your killer took your victim's placenta."

"He did what?" Patrick asked. He knew what he heard. His brain just refused to process it.

"After a child is born, the mother passes the placenta." Doctor Wilkensis informed them. "Your victim's placenta was gone.

As if everything they had now to go on wasn't enough to officially link the Ramsey's murder to Evangeline Carpenter's, this tidbit of information certainly was.

There had been skin left at the Ramsey's house after their killer had cleaned up after himself and left, but once it had been collected, it became apparent it wasn't all there. In fact, combined, there wasn't enough skin left behind to cover a single person. Their slaughterer had taken a good amount with him as a trophy.

Still, it wasn't substantial enough to claim their murders were committed by the same perpetrator. What Doctor

157

Wilkensis told them next, however, was, and it was exactly what they had been waiting to hear.

"I also found traces of Pancuronium Bromide in Evangeline Carpenter's blood. That's the same drug that was used to paralyze your two other victims."

With that said, it became official. The sadistic thing that stripped the skin from Arthur and Estelle Ramsey was the same monster that ripped the unborn child from Evangeline Carpenter.

The Nassau County Homicide Unit would now be on the hunt for a serial killer.

PART II

CHAPTER 18

It was an average mid-December day.

The usual crowd of holiday shoppers packed out the local malls and shopping centers. Busy buyers frantically bounced from store to store; trying to find the perfect gift for their loved ones as Christmas hastily neared. Yet, despite the utter insanity, the general mood was one of merriment. After all, it was the holiday season. Outside, the world was covered with a mesmerizing thin blanket of the season's first snowfall. Kids stared out their windows, in awe, as outside, every color they had ever known turned to an angelic white. Inside, Christmas trees stood tall. Each branch trimmed to perfection; wrapped in tiny lights and decorated beautifully. Wrapped presents began to build up under the tree, and children wrote Santa Claus with overwhelming hopes that on Christmas Day, he would add to the already towering mounds.

All-in-all, it was an average mid-December day.

Patrick Sullivan stood outside a department store window. He sipped at a hot cup of freshly brewed [black] coffee as he gazed through the pane of glass at a young woman, who was quite pregnant, having a conversation with an elderly couple.

Although he could not hear what was being said on the opposing side of the glass, he had the perfect image painted before his mind's eye of the conversation taking place. The young woman, who had been holiday shopping, bumped into the couple. The elderly woman, who, once upon a time, bore her own children, approached the beautiful young woman, and asked her how far along she was. The mother-to-be, who was welcoming all of her firsts when it came to pregnancy, answered proudly. The elderly woman raved of the joys of pregnancy, and assured the young woman that motherhood was nothing short of wonderful. The young woman stood there; listening to this kind lady's words. She rubbed her swollen belly in anticipation; feeling the love that was radiating from her womb.

Patrick stood on the outskirts of this serene picture; soaking up its beauty as much as he could, because when it was gone, he'd have to return to the ugliness that existed in the world.

"Beautiful, isn't it?" he heard a deep voice next to him say.

Patrick reluctantly pulled his attention from the people inside the department store. To his left stood Wallace 'Baby Tooth' Freewaters. The warm feeling of sublimity that had been rushing through him turned to ice as he stood in the cold presence of death. He knew then what he had been looking at was nothing more than a mirage. The three people inside that department store weren't happily enjoying the holiday season. They were all dead. Savagely murdered by a monster, and now buried six feet beneath the dirt.

"It was," Patrick answered Baby Tooth. "Until you got here."

He turned his attention back towards the scene on the opposite side of the window. What had just been a perfectly painted picture with Evangeline Carpenter and Arthur and Estelle Ramsey was as now tainted by the reflection of New York City's most infamous drug lord of the modern era.

Baby Tooth wore a long black pea coat and scarf over his thirty five hundred dollar suit. The left side of his face was completely destroyed. All the bad things in life that, somehow, disappeared during the holiday season seemed to have been deposited into the ugly face of Wallace Freewaters, because when Patrick looked at it, all he felt was despair.

"You know, Patty-boy; it really hurts my feelings when you say mean things like that. After all, I'm only here to…"

"To help," Patrick finished. "You've said all this before. I still don't believe you. Also, I can't hurt your feelings, Baby Tooth. You have none to hurt."

"See! There you go; being hurtful with your nasty words. Cheer up, Patrick. It's almost Christmas!"

Patrick saw in the window's reflection, Baby Tooth throw his arms merrily into the air and smile. In that obnoxious grin, he saw that God forsaken baby tooth. He wanted to smash his bare fist through the department store window just so he wouldn't have to look at that face and that tooth anymore.

"What is it you want, Baby Tooth?" Patrick asked; emotionally spent. He wanted to get this over and done with as quickly as possible.

"I told you, Patty Boy. I want to help you."

"Then tell me, Baby Tooth." He was way past keeping his cool with Baby Tooth these days. "How the fuck is it that you—of all the people that exist in the entire world—can help me?! Please… tell me, because I'd really love to know."

"Control that temper. Being a hot head gets you nowhere. Then again, we both already know that."

"Just get to your fucking point."

"The point is this, Patrick." Baby Tooth pointed at the scene unfolding inside the department store of the Ramsey's telling Evangeline Carpenter of the bliss that awaited her at the end of her nine month pregnancy. "This is not the life these people lead, and you know it. This is what you've created for them so they can have a happy ending. Only there is no happy ending for any of them. Those three are dead, and you need to accept it, and stop living in this bullshit lie."

Patrick wanted to sink his fist into Baby Tooth's mouth right there, knocking out what remained of his teeth, just to shut him up. He didn't want to hear what Wallace Freewaters had to say. He didn't want to hear the truth. He wanted so badly for those three people to have an alternate ending to their lives, but they wouldn't. You couldn't change death.

"You aren't doing them any good like this," Baby Tooth continued. "This, right here, is you becoming too emotionally invested, and because of that, you aren't looking at things objectively. You're letting your taste for vengeance take control of you, and that has never gotten you anywhere, Patty Boy. Not back then, and it won't now."

"When did you become so insightful?"

"Shit, nigga; I got all sorts of crazy-ass shit going on inside this cracked cranium," Baby Tooth said; returning to the speech and tone Patrick was so accustomed to. "I'm actually quite sophisticated. You'd know if you listened when I talked."

"Yeah, because I want to take advice from a drug lord, who has, undoubtedly, killed plenty of people in cold blood."

THE REPLACEMENT

"That's neither here nor there," Baby Tooth responded; dismissing the comment. "All that matters is that I'm here to get your punk-ass back on track."

Only Patrick didn't want to accept Baby Tooth's gracious offer of help. For starters, he didn't want to accredit Baby Tooth with steering him away from the path of vengeance, and preventing him from doing something that could potentially ruin his life. He, also, wasn't entirely sure he wanted to stray off his current path. The idea of seeking out the rightful form of revenge on behalf of the Ramsey's, Evangeline Carpenter, and her unborn offspring seemed nearly orgasmic at that moment.

"This is getting us nowhere," Baby Tooth said; frustrated that his advice was not fully registering with Patrick, who was still admiring the happy scene playing out through the window. "If you won't do anything about this, then I will, nigga."

"Wait… What does that mean?"

Baby Tooth was hastily walking towards the entrance to the department store. Whatever it was he meant to do, it would not be good.

"Sometimes, Patty Boy, a nigga's got to do what needs to be done to help a friend in need," Baby Tooth yelled back, and then entered the store.

For a few long moments he was out of Patrick's sight. Patrick wanted to take chase before Baby Tooth could cause any damage, but he found himself paralyzed by an overwhelming sense of dread.

When Baby Tooth reappeared, he approached the Ramsey's and Evangeline Carpenter. He smiled kindly as they greeted him. No one took notice that the man who had just walked up to them only had half a face that resembled anything human. He placed his dark hands on the pregnant belly of Evangeline Carpenter, and muttered something that Patrick could not make out. Evangeline returned the smile, and said something back—Patrick thought it was *Thank you*. Baby Tooth then took two step back from the mother-to-be, reached into his jacket, and produced a handgun. Before Patrick could ever think to react, Wallace Freewaters fired a single round into the stomach of Evangeline Carpenter.

The horrid scream that bellowed from Patrick's mouth was enough to shatter his paralysis. He slammed his fist hard against the glass window, and watched as Evangeline Carpenter clutched the womb, which served as the home of her first child for the first nine months of its existence. A few moments later, she collapsed to the floor and died.

Patrick rushed to the door to intervene before Baby Tooth could do anymore fatal damage, but he found it locked. He made an attempt to break through the glass with his bare fist, but that quickly proved feeble. He'd have to blow a hole through the glass, but when he reached for his own gun, he only found an empty holster. He rushed back to the window where he had been standing the entire time, and saw that Baby Tooth was now holding Patrick's gun in his other hand. He smiled, and then turned his attention to the Ramsey's.

"Don't do it, Baby Tooth!" Patrick yelled through the glass, but Baby Tooth chose to ignore his pleas.

Baby Tooth raised his arms—Patrick's gun in one hand, and his own weapon in the other—and fired a single shot from each pistol into the faces of Arthur and Estelle Ramsey.

"NOOOOOO!!!" Patrick screamed, as Ramsey's both die instantaneously from the bullet to their brain.

He collapsed to the ground, and began to weep. Moments later, Baby Tooth was standing over him. Patrick wanted nothing more than to leap up, and choke the life out of Wallace Freewaters, but he couldn't. He was too overcome by his despair.

"I'm sorry, Patrick. I had to," Baby Tooth said, sincerely. He dropped Patrick's gun on the pavement, and walked away.

"I hate you," Patrick yelled. He repeated it over and over; screaming until his voice went hoarse, but it made no difference. Baby Tooth just kept walking away without a single care in the world.

Patrick snapped out of his hellish nightmare laying on his couch. Sitting across from him, her eyes wide with a mixture of shock and worry, was Claire.

"Are you okay, Patrick?"

"Yeah," Patrick responded; trying to establish a clear line between his dream and reality. "Why?"

"Because you were yelling. I tried to wake you, but you just kept screaming. What were you dreaming about?"

"Nothing," he answered, but knew there was no way Claire was going to buy into that shoddy lie, "Well, something… I just don't remember. I know I didn't like it; whatever it was."

Before Claire could offer a response and call her husband out on his pathetic attempt at a lie, the phone rang. She got up to answer it, and returned within a few seconds with the phone in hand.

"It's Detective Murphy. It sounds important."

Patrick composed himself, and took the phone from Claire.

"Patrick," Detective Murphy said once Patrick had said hello. Claire was right; there was a clear sense of urgency in his voice. "I need you to be ready to go in like a minute, because I'm on my way to pick you up."

"Why, what's going on?"

He already knew the answer to his question. He wasn't sure why he even bothered asking.

Patrick was wrong, though, and when he heard the words from Detective Murphy enter his ear, and register with his brain, he was up and out of his seat like he had just been set afire.

"They found one, Patrick," Detective Murphy had told him. "And she's alive."

CHAPTER 19

Less than three minutes after he had hung up with Murphy, Patrick was descending the stairs in his house two steps at a time, and was out the front door with the speed of an Olympic runner. He almost turned back around to grab a coat, but then remembered the weather was still uncommonly warm for the time of year. Only in his dreams was it wintery cold and snowing.

Murphy was pulling up as Patrick was making his way down his path; attempting to button the last button of his shirt. He slid into the passenger side seat, and slammed the door shut. Without a single word exchanged between the two, Murphy flipped on the flashing lights of his Lincoln Townscar, and depressed his foot onto the gas pedal.

There wasn't much conversation during the first half of their drive. They were both likely too busy with the endless thoughts racing through their minds to formulate speech. The only words exchanged were Murphy telling Patrick of what he knew so far. A 911 dispatch received a phone call from someone who clearly was incapable of speaking. The only sounds the operator could hear coming from the other end of the phone call was a gurgling sound; as if the caller had been choking. When police arrived, they found the young girl clinging to life. They immediately contacted Homicide, not only because this was clearly an attempted

Murder but because they had a strong feeling that the victim was a survivor of a Surgeon attack.

The Long Island Surgeon (The Surgeon, for short) was what the media outlets had named him once the gruesome details of what he did to his victims became public knowledge. The Nassau County Police Department never expected to keep the fact that there was a serial killer at large a secret. They just hoped to contain it as long as possible, because they knew how the public would react.

At first, there was irritation. Long Islanders did not like the fact that the police were withholding the fact that there was a demented sicko going around; slaughtering elderly couples, and pregnant women. Irritation was soon followed by panic. Following a press conference with the Homicide Unit's captain, the District Attorney, and Jonathan Hawkins, who let the public in on what details of the Surgeon's murders they felt comfortable divulging, fear took hold over the populous. People became terrified with the idea that this serial killer followed no pattern, and selected his victims at random. Anyone could possibly be the next to fall to the Long Island Surgeon. All the police could do was stress the point that they were doing all they could to catch this killer, and, until he was caught, people should remain cautious, and to remember to lock up their homes at all times.

Not only did revealing the truth to the public result in negative feedback, but it also created false trails in the Homicide Unit's pursuit. Twice in the two weeks between the discovery of Evangeline Carpenter's body and the car ride Detectives Murphy and Sullivan were now taking, there were reports of Surgeon attacks. Each time, they had proven to be false.

The first attack was in Roosevelt—one of Long Island's nastier, unsavory towns. There had been a shootout over something meaningless, and the shooters thought that calling in the murder as a Surgeon attack would be a brilliant way to throw the police off their trail. The cretins failed to realize the fact that when the police did show up, they would notice that the crime scene was a shooting, and not at all a Surgeon crime. Needless to say, it didn't take long for the police to investigate, and track down the true perpetrators of the crime.

The second of these false trails was far more cleverly put together compared to the slapstick effort of the first.

A married couple had gotten into a heated argument, and, as a result, the wife ended up dead from a blow to the head with a brick. The husband, in a fit of panic, decided he could transform himself from perp to victim by making his wife's murder resemble a Surgeon murder. He had managed to cut off his wife's face, but in the process, threw up multiple times all over the crime scene. This, he accredited to the shock of finding his wife dead in their living room, but the dent in her head, the discovery of the murder weapon in a dumpster a block away, and the complete lack of Pancuronium Bromide in the victim's blood work made it relatively easy to pinpoint who the real perpetrator was. All it took was a light interrogation from Hawkins to get a confession.

As far as the actual pursuit of the Long Island Surgeon, the case had gone cold real fast.

Both, the Ramsey's household and Evangeline Carpenter's apartment were squeaky clean. Forensics found absolutely nothing in the form of evidence. The Long Island Surgeon was calculating, and absolutely thorough in his work.

The extension of the search of hospital inventories for missing units of Pancuronium Bromide also proved to be frivolous. There had been zero reports of any drugs missing from any of the additional hospitals they had subpoenaed.

So, in the most simplistic of terms: their pursuit had come to a screeching halt, and it was eating away at all of them; especially Hawkins.

Patrick had seen over the last two weeks that the realization that his last case on the force might go unsolved was getting to Jonathan Hawkins. He pushed Patrick and Murphy to find answers when there were none to be found. If no new leads to follow were discovered by the time he retired, there was nothing he could do, except walk away from his stellar career with a single blemish on his perfect record. That became an extremely bitter pill to swallow.

"Listen, Patrick," Murphy said, as they merged on to the Meadowbrook Parkway from the Southern State. "About what happened between you and Ace the other day… there's a reason why he reacted like he did."

Jonathan Hawkins had kept his promise to treat Patrick as an equal for almost a full two weeks. He pushed his replacement to work to, and even beyond, his full potential, and used positive reinforcement to do so, instead of criticism, dismissal, and insults. This motivated Patrick to push the boundaries of his ability in order to be a better detective.

Hawkins was grooming Patrick for greatness, because greatness was what you had to achieve to become an adequate replacement for Jonathan Hawkins.

Unfortunately, this camaraderie would disintegrate over a single disagreement.

Of all the questions that seemed ultimately unanswerable, the one question that kept creeping its way back into their palavers was how was The Long Island Surgeon choosing his victims?

Yes, the victims had all been chosen at random—they knew this, because they tried, and failed at discovering a connection between the Ramsey's and Evangeline Carpenter—but it didn't fit the profile of your typical serial killer. They usually honed in on a specific target group. Jeffrey Dahmer only murdered homosexual males, while Jack the Ripper and the Gilgo Beach Killer both targeted prostitutes. Apparently, that was not the case with this serial killer. His victims, so far, were on complete opposite sides of the spectrum. The Ramsey's were an elderly couple, who were enjoying their last years together after raising a loving family, while Evangeline Carpenter was young and about to embark on parenthood, and start a family of her own. They had absolutely nothing in common.

Except they did, Patrick noticed. The missing link he had been searching for was right there in front of his clueless face. He had just been too blind to see it.

Happiness was the answer they were searching for.

"They were happy…" Patrick had said aloud on the afternoon he and Hawkins' mended relationship began to bend towards its break.

"Excuse me?" Hawkins said. Patrick had his full attention.

"Why is he killing these people?" Patrick asked his partners.

"I don't know," Hawkins responded in a tone drenched with sarcasm. "Maybe because he's a sick fuck."

"No, I know that, but why is he killing these particular people?"

"In case you haven't noticed, kid; that is exactly what we are trying to find out." His tone now switched over to extreme irritation. Apparently, Hawkins was the only one allowed to push the people around him to reach conclusions all on their own.

"He killed them because they were all happy. It's not a physical attribute that we're looking for in the victims. It's emotional. It's happiness. They were all happy." He stood up, and began to pace back and forth as the ideas flowed like a river from his brain, and out his mouth. "Look at the Ramsey's. They are the picture perfect example of happiness. Married for decades, had children who are married, and have produced beautiful grandchildren for them."

"And a gay son who they hadn't talked to in years." Hawkins cut in; trying to spear a harpoon through Patrick's theory, and kill it before it was even off the ground.

"That is true," Patrick fired back. "But they still loved their son. They tried to mend the fence, and make him feel accepted. They tried as hard as they could to make Stephen Ramsey happy, because they loved him."

He then moved on with their next victim.

"Then there's Evangeline Carpenter. She was engaged to be married, and about to give birth in only a few weeks to a baby boy. What could bring a woman any more happiness than starting her family? You can ask my wife; she'll tell you that there's nothing that comes even close."

Hawkins didn't speak, at first. He looked to be considering Patrick's newfound theory, but his eyes told a different story. He wasn't buying into it. Jonathan Hawkins didn't think this theory merited their time or attention, but, to Patrick, it was the only theory that made any sense.

"So you think this person—this surgeon—is choosing his victims because they lived happy lives?" Hawkins asked. The tone he chose made it sound like what he really wanted to say was, *do you actually believe this ridiculous horseshit that is coming out of your mouth right now?*

For the first time in two weeks, Patrick felt the urge to slap Hawkins in his mouth. Instead, he decided he would defend his theory, instead of letting it be shot down so easily.

"It explains a lot," he went on. "How he chose his victims... Why he did to them what he did.... It even explains why he uses all these drugs."

"How do you figure, Patrick?" Murphy asked.

Carl had remained quiet throughout the duration of the conversation, which was now on the fast track to becoming a full blown argument, but now he decided it was time to chime in. This was probably so Patrick's theory could have a fighting chance. If Carl made an inquiry, Hawkins wouldn't speak up against it. He had too much respect for his longtime partner. Patrick thought it was the respect he was starting to earn, but, apparently, he was wrong

"He drugged them so they could see the things that mattered most to them—the things that made them truly happy—destroyed. Arthur Ramsey had to watch, paralyzed, as the woman he loved his entire adult life was skinned. He went so far as to make Arthur Ramsey believe his wife was still alive and suffering after she died. Then, he dopes Evangeline Carpenter up on pain killers so that she wouldn't pass out from the excruciating pain of being cut open. He made her watch as he ripped her open, and took her baby from her."

Hawkins didn't offer a response, but Patrick could tell he still wasn't buying it.

"It even goes past the initial killings," Patrick went on; refusing to not let his point get across. "Look at what he did to the bodies, postmortem. When he had finished stripping the Ramsey's of their identities, he propped them up on the couch, slid their wedding band back onto their fingers, and interlocked their hands. With Evangeline Carpenter, he chose to cut open her vagina as means of getting to her son. He could have as easily gone in through her stomach, but he chose to rip her child out of the place that was meant to welcome him into the world. Then, to top it all off, he takes her baby, and places it in her arms to create the illusion that she's just holding him as he slept."

"Hmmm..." Detective Murphy said. Patrick could see that Carl was seeing precisely where he was coming from.

"You're not actually buying this shit; are you, Carl?" Hawkins said.

"I don't know how you can't," Patrick said.

"Easy, because it's stupid."

Patrick wanted to bury his fist right in Hawkins' face; feeling blood splatter onto his knuckles as he broke Hawkins' nose from the impact of the blow. How could Hawkins, a man who was supposed to be the very best at what he did, dismiss a theory that made perfect sense so easily. They had already spent countless hours trying to find a link between their victims, and when Patrick had found it, his reward was getting insulted.

"Whatever happened to respecting what I had to say?" Patrick asked; calling out Hawkins on the promise he was clearly breaking.

"Kid... I'd love to respect your opinion," Hawkins didn't even make an attempt to sound even slightly sincere. "But I just can't sit here, and feed into this absurd theory you have conjured up. Here's the truth: sometimes people are sick in the head, like this Long Island Surgeon. He has no underlining motive, like he despises happiness, and wants to hurt those who are happy. He's just some sicko who has finally went over the edge. So stop wasting my time with your psycho-babble bullshit."

With that said and out of the way, Hawkins left the room; closing the matter, indefinitely.

"Don't worry," Patrick told Murphy as they now drove northbound on the Meadowbrook Parkway. "I get it completely."

THE REPLACEMENT

"No, you don't," Detective Murphy told Patrick matter-of-factly. "There's a lot that you don't know about Jonathan Hawkins."

As they drove towards Route 24, Detective Murphy opened a door to Jonathan Hawkins' past to help Patrick understand the man he was being groomed to replace.

Before he became the Ace on the River, Jonathan Hawkins had been a detective with the homicide unit in New York City. There, he began to lay down the foundation in which his legacy was built.

However, back then, Carl Murphy was not the man Jonathan Hawkins called his partner. In the early days of his legendary career in law enforcement, he was partnered with a man by the name Mark Randalls. Through hours of working side-by-side, Randalls and Hawkins developed a strong bond. On the day of their fifteenth wedding anniversary, when Jonathan and Maryanne Hawkins renewed their wedding vows with a proper ceremony, it was Mark Randalls who stood in as his partner's best man. Like he would eventually do years later with Carl Murphy, Hawkins saw Randalls as not just a partner, but a close friend, and a brother.

All of that changed, however, in one night with a single violent act.

One evening, after the usual long day Hawkins put in at the job, he received a phone call from his captain. He had the unfortunate displeasure of informing Jonathan Hawkins that his partner and friend had been arrested for murdering his wife. Apparently, he had beaten her within an inch of her life with a frying pan, and then finished her off with a single gunshot to the head.

Hawkins couldn't believe the news—he refused to—but Mark Randalls had been found outside his city apartment, his service pistol still in hand, covered in blood.

The details of that night, and what could possibly provoke a man with absolutely no history of violence to suddenly snap and kill his wife never fully came out. Randalls had claimed, even to the day he died, that he couldn't remembered a single detail from that night. It was that reason that aided Mark Randalls in living out the rest of his days in a psychiatric ward, opposed to an eight by ten cell at Riker's Island.

Mark Randalls managed to squeeze by, with the help of his lawyers, with an insanity plea. He claimed that the horrific things he had been exposed to over the years with the NYPD, namely their homicide division, took an immeasurable toll on his psyche.

He took the stand in front of a jury of his peers, and broke down in tears before them. He spoke of how he had loved his wife, and there was no repenting for what he had done. With tears running down his clean shaven face, he told the jury of the nightmares that plagued him at night. The reoccurring faces of the dead men, women, and children that he had seen over the long harsh years ate away at him until, finally, it was too much for him to handle.

In the end, Mark Randalls was found guilty, and convicted for the murder of his wife, Cynthia Randalls. The plea of insanity paid off, however, because the judge assigned to the Randalls versus the People case sentenced him to life in a psychiatric prison. His stay would only last six years. One rainy day, Mark Randalls got his hands on some drugs, and later that night, he overdosed on them, and died.

As the days following the verdict turned into weeks, which eventually transitioned into months, and then years, Mark Randalls was forgotten by everyone, except Jonathan Hawkins. When he learned of what his partner had done, he was as shocked as everyone else, if not more.

He had worked side-by-side with that man day in and day out, and he never would have guessed Mark Randalls capable of even striking his wife. He and Maryanne would have the Randalls over for Saturday dinners, summer barbeques, and even spent holidays with them. Mark and Cynthia were as in love as Hawkins and Maryanne had been, or so it had seemed.

The man who Hawkins had known and worked with, and the man who had beaten and shot his wife were two completely different people. He just couldn't believe it.

Above that, what Hawkins really couldn't believe was the bullshit insanity plea that got his ex-partner out of prison, and into a psychiatric ward.

He had known that man inside and out, and there wasn't a snowball's chance in hell that Mark Randalls, at any point in his career or life, went insane because of the pressures of his job. That was just a flat out lie. Throughout his career, Hawkins had seen the officers who couldn't handle the dead bodies, grieving families, and faces of men who had murdered in cold blood. Mark Randalls was not one of those men. He was one of the people who, as Hawkins would call it many moons later in Patrick Sullivan's front yard, had the fire burning inside of him. He was the man who others went to for guidance when they were feeling crushed by the pressures of the job, and all that came with it.

Hawkins saw his partner's claim of insanity as one thing and one thing only: a coward's way out of dealing with what he had done.

"Ever since then," Murphy explained as they pulled off the parkway. "Ace always viewed murders one dimensionally: they were sick, twisted people, who are cowards that kill in cold blood. He doesn't believe too deeply into the psychiatric side of homicide."

"So, just because he has a bad chip on his shoulder means he can just compromise the investigation? You're okay with this, Carl?"

Patrick couldn't believe that Carl Murphy was trying to make excuses for his partner's outlandish behavior. He didn't give a damn what happened in Hawkins past, or what his ex-partner had done. It shouldn't affect the case, but it was. It greatly crippled what had the potential of being a key theory of profiling the serial killer they'd been chasing almost blindly for weeks now.

"I'm not saying that I'm okay with it, or with the way he talked to you. I'm just saying there are certain things you accept about Jonathan Hawkins, because of how good he is."

"How good could he be when he won't even accept a reasonable theory? Everything I laid down for the two of you was nothing less than solid, and he just shot it down, and all because he doesn't believe that psychology mixes in with homicide."

"He'll get it, Patrick," Murphy said with a voice filled with confidence. "Just work with him. If our killer is, in fact, choosing his victims because they were all happy, Ace will figure it out. He'll just find a way to turn it away from psychology."

"In the process, he'll make me look like a foolish amateur."

"Those aren't his intentions, Patrick."

"Sometimes I'm not so sure."

"Listen, Patrick," Murphy said. "I know how Ace can come off, and I know that he is stubborn when it comes to his own opinion—you've seen that first hand on more than one occasion—but he really is the best at what he does, and the victims are always his priority. Don't think that he's holding some personal vendetta against you just because you've spoken up to him a few times. If anything,

180

he respects it. He's just confident in his abilities, and that's why he presses for his own theories over everyone else's. He doesn't want to make you look or feel stupid, Patrick. Believe me when I tell you this: above all else, he wants you to succeed."

Patrick didn't have a response to this, and Carl decided it was best to just let it be.

Truth was, Patrick just didn't know what to think of Jonathan Hawkins anymore. He thought he had it all figured out, but there he was; at step one again. He would just have to let time decide what to make of the whole Hawkins situation. He couldn't let himself be bothered by it. He needed to focus. There were more pressing matters to deal with now, like their surviving Surgeon victim.

Minutes after their conversation had concluded, they pulled into an apartment complex. Everything seemed so calm and peaceful as they made their way past the first few units, but when they turned the corner, Patrick couldn't believe the scene in front of him.

CHAPTER 20

Even though two long and grueling weeks had gone by, the memories of the first two crime scenes had remained so fresh in Patrick Sullivan's mind, it seemed as if he was still standing in the Ramsey's home, or Evangeline Carpenter's two room apartment.

He was currently envisioning what each scene looked like at first glance upon his arrival. The Ramsey residence looked so peaceful, he barely believed it to be a crime scene. That was until he pulled his vision away from the quaint suburban home, and saw the combination of police tape and bystanders. He got the same impression when they pulled up to Evangeline Carpenter's on Thanksgiving morning. This time, the crowd was of smaller size, because of the early hour, and the police perimeter was just beginning to be set up. Those mornings had been so quiescent, Patrick had to remind himself that there were lifeless bodies inside those homes.

The scene Patrick and Detective Murphy were driving up to was the polar opposite of those first two crime scenes. The night sky was lit up by flashing lights from, both, police cruisers, and an ambulance. There was a large crowd of people standing outside the apartment. Unlike the crowd that stood outside the Ramsey's house, who all spoke in low voices, and were there more out of curiosity than anything else, this crowd was loud; demanding answers from police to questions that just couldn't be answered. To the crowd, whether it was announced to the public yet or not—which it wasn't—this was a Surgeon attack. The very mention of his name, sent people into a frenzy, and this crowd was no different.

The police may have been able to keep the first two scenes under control, but this was unstable; teetering on the edge of chaos. Unless they were able to find something that led them to the Long Island Surgeon and put an end to his reign of madness, the situation with the public was only going to worsen.

Detectives Sullivan and Murphy pushed their way through the growing crowd, both in size and in anger, with their badges held above their heads, and made their way to the apartment.

As they neared it, the door exploded open, and paramedics came rushing out; pushing a gurney. Upon that gurney laid a young woman. She was petite with hair that, if not for the blood that turned it dark red, would have been blonde. Paramedics applied pressure to her chest; attempting desperately to slow her bleeding down, while another held an IV bag that was hooked up to the dying girl.

"We have a female in her mid-twenties," one of the paramedic radioed as they rushed the girl to the ambulance. "Multiple stab wounds. Likely suffering from internal bleeding. We need an O.R. prepped immediately."

"No!" Hawkins' voice commanded.

He exited the apartment behind the paramedics. Patrick then heard him say something that could have only been his mind playing tricks on him. No sane human would ever utter such a line, but it wasn't a trick.

"She can't go anywhere, yet. I need to talk to her first."

"Detective, this woman needs to be in surgery now," the paramedic said; stunned by Hawkins' request. "She's more than likely bleeding internally, and she will die if we don't stop it."

"And I need answers from her," Hawkins shot back; putting his own professional agenda over the jobs of the paramedics, and, apparently, the life of another human being. "You need to slow down her bleeding as much as possible right now, and bring her to so I can question her. After that, you can bring her to the hospital."

"Are you completely insane?" Patrick asked. He was livid, and he didn't give a damn how obvious it was. "If she doesn't get to surgery, she could die!"

"She could die, regardless. Whether in five seconds on this gurney, or on the ride over to the Medical Center, or on the damn table, she might not see tomorrow morning. She's our best chance to getting anywhere with this case, and we need to get something out of her while we still can. If we wait, and she doesn't come through this, we may not have that chance again. Then we're stuck in the same place we've been for weeks… square one; with absolutely nothing!"

"I don't care," Patrick yelled. "I'm not going to let this woman die, because you need your answers."

"Goddamn it, kid; how many more people are going to die if we don't? Are we going to sit around for another two weeks, tossing theories back and forth; working with only the bare minimum as far as actual evidence is concerned? Maybe you're willing to do that, but I'm not. Not when we can get something substantial to work with, so then maybe we can catch this bastard, and stop him from killing again. I don't want this girl to die, but she could, no matter what those doctors try to do to save her. If that's the case, at least let her have a chance to help the people who haven't died by this Surgeon's hand yet."

Patrick had heard enough. There was no explanation, nor reasoning that could pass Jonathan Hawkins' lips that would convince him that he was right.

Instead, he was going to punch Hawkins in the face. He was convinced of it. It had moved past just an urge, and had transitioned into a reality. There was no longer any questions about that. Patrick Sullivan was going to bury his fist in Hawkins' eye socket; shattering the bone. He felt his hand clinch up, and his body moving into position to deliver the blow, but he couldn't say with certainty whether or not he was going to follow through. Carl grabbed hold of his arm.

Patrick wasn't sure if Murphy saw his new partner about to do something that would result in serious repercussions. If he did, he made his grabbing of Patrick's arm come across as if he was just trying to lure him away from an argument that had potential to escalate.

"Let's go inside, Patrick, and have a look at the scene."

"You can't possibly agree with this, Carl?!" He would have never thought Carl, no matter how much he respected Jonathan Hawkins, would agree to this.

"Let's just go take a look at the scene," was all Carl Murphy had to say.

He was going to look the other way while Hawkins did something ethically wrong, and downright despicable. All because Jonathan Hawkins was so damn good at being a cop that his calls had to be the right one. Well, good cop or not; this was not a good call, and what they were about to do was wrong. The Lord, Jesus Christ could come down from his Kingdom above, and say, flat out, that Jonathan Hawkins was always right, and Patrick wouldn't care. This girl deserved a fighting chance, and Hawkins was ripping it away from her. All because he wanted answers.

"Yeah, kid," Hawkins said. "Go check out the crime scene. I'll question her. It'll be quick—I know exactly what I need to ask. After that, she'll be on her way to the hospital."

Before he could answer or knock Hawkins' teeth down his throat, Murphy gave Patrick's arm another hard tug. This time, instead of resisting, he allowed himself to be pulled away. This was a battle he couldn't win. Even if he knocked Hawkins out, there would be no victory. The girl would still be interrogated, instead of being brought to the hospital, and Patrick would surely lose his job.

In this continuous war, Hawkins was an entire armed cavalry, and Patrick was a single soldier with a dull wooden stick.

"You get that girl stable and able to talk," Patrick heard Hawkins order the paramedics as he entered the apartment. "She's not going anywhere until I talk to her."

When he entered the two first crime scenes, Patrick was able to take notice of the small details that made his victims actual human beings. Things, like restored antique furniture or a fridge with a sonogram photo on it, made these places homes, and not just crime scenes. When he entered this apartment with Carl Murphy, he did not take notice of any of those little things. All he could see was the aftermath of the slaughter that had taken place.

The white carpeting in the living room was now stained red with splatters of blood. In the center of the room, like a bulls-eye, was a pool of blood so dark that it almost looked black. Leading away from the puddle was a long streak of crimson that stretched across the carpet, and into the kitchen. Patrick followed the bloody path right to a woman's bag. The contents of the bag were strewed out across the tiled floor, and a cell phone, now caked with dry blood, lay amongst the wallet, concealer, mascara and chap-stick that had spewed from the bag.

THE REPLACEMENT

She crawled across the living room— slowly dying—to her bag, and called 911, Patrick told himself as he assessed the scene. *She refused to give up on living... Good for her.*

"Here's what I'm thinking," Detective Murphy said as he walked up to Patrick. "She came home early, for whatever reason, while he was setting up."

Murphy pointed to the mess on the floor. A metal tray had been tipped over, and just like the purse, its contents were thrown across the carpeting. Scattered around the fallen tray were a variety of stainless steel and sharp-as-hell surgical tools. Patrick couldn't begin to imagine what this monster—surgeon—had planned for this poor girl.

"She freaked, and tried to run," Murphy continued. "He went after her—probably knocking the tray over in the process—grabbed her, and slammed her into the wall." He pointed to an indentation in the plaster of the wall that was put there by a large object; like a human head. "She fell to the floor, probably knocked half unconscious; based on how hard it looks like she hit that wall. He went to the kitchen, grabbed the knife from the wood block on the counter, and made his way back to her." About a foot away from the dark pool of blood was a large kitchen knife. The entire blade had been painted red with the blood of an innocent girl. "He proceeded to stab her multiple times until he was satisfied that she was dead, or at least had no chance of surviving. He then fled the scene."

It all made sense to Patrick, and he agreed with every word Murphy had said. He then followed up with his own theory of what happened once the Surgeon had left the poor girl to die. Murphy nodded in approval as it was explained to him how this girl must've fought with everything she had against death's cold embrace, and crawled across the room to call for help.

He felt a bond between him and Murphy beginning to form strong right then. Murphy had for Patrick the one thing that Jonathan Hawkins lacked, and that was respect. In two weeks, Hawkins would be gone; retired due to heart conditions, and then it would only be Patrick and Murphy. In the end, they were going to be partners; not Hawkins and Patrick. Right then, in that single moment of clarity, Patrick felt good about the future.

"Detective Murphy... Detective Sullivan," a member of the forensics team called from across the room. "I think that you should come have a look at this."

The two detectives made their way over to the far side of the living room, where the member of forensics was on one knee next to the couch.

"I found this under the couch. It must have rolled under when the tray was tipped."

In his hand was a tiny glass bottle with a label on it that read in tiny letters: *Pancuronium Bromide.*

As if they hadn't already known by everything they'd seen already, they now had their concrete proof. This was a Long Island Surgeon attack.

He's never going to stop, was the cold thought that passed through Patrick's mind as he stared at the drug that had caused so many people's suffering. *Unless we catch him, this insanity will never end.*

He saw in Carl's face that he had been thinking the same thing, but neither would get to say what was on their mind out loud. It was then they heard the commotion from outside.

"I need help!" Hawkins yelled from the ambulance. "She's crashing!"

Patrick and Murphy rushed to the outside, as Hawkins was jumping from the ambulance to allow paramedics to attend to the girl, who was probably about to take her last breath.

Jonathan Hawkins stood outside the ambulance with his hands on his head. He actually looked scared. Or maybe it was guilt, Patrick wondered. Was Hawkins now considering the idea that maybe he had made a wrong call, and cost a girl her one chance of survival in the process.

"What happened?" Murphy asked; as he and Patrick rushed over to Hawkins.

"I don't know."

You know exactly what happened, you fucking bastard, Patrick thought. The overwhelming urge to knock out Jonathan Hawkins came rushing back over him, like a vicious tidal wave. He even felt his hands beginning to knot into fists, but managed to contain himself. *That poor girl crashed, and is now dying, because you needed your God damn answers above everything else. After she tried so hard to survive, you went and took that away from her, you son-of-a-bitch.*

"They stabilized her," Hawkins explained to them. "I went in there to try to talk to her, she took one look at me, and started crashing."

"Damn it," Murphy said.

"I didn't mean for this to happen, Carl. I just wanted answers, so we can catch this guy."

"I know, Ace."

The rear door to the ambulance burst open, and one of the paramedics stuck his head out.

"We got her back," he yelled to the detectives.

Patrick wasn't sure if it was because he assumed it was what he would do next, or if he actually saw a slight movement in Hawkins towards the ambulance, but he grabbed his arm hard, and whipped him around.

"She's going to the hospital. You can wait for your damn answers."

Hawkins just stared his replacement down for a few moments. Patrick was sure Hawkins was going to take a swing at him right then. He would welcome the blow. It was just the excuse he needed to unleash the anger he'd been trying so hard to withhold.

"Ace," Murphy said; trying to step in between the two. "She needs to go to the hospital."

"I know," Hawkins answered; yanking himself free of Patrick's grip. "I was just about to tell them to take her to the hospital, then the *kid* grabbed my arm."

He turned back to the ambulance, and waved to the paramedic to take her to the hospital. The young man needed no more instruction. He slammed the doors, and seconds later, the ambulance was rushing out of the apartment complex towards the Nassau County Medical Center.

The whole time, until it was out of sight, Hawkins eyes were locked on to the ambulance. Patrick wondered what thoughts were passing through the man's head. He doubted it was guilt.

Jonathan Hawkins was probably worried that he was going to lose the one solid lead to catching the person who had the greatest chance of actually eluding him throughout his entire illustrious career.

CHAPTER 21

Patrick got home that night just after one. Claire had been fast asleep on the couch; the television playing an infomercial for the world's most amazing food processor. It seemed as if she had attempted to stay up, and wait for Patrick to return home, but had succumbed to the sandman. She looked peaceful as she slept that Patrick couldn't find the heart to wake her. Instead, he draped a soft fleece blanket they kept out during the winter months over her, and retreated to his own bed for sleep. Despite the fact his mind had been racing nonstop, he found no trouble with his descent into slumber.

He didn't expect to sleep in the following morning, but never had he expected to be woken up by a frantic phone call four and a half hours after he closed his eyes.

The three detectives had held palaver once the girl, whose name they had learned was Julianne Frankles, had been taken to the hospital.

Upon his second visit into the girl's apartment, Patrick was able to turn his attention away from all the blood stains, splatters, and surgical tools, and see the things around the apartment that made Julianne Frankles an actual human being; something Hawkins failed to acknowledge. To him, she was just a piece of the puzzle he so desperately needed to solve.

First thing Patrick saw was an electric piano against the far wall. Next to it, stood a music stand that had pieces of sheet music resting upon it. Their victim had hobbies. Maybe music was even a passion of hers. He then took notice of some shelves mounted to the wall. On them, were various pictures of their victim posing with her family and friends. One framed photo was even of Julianne Frankles laying in a field of summery green grass with a dog on top of her; licking her face. She had an ecstatic look on her face that showed she was savoring every ounce of love that animal had to give. In fact, in all her pictures, Julianne Frankles looked so happy to be alive, and, now, she was battling with death.

While Patrick was assessing the apartment, Murphy laid out the theory of what had gone down for Hawkins. Hawkins fully agreed with his two partners that their theory was likely what had exactly happened.

When they concluded at the girl's apartment, they headed over to the Medical Center, where they would wait. There was no new information for them when they arrived. Julianne Frankles was immediately rushed into surgery, and was currently being operated on. Waiting and patience was now the name of their game, and it was killing them.

After an hour of silence—all three clearly wondering the same thing: Was this girl going to make it, or would her fight be in vain?—a group of five near hysterical girls rushed into the waiting room. They were all friends of the victim, and had heard the devastating news from a tenant who lived in the same apartment complex. The three detectives split up, and questioned the young women; trying to learn what they could about their victim.

Julianne Frankles was a post-graduate student in psychology, who had come all the way from Nebraska to earn her higher education at Hofstra University. She was an extremely loving and caring person, her friends told the detectives. She was passionate about her schooling and doing what she needed to be done to achieve exactly what she wanted out of life. She welcomed her future with open arms, because it couldn't be anything but bright.

Her true passion, as Patrick had guessed back at her apartment, was music. Julianne Frankles was a hell of a piano player, and an even more extraordinary singer. She had a voice like no other, her friends recalled. There was just a presence and a power that couldn't be described when she was behind a piano or microphone.

"She loved psychology," one of her friends told Patrick; trying her best to articulate through her uncontrollable sobs, "But it was singing—music, in general—that made her truly happy."

That one line struck a note with Patrick. His mind instantly reverted back to his theory regarding how the Long Island Surgeon chose his victims. The same theory he wasn't allowed to bring up, because Jonathan Hawkins was too sore about his own past to accept certain truths… Like the fact Julianne Frankles had been chosen by the Surgeon because she was happy with the way her life was going.

Hawkins, himself, had also learned some very important information from one of Julianne Frankles' friends. Something that would give the detectives a clearer idea of why this attempt by the Surgeon had gone so awry.

Julianne Frankles went to the Hofstra campus library (located a mile away from her apartment), every Monday, Tuesday, and Wednesday to do research, write papers, or just to get away from those tempting home distractions to study for her classes. She did this during the semester without fail. She always stayed there, working hard towards her future, until ten o'clock. However, this week, her friend had told Hawkins, Julianne had been battling a cold—something that was pretty uncommon that year on

Long Island, given that there hadn't been a single day of cold weather.

With this tidbit of information, the detectives were able to piece a large chunk of their puzzle together. With a pounding head and clogged nose preventing any real intake of knowledge, Julianne Frankles decided she would call it an early night, and head home to try to get some rest. This was the factor that the Surgeon did not take into account, and it was probably what saved Julianne Frankles' life.

If she had stayed at the library until her usual time; trooping it out through sickness in order to study, she surely wouldn't have stood a chance against the man who would have been lying in wait for her when she returned home. However, when she showed up early, instead of her usual time of after ten, she caught her attacker off guard, and forced him to change his plans. He chose stabbing her to death over whatever hideous thing he originally had in store for her.

Something he failed at doing. Now, if Julianne Frankles made it through surgery, the three detectives chasing down her attacker had someone who could provide them with more than they had managed over the past few weeks. Namely, a positive identification

Just after midnight, four hours after she had been wheeled into surgery, Julianne Frankles was pronounced stabilized by the surgeon—the one who intended to save her life, instead of ending it. This was great news for not only her friends, whose tears of fear transformed into tears of relief, but for the three men waiting anxiously to find her attacker.

"When can we see her, doctor?" Hawkins asked the moment that followed the announcement that the young girl's surgery had been a success.

THE REPLACEMENT

If Hawkins had been relieved at all that the girl had made it through surgery, he didn't show it. He jumped right to business. There was no time to show any human emotion when there was a case to solve.

"I'm sorry, detectives," the doctor told them. "It's still going to be a little bit. She's in recovery now, and still unconscious. I want to give her a few more hours."

"Well, doctor, with all due respect; we may not have a few more hours," Hawkins argued. "Every minute we waste is another minute that the man who did this to her—who's done this to other innocent people—slips away from us."

"Well, again, I'm sorry, detective, but I must insist. You will have to wait until she comes to on her own to speak to her."

Patrick expected the argument to continue, and inevitably escalate, but it didn't. Hawkins simply accepted the doctor's request that they wait.

"Well, we appreciate what you were able to do for her, doctor. You saved a life tonight. Could you please let us know when the girl is up, and able to talk?"

"Of course, detectives. I appreciate your patience."

Once they had concluded their meeting with the doctor, Hawkins let the girls know that they would be able to see their friend in just a few hours; right after the detectives had spoken to her. After about an hour of waiting, Hawkins suggested Patrick and Murphy call it a night.

"It's going to be a few hours before the girl even wakes up," he told his partners. "And the two of you look absolutely spent. We don't need three detectives who are so tired that they're borderline useless. The two of you go home, and try to get at least a few hours of sleep. I'll try to get a few hours of sleep here. When she wakes up, I'll call."

Patrick didn't trust this. Not coming from Hawkins. It was suspicious, and he knew Hawkins was up to something. After the stunt he pulled earlier, Patrick took the man's sincerity as nothing but deception. He had given into the doctor's request way too easily, and now he was trying to send Patrick and Murphy away. He was planning something that he knew that his partners—namely, Patrick—would not approve of.

"Don't worry, kid," Hawkins said; as if reading Patrick's thoughts. "You don't have to worry about me doing something shady. I just want some of us to be on our feet, and alert come tomorrow morning. Plus, the two of you have families. Try to spend some time with them; even if it's a few hours in the morning."

Hawkins assurance did little to appease Patrick's suspicions, but he had to accept it. Battles needed to be picked with Jonathan Hawkins, and this was not one of them. After a little resistance from his longtime partner, the two finally agreed to the request, and that was what landed Patrick in his bed; descending rapidly into twilight at one-thirty in the morning.

When his cell phone rang, Patrick was dreaming. He was in a hospital room; standing on one side of Julianne Frankles' hospital bed. He was gripping her arm for dear life… Literally.

On the opposite side of the bed, also with a firm grasp on the arm of the sole survivor of a Long Island Surgeon attack, were Arthur and Estelle Ramsey, and a pregnant Evangeline Carpenter. They were pulling at Julianne Frankles; trying to pull her off the bed to join them. Patrick pulled on his respective side; trying to keep her from being pulled away. They were playing a game of tug of war with another human being. On one side was Patrick; trying to pull Julianne Frankles towards life, and on the opposite side were those who weren't as fortunate as her; trying to pull her into the black precipice of death.

"Come on, Patty Boy!" Baby Tooth yelled from over his shoulder like the world's ugliest cheerleader. "Pull! Pull!! Pull!" You can do it!"

"You think you can help?" Patrick asked; his face turning red, and beginning to sweat. "After all, you're always claiming to be trying to help me out."

"Not that kind of help, Patrick. Sorry, nigga."

As Baby Tooth went back to his useless cheering, Patrick continued to pull; trying to keep this girl alive, but he was failing. He could feel her slipping away. No matter how vice-like he made his grip, it was never tight enough. Julianne Frankles was slipping away from him.

Right as his sweaty hands were about to lose their hold on her wrist, Patrick's phone rang back in reality, and he was ripped out of his dream; to a place where Julianne Frankles was still alive.

"Hello," he said in a groggy, still-half-asleep tone.

He heard nothing on the other end, except loud noises, and a deafening static. He called into the phone again; this time in a louder, more awake tone. This startled Claire awake, who must have woken up at some point in the night from her sleep on the couch, and joined Patrick in their bed. He barely took notice to her, though. The voice on the other end was breaking up, and the words were inaudible. He knew the voice, though. It was Hawkins.

"Kid," Patrick managed to make out through the static and chaos in the background. His heart stopped in place, and his stomach twisted in knots. He knew exactly what was going on. "...Hawkins... Surge—... Girl... Get... th—... —ospital... now!"

Hawkins speech continued to be fragmented; thanks to poor reception, and Patrick wasn't going to wait to decipher what was coming through the other end of the phone. He had heard enough.

Patrick yelled that he would be there as soon as he could, hung up the phone, not knowing if Hawkins had heard him or not, and leaped out of bed. He took no notice of Claire, who was now sitting up in bed. He just peeled the clothes that he had worn only a few hours ago off the floor, and threw them back on. He jetted down the stairs, and out the door.

As Patrick Sullivan was pulling out of his driveway, a single thought passed through his mind.

The girl's dead. Somehow he got to her, and finished what he started.

Patrick was right.

CHAPTER 22

The horror scene at the apartment complex seemed tranquil compared to what Patrick saw when he arrived back at the Nassau County Medical Center. Evacuation had begun, and as he watched people slowly filing out of the building, the thing that he had already known was becoming more real with every passing moment.

Julianne Frankles was dead. The Long Island Surgeon paid her a visit in the night to finish what he intended to do the night before.

Patrick pushed his way through the crowd; like a firefighter running into a burning building while everyone else was trying to flee. As if this serial killer didn't already have Long Island in a state of scare, the fact that he had just attacked a hospital would send people over the edge. No one cared that there was a police officer trying to make his way into the hospital. Their only concern was getting out of there before they were the next victim of the Long Island Surgeon.

Patrick knew, of course, this was ludicrous. The Surgeon had gone into that hospital with one person in mind, and one agenda. Now that he had succeeded, he was long gone. These people had nothing to be scared about, but they were too worked up to listen had anyone tried to explain that to them.

When he finally managed to penetrate the crowd, and made his way in, he immediately saw Detective Murphy.

"This place is a madhouse," he said as he approached Carl.

"I know. I've been waiting for you. Ace is upstairs. It's bad, Patrick."

"Let's go."

They made their way up the private elevators to avoid the crowd. Julianne Frankles was placed in a private room following her surgery, instead of the Intensive Care Unit. The detectives wanted her isolated as much as possible. Little luck that decision did them, in the end.

The two exited the elevator, and made their way down the mostly deserted corridor. They turned the corner, where the nurse's station was located, and saw a body covered in a white sheet laying on the floor.

"One of the nurses," Murphy told Patrick. "Single gunshot wound to the back of the head."

"Executed…"

A painful reality dawned on Patrick. It wasn't just Julianne Frankles who was at risk in the night. There were going to be people in the way; people who stood between the Surgeon and the woman he most desired, and to get to her, they would have to die.

"Yeah, and she's not the only one, either."

"How many?" Patrick asked. He didn't want to know.

"Another nurse… Two security guards… one of our own… and the girl herself, Patrick."

"Six people?!" Patrick was beside himself. He didn't want to believe it. Six people dead within such a short duration of time. Six innocent lives cut short. Six families destroyed.

They made their way further down the hall to the room that had been Julianne Frankles'. They passed the second nurse; also covered by a white sheet. The same ill fate as the first. When they finally arrived at the room, there was another covered body lying in front of the door. A group of officers were standing around it.

"Officer Daniel Branson," Murphy said. "Thirty four years old. Beautiful wife. Two kids... one more on the way..."

Ten feet to their left was Hawkins. He was engaged in deep conversation with someone from hospital security. When he finally noticed his partners, he waved them over.

"He deleted the security tapes," was the first thing he said. "The son-of-a-bitch deleted the security tapes."

"Is that even possible?" Patrick asked.

"Yeah," Eli Burke, the head of the hospital's security, informed Patrick. "He got into our main security room, killed two really good men, and deleted the footage."

"Aren't there backups?" Murphy asked.

"Our backup system has been down for weeks. They keep saying they're going to send someone to fix it, but they never do."

"Well, I'd call that a convenience," Hawkins said; his voice thick with the sarcasm. "Just not for us."

"How'd he get into the room?" Patrick asked. "I mean, I get that one of your guys let him in, but I doubt they would just open the door for anyone."

"No, usually not, but we don't usually have a reason *not* to open the door if someone does knock."

"Your men didn't assume that there was a man with murderous intentions on his mind standing on the opposite side of that door." Hawkins said.

"This is a complete disaster," Burke told the detectives.

The head of security was beside himself, and falling apart right there. Six people dead under his watch, and he was clearly not equipped to handle such a monstrous catastrophe. Who would be, though? All three detectives were as equally in shock at what had gone down in such a small window of time.

No one could have guessed this would happen. Not even Hawkins, and he likely had a gut feeling the Surgeon might try to finish off what he started once he learned from the news that the girl had survived. Still, with all his years of expertise and his amazing abilities, this was even beyond Jonathan Hawkins' comprehension.

Hawkins gave Burke some comforting words of reassurance that he shouldn't take this personally, and none of this was his fault. He told the head of security that they would be in touch if they further needed his assistance, and then parted ways with Eli Burke. The three detectives headed to the next stop on their tour of this massacre; the room of Julianne Frankles.

The two nurses, officer Branson, and the two security guards, as Patrick had been told by Hawkins, were all clean kills. It was a single gunshot executed with perfect precision that had ended those five lives. The scene they walked into when they entered the room where Julianne Frankles had been recovering from surgery was anything but clean.

Around the bed, the white walls of the room were splattered with the blood of the woman, who only a few hours ago had been known as the sole survivor of a Long Island Surgeon attack. A title she no longer possessed. The bed sheets that had covered her as she slept, and the gown she wore were shredded, and saturated in blood. It would have been impossible to even venture a guess at what their original color may have once been. On the floor, lying at the foot of the bed was a singular surgical knife and a bone saw. Both instruments, once a shining silver, were now coated with Julianne Frankles' blood. They were the tools that ended her fight with death.

THE REPLACEMENT

The true horror of this unimaginable scene—as if everything they had seen that morning already wasn't enough to deem it one of the most disastrous events in Nassau County history—was not the site of the lifeless body of the career ambitious college student of Psychology in the bed; her stomach infested with an overkill of stab wounds. It was the site of Julianne Frankles' face that would haunt all those who looked upon it that morning until their dying days.

It wasn't enough that the Long Island Surgeon had to end Julianne Frankles' life after she had fought so hard to preserve it. It wasn't enough that he had to snuff the one light of hope in this dead end murder case. No, he had to do it in his usual unimaginable, gory fashion. The site of his victim needed to leave a lasting impression, and Julianne Frankles was no exception to this.

The Long Island Surgeon ripped the jaw clean off her face.

As they examined what remained of Julianne Frankles' face, Patrick imagined, as he was sure Murphy and Hawkins had been, too, exactly what had happened to this poor girl in the final moments of her life.

Despite the brutality of his past murders, everything the Surgeon had done had been considered clean and accurate. What he did to Julianne Frankles was far from either of those. This was done out of anger. Her face was riddled with stab marks; indicating that he mercilessly jammed the surgical knife into her face, repeatedly. Hanging from where her jaw had once been was a mess of skin, muscle, and nerve endings. Once he was satisfied that he had done enough damage to the girl, he got the bone saw, and after using that, he ripped her jaw right from her face. Although he had no evidence to support his theory, Patrick knew the final act was done with Surgeon's bare hands.

"He took the jaw," Hawkins said; pulling Patrick back to reality. "Just like he took the Ramsey's skin, and Evangeline Carpenter's placenta. He took it for his souvenir."

And that wasn't all he took.

Patrick noticed Julianne Frankles' limp arm dangling from the bed. The tips of her fingers were all dripping blood from them. Only, he noticed upon closer examination, that it wasn't the tips of her fingers that were bleeding, because they had all been removed from all ten fingers.

"He cut her fingers off," he pointed out to the Hawkins and Murphy, and he knew exactly why.

You took her fingers, because she needs those to play the piano, Patrick told the killer who was long gone from the scene of the crime. *Just like you took her jaw, because she loved to sing. You made sure, even in death, this girl was stripped away of the things that made her happy, you miserable monster.*

This all sent Patrick over the edge. He backed away from the body slowly in a full blown state of disbelief. He ran his hands over his head; not believing everything that had gone down. The whole thing was spiraling rapidly out of control for, both, the Homicide Unit and the Long Island Surgeon.

It wouldn't be the end, either. It was going to get worse. This, Patrick had no doubt of.

"Where were you?" Patrick snapped at Hawkins. He wasn't sure if it was rage or frustration, and, honestly, he didn't care. Whatever it was, he was going to unleash it on Jonathan Hawkins. "You sent us away, because you said you would stay here and watch over her. Instead, you left, and now she's dead."

"Patrick," Detective Murphy started to say. "Let's just take a minute here."

"No, Carl, I don't want to take a minute." Patrick snapped. "Where the hell were you, Hawkins?! I'd love to know, because six people are dead and you are not. You weren't even here."

For the first time since knowing Jonathan Hawkins, Patrick saw the slightest hint of shame in his eyes.

"I went home," he told Patrick. Despite the contradicting story his face told, his voice did not waver from its usual steady tone of confidence. "I went home to change into fresh clothes, because I didn't think I would have much time to do so come morning."

Patrick noticed that Hawkins had indeed changed from a maroon colored drastically overpriced button-down shirt to a grey drastically overpriced button-down shirt.

"I left Branson to guard her room while I was gone," Hawkins continued. "He was one of the best. I thought she would be safe."

"Well, she wasn't. Now they both are dead, but I hope that you're comfortable in your fresh outfit."

Patrick turned, and left the room. He had seen enough—enough of the ghastly ending of Julianne Frankles, and enough of Jonathan Hawkins. He was already half way down the hospital corridor when he heard Hawkins call after him.

"Where the hell do you plan on going? We have a shit load of work to do."

Patrick turned, and walked back to Hawkins.

"You, of all people, are going to lecture me about work. Are you going to scold me for shunning my responsibilities, Hawkins? There's no need for that, because I'm not going anywhere. I'm going to stay right here, where I belong, and do whatever it takes to do right by that girl in there. That girl, who only a few hours ago had survived the fight of her life. That girl, who is now *dead.* I'm going to stay put, and I'm going to do right by her. If only you could say the same."

"You think for one second I would have left this hospital—hell, you think I would have left her bedside?— if I had any suspicions, what-so-ever, she was in any danger?"

It was Hawkins now who seemed to be taking a page out of Patrick's play book by letting his emotions get the best of him. They were too busy being locked into a dead stare, like two boxers before a big fight, for Patrick to find out for himself, but he was willing to bet Hawkins' hands were balled into two tight fists. He was definitely ready to knock Patrick on his ass. Patrick would've welcomed it, too. He needed just one excuse to drive his fist into Hawkins face.

"You'd be insane to think otherwise, kid," Hawkins went on saying. "I thought she'd be fine for the hour I was gone, and I knew she was in good hands. Don't you dare presume that this doesn't weigh heavily on me, because it does."

"The two of you need to cut the shit," Murphy said; getting between the two of them. "You both are acting unprofessional, and disrespectful. We're standing in the middle of a multi-person crime scene, and all you two seem to care about is knocking the other's teeth down his throat. It's disgusting."

The two, without saying a word of apology to Carl or each other, backed down. They refused to break their stare, though. Wordlessly, Hawkins and Patrick delivered their respective message loud and clear to the other.

We're not through yet.

Hawkins was the first to walk away. Patrick didn't know where he was going, nor did he care. He walked slowly over to the window of Julianne Frankles' room. He stared at the slaughtered body of a girl, who had once had her entire life in front of her, but now had nothing. He wondered how one man—just one single human being—was able to do all this. Not just what would become known as the Nassau County Medical Center Massacre, but all of it? Everything starting from Arthur and Estelle Ramsey, running through Evangeline Carpenter and her unborn son, and ending with the six lives he had taken in the small window of only one hour.

He stood there, looking through the glass, and for the first time in this case, for the first time since Vivian Chambers, Patrick thought it was all hopeless.

Completely hopeless.

CHAPTER 23

Both, Patrick and Hawkins gave themselves a few minutes to calm down enough for them to be able to work together. Once they were ready to play civil with one another, they were faced with the daunting task of piecing together the events of that dreadful hour where the Long Island Surgeon had more than doubled his victim count.

They started with the security surveillance room. That was likely where the Surgeon had started his bloody spree. He would have to take out the guards, and, more importantly, the security cameras. The hospital and those who'd be pursuing him, needed to be blind to his movements.

Julianne Frankles' room had been a crimson mess, but the security room was almost squeaky clean. These kills were as clean as clean could be. They weren't his target. They weren't the point he was trying to make to the world. They were simply collateral damage, so no need for the theatrics with these two.

Patrick stood staring at the small monitor screens, which were now completely back up, and recording the activity throughout the entire hospital. Only now, it was completely pointless. Everyone who could be evacuated had been, and there was no longer a psychotic serial killer running rampant through the halls.

THE REPLACEMENT

The two bodies of the fallen security guards had been removed from the room, and taken for the short elevator ride down to the basement; to the morgue. There wasn't much in this room for the detectives, except to be used as a starting point. They knew how the guards were executed—single shots to the head —and they knew exactly why he had killed the guards, and needed access to the room.

Still, Patrick stood there, statuesque; staring deeply into those monitors, like one who would stare into the eyes of their lover. He was fixating on them. Hawkins and Murphy stood behind him; not speaking. They knew Patrick was on the brink of finding something, and if it was something that could help them, they were more than willing to wait.

"C'mon, kid," Hawkins said; trying to urge on the man he had almost gone to blows with moments before.

Patrick saw nothing, though. It was all wishful thinking, he realized. He was on the cusp of giving up; realizing he probably was wasting their time staring at those stupid monitors, when, suddenly, out of nowhere; he saw that dismal beacon of hope appear in the vast ocean of hopelessness they'd been shipwrecked in for so long. It was faint, but it was there, and it was enough to keep him going.

"Did he turn off all the cameras?" Patrick asked Eli Burke as he spun around towards the others in the room.

"Not all of them," Burke replied.

"And the surveillance footage that had been deleted," Patrick continued; growing more excited as the questions left his mouth. Everything was falling into place. "Was everything wiped or just certain parts?"

"He only deleted some of the footage from certain cameras," Burke answered; not quite sure where Patrick was going with this.

Hawkins knew, though.

209

"If we can figure out which cameras he turned off, then we can figure out the exact route he took through the hospital!" he exclaimed.

"And if we figure out what he had deleted from the tapes, then we can figure out where he was in the hospital before he got into the security room," Patrick finished.

"Thus mapping out for us his exact movements!" Hawkins concluded. "You're a freaking genius, kid!"

It may not have been a lot to go on, but it was a huge breakthrough compared to what they had up until that point. The Long Island Surgeon might as well have been a phantom; he was that good at covering up his tracks, but now, because he needed to finish what he had started at Julianne Frankles' apartment, he left them with a clear path of his movements during that horrible night.

The three detectives, along with Eli Burke, ciphered through the security footage of that gory night.

First they looked at the security cameras that had been turned off once the Surgeon had killed the guards. The two cameras in the corridor leading out of the security room to the elevators had been shut off. Then, he switched off every elevator camera, and completely wiped out all surveillance that had its electronic eye on the floor Julianne Frankles had been recovering on. With everything gone dark, he was free to move as he pleased; killing whoever got between him and Julianne Frankles.

Next, they attempted to figure out the footage that had been deleted; erasing all evidence that he was an actual corporeal being moving through the hospital. Finding out the Surgeon's movements after the security guards were killed was the easy part. Finding where he been before executing two innocent, hard-working men proved to be a more daunting task. The Surgeon seemed to have only deleted specific parts of surveillance footage, and they seemed to be sporadic at best. He only cared about particular locations and times to delete his movements from the digital records.

"It makes no sense," Murphy said after they had gone through, and tried to piece together a path from the deleted footage for the third time. "There's no rhyme or reason to this."

Carl was right, but Patrick still concentrated on trying to get inside the head of the man who had been making a fool out of him, and the entire Nassau County Police Department for the last month. He was too smart to be sloppy, and they all knew that. There had to be a reason for this chopped up editing they were staring dumbly at.

"He only deleted footage where he was singled out," Patrick finally said; realizing what the Surgeon had done. "The cameras are all set up to follow a path, so that there are no blind spots in the surveillance. He deleted the shots where it was only him alone in the frame. He didn't bother with the footage of crowds. He knew he could blend in with the other people."

"Holy shit," Hawkins said; staring at the footage more closely. "I think you're right. That son-of-a-bitch."

"He's playing with us," Patrick pointed out. It was true that he had come there with a sole mission of destroying the life of Julianne Frankles, but he wouldn't leave without telling the three men chasing him that he was far smarter than any of them. "He could have easily deleted all the footage, but he wanted us to know that he is somewhere in there, and we have absolutely no idea who he is."

"Couldn't you just go through the footage, and see who shows up in all the frames?" Eli Burke asked.

"I wish it was that easy," Patrick answered. "He moved when people moved. Numerous people show up in these frames more than once. He was smart about this. He's smart about everything he does."

"Hey, kid; did he shut off or delete any of the cameras on any of the hospital entrances?" Hawkins asked.

Patrick went through the hospital's security footage one more time.

"No, he touched nothing on any of the entrances or exits in the entire hospital. They're all intact, and nothing was deleted."

"Because he didn't need to..." Hawkins pointed out. "That sneaky son-of-a-bitch."

Hawkins was right; the Surgeon had no need to turn off any of the cameras at the entrances and exits. After he killed those six people the hospital erupted into a state of chaos, he could easily blend in with the crowds rushing for the doors.

He could have been in the crowd that I was pushing myself through to get in, Patrick thought. *He could have been one of the people I shoved out of my way. He could have been right there; in my grasp, and he slid right past me.*

Patrick tried to dismiss this thought; figuring it to be unlikely, but it lingered in the back of his brain, like a nagging headache. The idea that the Long Island Surgeon could have been within arm's reach, but got away, like a thief in the night, made Patrick feel sick.

"Okay, getting out undetected was easy—we all can see that," Murphy said. "But getting in unnoticed would be a bit trickier, and certainly it would be riskier to not delete the footage."

"Not really," Hawkins pointed out. "Plenty of people came and went since Julianne Frankles was admitted last night. I'm positive some of them were here up until the hospital got evacuated. He could have been anyone of those people. We have no way of telling. He's safe, and he knows it, so he didn't bother at all with worrying over the entrance and exit cameras. He doesn't waste his time with the futile details."

Hawkins was absolutely right. The Surgeon could have entered that hospital at any time in the night, and simply waited for the opportune moment to strike. He could have been there moments after he learned Julianne Frankles had survived his attack. After all, it was all over the news within minutes of being called in. All the news outlets had foolishly reported that the girl had survived, and had been taken to the Nassau County Medical Center to undergo emergency surgery in an attempt to preserve her life. There was no doubt in Patrick's mind that the Surgeon had begun plotting the perfect finish to what he started the moment the news hit his insane ears. Once he had schemed, he would be en route to the Medical Center, where he would play out his despicable design.

What really ate away at Patrick was the thought that the Surgeon could have been there at the exact moment they were; waiting on any word of Julianne Frankles' condition. He could have been one of the many people in that same waiting room where Patrick, Hawkins and Murphy sat alongside the victim's close friends. He could have watched each of them, laughing to himself; knowing all their hoping and praying would fall on deaf ears, because by the end of the night, Julianne Frankles, along with anyone else who stood in his path to her, would be dead.

The thought rampaging through Patrick's mind turned from an idea into a cold hard fact. He was convinced—he knew—that the Long Island Surgeon had been in the hospital for hours; waiting. Waiting for his perfect moment. Waiting to end more lives that didn't deserve to be ended.

Within a week's time, Patrick Sullivan would learn that he was absolutely right.

CHAPTER 24

One week.

One week of silence.

The murderous spree of the Long Island Surgeon would come to an unforgettable, crashing end at six in the morning on Christmas Day, but it was now the twenty-third of December, and the week that followed the tragic events at the Nassau County Medical Center could only be described as silent.

Like he had done the two weeks between the deaths of Evangeline Carpenter and the two attacks on Julianne Frankles, the Long Island Surgeon had gone underground; becoming completely ghost-like to the public, and the three detectives who were in pursuit of him.

It was not only the Surgeon who had become muted after such a loud explosion. The public had also become silent following the Nassau County Medical Center Massacre. There was a hush over Long Island after six people had been killed, and the perpetrator had escaped completely undetected. It was fear that silenced the mouths that once so angrily demanded justice. Fear that they may be the next victims of Long Island's most infamous serial killer.

Other than providing the detectives with the Surgeon's path through the hospital as he one-by-one ended six people's lives, the video surveillance footage did not give them much. However, their focus was concentrated on the Nassau County Medical Center; namely, its staff.

They had finally found the link between the Surgeon's victims that they had been looking for. Each victim, excluding the ones who stood between him and Julianne Frankles, had all at one time in the past year been checked into the Nassau County Medical Center. Estelle Ramsey— with her husband by her side—for an episode with her heart, Evangeline Carpenter started experiencing Braxton Hicks contractions one week before her murder, and Julianne Frankles had made a visit to the Emergency Room to get stitches during the summer, when a softball smashed her above her left eye.

This new vital information, combined with the use of Pancuronium Bromide in the murders—a paralytic drug that could have only come from a hospital—led the detectives to strongly believe that the Long Island Surgeon had to be someone who worked for the Medical Center. No one else could have access to the victims' file, nor get their hands on the paralytic drug.

Throughout the week, as the Medical Center tried to get back on its feet, and fight off the constant press, Patrick, Hawkins, and Murphy had questioned the entire hospital staff; ranging from Dean of Medicine all the way down to the custodial staff. They even had to question their good friend, Doctor Margareta Wilkensis.

Countless hours of interrogation throughout the long days and exhausting nights, and they came back with absolutely nothing. They had considered a few people briefly, but dismissed them almost immediately. There was not a single employee of the Nassau County Medical Center who they believed could be their man.

Still, it had to be someone in that hospital. There was no doubt about that. No matter how hard they got pushed away from the idea, they kept coming back to it.

On top of their lack of finding a suspect, there was the issue with the hospitals inventory of Pancuronium Bromide, and that was there was absolutely no issue at all. The Nassau County Medical Center had been one of the first hospitals to respond to the court ordered subpoena, and just like all the other hospitals that had responded, they had reported no missing units of the paralytic drug from their inventory records. Still, the records were all looked over again—and then again—and each time, they came back with the exact same result; no Pancuronium Bromide had been removed from the hospital. Thus, pushing the detective further away from their theory that the Surgeon was somehow linked to the hospital.

"It's doesn't mean that it wasn't stolen from the Medical Center," Hawkins told Patrick and Murphy during one of their long, endless nights during that week. "This guy's smart—smarter than anyone I've ever come against—and I wouldn't be surprised if he changed the inventory logs so it would show up that nothing was missing from the hospital, in case anyone went looking."

It was a possibility to take into consideration. After all, he had the know-how to delete every vital piece of security footage from that night. Still, it was a stretch, but stretching was all they could do at this point to hold onto their one feasible lead in the entire month they had been chasing the Long Island Surgeon.

Not to anyone's surprise, based on previous results of his first two crime scenes, the forensics team picked up nothing at Julianne Frankles' apartment, or the hospital. Both scenes should've been sloppy, and potential evidence should have been overlooked and left behind, but instead both were squeaky clean.

Their progress, and endless hours of hard work seemed to be coming full circle… Right back to square one.

To make matters worse for the Homicide Unit, halfway through the week, Detective Murphy was pulled from the case to help Missing Children's. In a matter of days, four children had gone missing in Nassau County—one from the mall, one from the supermarket, and two right from their own homes! This caused a brief stint of hysteria amongst the general public, who believed that the missing children and the Long Island Surgeon were indefinitely linked. This theory would be squashed quickly by the Nassau County Police Department. Missing children did not fit any pattern of the Surgeon, and it was highly improbable (if not impossible) that a link existed between the two. Only now, not only was the police department chasing a crazed serial killer; they were now chasing a serial kidnapper, as well. It wasn't exactly what they needed on their already overcrowded plate.

Although promised that he would be returned immediately if there was a break in the Surgeon case, losing Murphy served as a severe disadvantage. Not only because they were down a detective—a damn good detective—but Patrick and Hawkins still had to deal with the constant elephant in the room; the fact that they loathed each other. Without Carl there to keep the peace, and put them in their places when he had to, it was inevitable that one of them was going to snap on the other.

Things between them had cooled down after the altercation outside Julianne Frankles' hospital room. They had remained civil towards one another as they worked to question the gargantuan staff of the Nassau County Medical Center, but the tension was still thick in the air, and it wasn't going anywhere.

As the two were forced to interact more directly with each other, Patrick noticed a sudden shift in Hawkins' behavior. He barely seemed like the same man Patrick had come to know, and detest over the past month. Something had changed. He constantly seemed distracted; trapped within his own thoughts, and his wiseass remarks and insults were almost nonexistent. It seemed as if the fire that once burned so wildly inside him—the same fire he once said he saw blazing inside Patrick—was beginning to burn out.

Patrick could only speculate to why the sudden change in his partner. He would never ask Hawkins, nor would he expect to get an honest answer, but if he had to venture a guess, his go-to theory would be that the realization that this case may go unsolved as he was heading into retirement, was eating away at Hawkins like a corrosive acid.

Maybe, however, the deaths of six people, namely Julianne Frankles, was beginning to weigh down on Detective Jonathan Hawkins. Patrick knew a thing or two about the crushing weight of the dead, and he wouldn't be surprised if guilt was beginning to plague the conscious of Hawkins.

After all, he was the one who said he'd stay at the hospital, and look after the girl. It was he who took responsibility for her safety and wellbeing, and she ended up dead; her torso shredded, and her face and fingers mutilated. Now, it was he who got to carry the burden of her death, and all those who died, because they merely stood in the path of a crazed psychopath.

If there was any proof to support Patrick's latter theory, it was during their meeting with Doctor Wilkensis, as they sat in her tiny office, which somehow seemed more claustrophobic than usual. There had been no pain killers in Julianne Frankles' system to help ease her suffering as she passed from one plane of existence into the next, the coroner told the two detectives. The Surgeon stabbed excessively in the chest, stomach and face with a surgical scalpel, and then sawed off her fingers tips and ripped the jaw from her face; using the scalpel to cut away muscle and nerve.

Hawkins winced at each and every gruesome detail as they flowed from the mouth of Doctor Wilkensis, and filled the room like thick cigar smoke. The doctor's words were like tiny knives, and every time she spoke them, they stabbed Jonathan Hawkins right in his chest. If there was any guilt for leaving the girl's side to change clothes and grab a cup of coffee, it was while they sat in that office.

Would it have even mattered? Patrick wondered.

Would it have made a difference in Julianne Frankles' fate had Hawkins been there when the Long Island Surgeon made his move? Patrick guessed not. Hawkins was good; there was no denying that, but Patrick believed the Surgeon was better. He had proved that time and time again throughout the entire month they had been hunting him.

Could Hawkins have saved the girl from death, or would there just have been one more victim added to the increasing body count?

Patrick was sure that if it was, in fact, guilt that caused Hawkins' sudden change, those same thoughts were plaguing his mind as well.

Patrick had awoken on the morning of December twenty-third at six in the morning. There were only a mere forty-eight hours until everything, including life as he knew it, came to an explosive ending, but right now, he was coming up from slumber to something extremely pleasant... Claire straddling him; naked, and kissing his chest.

The feel of her smooth lips on his firm pec sent a sensation of euphoria coursing through his body, right to his penis; making him hard. Unable to contain his desire, he sat up, and pulled his wife closer; letting her feel exactly how good she was making him feel. Claire, at the feel of her husband rubbing against her, let out a soft, pleasurable moan. They kissed furiously, and Patrick ran his hand up her back and neck; into her thick brown hair, where he squeezed, and gave a light tug. This caused Claire to bite down on his bottom lip.

Unable to contain themselves any longer, the two worked together to remove Patrick's boxers-briefs. When they were off, and kicked onto the floor, Patrick slid into his wife. Neither of them needed much time after that.

After they had made love, and both had come, Patrick laid in bed; completely relaxed. The Long Island Surgeon was the furthest thing from his mind. He was letting these few moments of soaking up Claire's beauty last as long as possible before he had to get up and face reality.

When he arrived at the station a few minutes later than usual, he still must have been glowing from his wake up call, because Hawkins had cracked his first wiseass remark in days.

"Damn… Obviously, someone had a good morning," he said as Patrick sat down at Murphy's desk. "Claire's been helping you deal with the stresses of work, I see."

Patrick's response was merely a smirk, but it did all the talking.

"Good for you, kid," Hawkins said with a wink.

A half hour later, Patrick's cell phone began to ring. It was Claire calling. Just the sight of her name and picture displayed on his phone brought a smile to his face. With everything that had been going on, he barely had time to reflect on how much he adored that amazing woman, and couldn't survive without her.

The moment Patrick hit *accept* on his phone, and heard Claire on the other line, every joyous emotion he had felt that morning—in his entire life—melted away.

THE REPLACEMENT

He didn't even get through saying hello before he heard Claire on the other end; crying. Only crying wasn't what he would call what he was hearing from his wife. It was full blown hysterics.

Claire wasn't sad. She was terrified.

"Claire, what is it? What's wrong?"

His first thought was Connor. Something bad had happened to Connor. He was beginning to freak out before he even knew what was going on. He tried to gain composure, but as Claire continued to cry into his ear instead of answering his questions, Patrick found himself losing control.

"Claire, what's going on?! You need to talk to me!"

The two words that came from her mouth were spoken in barely a whisper, but they were enough to make Patrick's whole body go numb.

"The kids…"

There were a few more seconds of crying on Claire's end before she spoke again, but Patrick knew what was going on. They had made a big mistake—the police department—and jumped the gun, and they were all fools for being so careless.

"They're here, Patrick…" Claire continued. "At the school… The missing children are here."

CHAPTER 25

"You need to drive faster!"

They raced down the streets; sirens and lights blaring; attempting to take the quickest and least congested route to the school where Claire taught Kindergarten. However, the combination of school traffic, and the work commute was slowing them down.

"Kid, if we crash and die, that's not going to make matters any better," Hawkins explained as he weaved in and out of the traffic; blowing through a red light.

Claire didn't say anything else after she had told Patrick the missing kids were at her job. She couldn't have even if she wanted to. She was completely overcome with hysterics. He just told her to stay at the school, and he would be there as soon as he can.

"The missing kids," he told Hawkins; springing out of his seat the second he hung up with Claire. "He killed the missing kids."

Hawkins, who had been on the edge of his seat during Patrick's entire thirty second phone conversation, jumped from his own seat, and followed Patrick out the door.

"I'll drive," Hawkins said as they ran to the car. "Call Carl. Tell him what's going on, and have him meet us at the school."

THE REPLACEMENT

They pulled into the school parking lot twenty minutes shy of the eighth hour of December twenty-third. Hawkins made no attempts at a parking spot. He pulled right onto the grass, and parked right in front of the kindergarten entrance to the school. He threw the gear shift into *park*, and cut the engine. Patrick had his door ajar even before the car had come to a complete stop. He was out the door; running to the school entrance, before they had even come to a full stop.

He entered the school, and immediately saw Claire at the end of the hallway; standing with two women. One was a fellow teacher, and the other was the principal. He could tell by their faces, that all three women had seen what was in store for Patrick, Hawkins and Murphy inside Claire's classroom

"Claire!" Patrick shouted; running down the hall to his wife. "Baby, I'm here."

The moment he was in arm's reach of his wife, she threw herself into his embrace, and began to sob uncontrollably. She attempted to speak, but was so far beyond articulation, she couldn't even get out the simplest of words.

"It's okay, baby," he told Claire as she wept. He lifted her face from his chest, and looked into those wet blue eyes. Her face was stained with dark streaks from the combination of makeup and overwhelming tears. "It's going to be okay."

And for the first time since Baby Tooth, Patrick had to lie to his wife.

It wasn't going to be okay, and he knew that better than anyone.

They are going to be with her forever, Patrick thought as he forced himself to tell Claire this ridiculous fable. *She is going to see them every night as she sleeps. Every night, when she closes her eyes, she is going to find herself back in her classroom; staring at those dead children. Only then*

223

they might not be dead. They may be asking her for help, or pleading with her to save them.

He pushed away a piece of hair from Claire's face, and kissed her salty lips. "It's going to be okay."

Hawkins came down the hall, and took a look at Claire. Patrick could see the disbelief in his face. The woman he was currently staring at was a shell of the woman who had invited him over for dinner only three weeks ago.

"Jesus," he said in barely a whisper. "I'm so sorry, Claire."

She attempted a smile of thanks, but it was just a lost cause.

Hawkins turned his attention to Regina Farney, the principal of the school.

"We're going to have to shut down school today."

"I already have the secretarial staff, along with some of the teachers contacting parents to tell them there had been an incident at the school, and it would be closed today," the principal responded.

"Don't have them divulge any details as to why school is canceled," Hawkins told Regina Farney, who seemed to be handling the pressures of discovering children who had been missing for almost a week dead in one of her classrooms. "We don't need this reaching the public's ears before it has to, which won't be very long, I'm guessing."

"Agreed; my staff have already been told not to mention any information to parents that might cause a panic."

"Good, you seem to have everything under control."

"I'm barely holding it together."

"You're doing just fine," Hawkins assured her. He turned back to Claire and Patrick. "Claire, the department psychologist is on his way. I want you to sit, and talk to him. You've been through a lot and he can help you."

Claire nodded, but Patrick wasn't even sure if anything Hawkins had just said even registered. She was just too in shock to comprehend and fully process anything at the moment.

"When the psychologist gets here, I really need you in there with me, kid."

"I need to stay with my wife."

Patrick understood Hawkins' need for every man on deck for this battle, but Patrick wasn't about to leave his wife alone. Not while she was in this porcelain state.

"No," Claire said in a low, raspy whisper. "You need to go."

"You need me, Claire."

"I need you to find the bastard who… who… did that…" She pointed to her classroom. She just couldn't bring herself to produce the actual words out loud. She couldn't tell her husband that he needed to help find the individual who was perverse enough to kill children.

"Okay," Patrick answered. "I'll be in there once the psychologist gets here."

Hawkins nodded, then walked in to Claire's classroom. It was once a place that had been a safe haven for children; a place to help further the youth of America, but now it was a crime scene.

Carl arrived on scene minutes later. He immediately asked Claire how she was holding up. Her response was the same as it had been for Hawkins. He then joined his partner in the classroom. The psychologist showed up shortly after the forensic team had arrived. He was compassionate with Claire; promising her she didn't have to talk about anything she didn't want to, and he was just there to listen. He slowly pulled Claire by the elbow from Patrick's arm; not forcing her from her husband, but leading her along. She followed with no resistance, but the moment their embrace had been broken, Patrick wanted to hug his wife once more just to shield her from the disgustingness of reality. He fought the urge, and watched as the department psychologist led his wife down the hall to the outside. He then joined Hawkins and Murphy.

As he walked to the classroom where there were now the bodies of four dead children, Patrick thought back to the moment he first laid eyes on the bodies of Arthur and Estelle Ramsey. Back then, he thought he had an idea of what he may see, having some exposure to murder in his years with the city, but when he saw the skinned bodies of the Ramsey's, he knew that he was wrong about that.

Now, Patrick, once again, found himself having an idea of what he would see inside that classroom. He had enough exposure to Surgeon murders that he was well familiarized with his style. The Long Island Surgeon knew one thing, and one thing only; brutality and blood. Patrick didn't want to think about what horrific things that monster could have done to those poor children.

When he entered the classroom and saw the scene, Patrick again realized he was completely unprepared for what he was looking at.

The scene wasn't bloody. It wasn't the massacre he had become accustomed to seeing at Surgeon murder scenes.

It, in many ways, was worse.

The children had been propped up at the desks with their arms folded across the tops. Their heads were placed down in their folded arms, and their eyes had been closed. It looked like they were simply taking an afternoon nap, or playing a game of Heads-Up-Seven-Up. The Long Island Surgeon hadn't bothered with his usual gore. There was no need to this time, because this had been sickening enough.

Up until then, each time Patrick laid eyes on a victim of the Long Island Surgeon, a fiery hatred consumed him. This time it wasn't loathing and the overwhelming need for revenge that flooded Patrick Sullivan's emotions.

It was sadness.

He felt the tightly wound ball of sorrow rising in his throat; choking him. He felt his eyes watering up with tears that he couldn't let spill.

They hadn't worked hard enough. No matter how many hours they put into the case, no matter how much time they spent dwelling and fixating on every detail put in front of them, it was just not enough. Now, the ultimate price had been paid, and four children, whose parents prayed to and pleaded with anyone who would listen that their kids might be returned to them unharmed, were dead.

Except there weren't four dead children in Claire Sullivan's classroom that morning.

There were five.

There had only been four children reported missing as of that morning, and they surely would've heard of a fifth. Still, there was a fifth child in that room with them.

Hawkins and Murphy stood over the fifth child's desk. The same sadness that swallowed Patrick, plagued their faces. There was also disbelief mixed in there as well. Was it the disbelief that this whole thing had gone so wrong, or was it something else all entirely?

When he heard the entrance door to the school crash open, and the frantic screams of a man coming down the hall, Patrick knew that it was indeed something else.

"Shit," Hawkins said to Carl. "We can't let him in here."

"Officer Henderson; you can't be here right now," an officer in the hallway called out, but it was useless. "Officer Henderson!"

Hawkins and Murphy both rushed to the classroom door; hoping to intercept Officer Henderson before he got to the classroom.

"My son; is he in there?!" Patrick heard the hysterical man ask, as he neared the room. "Is my son in there?! Is he d-d-dead?!"

"Mitch, I can't let you in there," Hawkins said.

"Is he in there, Ace?" Officer Mitchell Henderson asked; petrified his son was one of the children amongst the dead. "Is he dead, Carl? Please tell me he isn't in there; dead."

He's the fifth kid, Patrick thought; staring at the tiny face that had now turned white from death.

Patrick had met Officer Henderson the night at O'Reilly's Pub. There was without a doubt a father-son resemblance. It explained the disheartened looks on Hawkins and Murphy's faces as they stood over his body.

The Surgeon had killed a child of one of their own. He was making it personal.

Officer Henderson must have found his son missing that morning, and, before he even had a chance to report it, he found out about the dead children, somehow.

"Mitch, NO!" Murphy yelled from out in the hallway.

Patrick didn't think. He just reacted. He made his way across the room, and tackled Officer Henderson to the ground as he entered the room. It was too late, though. Mitch Henderson had seen his deceased son at the desk; looking like he was peacefully asleep.

"NOOOOO!!" Officer Henderson cried; trying to break free of Patrick. It felt like Patrick was wrestling a bear, and the bear was winning "Luke, NOOOOOO!! MY SON!!"

He almost broke free of Patrick's hold, but Hawkins and Murphy jumped on top of him in order to keep him down. Even with three men trying to restrain him, Officer Henderson almost broke free from them twice. This didn't surprise Patrick one bit. If it was Connor there—God forbid—there wasn't a force on Earth that could keep him down.

"LET ME SEE MY SON, YOU FUCKING PRICKS!!" Officer Henderson screamed. That was when the punches started flying.

THE REPLACEMENT

Most of the bombs missed their targets, but one particularly powerful one landed dead on Hawkins' jaw. He stumbled back holding the side of his face, and Officer Henderson saw this as an opportunity. He heaved his entire body forward with all the force he could muster, and managed to break free of Detective Murphy's grip. Patrick felt the grieving father's arm slipping from his grasp, and Hawkins must've seen it, too. He forgot about his throbbing jaw, and dove on top of Officer Henderson; pinning him to the ground as Patrick and Murphy regained their tight hold on him.

After his last failed attempt to get to his son, Officer Henderson stopped thrashing around. He stopped throwing punches at anything that got in his way. He just succumbed to his grief, and broke down crying.

The three detectives slowly relinquished their hold; cautiously. They would be ready to pounce if Mitch Henderson decided to make one more move towards his son, but that attempt never came. He just sat there bawling over the death of his only child.

"L-L-L-Luke..." he wailed in deep sorrow. "My baby boy is dead."

Carl put an arm around the grieving man; trying his best to comfort him. Patrick stood over the two, and Hawkins knelt beside his fellow officer; rubbing his jaw that had turned a deep red.

"That's a hell of a punch you pack, Mitch."

"I'm sorry about that," Mitch Henderson said. "I shouldn't have."

"You have nothing to apologize for," Hawkins assured him. He put his hand on the shoulder of Officer Henderson. "I'm so sorry, Mitch. Luke was such a good kid. I loved him. We all did; you know that."

"I just can't believe my baby boy is dead," Officer Henderson said. He was beginning to calm down physically, but Patrick had no doubt that inside, he was ripped to shreds by the razor sharp claws of despair. "This isn't fair."

"I know it's not, Mitch... I know it's not."

Mitchell Henderson lifted his head from his knees, and looked right at his son. Patrick, again, was ready to act if he made any movements towards the body. He noticed Hawkins and Murphy had readied themselves for the same thing. There was no move. Officer Henderson just stared in disbelief at his son, who no longer had that amazing childish life flowing through him.

"He looks like he's sleeping," he said; tears flooding his eyes once again, and streaming down his face. "What am I supposed to tell Erin? How am I supposed to tell my wife that our son is dead?"

Mitch Henderson lowered his head back between his knees, and began weeping again. The three detectives looked at one another as the man in the middle of them grieved deeply. They didn't know what to say. There were no words for what was happening. Finally, Patrick made the first attempt to speak up.

"We're going to get him," he told Officer Henderson. "We are going to catch him, and he is going to pay for what he's done... to your son, and everyone else who has crossed his path."

Officer Henderson, face red and streaked with tears, looked from Patrick, to Murphy, to Hawkins. The look in his eyes desperately pleaded one question: *Is that true? You're going to get the bastard who destroyed my family?*

"We won't stop, Mitch," Hawkins promised. "Not until we get him, and we put him in the ground."

Should Hawkins have promised they'd kill the Long Island Surgeon once they found him? Probably not, but it was what needed to be said. They were driven far beyond conventional justice, and Patrick was glad he was no longer the only one who felt that way. The Surgeon didn't deserve life, even if it was behind bars. He deserved one thing, and that was death. If Hawkins intentions were to make sure that happened, then Patrick applauded him.

Truth was, if Hawkins wasn't going to do it, Patrick knew he would.

"Mitch, you need to let us work, though," Murphy said; his arm still around the grieving father. "As much as you want to go hold your son, you can't. Not yet, at least."

"Let me just get close to him, please," Officer Henderson pleaded. "I won't touch him—I know I can't compromise the crime scene. I just want to be near him for a second."

They looked at one another; silently conferencing. They were considering the request, and if it was wise to allow it.

"We're coming with you, Mitch," Hawkins said. "But if you make any movement to grab him, we're going to have to take you down, and restrain you. I don't want to have to do that, friend."

"You won't," Officer Henderson promised.

The three detectives helped Mitch Henderson to his feet, and walked him slowly over to the desk where his son, Luke, who died at the age of only five years old, sat; propped up like a doll.

"Goodbye, baby boy," Officer Mitchell Henderson of the Nassau County Police Department managed to say through his heavy sobs. "Mommy and Daddy love you. We love you so much."

They escorted Officer Henderson from the classroom, and Hawkins told two fellow officers to take him outside to get some air. He then instructed them to immediately get the department psychologist, who seemingly had his plate full that morning; first with Claire, and now the grieving father of one of the victims. They watched; their faces expressionless—there was no expression that could register what any of them were feeling at that moment—as Officer Henderson was slowly escorted down the hall to the outside; crying for his loss.

When they reentered Claire's classroom, Patrick took a look around. Not at the dead children—he had seen enough of them for right now—but at the classroom, itself. It was such a beautiful place; decorated for the time of year. Stretched across the rear of the room was a huge bulletin board. Its border was holiday themed, and it was decorated with drawings made by Claire's kindergarten class. There were children's renditions of a winter wonderland filled with snowmen.

It's exactly what a classroom is supposed to look like, Patrick thought as he scanned the room. *Now it's tainted by death's ugliness.*

He turned around to face the front of the room, and the moment his eyes landed on the chalkboard, whatever happiness this room had left in it was now gone. He had been in the room for almost a total of ten minutes, but it had been so chaotic, he hadn't even noticed the message left for them on the chalk board.

The Long Island Surgeon had done something he had never done before up until then. He left them a message; written in big bold letters across the chalk board.

It read:

SHE DROVE ME TO DO THIS!
BLAME THE GIRL, NOT ME!
THEY ARE DEAD BECAUSE OF HER!

CHAPTER 26

That day had been brutal, and seemed not to ever want to end, and once December twenty-third had concluded, and the clock finally reached midnight; ushering in the twenty-fourth of December, the onslaught of brutality continued.

And things seemed as hopeless as they always had.

Patrick had stared at that chalk board intensely; taking in the message. He was desperately trying to get into the head of the Long Island Surgeon. He placed all the blame for the death of these five children on Julianne Frankles. That, of course, had been an outlandish claim, but that had been Patrick's rational thinking at work. The Surgeon was irrational, to say the least, and completely off-the-rocker psychotic at best. There was a reason for everything they were looking at that morning, and Patrick Sullivan knew exactly what it was.

The Surgeon's original plans for Julianne Frankles had completely blown up in his face when she returned early that night from the campus library, due to sickness. He was then forced to change them on the fly. Things then got even worse for him when the girl he had stabbed repeatedly, and left for dead survived the attack. Now he had to go, and make sure he finished the job before the girl could aid those pesky detectives in their investigation. Only this time, his attack had to be thought up, and executed on the fly. Every environment he had put himself into when it came to killing had been controlled. Making his way through the Nassau County Medical Center in order to end the girl's life was completely out of his control. He had little time to prepare, and even less time to act. No matter how good he was at becoming a phantom, the Long Island Surgeon was apt to make a mistake somewhere that night. The three detectives in charge of the investigation of his crimes would know this, and they would tear down the Medical Center until they found what they needed in order to find and apprehend him. He needed to do something to throw them off his scent.

Murdering five children, and making it as personal as he possibly could was the answer he found to his predicament.

Not only had the Surgeon killed five children, which was probably enough to throw any detective off their game, but he had killed the child of one of their own. On top of that, he personally targeted, and tried to get into the head of one of the investigating detectives.

That detective was Patrick Sullivan.

It wasn't just coincidence that five children showed up dead in Patrick's wife's classroom. No one had once suspected that. The Long Island Surgeon had chosen Claire's classroom to set up his little display, because he knew it would get into the head of Patrick, and he was successful at that.

Why me? He had asked himself earlier that morning, as he and Hawkins were driving to the school. His question was answered by the familiar deep voice of his friend, Baby Tooth.

Because, Patty Boy, this nigga is trying to get inside your head. He's trying to fuck with you, and it's working.

THE REPLACEMENT

Look at how pissed off you are. He made this shit mad personal, and got that pretty wife of yours involved. Not even I would stoop that low. I bet you are itching just to bury the butt of your gun in this sorry fucker's skull. Too bad you can't find him, and now you're never going to, because he's got you off your game already, and you haven't even seen the dead kids yet.

Patrick shared his theory with his partners, and they both agreed to what the Long Island Surgeon's intentions were.

"We can't let him get under our skin, kid," Hawkins said. "The minute he does is the minute he finally wins."

He won the moment he killed Arthur and Estelle Ramsey, Patrick thought, and almost said out loud.

What came next was the daunting inspection of the five bodies. The cause of death for each child was apparent; strangulation. There was dark purple bruising around each of their fragile necks.

They might be able to get an idea of what sort of object was used to choke the life out of these children by the marks left behind, but it would do them little good. The Surgeon was too smart to use something the police could narrow down, and if they could pinpoint the exact object used, it would certainly be something that was commonly used, and sold everywhere.

The mutilated bodies of the Ramsey's, Evangeline Carpenter, and Julianne Frankles had been difficult to look at, but this was nearly intolerable. Patrick stared at the children, who looked so at peace, one by one, and with each body he inspected the ball in his throat expanded, and choked him. He desperately wished for that familiar feeling of rage to resurface, and consume him. He much preferred it over the current urge to curl up in a ball, and weep for these children. The anger never came, though. It was there; lying dormant somewhere inside him, but the feeling of despair was too pungent that morning.

Or maybe his rage wasn't there, because it was too busy taking over Hawkins.

Patrick always thought he'd be the first to snap in this case; given his lack of experience in homicide, his immediate compassion for the dead, and, not to mention, his history of letting his emotions get the best of him. He knew that no matter how hard he tried to cap the volcano within, it would eventually erupt; spilling boiling enmity all over the world around him.

However, Patrick was not the first to lose his cool in this high pressure case.

It was Jonathan Hawkins.

He had been staring at one of the bruised necks when he heard Hawkins finally lose control. He looked up, and saw the man, who was usually calm and collected; no matter what situation they were in, flipping out on one of the forensics people. Apparently, a member of the forensics team wasn't working hard enough—at least not to Hawkins' standards—and that set him tumbling off the deep end.

"There are five dead children here!" Hawkins screamed in the young man's face. "One of them is the son of a fellow police officer. A man whose house I have been to. A child I've sat down with, talked to, and played with. He's dead—all these children are *dead*—and you're sitting around here with your fucking thumb stuck up your inexperienced ass!"

"I'm sorry," the young man said. He probably wanted to offer an explanation to why he looked as if he wasn't working, even though Patrick was sure that no one, besides Hawkins, actually believed the young man was slacking in his responsibilities. He never got the chance to offer such explanation. Hawkins shoved the young man, and he stumbled backwards; probably would've fallen flat on his ass if it had not been for the bookshelf that ran along the windowsill to break his fall.

"Don't apologize," Hawkins screamed. "WORK! Give me something… Anything! All of you; give me something to work with, because after a month, and fourteen people dead, you have given me absolutely jack shit to go on! I'm beginning to think that each and every one of you are completely inadequate at your jobs!"

Murphy then stepped in; pulling Hawkins from the classroom, but not before he could get off one last insult to the forensics team on their lack to produce. Patrick apologized to the young man Hawkins had initially blown his gasket on, and assured him, along with the rest of his team, that the Homicide Unit knew they were doing all they could, and appreciated their work.

Hawkins was taken outside by Murphy to cool down. Patrick didn't know what words were exchanged between the two, but when he joined them, Hawkins was, for the most part, back to his normal, composed self.

Still, Patrick could not believe what he had just seen. Hawkins, of all people, had lost it. He had always been the man to look up to, because he was a master of his craft. He knew precisely how to conduct himself during a murder investigation, no matter how much pressure was put on him.

Well, every man has their breaking point, and the events of that morning were Jonathan Hawkins'. The realization that no matter how great he was, the Surgeon might just be that much better had been enough to drive him over the edge.

When Patrick joined them, Hawkins apologized for his behavior inside. Patrick assured him that no apology was necessary; at least not to him. Hawkins owed the entire forensics team inside that classroom an ample apology, which he planned on delivering. That would have to wait, though. They had to move on with their morning

The next order of business in their investigation was getting a statement from Claire Sullivan.

At first, both, Hawkins and Murphy suggested one of them talk to Claire, because she was Patrick's wife, and they were worried he might not push her if need be, but Patrick was adamant about being the one to do it. On that point, he remained stern. There was little argument from his partners once they realized this wasn't a negotiation. Hawkins and Murphy went to check up on a grieving Officer Henderson while Patrick took on the responsibility of forcing his wife to relive what would likely remain the most haunting morning of her life.

Claire sat on a bench overlooking the school's playground. She did not take notice of her husband's presence, and if she did, she chose to ignore it. She just stared at the playground that would, on any other weekday, be swarming with young children, who were trying to get a few minutes of playtime in with their friends and fellow classmates before heading in for the school day.

Today, there were no kids crawling all over this playground. Today, it was barren, because school was closed.

Patrick wondered what was going through his wife's head right then. Was she thinking about those five dead children, and how they would never climb the monkey bars again, slide down the slide, or even swing on the swings? Perhaps, she was. He knew for sure that he was, and again, that ball of sorrow that should've been infinite rage choked him.

He cleared his throat, and swallowed, so not to choke to death on his sadness. As he did this, Claire became aware of, or decided to finally acknowledge, his presence. The usual color had returned to her face, and she no longer looked like a woman trapped in the tangles of overwhelming fear. She, once again, looked like the woman Patrick Sullivan had known and loved for the past six years.

Right then, he realized that Claire was going to be alright.

Yes, Claire would always remember the day she found five children dead in her classroom, but she wouldn't let it destroy who she was. She had too much to live for to let that happen. She was the strong one in the marriage, Patrick would never deny that. She stood at a crossroads, and Claire Sullivan chose to continue living her life, rather than letting it be consumed by the hauntings of the dead.

Something her husband found extremely difficult to do.

"I just have to ask you a few questions," he said; taking a seat next to Claire on the small park bench.

"I know."

Claire relived the events of her morning that led up to her phone call to her husband.

She came in a bit earlier than usual to set up for her class's holiday party. When she entered the classroom, the lights were all off, and the shades had been drawn. Something did not sit well from the moment she had stepped into the room. She wasn't exactly sure what she was looking at when she flipped on the lights, and saw the bodies of five children, who all looked like they were asleep; enjoying delightful dream. For a moment, her brain had failed to register the reality before her. Patrick knew that feeling. He had felt it every time he laid his eyes on a victim of the Long Island Surgeon.

It was only a second before Claire became aware of the horror she had just walked in on. She tried to scream, but shock had frozen her lungs. Her legs went numb, and she fell against and slid down the wall. When she found the ability to articulate once again, she reached into her bag, and called Patrick.

When their phone call had ended, Claire finally allowed herself to break down, and that was when she started screaming. This brought two other teachers, who had also come in early to set up for their day. They saw the inconceivable scene upon entering, and immediately lifted Claire up, and quickly removed her from the classroom.

"Thank you," Patrick said, once Claire had concluded. "That's all I'm going to need."

Despite everything, a smile stretched across her face, and she let out a lighthearted laugh.

"What's so funny?"

"That was very cop-like of you, Patrick," Claire told her husband. "I've never really seen you in your element."

This was because Patrick chose to keep his work life and his home life separate. There was no need to bring home the things he saw. Of course, that barrier was breached when he met Wallace 'Baby Tooth' Freewaters. Now, that he was back in law enforcement, and investigating some of the most demented and violent crimes humanly imaginable, his desire to leave the cop at the precinct, and let the doting husband and caring father come home to his family was stronger than ever.

"What do you think now that you've seen it?" Patrick asked.

"I like the whole serious detective thing you have going on. It's cute."

Patrick found himself admiring Claire's amazing ability to bounce back from witnessing something as horrendous as she did.

"Wait here a second," he said. "I'll be right back."

He walked over to the ambulance, where Hawkins and Murphy were standing with an inconsolable Officer Henderson.

THE REPLACEMENT

"I'd like to take Claire home, and spend a few hours with her to make sure she is okay," Patrick told his partners, as he had pulled them aside.

He expected resistance to his request; mainly from Hawkins. They needed to, more than ever, steer the course, and losing Patrick, even for a few hours, would be hurtful towards their investigation. Still, he would need to try.

To his surprise, there was no resistance from Jonathan Hawkins. He agreed to the request with zero argument or objection.

"Spend some time with your family, kid. Carl and I will handle informing the parents of the victims, but we need you back as soon as you feel comfortable leaving Claire alone. We can't waste time on this. Who knows what he's going to do next."

"I just need a few hours," Patrick assured Hawkins.

The resistance he had been anticipating came to him in the form of Claire. She let him know that he didn't need to see her home, and what he needed to do was devote all his time to the case. Regardless of her objections, he insisted, and Claire gave in to her husband's stubbornness.

On their way home, they picked up Connor from his daycare, so they could all share an afternoon together; as a family. When they arrived home, Patrick unloaded the barbeque, which he thought he should have never bothered packing away in the first place, because of the warm weather, from the shed. On it, he grilled Claire and himself some hamburgers, and Connor a hotdog.

While they ate their lunch, Connor rambled on about the kind of subject matters that could only go on within the innocent mind of a two year old child. Claire and Patrick laughed together at their son's cuteness, and flirted with one another from across the table. They were a married couple, who were very much in love with one another and their son. It was almost as if the events of the morning had never happened.

Still, they lingered in the back of Patrick's mind, like a nagging headache. Soon, he would have to leave his home and family behind, and face reality once again. Until then, he would not let anything ruin the little time he had with his wife and son.

After lunch was gobbled up, Patrick cleared the table, and took care of cleaning the dishes while Claire played with Connor, and relaxed in the yard. Once everything in the kitchen was up to the usual standards of cleanliness, he joined his family in the yard.

He spent the next hour he had given himself before returning to work playing with his son. He would squat down in the grass, like a catcher in baseball, as Connor ran ecstatically across the grass into his arms. Patrick would take hold of his son, and then jump up from his squat; extending his arms, and lifting Connor high above his head as his only child burst into a fit of extreme hilarity. When he brought Connor back to ground level, he showered his tiny face with kisses, while Connor demanded they do it again, and Patrick was happy to oblige to this request.

They played for the remainder of the time Patrick had with them—father and son—while Claire sat on a lawn chair; watching and laughing right along with the two of them. It was the embodiment of perfection. No man could ask for anything more out of life. In that moment he wasn't Patrick Sullivan, detective of homicide; a man haunted by faces of the dead, a sadistic serial killer, and the demons of his past. He was Patrick Sullivan; husband and father, and a man who was so in love with life.

Playing with Connor in the grass, as Claire looked on, would be the image Patrick Sullivan desperately fought to hold onto for the remainder of his days. It would be the last moment in his life where he truly felt happy.

THE REPLACEMENT

When the time that he held so dearly with his family had finally expired—he gave himself an extra twenty minutes than he had originally planned—Claire drove him back to the 8th Precinct, while Connor; exhausted from his afternoon of playtime with his daddy, slept in his car seat.

As they drove through the maze that was the streets of Levittown, Patrick stared out his window at the houses decked out in Christmas lights. They would soon be beautifully lit up once the sun set.

Everything looks so perfect, Patrick thought as the car passed from one house to the next.

That was the moment the walls he had temporarily put up to keep out reality for just a few hours came crashing down. Nothing at all was perfect. Somewhere in this neighborhood, or the surrounding ones, parents were learning that their children, who had so little chance to experience life, were dead. They were murdered by the very man the Nassau County Police Department swore had zero involvement with their abduction. There would be no Christmas for these families. Not this year, and not ever again. The holiday that brought families and friends together would forever be tarnished for the families of five dead children. All it would be now is a reminder of the child they would never get to see grow up.

In that moment of horrific realization, Patrick found himself selfishly thankful for all he had. He placed his hand on Claire's thigh as she drove. She freed one of her hands from the wheel, and took his hand in hers, and squeezed affectionately.

"I need you to pack a bag, and head to your parents for a little bit," he told Claire. "Just to be safe."

"Do you think he's going to come after us?"

"No, I don't. I still want you to go, though"

Patrick truly believed the Long Island Surgeon would not target Claire. He was merely using her as a scare tactic.

Still, he wouldn't take the chance. He needed his family safe, in case he was wrong.

After Claire agreed to her husband's request, they spent the remaining few minutes of the car ride in silence; hand-in-hand. It wasn't an awkward silence, but one of appreciation they shared for each other. Patrick and Claire Sullivan didn't need words to express how much they were grateful for the other. Sometimes words just dilute what we are feeling, because no combination of them can truly explain what we want to express in that moment.

"Patrick," Claire said, as he was unbuckling his seatbelt once they pulled up to the precinct. "Can you promise me two things?"

"What?"

"That you'll be careful, and that you'll catch that bastard."

Claire looked at Connor; sleeping in the backseat. Patrick knew exactly what his wife was thinking as she stared at their son.

It could have been him.

Claire wanted The Long Island Surgeon to get what he deserved, but not for what he had put her through. She wanted revenge for those people who were now childless.

"I promise," he told her; leaning over the center console to give her a kiss. "On both counts."

He stole a quick glance at Connor, who had his thumb in his mouth, and got out of the car.

The media was setting up outside the 8th precinct when Patrick walked through the front door, which could only mean one thing; word of the morning's atrocities had gotten out. This meant it would be all over the news within hours, if it hadn't already been. Soon Long Island, and the rest of the nation, would learn that The Long Island Surgeon had killed again, and this time it was children who had paid the ultimate price for the Nassau County Police Department's inability to bring him to justice.

As he entered the police station; ignoring the reporter's pleas for a statement, Patrick prayed that Hawkins and Murphy had been able to speak to all the families of the deceased children before they could learn of their child's demise from the news or internet.

His two partners were sitting at their desks when he arrived. They had gotten back from their daunting task only minutes before Patrick, himself, had arrived. The two of them, along with the Homicide Unit's captain, and the District Attorney, who had publically vowed to make the Surgeon case her office's number one priority since the incident at the Medical Center, made their visits to each of the parents of the dead children.

Patrick's prayers had been answered, and his colleagues had been able to get to each family before the tragic news had been broken to the public.

"A janitor at the school went to the media," Hawkins said without even having to be asked. "It was bound to happen. There was no way we were going to be able to keep a lid on this for that long."

"So what's next?" Patrick asked. "What now?"

"We wait," Hawkins answered.

And wait, they did.

They waited for the forensics team or Doctor Wilkensis to bring them something; anything. The minutes dragged on; turning hours into eternities, and all they could do was wait for any news that would aid them in their investigation.

They spent the early afternoon trying to pass the time by exchanging ideas and theories, but not much came of it. They already knew why he had targeted those children, and killed them. They were getting close to finding his one mistake, and he wanted to throw them off their game by making it personal.

The one question that was raised that left them answerless was how the Surgeon was able to abduct *five* children so easily. Parents these days educated their children more and more about not talking to strangers, or getting in cars with people they didn't know. So how was he able to snatch up five children with such little effort?

At three o'clock the District Attorney and the Homicide Captain held a press conference outside the station. They spoke of the tragic events of the morning, and promised the public that they were doing everything they could, and exhausting all resources and manpower in the pursuit of The Long Island Surgeon.

"We will not let these injustices carry on any longer," the District Attorney told the media. "Too many have died on our watch, and Captain Stints and I promise that the Nassau County Police Department, along with my office, will put an end to this horror."

Her promises fell on deaf ears, however. The public was no longer silenced by fear. Now, they were fueled by rage; demanding that this be quelled immediately, because it had gone on way too long. There were no more promises to be made that everything was being done that could be done that would calm Long Island residents. Too much blood had been spilled, and it was time for all this to end.

At five fifteen, right after the story had broken nationally; Patrick received a phone call that he really wished he had chosen to ignore.

"Detective Sullivan," he said when he picked up the phone.

"HA!" a voice boomed from the other end. "Detective, huh? Is that what you call yourself? How are you supposed to serve and protect the public when you can't even protect my God damn daughter from the shit you get yourself involved with?!"

Patrick was used to such tirades from his miserable father-in-law. He had been dealing with them since the first day Claire had brought him home to meet her parents. However, today was not the day to fuck with Patrick. He needed to end this conversation as quickly as possible before he ended up saying something he couldn't take back.

"Listen, Ted; I really can't…" But that was as much as he was able to get out.

"No, you listen to me, you little shit. It's bad enough that my daughter never wised up, and ditched your pathetic ass. Now, you are putting her in harm's way. I always knew that you were a useless human being, so it's no surprise to me that you are completely incompetent as a husband. I don't know how you ever became a cop; let alone a homicide detective."

And then Patrick snapped.

"You know what, Ted… FUCK YOU! You have no idea what the fuck you are talking about. You sit there in your office with the amazing city view, and act like you know it all. Truth is, you know absolutely shit. You don't know me, you don't know your daughter, and you certainly don't know how the world works. I'm a better husband than you ever were, or will be. I actually love my wife, and she loves me right back. So, think what you want, and feel free to say whatever comes to mind, but do me a favor, and tell it to someone who actually gives a fuck, because I don't! I'm too busy trying to catch a serial killer, and save lives. You know, something you would never bother doing, because you care for no one but yourself." Patrick paused momentarily; thinking if he had left anything out of his speech. When he finally remembered, he shouted into the phone: "ASSHOLE!!"

He heard Ted Johnston yelling something on the other end of the phone, but he didn't care. He simply hung up on his father-in-law. When he looked up, Hawkins had a huge amused grin stretched across his face.

"Good for you, kid," he said. "You show that prick who's got the biggest balls of them all."

As Hawkins got up and walked away, a smile of his own stretched across Patrick's face. That had felt great

His momentary high dissipated as the hours slowly crept on. There was no news from the forensics team, nor was there any from Doctor Wilkensis, and there were no more theories to be passed around. All that remained was silence, and the dreadful wait.

As the clock turned to midnight, and the morning of Christmas Eve was upon them, Patrick Sullivan believed that failure was eminent.

All that changed with a single phone call at one-thirty that morning.

"Hawkins," Hawkins said as he answered the phone. "Margareta, wait one second. I'm going to put you on speaker phone."

He put the coroner on speaker phone, and told her she was on the line with Murphy and Patrick as well.

"Semen!" Doctor Wilkensis voice said; coming from the speaker. "I found semen on two of the children."

And there it was.

The Long Island Surgeon had made his mistake. He left his DNA at the scene of the crime.

"Did you run it through the department database?" Hawkins asked.

He could barely contain himself at this moment. None of them could. It was all going to come to an end. The nightmare was on the cusp of finally being over.

"I did," Doctor Wilkensis said. "I faxed it over to you right before I called.

THE REPLACEMENT

Hawkins took off like a bat out of hell to the fax machine. He grabbed the paper from it that the coroner had sent over. When he turned back towards his partners, the look of excitement mixed with anticipation had been drained from his face. All that remained there was shock and horror.

"What is it, Ace?" Murphy asked.

Hawkins said nothing as he walked back over to the desk. He just handed the paper to Carl to look for himself.

"Oh my God," Murphy said; his voice was filled with the same shock and disbelief as his longtime partner. "Are you a hundred percent sure of this, Margareta?"

"I am," answered the coroner.

Murphy stared at Hawkins, and Hawkins stared right back. Again, sometimes there just aren't words for certain moments. This, clearly, was one of them. Carl Murphy slowly raised his arm, and handed the paper to Patrick; not taking his eyes off of Hawkins.

Patrick took the single piece of paper that had these two seasoned veterans in a state of disbelief, and read the real life name of the Long Island Surgeon.

CHAPTER 27

When Patrick Sullivan stepped outside of the 8th precinct at ten-to-seven on the morning of Christmas Eve, the air was still and frigid. The sharp, cold winds stung his skin as they sliced viciously at his face, and, for the first time since March of that year, he saw his breath on the air whenever he exhaled. It seemed as if, in a blink of an eye, winter had finally come, and on this cold morning, Mother Nature was making up for lost time. The sky was blanketed by a depressing shade of grey clouds, and it looked as if Long Islanders would be having a white Christmas that year; at least the families who were still able to enjoy the holiday.

The sudden and drastic climate change felt eerily fitting for this particular morning and the man they were only an hour away from apprehending.

Gary Kaste.

That was the name Patrick read on the piece of paper he had taken from a stunned Carl Murphy. He was known to the public as the Long Island Surgeon, but the name he had been given at birth was Gary Kaste.

So you're an actual human being, after all, Patrick thought as he read the name repeatedly.

A human being; one who had been birthed and raised by other humans, was actually capable of committing the unimaginable crimes Patrick had seen over the course of the last month.

That human being's name was Gary Kaste.

Hawkins pulled the file on the Gary Kaste case for Patrick to familiarize himself with.

Twelve years prior to the emergence of the man who would inevitably have New York Times bestselling novels written about him, Gary Kaste was a pedophile; arrested and convicted for luring two young boys into the woods near their Long Island home, molesting them there, then assaulting when they tried to escape.

The investigating and arresting officer on the case was Jonathan Hawkins.

After being evaluated by a criminal psychologist, and deemed no longer a threat to society (*boy, were they wrong about that*, Patrick thought as he read), Gary Kaste was granted early parole ten years into his twenty five year sentence. Months later, after receiving numerous threats from the people within the community, the parole board granted him a relocation request. He now lived in a small trailer park outside of Westchester; away from most civilization.

As Patrick familiarized himself with the man behind the Long Island Surgeon mask, Hawkins and Murphy made phone calls to the Westchester and state police; coordinating with them. The three detectives would drive up, and with local and state law enforcement to aid them, they would move in on Kaste's trailer, and arrest him. Thus, bringing to an end, his long crimson reign of terror.

Patrick stood outside the police station; waiting for his two partners to square off all last minute plans for their operation. An icy chill, that may have been from the cold wind, or may have been from something else entirely, shot up his spine, and radiated throughout his entire body; covering him from head to toe with goose bumps. They had decided it would be best to wait until day break before attempting any kind of move. The area in which Gary Kaste lived was surrounded by rich, endless woods. If he managed to escape before they could arrest him, he would become a phantom in the thick woods of Upstate New York.

When Hawkins and Murphy joined Patrick outside, their moods were somber. They finally had the identity of the man who had brilliantly eluded them for so long, and that was reason enough to have a surge of excitement rush over you, but there would be no excitement; not yet, at least.

Gary Kaste was smart, cunning, all-encompassing, and, most importantly, infinitely dangerous. Despite the perfection of his crimes leading in to the Medical Center disaster, he must have been aware of the possibility he might be caught, and, surely, he had a thoroughly thought out escape plan in place.

There was more to the gloominess in Hawkins' mood, though. This likely had to do with their visit from Doctor Jennifer Hadley; Gary Kaste's psychologist.

Jennifer Hadley arrived at the police station at four-thirty that morning. All the phone calls had been made, and the plans were already in place. They were going to use the remainder of that morning until they left for Westchester to calm their nerves, and prepare themselves for what might be the most important morning of their professional lives. However, the unexpected arrival of the doctor squashed any hopes of calm few hours; especially for Hawkins.

"Detective Hawkins, Detective Murphy, Detective Sullivan; there is a Doctor Hadley here to see you," one of the officers had told them. "She says it's urgent she speaks to you."

THE REPLACEMENT

There was a mutual look of confusion between the three detectives. There could only be one reason why this stranger was at the police station at four-thirty in the morning on Christmas Eve. That reason had to be Gary Kaste.

"Send her in," Hawkins told the officer, then turned back towards his colleagues. "This should be interesting."

When Jennifer Hadley entered the room, all eyes were on her. Her hair was a mess of a bun, and she was dressed as professional as one could when they're rushing around in the dark, half asleep in the middle of the night.

"Detectives," the doctor said; greeting the three in a voice still groggy from sleep. "My name is Doctor Jennifer Hadley. I'm Gary Kaste's psychologist."

The three stood, and greeted the doctor with a handshake.

"You have the wrong man," Jennifer Hadley bluntly told the three detectives after pleasantries were exchanged, and they were seated again. She now had their undivided attention.

"Excuse me?" Hawkins said; as if he had misheard what the young doctor had said.

"Gary Kaste is not the Long Island Surgeon. You are about to arrest the wrong man."

"With all due respect, doctor," Hawkins responded, as if she had no right questioning the Nassau County Police Department Homicide Unit. "We have two of *five* dead children with his DNA on them that says otherwise."

"Well it's not true." Jennifer Hadley's confident tone did not waver, despite Hawkins' assurance that they had their man.

"Well DNA hardly lies—and by hardly, I mean *never*. So I'm sorry to disappoint, but Gary Kaste viciously killed fourteen people in cold blood; fifteen, if you want to count

Evangeline Carpenter's unborn child that he ripped out of her."

"It's impossible," the doctor of criminal psychology said.

"It's impossible that a sicko committed sick crimes?" Hawkins asked. There was a faint hint of humor in his voice that made Patrick want to slap him. "Not to sound rude, doctor, but that seems entirely feasible. Also, if you don't mind me asking... How exactly did you learn that we were planning on arresting Gary Kaste in connection with the Long Island Surgeon murders?"

Gary Kaste's parole office, the doctor explained, had contacted Jennifer Hadley after he had received a courtesy call from Hawkins, who had no problem informing the parole officer that the man he was supposed to be watching over, and making sure remained a law abiding citizen was actually out on a murdering spree throughout the end of November all the way through December.

"He was just as surprised by this news as I was," Jennifer Hadley told the detectives. "And thought I should know. He knew I'd come down here, and try to convince you that you had the wrong man; which you do."

"Well remind me to thank him for that," Hawkins said in a partially sarcastic, mostly annoyed tone.

"Doctor Hadley," Murphy said; willing to do what Hawkins clearly was not, and hear her pleas. "Why do you think Gary Kaste is innocent of the Long Island Surgeon crimes?"

"Because you guys don't know Gary Kaste,"

"I know him," Hawkins interrupted. "I got to know him pretty well when I arrested him for molesting two children, and then beating them pretty badly."

"Crimes in which he knows were wrong, and has had sincere regret over committing."

"Or so he'd like you to believe."

THE REPLACEMENT

Patrick was beginning to become annoyed by Hawkins' attitude towards the young doctor. Yes, he understood the desire to close the Long Island Surgeon case, but he also respected Jennifer Hadley's right to defend a man she felt was being wrongly accused for a very serious crime.

"With all due respect, Detective Hawkins," the doctor shot back to Hawkins' rude response. "It is my job to wean out the ones who are sincerely remorseful for what they did from the ones who are feeding me bullshit. Gary Kaste was remorseful then, and he still, to this day, regrets what he did to those children."

"With all due respect, doctor," Hawkins said; leaning forward in his chair. The sarcasm and annoyance was temporarily washed away from his voice, but Patrick knew that it'd soon be back. Right now, Jonathan Hawkins was going to try that classic charm to try to get this woman off his case, and let him do the job that he does so well. "If you were to tell me that Gary Kaste committed these crimes, and I didn't have the evidence that I did against him, I wouldn't believe it either. Yeah, I think he's a sick bastard for what he did to those kids, but I never in a million years would have guessed he was capable of the murders that I've seen over the past month. Hell, I'd like to think that no human being was capable of that, but I'm telling you, Gary Kaste would be the last person on my list of suspects. *However*, we have his DNA on two of the victims—victims who are young boys, by the way—so he's our man; no matter how much breath you want to waste saying he isn't."

Just like that, Hawkins had won the argument, like he always did. This woman, despite her initial objections, understood Hawkins completely. She knew that Gary Kaste was the Long Island Surgeon, and she would now back off to let the police do their job.

Except, that was not how it unfolded. Jennifer Hadley was not convinced.

"If I may make a point, please," the doctor said once Hawkins had concluded his speech.

"Go ahead," Patrick said before Hawkins could object.

"Your killer—this Surgeon—kills in cold blood. More importantly, he seems to hate happiness; based on his killings."

"Oh my god," Hawkins interrupted; now clearly annoyed. "Here we go again with the underlining meaning to why he's killing these people; he can't stand people's happiness. Give me a break. Hey, kid; if you weren't married to Claire, I'd suggest you and the doctor get hitched, because you share the same ridiculous theory on this guy."

"Ace," Murphy said. "Let the doctor say what she needs to say. We did agree to hear her out."

"I never agreed to this," Hawkins argued. "But go ahead. The floor is yours, doctor."

Doctor Hadley, maintaining a cool and professional composure, despite Hawkins' attacks and rude behavior, continued.

"The Long Island Surgeon kills people based on their happiness; the old married couple, the pregnant mother, the woman who was only months away from realizing her professional dream, and now the children. These are all picture perfect examples of happiness, and I've managed to notice this just from what I've read in the newspapers, or seen on the news."

Hawkins let out a sigh, as if he could not believe the hot garbage that was spilling from this woman's mouth, but he kept quiet.

"Gary Kaste," Jennifer Hadley continued. "Thought those children were beautiful. Now, I know that seems disturbing, but you have to understand these kind of people."

"Doctor, I'm not trying to disregard what you are saying right now, and I understand completely the point you are trying to make," Murphy cut in. "But after he molested these children he thought were beautiful, he assaulted them."

"Only because they tried to escape him. He panicked, and acted. In my professional opinion, he would have let them go had they tried not to escape."

"What a prince," Hawkins chimed in.

"I'm not defending him for what he's done, Detective Hawkins. I'm defending him against what's about to happen to him. My point is this: the man who is Gary Kaste, despite what despicable crime he has committed in the past, is not the man who is the Long Island Surgeon. They are, by nature, two completely different people."

Everything Jennifer Hadley had to say made perfect sense. Patrick remembered back to earlier that night, as he was reading the case file on the Kaste crime. He couldn't believe that the same man he was reading about was the man who had put all of Long Island in a state of worry. Now, as Jennifer Hadley compared her patient to the Long Island Surgeon, he felt that familiar feeling from earlier creeping back.

"May I interrupt with a comment, Doctor Hadley?" Hawkins asked politely enough, but continued with what he had to say before she could give him the floor. "Gary Kaste spent ten years in prison for his crimes. Crimes that you say he is remorseful for, but at the same time, crimes that he felt he shouldn't have been convicted of, because he thought he was in love with those two boys, if my memory serves me correctly."

"That was then, detective," Doctor Hadley argued. "He's well aware that his crimes were wrong, whether or not he had thought he was in love with those two boys."

"Or, like I said before, that's what he wants you to believe, and, please, hear me out before you hit me with that 'it's your job to wean out the sincere ones from the bullshit artist' lecture."

Jennifer Hadley made no attempt to argue. She let Hawkins make his point.

"Ten years is a long time to muster up a lot of hatred; especially for a crime you initially didn't think you were wrong for committing. It's a long time to sit on that hatred, and let it consume you. The Long Island Surgeon, whether it's Kaste or not, according to you and the replacement over there, has all this hatred towards happiness bottled up, and is unleashing it on the world. If you ask me, which I'm sure you wouldn't, and that's why I'm going to tell you, ten years in prison seems like a good amount of time to bottle up a shitload of hatred towards the world."

As strong as Hadley's point had been, Hawkins raised a seemingly stronger counterpoint. Gary Kaste molested and beat up two children, and it landed him in jail. Prison life for a child molester was no easy experience. It was possible that those kids, who he once thought were so beautiful and who he was in love with, were perceived as the reason why Gary Kaste's life was now destroyed. Patrick believed that was enough of a spark that could eventually ignite the inferno of hatred that fueled the Long Island Surgeon.

"I see your point, Detective Hawkins," Doctor Hadley admitted. "But Gary Kaste isn't capable of committing those sorts of crimes."

"Why," Hawkins asked. "Because he had you, and everyone else he's come in contact with convinced that he's barely functional as a human being? Did it ever once occur to you, doctor, that he's been bullshitting you all along?"

"No, but I'm glad I now have you to repeatedly tell me."

"What's Gary Kaste's IQ?" Hawkins asked.

"I don't know off hand."

"But you've run intelligence tests on him; have you not?"

When Doctor Hadley informed Hawkins she had ran numerous intelligence tests on Gary Kaste, including a standardized IQ test, a victorious smile stretched across his face. He had Jennifer Hadley right where he wanted her.

"What were the conclusions of your tests, doctor?" Hawkins asked.

"That Gary Kaste was far more intelligent than the average human being, but that means nothing. He's handicapped by his social awkwardness, among a laundry list of other psychological problems. It's not an uncommon occurrence."

"Or maybe he was smart enough to play the idiot for everyone around him. His high intelligence certainly points towards his ability to plot out, in detail, these murders, and then be able to cover all his tracks so well. That, piled on top of who Gary Kaste's cellmate was in prison, points right towards him being able to pull this off."

In prison, Hawkins told everyone, Gary Kaste shared a cell for seven of his ten years with a Doctor Marcus Lynbrandt. Marcus Lynbrandt was, once upon a time, a plastic surgeon, but that was an arrest and a conviction ago. The plastic surgeon had been busted for fondling, sodomizing, and raping his patients while they were still under anesthesia in recovery following their procedures.

"You can learn a lot about anatomy in seven years; especially when your cellmate is a doctor, and a fucked-up-in-the-head doctor at that," Hawkins told the doctor.

Victory saturated the tone of his voice. He knew he had the doctor, and anyone else listening, right where he wanted them.

"He didn't commit these murders," Doctor Hadley still argued. However, this seemed more directed at herself rather than Hawkins. She was trying to reassure herself that Gary Kaste was innocent, despite the overwhelming counterargument.

"Why are you so convinced that this man is innocent?" Hawkins asked. He was annoyed now more than ever with the doctor, who wouldn't just cave, and agree with everything he said, like he was so accustomed to. "Are you fucking Gary Kaste, Doctor Hadley?"

Patrick couldn't believe Hawkins even had the audacity to ask that question. He was just trying to embarrass this woman now by accusing her of being unethical. He went to speak up for these inexcusable remarks, but it was Murphy who intervened on the doctor's behalf.

"That is enough, Detective Hawkins," Carl said. "You are out of line."

"Of course," Hawkins said; throwing his hands up in an *I mean no harm* gesture, when clearly he did mean to cause harm. "My apologies, doctor. I'm sure you and Gary Kaste are not sleeping together."

She did not acknowledge the apology, nor the outlandish accusation, but Hawkins was beginning to get to her. Whether from his damn-near concrete proof that Gary Kaste was The Long Island Surgeon or the personal jab he took at her that got her upset, Hawkins took notice, and decided to take one last dig at Jennifer Hadley.

"Or maybe, Doctor Hadley," he stood up; towering over the doctor. "You refuse to admit Gary Kaste's guilty of these crimes, because you don't want to admit you are a failure. It's your job to make sure that anyone who is paroled is safe to be released into the general public. You

260

deemed Gary Kaste a non-threat, and you gave the okay for his release. Now you find out he's been killing innocent person after innocent person. That must be a hard pill to swallow. So, maybe you refuse to just admit that you are wrong, because you can't admit that you are, in a way, responsible for the deaths of each and every person Gary Kaste murdered."

The doctor remained speechless. She simply looked around the room from person to person. All eyes were now glued to her and Hawkins.

"Now, if you don't mind, Doctor," Hawkins continued. "My partners and I have a murderer to arrest. We appreciate you coming down here, but, unfortunately, it was just a waste of your time, not to mention ours."

Satisfied that he had done enough damage, he sat back down in his chair. He had hurt the feelings of this young woman, and he was absolutely proud of himself for doing so.

"Goodnight, Detectives," the doctor finally said. There was defeat in her voice. She made no eye contact with any of them, even though Patrick and Murphy had tried their hardest to be professionals. She just wished the detectives a good evening, turned around, and left.

Now, in the bitter December cold, whatever woes that troubled Hawkins' mind didn't matter. When the time came, he would put his issues—if there were actually any issues, to begin with—on the backburner, and make his duties to bring a murderer to justice his priority. Patrick had no doubts about that.

The one Patrick had to worry about was himself.

In less than a two hour car ride, The Long Island Surgeon, the man who up until then had been a specter to the Nassau County Police Department's Homicide Unit, would finally become corporeal. His mask had been stripped away, and Gary Kaste was exposed for the world to see. Soon, he would be flesh and bone, and soon they would be able to arrest him.

Or kill him.

That was the voice in Patrick's head he had been fighting to suppress ever since a warm November morning while staring up at a wall full of pictures in the living room of an elderly couple, who had just been found murdered. It was a voice that demanded revenge in its truest form. Now, he was just a car ride away from being face-to-face with the Long Island Surgeon, and Patrick Sullivan wanted nothing more than to succumb to temptation, and kill Gary Kaste.

After all, he had given in to temptation once before.

That was a long time ago, though; in what Patrick liked to think was another life. After everything that had gone down, he promised himself he would not let that enraged voice dwelling within his head get the best of him. Not after everything it nearly took from him.

For his own good, and good of his family, he would not let the urge to hammer down violent justice win again. When the time came, he would arrest the Long Island Surgeon. He would place the handcuffs around his wrist, read him his Miranda Rights, and he would take Gary Kaste into custody.

The car ride had been silent, for the most part. The only one who spoke during the long drive was Hawkins, and only to give precise instructions on how to handle the apprehension of Gary Kaste. He went over their plan repeatedly; starting from even before they got into the car. He wanted to be certain everything went smoothly, and without problem.

Although unlikely, there were some concerns that the local authorities would try to swoop in, and play hero; stealing the arrest as their own, and claiming they had brought the Long Island Surgeon to justice. Even though his victims had all been residents of Nassau County, the Westchester Police would try to say that, since Kaste lived within their jurisdiction, the arrest belonged to them. This would bring politics into the mix, and then things would get really messy.

This didn't surprise Patrick. In the end, to some people, it was about making a name for yourself, and having your fifteen minutes of fame. Despite what the suits told the media, it wasn't just about the victims. It was a popularity contest over who could earn the bragging rights to say they were responsible for putting Gary Kaste behind bars for the remainder of his pathetic life.

They had arrived in Westchester, and met with the local police chief to discuss their next move. Despite his obvious ability to run a police station, he might as well had clocked out, and gone home for the day. The moment Jonathan Hawkins stepped into that police station, he was calling the shots. It was his show, and no one was going to screw things up. Not when they were so close to closing the book on the Long Island Surgeon investigation.

Hawkins had left the task of securing the surrounding woods around Kaste's trailer park home to the local authority. After all, they knew the area far better than anyone, and if Kaste tried to make an escape through the woods, officers needed to be strategically placed in order to catch him.

Unfortunately, as it was proven later on, it wouldn't matter who secured the area. Bullets would fly, and blood would be shed. The arrest of Gary Kaste would go south real fast.

CHAPTER 28

Maybe they were so anxious to get it over and done with that they missed that single important detail. Maybe they just didn't plan enough. Perhaps, what it simply boiled down to was carelessness on all parties account. When things go wrong, you can look back from a thousand different standpoints, and still not be able to pinpoint what the issue was.

Above all else; what it probably boiled down to was that they had forgotten who they were dealing with.

They only convened for an hour at the police station before they headed out to the trailer park where Gary Kaste lived. He had been confirmed to be home that morning by two officers who had been given the charge of doing surveillance on his trailer. As they drove the winding roads just outside of Westchester County, Patrick felt his heart jackhammering in his chest, and his pulse pounding in the back of his throat. As the miles wound down, so did this case.

Soon, one way or another, it would all be over.

They pulled off the main road onto a single lane dirt road that led to the trailer park. Patrick had seen trailer parks in his life, and this barely qualified as one. It looked more like an oversized campsite. There were only four trailers; all parked in the back of the dirt lot. In front of each trailer were beat up metal mail boxes; each baring the name of the current residents. The one that read *Kaste* was the second one from the left. In front of one of the trailers there had been a young child playing in the dirt with his baby brother, who was completely naked; sitting in the dirt with a filthy tennis ball in his mouth. The older boy, who apparently had been deemed old enough to care for his toddler brother, took one look at the police vehicles piling into the parking lot, picked up his naked brother, and headed back inside their mobile home.

Patrick and Murphy got out of their vehicles, and walked across the dusty lot to Hawkins, who had ridden with the police chief. Their faces were as expressionless as the dead, but, still, they all screamed with anticipation.

"This is it, boys," Hawkins said to his colleagues. "You two, behind me." He ordered; pointing to Patrick and Murphy. He then pointed to the police chief "I need your men sharp, and ready for anything."

The Westchester Police Chief nodded.

Everything was in place; Hawkins had given all the orders, and everyone was ready.

There was no hesitation or calming of nerves needed for Jonathan Hawkins. This was him in his element, and it was now go time. He was about to embark on the last hurrah of his professional career. He took a step, followed it with another, and proceeded to walk towards Kaste's trailer.

They approached the trailer, and stood at the foot of the three rotting wooden steps that led up to the front door. No one spoke. They were assessing the situation, and, at the moment, everything seemed calm.

Wasn't it always calmest before the storm, though?

Hawkins climbed the stairs to the front door, and took one last look back at his partners. The expression on his face said the exact thing that was running through Patrick's head.

Here we go.

He balled his fist, and hammered down on the thick wooden door.

"Gary Kaste," Hawkins bellowed. "This is the police. Open the door. We have a warrant for your arrest."

There was no response… just silence.

"You have two options here," Hawkins continued. "Either, you except it's over and cooperate, or we bust this door down and come in there after you."

Still… silence.

"Dammit, Kaste; OPEN UP!!"

As Hawkins rained his fist down upon the door, Patrick noticed the wooden door to Gary Kaste's trailer park home did not quite fit its frame. It was a few inches too short at the bottom. Someone didn't bother to measure doorframe dimensions when they were looking to replace the front door. Seemingly, it was the most unimportant thing for someone to take notice of, given they were attempting to arrest a serial killer, but it was that small detail that saved Hawkins' life.

Patrick saw, through the extremely large gap at the bottom of the door way, two feet just standing there; facing the door in which Hawkins was currently slamming down upon. He didn't bother to think. Patrick just wrapped his arms around Hawkins, and pulled him backwards off the small stoop.

It was in the moment they were falling back towards the ground that the front door to Gary Kaste's trailer park home exploded into a thousand pieces from the shotgun blast that came from behind it.

CHAPTER 29

For his age, Jonathan Hawkins was certainly a man of impressive physique. He stood just south of six foot, and weighed a muscular hundred and seventy five pounds. So when he came crashing down on top of Patrick; sandwiching his replacement between himself and the unforgiving dirt ground, the wind was violently expelled from Patrick's lungs. A shower of tiny splintered wood pieces that, only a moment before had been a door, rained down on them as Patrick gasped desperately for air.

Despite the pain and agony he was currently experiencing, Patrick gave himself little time to recuperate, and even less time to think. Letting his instincts take control, he heaved Hawkins off of him; not even bothering to check if the guy was okay, or even alive. He just got up, pulled out his pistol, and took pursuit of Gary Kaste.

He entered the trailer more carelessly than he should have, but adrenaline had completely taken over. There was no longer time for caution or logic. His carelessness didn't matter, though. He entered an empty trailer. A quick scan of the tiny living room area showed that Gary Kaste was not there; waiting to open fire on whoever dared to enter. Instead, he had chosen to flee. At the rear of the trailer;

next to what was supposed to pass as a kitchen, there was a hole in the wall leading to the outside.

How could they have been so stupid?!

Gary Kaste had his escape planned out months before he murdered the Ramsey's. They had been cocky, and they were all idiots; each and every one of them. They actually thought they would be able to just mosey on up to Gary Kaste's front door, and simply arrest him. None of them had really truly anticipated things going wrong; not even Hawkins.

And why would they?

Gary Kaste was a socially awkward pedophile who was afraid of his own shadow. They had forgotten the monster that was known as the Long Island Surgeon, and that was their biggest mistake, because the Surgeon was always one step ahead of everyone else.

"He's on the run!" Patrick yelled out. Then, without giving a second thought to whether or not the other officers outside even heard him, he crawled through the hole in the trailer, and took pursuit of Gary Kaste.

Outside the back of the trailer home, there was nothing but the vast woods of upstate New York. Kaste had a few minutes head start, and that was really all he needed.

Patrick was now searching for a needle in a haystack.

Why didn't we set up a tighter perimeter?! Patrick thought; cursing all their incompetence, but he knew the answer… because they were all very stupid, and careless.

His body moved solely on autopilot. He should have been more aware of the threat that, at any given moment, he could trip on a root, or slip on some wet leaves; ending his pursuit real fast with a sprained ankle or broken leg. There were too many other thoughts clouding his mind for him to fret over where his footing was going to fall.

Someone is going to shoot him.

That thought, above all the others, made Patrick hasten his pursuit. Somebody would have ideas of grandeur—at least an idiot's idea of grandeur—and try to be a hero by shooting down Gary Kaste. Of course, when they told the story to the media, they would proudly claim they shot down, and killed the Long Island Surgeon after he had fired upon the police, and fled.

Patrick kept his eyes peeled for any sight of Gary Kaste; letting his body navigate him through the woods. It was a mistake that would eventually catch up to him.

His foot hit the ground, and as it came up for another stride, it got caught on a root. Momentum did the rest.

Patrick flipped forward, landed on his back, and tumbled down the small hill. During his descent, his body smashed against branches, roots, rocks, and the ground already freezing over from the newly cold weather. Each blow felt like a hard shot to a different part of his body. He landed at the foot of the hill with a big rock smashing into the small of his back. That blow had been so painful that Patrick lost the grip of his firearm, which he had managed to hold on to during his entire fall. Never minding the explosive pain in his lower back, he reached forward for his weapon.

"Don't freaking move!" a voice said.

Patrick froze where he was; just a fingertip away from his gun. He slowly looked up, and saw a double barrel of a shotgun not even a foot from his face. At the other end of the weapon was Gary Kaste; the Long Island Surgeon in the flesh.

"Okay…" Patrick said. He slowly moved away from his weapon, and raised his hands to the air. "Let's not do anything rash here."

"I didn't kill those people," Gary Kaste said. The tone that saturated his voice certainly sounded like a man desperate for someone to believe him. "I'm not the guy you are looking for."

"Then why did you fire at us, and then run?"

The answer to that question was obvious: Gary Kaste was not a mentally stable person. Now, the Long Island Surgeon, undoubtedly, could definitely be called a mentally unstable person, but not the same way as this man.

"You wouldn't have believed me!" Gary Kaste was working himself up more towards hysterics the more he talked. "You would have arrested me, and blamed me for all those people's deaths. I know there were kids who died; I saw the news. You think just because of what I did, I'm guilty."

"We have your DNA on the victims..." Patrick started to say.

"I didn't do it!" Kaste yelled, and for a moment Patrick was convinced his time was up. He thought for sure Kaste was going to pull the trigger, and put a gaping hole in his face.

The blast never came, and Patrick's life continued.

Instead, Kaste began to whimper.

There's no way this guy is the Long Island Surgeon, Patrick thought as he watched tears begin to stream down Gary Kaste's face.

These weren't the tears of a man upset over the fact he had been bested by the police, and caught. They were tears of a man scared. Scared that no one would believe him, because he was a convicted felon, who was mentally unstable.

"Lower your weapon, Gary. Let's talk about this."

"No! You're trying to trick me. You're just going to arrest me."

"Yes, I am, but that doesn't mean you are going to jail for murder. Listen, I'm going to lower my hands now,

Gary. I just want you to listen to me for a moment." Patrick slowly lowered his hands, and placed them in front of him where Gary Kaste could see them. "Like I said, we have your DNA on some of our victims, and you fired at us back at your place. There's no way you aren't going to be arrested, but we can prove you didn't kill all those people. You can walk away from this"

"No one is going to believe me."

"I believe you, Gary. Look at me…" As he looked into the glassy eyes of Gary Kaste, he knew more than ever that he was looking at a wrongfully accused man. "I believe you. I'm one of the detectives in this murder investigation. It doesn't matter what any of the other police officer's think; I can help prove you weren't involved in any of the Long Island Surgeon murders. You know you're innocent, and I know you're innocent. Together, we can sort this out."

"You're trying to trick me," Kaste said, but his sobs were beginning to taper. Patrick was getting across to him.

"I'm not, Gary. I can help you, but you need to work with me. The first thing I need you to do is lower your weapon."

"I can't go back to prison! Do you know what they did to me last time?"

"You don't have to go to prison." Patrick now had his hands up in a pleading fashion. "Just lower the weapon, and come with me. We can work this all out. If you know you're innocent, then you have nothing to worry about. I'm going to work with you, and this will all be sorted out."

He could see the change in Gary Kaste. He was still a nervous wreck, but the hysterics had subsided. He was going to cooperate. Patrick knew it… He could feel it. He even thought he saw Kaste beginning to lower his weapon.

That was when the blast came.

Patrick closed his eyes tight, and waited for death. He thought of Claire; his beautiful wife, who had saved him, and their amazing son, who was Patrick's greatest creation, and contribution to the world. He would hold onto that image until darkness came. He expected to see Baby Tooth there; waiting for him on the other side. There, they would spend eternity together; the way Patrick figured it would always be when he died.

There was no darkness, there was no Baby Tooth, and there was no death for Patrick Sullivan. There was just a warm splatter across his face and torso, and the thud sound of a body hitting the ground.

When he finally dared to open his eyes, Patrick saw that he was covered in blood. He also saw, lying in front of him on the cold winter ground, the body of Gary Kaste. In his back was a huge gaping hole from a shotgun blast. No question about it; he was dead.

Patrick looked up to see who had fired the shot at Kaste, and decided to play hero.

There, a hundred yards away, he saw Jonathan Hawkins with a shotgun in his hands.

CHAPTER 30

The locker room at the 8th precinct on North Wantagh Avenue erupted at the commotion. They couldn't believe what was unfolding before of their very eyes. While some reacted, and others stood by, dumbfounded, everyone was shocked. Patrick Sullivan, without giving a single word of warning, walked through a celebratory crowd of his comrades, approached Jonathan Hawkins, and grabbed him by the neck; slamming him violently into the nearby lockers.

He had spent the eight hours following Gary Kaste's death physically present, but, by no means, mentally. The image of Gary Kaste's face; one moment alive and fearful, the next dead and emotionless, was running on a loop in Patrick's mind.

Gary Kaste was dead, and it was because of Jonathan Hawkins

Kaste was surrendering, Patrick was certain of it. He had convinced the near hysterical man to trust him, and for that, he got shot in the back.

And what did Jonathan Hawkins get for shooting Gary Kaste?

The same thing he always got… praised as a hero.

The sight of Jonathan Hawkins standing there in the distance with that gun in hand filled Patrick with that familiar rage. It was the same ire he felt whenever he laid eyes on the victims of the Long Island Surgeon. The same one that had consumed him ten months earlier with Baby Tooth. He wanted nothing more than to charge Hawkins right there and then. He wanted to tackle him to the ground, and choke the life out of him.

He didn't give into sweet temptation, though. Instead, he decided it would be best to curb his anger, because the last time he let it take control of him, it was disastrous. He would just let it subside, and calm. This didn't happen, though. This time, it lingered for eight hours; simmering. He still managed to put up a hell of a fight against it. That was until they walked into the 8th precinct to cheers.

They were cheering for Hawkins, because he had taken down the Long Island Surgeon.

Or that's what they all thought...

Patrick knew the truth. All Jonathan Hawkins had done was kill a scared and innocent man.

Gary Kaste may have been many unsavory things—things which Patrick found to be absolutely disgusting—but the one thing he was not was the Long Island Surgeon, and for that, he did not deserve to die.

No one else knew that, though. They hadn't seen the innocence in Gary Kaste's eyes. To everyone else, Jonathan Hawkins was the hero that he always was. Once again, he was the guy who saved the day, and that was Patrick's breaking point.

That was when he decided there was no longer a need to keep his anger at bay.

"He was surrendering," Patrick yelled, as he resisted the guys trying to pull him free of Hawkins. "You asshole; he was surrendering, and you fucking shot him."

Hearing the actual words leaving his mouth, just made him even angrier. He tightened his grip around Hawkins' neck, and if it hadn't been for the four guys tugging at his arms, he wouldn't have stopped until the man was dead.

He was pulled away momentarily, but Patrick wasn't going to give up that easily. He struggled to free himself, so he could get his hands around Hawkins' neck once again. He lunged forward, but this time the seasoned veteran was ready for him. Patrick felt an explosion on his cheek, followed by a sudden throbbing. Hawkins had nailed him with a hard punch. That had been enough for the guys to create a good separation between the two.

"He surrendered," Patrick repeated; holding his cheek.

"It's not what it looked like to me. To me, it seemed like a man, who had already once fired upon us, had an officer down with a shotgun to his face."

"He was about to lower his weapon"

"Or so he wanted you to think."

Patrick took that notion in only momentarily. Maybe Kaste had been playing him for a fool, and he was the Long Island Surgeon; just pulling Patrick's strings like a puppet. This possibility was dismissed as quickly as it was considered. All Patrick had to do was think of the eyes of Gary Kaste.

"Listen, kid," Hawkins said in that tone he always used when he wanted to defuse a situation. "You saw what you saw, and I saw what I saw. What I saw was your life in extreme danger, so I reacted. You saved my life when I was about to be blown to pieces, so I repaid the favor."

"I had him. He was about to surrender himself over, and then you killed him"

"Who fucking cares," There was no more soothing tone in Hawkins' voices. He was straight up annoyed. "The man was a murderer, and a child molester. Not to mention, on top of all that, he was completely out of his mind. One way or another, I did this world a fucking favor by ending him."

Patrick was shocked to hear Hawkins' words met with approval from his colleagues. They had seen the writing on the wall. Gary Kaste was the Long Island Surgeon, and Jonathan Hawkins had single handedly ended his reign of terror, and, in the process, saved another cop's life. There was no wrong to be placed on Hawkins as far as this went.

None of them had been there with Gary Kaste, though. They hadn't seen the terror on his face, but, mostly, the truth in his eyes.

"What's the matter, kid," Hawkins asked; seeing the enraged look on Patrick's face. "You don't like what you hear? What are you going to do; pistol whip me… like you did to Wallace Freewaters?"

Baby Tooth's name coming from Hawkins' mouth, at first, shocked Patrick, but that didn't last long. The mention of the man who haunted his dreams, sent Patrick into another blind rage. He bolted across the room towards Hawkins, but was quickly intercepted by six other officers in the room.

"What's wrong?" Hawkins' tone was, both, mocking and malicious. "You don't want everyone to know the truth about you, and a certain New York City drug lord?"

"Shut your fucking mouth. You don't know a God damn thing about that."

How could he know? That file was closed, and tucked away. Hawkins had an ability to find things out, even things that were supposed to be buried deep in the past.

"What is there not to know? You pistol whipped a drug dealer so badly that he was hospitalized, and eventually died."

"SHUT UP!" He made another lunge for Hawkins but, again, was restrained.

"What the hell is going on in here?" Detective Murphy demanded as he busted through the locker room doors.

"The kid is trying to pick a fight, because he doesn't like that I saved his ass from being blown away."

"You don't fucking know that he was going to shoot me!"

"Who cares!"

"Enough!" Murphy exclaimed. "The party's over… nothing else to see. Everyone… out! Except you two."

He pointed to Patrick and Hawkins. Everyone else followed Murphy's instructions, and cleared out of the locker room.

"You had no right bringing up my past!" Patrick said the moment the last man had exited the room, and the door closed shut. He was ready to make another attempt to strangle Hawkins, but chose to restrain himself. Carl wanted them to talk, and Patrick respected Carl, so he would talk.

"Why?" Hawkins asked. That same malevolent tone in his voice he used to mock Patrick, as if he was trying purposely to provoke a response. "Does your past embarrass you, kid? Why'd you do it?"

Maybe it was because Hawkins knew all the right buttons to press, or perhaps it was the weeks of frustrations he had built up towards the man. Maybe it was the mention of Baby Tooth, who was still, to this day, a sensitive subject. Whatever it was, Hawkins attempts to get under Patrick's skin were working.

Since the assault on Baby Tooth, he had mastered controlling his emotions; especially anger. Now, however, in that locker room with Hawkins, it seemed as if nothing would calm the storm within himself. Detective Murphy must have seen this, because, before Patrick could even make a move for Hawkins, Murphy had an arm across his chest.

"Just calm down there for a minute, Patrick. Let's talk this out."

"Fuck that, Carl," Hawkins fired back; goading Patrick. "The kid wants to fight, let him fight. Clearly, he doesn't like the fact that I told everyone about his pal, Baby Tooth."

"Ace... SHUT UP!" Murphy snapped. "You aren't helping! The two of you get yourselves under control. I want to know what the fuck is going on here, because if you two can't work this out now, I'll have to get the captain, and you know it's not going to be as easily swept under the rug if he gets involved."

"First, the kid, over here, got mad, because I saved his ass from being blown away by Gary Kaste," Hawkins explained. "Then he got mad, because I let the cat out of the bag about his dark past. Do you know what our rookie did while he was working for the NYPD, Carl? You won't believe the wild side this kid's got."

"I really don't care what he did. If he wants to keep things in his past, he has that right. Why you choose to not only disrespect his wishes, but exploit his past, Ace, is beyond me."

Patrick couldn't believe what he was hearing. Sure, he knew Carl wasn't a pushover to Hawkins, but he never seen him put Hawkins in his place like he just had.

"I've known you to be hard on guys, and sometimes downright offensive," Carl continued. "But this is low, even for you."

Hawkins had no response to this. He even looked embarrassed. Not because he had gotten yelled at, but that he had disappointed Carl. Patrick may have been nothing but a replacement to Hawkins, but Carl Murphy was his longtime partner and friend. If he said or did something that really bothered Carl, Hawkins would do what it took to make things right again.

"What I do want to know," Murphy continued. "Is why the hell are you two trying to kill each other in here?"

278

THE REPLACEMENT

"The kid is mad, because I shot and killed Gary Kaste," Hawkins answered. "He thinks he was innocent."

That shocked Patrick just as much as Hawkins knowledge of Baby Tooth. He had believed Gary Kaste was innocent, but he had kept it to himself. Had he blurted something out that he couldn't remember during the scuffle with Hawkins? He didn't think so. Hawkins, somehow, just knew.

"Is this true?" Carl asked. He got the answer he was looking for when Patrick gave no response. "Patrick, I'm sorry if he had you fooled up in those woods, but Gary Kaste being innocent is impossible. Not only did we have his DNA on our victims, but you saw that shed."

He may have been in a cocoon filled with rage; ready to burst at a moment's notice following the shooting of Gary Kaste, but Patrick was aware of the things going on around him. He remembered changing out of the blood stained clothes, he remembered giving a statement about what had happened—he chose to leave out most of the details of the conversation—and he remembered watching them load up Gary Kaste's cold dead body to be brought to the nearest hospital. Patrick also remembered the shed. How could he not?

About an hour after the shooting, one of the local police officer's found a rundown shed not too far from Gary Kaste's trailer park. It had clearly been abandoned for some time; the two small windows were boarded up, and a fallen branch had crashed through the roof of it. However, there was a small padlock on the door that looked brand new. They got bolt cutters to break the chain, and when they entered the shed, what they found would leave an everlasting impression on each and every one of them.

Gary Kaste had put together an extensive shrine dedicated to the Long Island Surgeon—dedicated to himself.

Plastered on one wall were newspaper clippings from various newspapers on Long Island, New York City, and Westchester. Each article's subject matter revolved around the Long Island Surgeon, or his murders. There had been enough material collected to cover an entire side of the shed. On another wall, they found something far more disturbing than newspaper clippings. They found Polaroid photos of the victims; starting from the Ramsey's, going all the way through to the children found in Claire's classroom the day before. There were pictures of his handpicked victims taken from a distance; alive and going about their daily lives, and there were photos of them again, up close (so you could see the fine details of his gruesome handiwork) once they had been murdered. The only people missing photos from the wall were Julianne Frankles after she had been torn apart, and the rest of the victims from the hospital. Apparently, he didn't have time to take photos. He was too busy covering all his tracks.

What had been posted up on the wall for Kaste to admire wasn't even the worst of it; if one was capable of believing such a statement. Under all the photos—the shot of Evangeline Carpenter standing in a park with her hands on her swollen stomach; before her child had been ripped from her currently stuck out in Patrick's mind—there had been a long workbench set up along the wall. This must have been for when it was still being used as a shed, and not as a shrine to a vile monster's doings. Beneath the bench, they found a box filled with various surgical tools; perfect for mutilating victims, and, more importantly, several units of Pancuronium Bromide. Atop the workbench; replacing the tools, were several tee-shirts. They had once been white, but now they were all stained thoroughly with blood. The victim's blood. Gary Kaste had saved the shirts he wore while he murdered his victims.

Still, that wasn't the worst of it.

Also atop the workbench were various jars. The site of them sent some of the officers fleeing the shed; fighting off sickness. In the jars, which were all filled with Formalin for optimum preservation, were different parts of each of the victims. With the exception of the children, there had been something taken from each of the Long Island Surgeon's handpicked victims; the flesh that was ripped from Arthur and Estelle Ramsey's body, the placenta from the womb of Evangeline Carpenter, and the jaw and fingertips of Julianne Frankles. They were never found at the crime scene, and were presumed to be taken by the Long Island Surgeon as souvenirs. That theory was proven correct.

Patrick had heard of serial killers following, and admiring their own work, but this was at a whole new level.

As if the DNA found on the victims wasn't enough to convict Gary Kaste (had he lived to see a trial) of murder in the first degree, the contents of The Shed would definitely have been the deal breaker. There was no doubt that he had been the Long Island Surgeon.

Yet Patrick had doubted it. He had gone hours, and come all the way home; back to Long Island, thinking that Jonathan Hawkins had killed an innocent man. He had attacked Hawkins in front of all their colleagues because of it. He was played with, like a puppet, by Gary Kaste. He was manipulated when he should have known better. If it wasn't for Hawkins, Patrick would've let his guard down completely, and, as a result, would've been blown apart by a pointblank range shotgun blast to the sternum, or face.

"I'm sorry."

The apology had come out of his mouth, accidentally. Sure, he could see now that he had been wrong, and was duped by Gary Kaste, but he didn't think he could bring himself to actually say the actual words. He wasn't sure how Hawkins would respond to his apology. Would he accept it, and that would be the end of it, or would Hawkins, as he had a tendency of doing, rub it in Patrick's face, and not allow the subject to just be dropped.

If it hadn't been for Carl's presence, Hawkins might have acted the latter, and gloated, once again, how he was always right. Murphy was there, though, and that didn't happen.

"It's fine," was the response Patrick received. Then, to his complete and utter surprise, Hawkins extended his hand.

Patrick did not want to take that hand, and shake it. Despite everything, he flat out did not like Jonathan Hawkins. He may have been right in this situation—or most situations, for that matter—but that didn't change the fact that he was an arrogant prick.

Still, and probably for the same reasons Hawkins didn't instigate a fresh argument, Patrick shook Hawkins' hand, and, just like that that, the matter was squashed.

"That's more like it," Detective Murphy said. "You two may never get along, and whatever the reasons are; they don't matter. All that should matter to either of you is that you two coexisted, and caught what may be one of history's most sadistic serial killers. You two should be proud of that."

"You did everyone proud, kid," Hawkins said.

Still, Patrick thought. *After all this time, and everything that has happened, he can't call me by my name. He is still calling me kid.*

"Well, I don't know about you guys," Hawkins said; dropping the subject now completely. "I am exhausted. I plan on going home, and taking a nice long nap."

There were still some odds and ends to be squared away with closing the investigation, but everyone felt the same exact way after a month's pursuit of the Long Island Surgeon; it could wait until after the Christmas holiday.

"Are plans still on for tonight?" Carl asked Hawkins.

"Absolutely," Hawkins said. "In fact, why don't you join us, kid? Every year on Christmas Eve, the guys get together at Jacky Reilly's for a few drinks. This year was going to be a sort of unofficial send-off party for me, as well. Not to mention, we have something great to celebrate... the end of a torturous case!"

"It's definitely worth celebrating."

Although celebrating was the last thing Patrick Sullivan felt like doing. He never expected for victory to feel so much like defeat.

"Well, if you don't have plans with the family, then join us! It's time to put all the bullshit behind us, and to just enjoy life. Who knows how much time we have, right?"

"Right," Patrick agreed. "I'm going to have to pass, though. I'm sure Claire would love to have me home. I'm going to stick around here a bit; maybe box up some of the evidence, and then go home to my family."

"That's great, kid," Hawkins stood, and stretched his exhausted muscles, and aching bones. "You spend as much time with that wife and kid as you can. Believe me, I know from experience; they're gone before you know it, and all you're left with is regret that there wasn't enough time."

With that said, he left the locker room. Patrick wanted to feel bad for Hawkins; he really did. The guy had lost his wife so early on; taken away from him by forces beyond his control. No one deserved that, but Patrick still couldn't find any real compassion within himself. Hawkins, above all else, was a liar and a manipulator. He meant nothing he said. He hated Patrick just as much as Patrick hated him. His words were fiction; each one strung together with precision to get exactly what he wanted. Patrick understood that now, and how everyone else fell for his

JASON PELLEGRINI

elaborate act, he would never understand, because Detective Jonathan Hawkins was not a good man.

"Enjoy your holiday, Patrick," Murphy said. He put a hand on Patrick's shoulder, and then left the room; leaving Patrick alone with just his thoughts.

His body was beyond exhausted, but his mind was racing. So much had happened over the last twenty-four hours; he could hardly believe it was plausible.

Yet, it had happened, and it was now finally over.

The Long Island Surgeon was no more.

Patrick laid down on one of the cots to rest his eyes a bit before packing up the evidence into boxes, but so much was going through his head.

He closed his eyes, and saw Gary Kaste's face. That look of pure innocence. Only it was just a mask Kaste had put on. He had manipulated Patrick, and was likely seconds away from ending his life. Still, even after accepting the truth, when Patrick saw that face in his mind's eye, he doubted everything. All the facts in front of them were lies. Somehow, they were all lies, and the truth was still out there; waiting to be discovered.

But, of course that was all nonsense, and Patrick Sullivan was wise enough to know it. He was just too tired physically, and too wound up mentally from the encounter in the woods with Kaste to the fight just moments before with Hawkins. He just needed to rest a bit.

After a few minutes of lying there; staring at the ceiling, Patrick doubted sleep would come to him—his mind was just racing too quickly—but sometimes, no matter what is on your mind, your body wins the battle. This was the case for Patrick, because, after a few minutes, he slept soundly.

And he dreamt.

CHAPTER 31

He sat at a poker table.

The room was dimly lit, and masked with a thick cloud of cigar smoke. It had a claustrophobic feel to it. Even though he couldn't see any walls, he knew the room couldn't have been any bigger than a walk-in janitor's supply closet.

But it wasn't the tight quarters that gave it that closed-in feel.

He could feel the presence of the people behind him. Bystanders; watching the game of cards. They had crammed themselves into that small room. They stood so close that he would have felt their breaths on his neck. If they still breathed, that was. He couldn't see their faces, but he knew who they were. They were the dead, and the dead had no use for breathing. They were the ones whose deaths he had sworn to avenge. They were the elderly; taken before their time. They were the mother who would never get to be. They were the young, career driven girl with a strong passion for singing. They were the nurses, security guards, and cops who worked hard to support their families, and got caught in the crossfire. They were the children who never got to wake up to see what Santa brought them on Christmas Day. They were all there, and they were all watching him.

And there was one more.

He watched along with the rest of them. He was the one who tried to move on from the sins of his past, but, instead, ended up dead for them.

The game of poker they were playing was down to him, and one last person. They were the final two. His opposition sat in the adjacent chair; his face, like the others, was masked; making his identity a secret. The orange embers of a cigar glowed dimly as it burned away slowly in his fingers; filling the room with its heavy smoke. He didn't know how many people he had had eliminated to get here—the final two—but he knew the man sitting across from him was the real threat. He was the only true competition.

"The bet is on you, Patty Boy."

Patrick Sullivan looked up, and there, between the last two players in the game, was the dealer; Wallace 'Baby Tooth' Freewaters. He wasn't hidden by the cover of darkness, or smoke. His mutilated face was lit up perfectly by the weak beam of the light from the overhead lamp. Patrick could see every disfiguration he had personally given Baby Tooth. He was wearing one of his ridiculously overpriced suits, and an obnoxious smirk on his face. It made Patrick want to reach across the table, and break the other half of his face.

"Now, Patty Boy; control that temper of yours," Baby Tooth said. He knew Patrick well enough to know what was going through his head. "We have a game to play."

Patrick looked down at the table. There, face down, on the green felt, were a pair of playing cards.

"Why are we still playing?" Patrick asked; confused. He thought they were done playing.

"Come on, nigga," Baby Tooth responded, as if Patrick had just asked the world's most ridiculous question. "Quit playing dumb. You know damn well the game isn't over yet."

"But it's supposed to be."

"Well, what it's supposed to be, and what it actually is, are two completely different things. Now, bet!"

How could Patrick bet? He didn't even know what cards he had. He reached for them to take a look, but Baby Tooth slapped his hand away.

"We're playing this hand blind, Patrick," Baby Tooth explained. His grin widened, and Patrick saw that damn baby tooth in his mouth; the survivor of a fierce beating. It mocked Patrick, and he wanted nothing more than to rip it right out of that drug dealing, life ruining bastard's mouth.

He looked across the table at his opposition's chip pile, and then back at his. The two stacks were completely even; not a single chip difference. He thought momentarily, but there was nothing to think about as far as he was concerned. In a move that would cause so many others extreme hesitance, Patrick pushed his pile of chips towards the center of the table.

"All in."

"Whoa!" Baby Tooth exclaimed. "I knew you had balls in your pants, every now and then; I mean, after all, look at my face." He pointed to the swollen, bloodied, and broken disaster that was the right side of his face. "But I didn't think it would be tonight."

"This needs to end," Patrick said; staring emotionlessly across the table at the cigar smoke covered figure.

"Indeed, it does," Baby Tooth agreed. "So what's it going to be?"

Wallace Freewaters turned his attention to Patrick's opponent. The opposition raised his cigar to his face, pinched it between his lips, and puffed at it. As the orange embers lit up, Patrick was able to make out a hint of stubble on the man's face, but that was it. With the cigar held between his teeth, he pushed his own pile towards the center of the table.

"Call," He said. His voice was as deep as the depths of hell, and that is precisely where it had come from. It caused the skin on Patrick's arms to prickle with gooseflesh. It was pure evil.

"Things are heating up!" Baby Tooth was excited. "This is it, boys; all or nothing. Someone is walking away a winner, and someone is walking away a loser; not to mention a poor-ass nigga."

There was a brief moment where neither man moved, but it was Patrick's opponent who made the first move, and flipped over his two cards. They turned, and landed face up on the table.

Pocket tens.

Patrick's stomach dropped at the site of those two tens. In any hand played, you didn't want to see those two cards flipped over by your opponent, but when you were playing all-or-nothing, pocket tens spelled certain doom.

He looked down at his cards, which were still face down.

"Let's see those sons-a-bitches, Patty Boy!" Baby Tooth exclaimed.

Patrick took a deep breath, and flipped over his own two cards. What he saw were two cards; the ink on each smeared beyond recognition; only it was blood, and not ink. It made no difference, though. He knew which two cards represented him during this last hand.

Jack and King... off suit.

"Okay, boys," Baby Tooth said. His usual obnoxious tone was now dialed down to a more serious one. "Moment of truth. Here comes The Flop."

He threw away one, and then laid down three cards face up for everyone to see. Two of them had nothing but a big black X printed on them. Patrick knew what this meant; they helped no one. The third, however, was a ten.

That made three of a kind for the man sitting across the table.

"Ouch!" Baby Tooth cringed at the site of that ten, and Patrick couldn't blame him. His insides were doing the exact same thing. "Tough break, Patty Boy, but you still have a chance."

He threw away another card, and revealed The Turn.

A queen.

Patrick felt a spark of hope. He just needed one more card, and everyone knew which card that was.

"You see, Patrick," Baby Tooth said. "Sometimes you just need to take a chance. Not a lot of people realize that. They just play it safe, and go with the flow. If you don't take chances, you don't get shit done. Look at me... I took chances, and, because of that, I made myself a lot of money. Granted, in the end, that didn't work out too well for me—we owe that all to you, my friend—but I still took those risks. I went all in when I could have played it safe. The odds aren't always going to be in your favor—hell, I'd say nine times out of ten, you're betting against the odds— but you still need to make that bet, because you never know; just once it might pay off..."

Baby Tooth threw away the final card, and drew The River; the card that would decide the fate of this game. He looked at it; his face emotionally neutral, which was a rarity for Baby Tooth, being he usually had an obnoxious grin on his face. He looked at Patrick, then back at the card. He was letting the anticipation build, and it was.

"Drop it," Patrick said.

"You never know, Patty Boy. That's the brilliance of taking a chance; not knowing the outcome. Sometimes it pays off, and other times, it doesn't, but you're never going to truly know. Not unless you look the odds in the face, and bet against them. So take a chance, because you never know… you might just get lucky…" Baby Tooth dropped the card, and it fell to the table in slow motion. When it finally made touchdown, it was face down. Patrick reached for it. "You might just catch that Ace on The River."

As he was flipping over the card that would decide his fate, Patrick Sullivan opened his eyes, and woke from his dream.

CHAPTER 32

Patrick sat at his desk; not at Murphy's, but *his* desk. The one that was meant to be his once Hawkins retired. Well, to Hell with Hawkins. It was his desk as much as it was Hawkins', and he was going to sit at it all he wanted. Had he known, at the time, it would be his one and only time in that seat, he might have enjoyed his moment of sticking it to the man a little more.

In addition to basking in his small victory, he attempted to rid himself of the heaviness of sleep. He had been mentally and physically exhausted; not just from the past forty-eight hours, but an entire month long rollercoaster ride. It had all caught up to him, and he slept for a full seven hours. This did little to quell his fatigue.

It was now one in the morning on Christmas Day, and Patrick had nearly a full night's worth of sleep, but he still felt as if the weight of the Sandman was crushing him. He tried to give himself a jump start the only way that he knew how; coffee... black.

Still, even his one vice wasn't helping him be rid of exhaustion.

He thought about his dream; the poker game with dead spectators, and an equally dead card dealer. He knew what the dream had meant, but he was also aware that its meaning was not real.

Patrick had been tricked, and tricked well. After all the hard, concrete proof of Gary Kaste's guilt, a little part of him still believed the man to be innocent.

He just doesn't fit the profile, Patrick thought.

He had used that argument once before, on his first day on the case, while defending the innocence of Stephen Ramsey against Hawkins.

And he had been right then.

However, the case of Gary Kaste wasn't like the case of Stephen Ramsey. They had brought the son of Author and Estelle Ramsey in for questioning, because of a hunch based off of family history. They went after Gary Kaste, because of evidence, and once Kaste had been taken down, they found even more compelling evidence in The Shed.

So why was the truth so hard for Patrick to digest?

This back and forth inner battle was likely the explanation for his exhaustion, even after seven hours of sleep.

"Detective Sullivan," an officer said; pulling Patrick away from the ongoing quarrel in his head. "There is a young woman here to see you."

His first thought was Claire. It was just after one in the morning, and his cell phone had died earlier that day. She would, undoubtedly, be wondering where he was. He had called her shortly after they confiscated all the evidence from The Shed. He had told his wife it was over, and they had killed the man who had caused so many people so much pain and suffering. The man who tried to weave Claire into his little game no longer plagued this Earth.

He told her he wasn't sure when he would be home, but after so much time passing without even a phone call and her calls going straight to voicemail, Claire obviously decided to come down to the station to see if her husband was okay.

Only, it wasn't Claire who entered the room. It was Doctor Jennifer Hadley; Gary Kaste's psychologist.

"Doctor Hadley," Patrick said; shocked. He stood up to greet her with a handshake. "I didn't expect it to be you; especially at this late hour."

"I called first to see if, either, you or Detective Murphy were here. I planned on doing this over the phone, but when they told me that you were still here, I decided I would come down, and talk to you face-to-face."

"About what?"

"I saw the news all day, and I feel absolutely terrible."

"Listen, Doctor Hadley," Patrick started. "I know Gary Kaste was your patient, and you thought him to be innocent…"

"It's not that," she said; cutting Patrick off. He could hear the wavering in her voice, as if she was attempting to hold back tears. She took a deep breath; mustering up the courage to say what she needed to say next. "I'm the reason things went so wrong this morning when you guys tried to arrest Gary Kaste."

Immediately, in his mind, Patrick began to put the pieces together.

"What do you mean by that, Doctor Hadley?"

Jennifer Hadley told him that after she left the police department that previous morning, she had called Gary Kaste.

"I wasn't trying to tell him you guys were coming to arrest him, I swear. I just wanted to ask him about it."

"What would that have accomplished?"

She had no answer for Patrick, because she wasn't sure, herself. Maybe, she thought Gary Kaste would come clean, and confess guilt; telling her openly that he was the Long Island Surgeon. Maybe she'd be able gage by his tone and answers whether or not he was lying about his innocence. Perhaps, she was just looking for some type of peace of mind from her heated argument with Jonathan Hawkins. Whatever Jennifer Hadley hoped to accomplish by calling Gary Kaste, it did absolutely nothing positive for his apprehension, because two detectives were almost killed, and Gary Kaste was taken down by deadly force.

"You are aware that what you did is considered interference in a police investigation." Patrick spoke in hushed tones so that no one else—even though the station was nearly empty at that hour—would hear what they were talking about. "There are serious repercussions for this."

They had wondered how Kaste was aware they were coming for him at that exact moment in time. Knowing what he now knew, Patrick wondered if Hawkins had considered Hadley tipping off Kaste. If he had, he kept it to himself. The general belief was that after the children, Kaste knew he'd be found out, and that when they came to arrest them, he'd put up a fight.

"I know. I'm so sorry." Tears started to roll down the doctor's face. She was at the beginning stages of a freak out; probably at the idea of how much trouble she can get in for making a single phone call. "I wasn't thinking. I just wanted to talk to him. He started freaking out; telling me he didn't do it, but no one was going to believe him. He just hung up on me, eventually, and wouldn't pick up when I called back. I never thought he would take violent force against you guys. He's not even supposed to own a gun."

Yet he did own a gun, Patrick thought. *And yet he did use violent force against us. Shows how well you know the stability of your patients, Doctor Hadley.*

He wanted to say that out loud, but decided not to. He was just mad at the fact everything that went down could have been avoided, but he wasn't going to take his anger out on the doctor.

"You can't repeat this to anyone, Doctor Hadley," was what he said, instead. "If anyone finds out what you did, they'll have you arrested. You'll, without a doubt, lose your license to practice, and you'll possibly serve jail time. I'm not trying to scare you. I'm just trying to drive home how serious this is."

"You aren't going to arrest me?" She asked; stunned.

"No, I don't see the point."

In Patrick's opinion, arresting Jennifer Hadley would do nothing, but ruin yet another person's life, and too many lives had been ruined because of this case. He knew she meant no harm, and, despite how things went down, had no ill intentions. All she had was some poor judgment, and some of that probably had to do with Hawkins.

He was willing to forgive the doctor for her mistake, but others, like Hawkins, wouldn't be as forgiving. Carl, Patrick could see being forgiving, and willing to let it all be swept away under the rug, but not Jonathan Hawkins. He was a vengeful person, and would find some sick delight in making Jennifer Hadley suffer for causing him such an inconvenience. Yes, Patrick was almost certain that Hawkins had considered Hadley's tip off, but he kept quiet, because it was only a hunch. If he knew for sure, Hawkins would end Hadley.

"Thank you," Jennifer Hadley said; clearly relieved by the news. She used the sleeve of her winter jacket—something that just twenty-four hours ago she wouldn't have to be wearing—to wipe away the tears from her eyes and cheeks. Patrick passed her a few napkins, so she could wipe away her smudged makeup.

"Was this confession the real reason you came down here, or just an excuse, because you have something else you want to get off your chest?" Patrick asked.

He guessed it was the latter reason.

"I don't know," the doctor admitted. "I know now that Gary Kaste is guilty of those crimes, and I feel so stupid for thinking he was innocent; especially after hearing about that shed they found near his trailer."

She'd be so relieved to know she wasn't the only one who feels like a fool for being duped by Gary Kaste, Patrick thought.

"But part of me still can't believe it," the doctor continued. Patrick understood more than anyone precisely where this young woman was coming from. "I'm not bad at my job, Detective Sullivan; I'm really not. You could have asked me a million times over, and, each time, I would tell you the same thing; Gary Kaste, in my professional opinion, is no longer a threat to society, and I would have said it without a shred of doubt in my voice."

"He wasn't like everyone else," Patrick said; thinking how he had been manipulated by the Long Island Surgeon as well. "He was good at playing everyone for a fool. He had me going, too."

He could see the questioning look on her face, so he explained. He told her how he had looked into the eyes of Gary Kaste, and saw a scared and innocent man looking back at him. He had told her how he pleaded with Kaste to not shoot him, and how he thought he was going to actually lower his weapon before Hawkins took a shot at him.

"Do you still think he's innocent?" she asked Patrick, flat out.

Yes, Patrick wanted to say. He knew it would give her some peace; knowing she wasn't the only one who thought they had taken down the wrong man. Still, he couldn't bring himself to say it, because it wasn't the truth.

"It doesn't matter what I think," was his response, "The evidence doesn't lie. We have his DNA on two dead children, and found an entire shed filled with undeniable proof that he murdered those people. I'm sorry to say this,

Doctor Hadley, but Gary Kaste was the Long Island Surgeon."

He thought she wanted to push the matter; as if hearing him admit part of him, even against all logic, still thought Gary Kaste was innocent, would give her some sort of closure on the subject. Maybe then she wouldn't think she was crazy for thinking Kaste to be innocent. Patrick knew he felt relieved knowing he wasn't alone on the subject.

She didn't push the subject any further, though. Instead, she thanked Patrick, once again, for not having her arrested for her involvement in what had happened that morning, and excused herself because it was getting late.

"Doctor Hadley," Patrick said; suddenly, as she was walking away. He momentarily was about to tell her the truth about how he felt. She deserved it, but for reasons not even he knew, he chickened out. "Try to have a Merry Christmas; please."

"You, too; Detective."

When she was gone, Patrick was alone, once again, at his desk with nothing but his thoughts, his exhaustion, and one useless cup of, now room temperature, black coffee. He had just finished telling that woman that Gary Kaste was, beyond a shadow of a doubt, guilty, yet here he was; still having the argument in his head over it. He had actually said the words out loud; given a full explanation to another human being, and he still couldn't accept the truth.

Patrick was the one who needed closure.

"Oh, fuck it," he said to himself; kicking his chair out from under the desk, and getting up.

He knew what he had to do. He had been toying with the idea since he had woken up, but refused to give in. He kept telling himself there was no point; Gary Kaste was guilty, and he'd just be wasting his time. Still, it was the only way to put his doubts to rest. Patrick needed to know that he looked over everything thoroughly; every little detail.

In the basement of the 8th precinct on North Wantagh Avenue, there was a deep storage closet. This closet was primarily used to store boxes upon boxes of files, and other various documents and paperwork that the Nassau County Police Department frequently used. At the moment, all the evidence found in The Shed, with the exception the various body parts from the victims, were in that closet; waiting to be boxed up, labeled as *Case Closed*, and stored away in a warehouse. Patrick now stood in front of a table with everything they found that morning laid out before him. He was searching for something. He just had no idea what.

Most of what he had been looking at, he knew was useless. The newspaper clippings didn't tell him much; only that the Long Island Surgeon enjoyed his own handiwork. All the surgical tools had been bleached down, and cleaned thoroughly; leaving zero trace of blood or fingerprints behind, and the Pancuronium Bromide had no serial numbers or barcodes to track them. His only real hope lied with the bloodied shirts.

They laid across the table in large bags; each bag labeled with a letter. Earlier that evening a sample of blood was taken from each shirt, and shipped off to a lab to match the DNA with the victim. Those results, because the case was closed and weren't being rushed, wouldn't be back, likely, until after the holidays were over. Patrick didn't think that really mattered, though.

He donned a pair of gloves, and slowly removed each bloody shirt from their respective bag. The blood had been long dried up, but he wasn't paying attention to the blood. It wouldn't tell him anything. He was looking for something else.

Anything else.

He stared at the first shirt for about twenty minutes, which seemed more like two hours. He covered every square inch of it, and found nothing; except blood. He knew how precise the Long Island Surgeon was. He had seen all the crime scenes, and how unfathomably squeaky clean they had been. These shirts would likely prove the same. Still, he had to keep on looking. His stubbornness and determination paid off with not the second shirt, but the third one; or so Patrick hoped. Unlike the first two shirts, the third one had a small tear across the binding of the neck. This wasn't much to go on, but, then again, what did he have to begin with?

Patrick hoped blindly as he gently tore at the binding of the neck. He saw something after a few small tears.

He grabbed for tweezers, and realized his hands were shaking. He had found something. In a case that was, essentially, evidence free—with the convenient exception of Gary Kaste's sperm—Patrick had found something. He focused with everything he had to calm his nerves. He steadied his hand, and removed what he had found from the neck binding of the tee-shirt.

It was a fiber from a shirt. It wasn't one from the plain white tee-shirts they found in The Shed. Patrick studied it; knowing immediately what kind of shirt it came from, but hoping he was wrong.

It came from a maroon dress shirt... and an expensive one, at that.

Patrick's hand began to shake again. He tried to calm it again, but wasn't doing a very good job at it. His nerves were shot, and his mind was racing. He grabbed a small evidence bag, and, miraculously, managed to get the shirt fiber into it. He placed the bag and the shirt down on the table, and tried to gain his composure.

The thoughts running through Patrick Sullivan's mind were ludicrous. He wasn't thinking straight; certainly not logically.

Then he noticed something else on the shirt he had found that single fiber on. It was a stain, and not a blood stain.

Patrick picked the shirt back up, and stared at it. His first thought was semen, but ruled that out, immediately. For starters, the stain was way too large to be from semen, and, secondly, semen was only found at the school, and the children had all been strangled to death. There was no blood at that crime scene. He fixated on the stain, but nothing came to mind of what it could be. So, without fully knowing why he was doing it—maybe he was just that desperate for answers—Patrick brought the shirt up to his face, and smelled the stain.

There was the slightest metallic scent from the dried blood, and that might have even been his imagination. The stain, however, still reeked of what it was. He had recognized the smell immediately, and lost all the motor functions of his hands. The shirt fell to the table. His legs started to go next. Luckily, Patrick was somewhat aware of this, and allowed himself to fall back into a chair behind him.

He ran his hands repeatedly over his face; feeling a day's worth of stubble flow roughly across his palms. He was trying to calm himself down. His mind couldn't fully process anything at the moment; too many thoughts were going through it—realization, above everything else. It couldn't be true, though. There was no way. It was, flat out, impossible.

Patrick was getting ahead of himself; letting personal judgment, whether or not he was aware of it; lead him to this outlandish conclusion. Yet, as he stared at the stain on that shirt, and remembered the smell of it, he knew what he was thinking was true.

He tried to think of what to do next, but he didn't even have an inkling of an idea where to start. He was hoping to find something, but he never thought he'd find this. There wasn't a way to even begin to handle this now. Everything was taken to a whole new level; a new level of bad that he could have never comprehended the existence of.

Yet, here it was, and Patrick needed to handle it, and handle it now.

Without really formulating a real plan, Patrick rose to his feet. His legs felt like they were made of Jell-O, but he managed to gain control of them. He left the closet, and walked into the locker room. His cell phone had been dead, but he couldn't use the station's phone; not to make this call. No one could know about this—not yet, at least. He went to his locker, and grabbed his phone charger. He only gave his phone about thirty seconds to charge; just enough power to let it start up, before he dialed Hawkins' number.

After four rings, he heard Hawkins' voice on the other end.

"Yeah," Hawkins said as his greeting.

Patrick froze. He didn't know what to say, but he needed to say something, and say it soon.

"Kid, you there?" Hawkins asked. "I can't hear you."

"Yeah, I'm here," Patrick managed to get out. There was noise in the background. He guessed Hawkins was still out with the guys; celebrating.

They aren't celebrating the same thing, though, Patrick thought.

"What's up, kid?"

"I need to speak to you."

"Okay... what's up?"

"In person." He hadn't thought any of this through. The words, without having any plan, were falling out of his mouth before he could even stop them. "Not over the phone."

"Can it wait?" Patrick could hear the confusion in Hawkins' voice from the request. "I'm out right now."

"No; it needs to be now."

"Listen, kid; whatever it is you need to tell me, I'm sure it can wait until after Christmas if you can't tell it to me over the phone."

"No, Hawkins." He felt his anger pushing through, but he kept it at bay… for now. "It needs to be tonight."

"Well, I'm not exactly in tip-top condition to drive. I don't plan on starting my retirement with a D.U.I."

He knows, Patrick thought. *He knows why I want to see him.*

"How long do you need?"

"C'mon, kid; I'm having fun here. Is it really that important? Can it wait?" Hawkins was playing dumb, but Patrick was no longer falling for any of his games.

He had already played them for far too long.

"No, it can't."

"Okay," Hawkins said reluctantly. He took a few seconds to think. "I need a few hours to sober up, so I can drive."

"That's fine."

"I'll meet you at the station."

"No," Patrick said. "Not at the station. Somewhere else."

There was silence. Hawkins was speechless. His mind was probably racing as much as Patrick's.

"Okay, fine. Where then?"

Patrick said the first place that came to his head. He wasn't fully sure why he had chosen it, but later on he was glad he did. He asked Hawkins if he knew the place, and Hawkins said he did. They hung up; agreeing they'd meet in a few hours. That was good. Patrick needed a few hours. He needed a plan, and a good plan at that.

After all, he was about to come face-to-face with the Long Island Surgeon.

.

CHAPTER 33

In 1961, Mitchel Air Force Base was decommissioned, and closed down. Since then, a few major Long Island landmarks have been built on this historic piece of land that dates back as early as the American Revolutionary War, when it was an Army enlistment center. Two of these landmarks are Nassau Community College, and the Cradle of Aviation. Located between the two properties are two large closed down airplane hangars; leftover from when the Air Force base was decommissioned. They aren't open to the public, and serve very little use.

That was where Patrick told Hawkins to meet him.

When he told Hawkins over the phone the location where they would meet, Patrick wasn't quite sure why he had picked it. It was abandoned and secluded, but there were plenty of other locations on the Island that had the same atmosphere. That was just the one that popped, immediately, into his head, so he went with his gut. In the end, he was glad he chose it as their meeting place.

Adam Burton; an overweight and asthmatic longtime friend of Patrick's, worked as overnight security for Nassau Community College. Patrick had made the phone call, and told Adam he needed use of one of those hangars; for police business. Adam, who always had dreams of becoming a police officer, like so many of his childhood friends had done, was more than happy to accommodate the request. He did not question Patrick's bizarre request. This was because he longed to live vicariously through his friends serving in law enforcement. So it was obvious by the look of disappointment on his face, he wasn't thrilled when he was advised to go off, and do a long sweep on the complete opposite side of campus.

Now, at three forty-five in the morning, Patrick waited alone; as patiently as anyone put in this incomprehensible predicament could wait. He was waiting for Jonathan Hawkins to arrive.

The truth was, his heart was pounding so hard, he could feel it throughout his entire body. His mouth was bone dry, and, even though the temperature inside of the metal, non-heated/non-insolated airplane hangar was in the lower thirties—a near whopping twenty-five degree difference from just over twenty-four hours before—he was sweating.

He had been planning for this altercation since he hung up the phone with Hawkins, but, in reality, Patrick Sullivan had been preparing for it ever since he first saw the skinless bodies of Arthur and Estelle Ramsey. He had known since that warm November day that before it was all said and done, he would have a face-to-face encounter with the Long Island Surgeon.

And it was about to happen.

Hawkins had kept Patrick waiting for two hours before finally sending a text that simple said 'Meet'. That was fine. Patrick used that time to plot. He had formulated a plan that, at best, had a fifty percent chance of going his way. He had also spent those two hours reflecting.

He had worked beside this man for an entire month; chasing the ghost Hawkins had created. All the while, Hawkins was the real killer, and he stood there, in the thick of things, every step of the way, and Patrick had not even the slightest conception that he was in the presence of the Long Island Surgeon. Even Carl Murphy, a man who knew Hawkins better than anyone else, had no idea his partner was a vicious serial killer. Everyone had played the part of puppets to Jonathan Hawkins.

As Patrick looked back over the case, now knowing the hideous truth, so much of it made perfect sense.

The crime scenes, even the hospital, which should have been a disaster area, were all in tip top shape. Not a shred of evidence was left behind that would indicate who might have committed these murders. Of course, Hawkins would know exactly how to cover his tracks. Not only had he been doing this professionally since before Patrick was taking his first steps, but he was the very best at it. His demands that paramedics attempt to save Julianne Frankles right there in the ambulance, instead of taking her directly to the hospital, so he could question her was nothing more than a smoke screen. He needed to be alone with her, so he could make sure she didn't survive. If the girl lived, and woke up in the hospital, Hawkins would have to take part in questioning her about her attack. She had seen his face, and she would be able to identify him. Then he sent, both, Patrick and Murphy away from the hospital to get rest. What Hawkins really needed them gone for was so that he could finish off the poor girl, who fought so hard to live.

Throughout those two hours of his reflection over the case, especially everything that happened with Julianne Frankles, Patrick started to beat himself up over the fact he hadn't caught on to any of this. He could have saved so many lives, including five children, and an unborn life. In truth, however, he knew there was nothing he could have done differently. He and Carl were doing everything that they could for those victims. Hawkins was just always one step ahead of them.

He heard the car pull up. He heard the door open. He even heard the feet shuffling on the ground as Hawkins got out of his car. He heard it all. He heard the car door slam shut, and then he heard Hawkins' footsteps, as he neared the hangar.

This was it.

The door opened, and Jonathan Hawkins entered. He looked like the same man Patrick had been working with over the course of the last month; only he was now completely different. He was a monster wearing the disguise of a man. Patrick thought he could never hate anyone like he hated Baby Tooth.

He was wrong.

Hawkins had already managed to make Patrick hate him before any of this, but now, seeing him walk in from the cold night, Patrick felt new depths of hatred that he never thought could have existed. It wasn't human.

"Whatever it is that you felt was so important that you needed to drag me away from a warm bar; filled with friends and alcohol, to meet in this frigid shit box better be good, kid,"

He kept that usual obnoxious Hawkins tone as he spoke; his words echoing off the walls of the enormous empty building.

He's playing dumb, Patrick thought, as he watched Hawkins draw nearer. *He knows that I know, yet he is still keeping up with this whole charade. Let him. It's all coming to an end right now... one way or another.*

"Are you going to tell me what all this is about?" Hawkins asked; gesturing at the, admittedly, shady meeting spot in the dead of night. He stopped, and kept a distance of about ten feet between him and Patrick.

He's being cautious, Patrick noted. *He doesn't know it, but he's keeping his distance on purpose.*

Jonathan Hawkins was nervous.

"Gary Kaste wasn't the Long Island Surgeon," Patrick said.

He had known from the beginning that this would be his opening line. He wasn't going to outright accuse Hawkins. Things might escalate too quickly if he did.

"Oh, come on, kid," Hawkins said; agitated that this subject was coming up yet again (as if he didn't know this would be the topic of conversation going into this meeting) "Are you still on this? I thought it was settled. You clearly are a lot dumber than I thought, because a dimwit could see that Kaste was our guy. Look at the evidence."

"He was set up. It wasn't him."

At this, Hawkins actually laughed.

"Set up… that's a good one. Listen, kid; I'm not having this argument, again. Gary Kaste was the Long Island Surgeon. He's dead, and the case is closed. Let it go. I can't believe you dragged me out for this!"

Hawkins turned away, and started towards the door. As far as he was concerned, the conversation was over. Patrick, on the other hand, wasn't near done.

He drew his weapon, and raised it to Jonathan Hawkins; aiming it at the base of his skull. Based on his nerves, his hand should have been shaking like crazy, but it remained steady. In the vast hangar, the small sound of the safety being disengaged sounded like someone had just pounded down on a snare drum.

Hawkins froze in his steps once he had known a gun was pointed at him.

"Turn around slowly with your hands up, Hawkins."

"What are you doing, kid?"

"I said, turn around."

"Don't do anything stupid, kid."

"Turn… A-round…"

Hawkins shoulders dropped, and he let out a sigh. He didn't turn around, like he had been asked, but Patrick knew he was done playing his games.

"The children weren't supposed to die…"

There is a fine line that separates thinking you know something, and actually knowing the truth. It is a line as thin as a strand of hair, and it's called hope. It's the hope that maybe—just maybe—our assumptions will be proven wrong. It is the line that so many people desperately hold on to, and once it is gone, the affects it has on us are everlasting.

When the words came out of Hawkins' mouth; forming that one single sentence, the line for Patrick Sullivan had dissolved away, and he was now facing the unadulterated truth.

His first instinct was to pull the trigger of his pistol, and end Hawkins right there. He craved nothing more than to put a bullet in the back of that man's head, and snuff out his pathetic existence. He needed to squash that craving— at least for now. He had to stick to his plan.

But, more importantly, Patrick needed to know why.

"They weren't part of the plan," Hawkins continued. "It wasn't supposed to happen like it did."

Patrick actually thought he could detect sadness in the voice of Jonathan Hawkins. He remembered how Hawkins had acted that morning in Claire's classroom. How he had actually taken physical action against another officer. At the time, Patrick thought the reasoning had been the case getting to Hawkins, but now, he wondered if Hawkins had lashed out the way he had, because he was becoming unhinged. Had he gone too far, and passed his limits? Did the site of the five defenseless children he had murdered, just to frame an innocent man just so he could cover his ass, begin to eat away at him?

When he spoke again, his tone shifted from melancholy to infuriate.

"It was that *bitch*, Julianne Frankles' fault. She ruined everything. She's to blame for all of this. Everything was going smoothly—exactly according to plan—and she had to ruin it by coming home early that night."

Patrick remembered the chalkboard in Claire's classroom. He could see the message written on it as clear as if it was right in front of him.

SHE DROVE ME TO DO THIS!
BLAME THE GIRL, NOT ME!
THEY ARE DEAD BECAUSE OF HER!

Hawkins had actually believed that to be true. In his head, Julianne Frankles was at fault for those children dying. As if he hadn't already murdered three other people and prevented an unborn child from ever experiencing its first breath. As if he wasn't setting up that night to murder Julianne Frankles in some morbid fashion. None of that apparently mattered. The fact that Jonathan Hawkins was a serial killer meant nothing.

Somehow; it was just about Julianne Frankles.

And Patrick knew why.

If she hadn't come home early, and survived Hawkins' attempts at murder (twice), she wouldn't have been sent to the hospital, and she wouldn't have forced Hawkins into an environment beyond his absolute control. If he didn't have to go to Nassau County Medical Center to eliminate his problem, there would have been no mistakes and no evidence that could expose him as the Long Island Surgeon.

They were precisely where they were, because of Julianne Frankles, and her tenacious will to live.

"Hawkins," Patrick said; trying to keep control of the situation. "I need you to turn around."

This time Hawkins listened. He turned around, and, in his hand, was his own service pistol; pointed straight at Patrick's belly.

"Drop the weapon," Patrick said; his finger now on the trigger of his own gun

"Come on, kid; you know that's not going to happen."

Patrick did know this. Hawkins would never comply with his command. In fact, he was counting on it. Telling Hawkins to surrender his weapon was just part of his plan. Right now, Patrick was putting on a performance, and Hawkins was buying right in to it.

"So how'd you find me out?" Hawkins asked.

Perhaps, it was cockiness, or maybe it was just how he was used to things always going, but Hawkins believed he was the one in control of the situation. Sure, he had a gun, but so did Patrick, yet that didn't seem to faze him.

"I'm not answering your questions," Patrick fired back defiantly. "Not yet, at least."

"I could just shoot you, and be done with all this."

He wouldn't, and Patrick knew it. Hawkins wouldn't kill him, at least not yet. Not while he withheld answers to questions that Hawkins wanted. He could play off that he didn't care this way or that all he liked, but, the truth was, it would eat away at Hawkins not knowing what his mistakes had been.

Patrick had more control of the situation than Hawkins could have ever imagined.

"Go ahead," Patrick said; calling Hawkins' bluff.

In the end, Hawkins didn't shoot, like Patrick had predicted. He still kept the aim of his gun, however, fixated on Patrick's stomach; letting Patrick know that at any moment he could put a bullet in his belly.

"It doesn't matter," Hawkins said. "There's too much on Kaste—including the guy's DNA—whatever you found won't hold up in court."

"Who said anything about you going to court?" Patrick responded, coldly. "I have no intentions on letting you walk out of here."

"OH!" Hawkins exclaimed; shocked by this threat. "Look who has a pair. You know, kid; I have to admit, I was shocked when you came at me in the locker room today. I knew you knew Kaste was innocent, but I never thought you'd come at me. I was impressed then, but, now, forget about it! You'll never do it, though."

"You'd be surprised at what I'm capable of."

"Yes, I'm aware that you beat up the big bad drug dealer," Hawkins said; his words saturated with sarcasm. "I hate to tell you this, kid, but I plan on walking out of here alive tonight."

Patrick was thinking the same exact thing. Only in his scenario, he was walking out alive; not Hawkins. He needed to tread carefully, though. Every move he made from this point out would be crucial to his survival.

"Why'd you do it?" He asked Hawkins point blank. That was exactly what it came down to, in the end. Patrick needed to know why.

"Why did I do it?" Hawkins repeated; annoyed by the question; as if Patrick should know the answer. "For almost forty fucking years, between the NYPD and the Nassau County Police Department, I have served, and I have protected. I have saved lives, and I have brought criminal after criminal to justice; sometimes when no one else could. You name 'em—drug dealers, sex offenders, murderers—I have brought them down, and I have helped clean up the streets; making this world a safer place to live in. So, how do they repay me? They send me packing before I'm ready to go! After all my hard years, they force me out on my ass.

"I built a legacy, here. To all those people we have the privilege of serving day-by-day with, I am a hero. More importantly, I made a promise to my Maryanne that I would do everything in my power to ensure others would remain safe."

Patrick remembered the story. Hawkins had told it to him and Claire over dinner; the night he had the Long Island Surgeon as a dinner guest. That thought made him feel sick to his stomach.

"You killed innocent people," Patrick said; pointing out the obvious flaw in what Hawkins' explanation.

"Collateral damage," was his reasoning. "In war, innocent people die."

"This isn't war."

"Yes, it is! Don't you see that? Every day of our careers in this line of work, it is war. It never ends. We fight the constant battle. Those people died for the greater good. Their death's had a purpose!"

"Enlighten me, then; what was their purpose?"

"To ensure all my hard work wasn't for nothing! I devoted my life to this, and if kicking me to the curb is how they want to repay me, then fine; but I'll be God damned if they think I'm going to sit back idly, and let any schmuck take my place. If I was retiring, I needed to know my replacement was fit to fill my shoes."

Patrick wanted to shoot him there. He should have shot him there, but he didn't. Understanding began to take a form, and Patrick Sullivan wished that it hadn't. He wanted answers, because he needed to know why, but, now, he simply wished he could take it back.

"A test?" Even as the words left his mouth, Patrick couldn't fully grasp the idea. "You were testing me?"

"Once I got you on board, I needed to know you were capable of handling the job." Hawkins stopped, saw the look of confusion on Patrick's face, and began to laugh. "Come on, kid; you didn't think you got this job on your own, did you? You never even took the Nassau County Detective's Exam!"

Patrick had wondered that when he received the offer to take the position in the Homicide Squad, but he didn't ask questions. He was desperate for a job, and wasn't about to ruin the chance he had gotten to right the wrong he had done to his family.

"The Captain only saw you as a favor to a friend," Hawkins continued. "Even before he met you, he had no intentions of letting you come on board. He was going to tell you to take the exam, and they'd take it from there— pretty much he was going to tell you to hit the road. You had left the NYPD, for Heaven's sake, and don't think anyone believes it was on your own accord. That file may have been closed, but we're not idiots."

Hawkins explained that all the interviews for the position of the replacement were taped. The Captain, out of respect to Hawkins, who poured his entire life in to law enforcement, allowed him to take part in the hiring process. The Captain may have had no real plans of hiring Patrick, but when Hawkins saw the tape from the interview, he had different feelings on the matter.

"You had that fire," Hawkins told Patrick. "You remember the one I'm talking about, don't you?" Patrick did remember. "No one else had it, but you. You were truly different from everyone else, kid."

So Hawkins made a few phone calls, and got Patrick's file from the NYPD. His real file. The one that mentioned him pistol whipping Baby Tooth on a Bronx street corner. The one the NYPD swore no one would ever see to protect their asses from bad media, and, less importantly to them, Patrick's own reputation.

"Just so you know; I don't know why you did what you did to that drug dealer, but I'm proud of you. He deserved it."

Whether or not Hawkins approved of Patrick's history with Baby Tooth meant absolutely zero to him. He bit his tongue on the subject matter though, and let Hawkins continue on with his twisted justification for murder.

"So once I was sold on you coming in, the Captain looked the other way as I made sure you had all the proper documents to come on board."

Hawkins was even bold enough to wink at Patrick after his last remark. As if they were two colleagues enjoying conversation over a friendly round of drinks, and not two people who hated each other—one of which was a serial killer—with guns pointed at one another.

Patrick remembered his first day. He wasn't even finished up with the academy. They just pulled him, and threw him into an active murder investigation. That had been Hawkins' doing, for sure. Then the following day, Hawkins had gotten him out of his meeting with Officer Summers, because they needed to meet with the coroner. He just signed all the proper paperwork, and was sent on his way.

Hawkins was the kind of guy people had unlimited amounts of respect for, because of his dedication and years he put in. They were willing to look the other way when he needed to bend, and sometimes break, the rules. He explained to Patrick that all he needed to do was change the information on an already taken exam to Patrick's info, and the deal was sealed. Everyone else, including the captain of the Homicide Unit, just turned a blind eye to Hawkins' doings.

Guilt actually filled Patrick as he learned that he had gotten the job at the expense of someone else. Their hard work and possible dreams were erased, just like that, because Jonathan Hawkins willed it. He wanted the job, but not like that. His guilt would have to wait until later, though.

"But once you were on board, kid," Hawkins continued. "I needed to see if you had what it took. I needed to see you in action. There was only one way to do that."

To murder, and massacre innocent people.

Hawkins didn't say that part, though, because that sick monster didn't see it that way.

"So this was a test…" Patrick said; summed up. "It looks like I passed."

"This," Hawkins said; gesturing his gun back and forth between he and Patrick. "This wasn't supposed to be part of the plan. The Long Island Surgeon, or whatever you want to call him, was never supposed to be found. I was fine retiring with one blemish on my record. The murders would have stopped, and he would've gone down in history just like Jack the Ripper or the Zodiac Killer; never discovered. Then things went bad with Julianne Frankles, and now here we are."

"You're psychotic," Patrick said. Hawkins was actually speaking as if he and the Long Island Surgeon weren't the same person.

"Watch your tongue, boy," Hawkins warned.

Anyone in the right state of mind could see that Hawkins was psychotic… except for Hawkins. He thought he was as right as rain. He truly believed what he did was for some greater good. He was making sure Patrick could continue the quality police work that he had done over the long years of service. So, clearly being called psychotic, when he was doing something so genuine and good, was something that bothered him. It was a button he didn't like pressed. So Patrick knew it was exactly what he needed to do. It was time for the next part of his plan to go in to action, and he knew exactly how to get the ball rolling.

"I wasn't too far off," Patrick said. "Was I?"

"What the hell are you talking about?"

"Maybe that's why you were so bothered by me mentioning it. Carl said it had to do with your last partner, and how he pretty much cheated his way out of a murder conviction, but maybe it really got to you, because you knew it was the truth."

Patrick remembered back to that day, only a few weeks ago, when he suggested to his two partners that the Long Island Surgeon picked his victims because they were happy with their lives. He remembered how quickly Hawkins had been to dismiss the theory; as if it was the most preposterous theory ever formulated. He remembered how crude and unprofessional he had been about it, too. Carl had told Patrick later on that it was because of what had happened with Hawkins' old partner, and that may have been true on some levels, but now, with the truth exposed, he realized that Hawkins had acted the way he did, because he was the one being talked about. He was the psychopath being accused of hating all the beautiful things in the world. Every word Patrick had spoken of the Long Island Surgeon had been directed right at Jonathan Hawkins.

"Kid, you're really asking for a bullet in the brain. I suggest you bite your tongue now, before I rip it out of your damn mouth."

Patrick could see the anger building up inside Hawkins coming to the surface. It was in his face. He truly believed that everything he had done was for a greater good; to assure the man taking up the reigns was worthy enough to be called Jonathan Hawkins predecessor. So the fact that

Patrick, out loud, was calling him a psychopath was not going over well.

But, then again, what psychopath is actually aware they are insane?

To them, they are probably more normal than the people calling them psychotic.

Patrick knew though that Hawkins' threats were empty ones. There would be no bullets in the head, and he was certainly not going to rip Patrick's tongue out. There were questions Hawkins needed answers to, and he wouldn't end Patrick's existence until he got those answers.

As long as Patrick withheld the information Hawkins desired so badly, he would remain alive.

He needed Hawkins madder, though. He needed to continue pushing Hawkins towards his breaking point.

"You didn't like the truth, did you?" Patrick continued; ignoring the empty threats. "I can see it in your face now—the anger—but what are you angry at; me for calling you psychotic when you don't think you are, or are you mad at yourself, because you realized that you are completely bat shit loco."

"Shut the fuck up!"

Patrick saw that he wanted so badly to pull that trigger, and end Patrick right there and then, but he couldn't.

Despite his fury, Hawkins couldn't put one between Patrick's eyes.

"Because, no matter what you tell yourself, you are completely crazy. You're a complete lunatic. Whatever humanity you've ever had is gone, because you're nothing but a monster." He then realized what he needed to say to get Hawkins precisely where he wanted him. "You had a human side once—I truly believe that—but it's gone, because all the things you have ever loved have been taken from you."

"Shut your mouth!" Hawkins voice wavered in its previous sternness. There was a shakiness to it now.

"Look at the people you killed, Hawkins; an elderly married couple, who had spent their entire adult lives together. They raised a family… they had grandkids. You lost your wife to cancer. You never got to have what the Ramsey's had, so you murdered them, because they had happiness.

"Then you murdered a pregnant woman. You and your wife couldn't have children. You never got to feel what it's like to become a father. So you take away not only her life, but you make her watch as you open her up, and took out her unborn child; just so she knew, before she died, her child had no chance."

"I can't believe you're the one calling me crazy, kid! You're the one with the obvious death wish." Hawkins hand in which he held his firearm was actually beginning to shake. Patrick needed to keep the momentum rolling.

"And then you massacred Julianne Frankles, and it wasn't because she caused you so much grief by ruining your plans. She had worked so hard in school to get where she wanted to be in her life, and she had such a passion for singing. You had just lost everything you had worked for over the years. Your true passion was ripped away from you when that doctor said you had a heart condition that would force you in to retirement. So what did you do? You projected that hatred on to Julianne Frankles."

He knew what his closer was going to be before he even started his speech. He had delivered the cold hard truth, and now it was time to finish this step of his plan.

"I never met your wife, and I truly am sorry she is dead—no one deserves to die from cancer—but that night at dinner you had talked about how you devoted your life to solving homicide crimes for her; in her memory, and all of this was for her; to keep what you were doing alive, even after you retired. Well, guess what, Hawkins; if your wife could see what you've become, and what you've done, she wouldn't be proud. She wouldn't even recognize the man she married. All she would see is someone filled with hatred. The only thing she would see in front of her was a monster."

That was when Hawkins shot Patrick.

CHAPTER 34

Patrick had always heard that the most painful place on the body to get shot was in the knee. He knew that Hawkins wouldn't shoot to kill, but he also knew that Hawkins would want him to be in pain, so he wasn't going to get a bullet in the thigh or shoulder. When he made the insane plan of getting shot, Patrick had expected the likelihood of it being in his knee near a hundred percent, so he was expecting a significant amount of pain.

However, when the bullet hit his patella; disintegrating bone, and shredding muscles, tendons and nerves, the pain he experienced was other worldly. He collapsed instantly; grabbing his knee, which was no longer there, and started screaming bloody murder. There weren't many residential areas near the Nassau Community College/Cradle of Aviation area, but his horrific screams in the cold dead of night would be waking up people towns miles away.

He thought he was going to pass out from the pain. It was nothing anyone, other than those who had felt it, could begin to comprehend. Blood was pouring from the wound; staining his pants and covering his hands in a crimson mess. In that moment, he regretted his plan. He regretted it more than anything. He wished for death, because then, and only then, would the pain stop.

Hawkins walked over, and put the gun right up to Patrick's temple. He wanted to pull away from it, but he was too disoriented from the raging pain coursing through his entire body to actually move.

"I'd stop that God awful screaming if I were you, kid," Hawkins suggested; pressing his firearm harder against Patrick's temple. "Otherwise, you're going to be silenced permanently."

Patrick clenched his jaw, and grit his teeth together as hard as he possibly could. He managed to reduce his blood curdling screaming to hard moans, and very heavy breathing. It wasn't fear of getting shot that made him quiet himself down. He still knew he was safe from death, even though he welcomed it over the pain he was feeling. He was afraid that the gun shot and the screaming would draw Adam Burton back over to the shutdown hangar. If that happened, his longtime friend would receive a single gunshot to the head; compliments of Hawkins.

Secondly, Patrick had a plan, and as much as he was thinking that parts of his plan—like getting shot in the knee—weren't as smart as he had thought them to be only moments earlier, he had to move forward with it.

"That's more like it," Hawkins said. "It hurts, kid; doesn't it? I've always heard horror stories about gunshot wounds to the knee." He looked at Patrick's destroyed knee, as if inspecting it. "Yup; you're definitely going to need a new knee cap."

He put his foot to Patrick's chest, and pushed him down to the floor. Patrick started to scream out in pain, but silenced himself the best he could. Hawkins dug his knee into his stomach; driving the air out of him. He then ripped open Patrick's shirt; followed by his undershirt. He inspected Patrick's torso.

Just as Patrick had expected him to.

"No wire, kid?" Hawkins said; legitimately surprised. "I'm disappointed in you. I thought you'd want my confession on tape."

"I don't give a shit about your confession," Patrick managed to say through his blinding pain, and frozen diaphragm.

"Oh, that's right; I'm not going to walk out of this alive. I almost forgot." His tone was almost comical.

He got up, and kicked Patrick's gun, which Patrick had dropped upon getting his knee cap blown off, across the floor.

"You can use your shirt to tie off your leg. I wouldn't want you to die on me... at least not yet."

Hawkins gave Patrick a few minutes to remove his shirts. The whole ordeal was a struggle. Every little move sent pain rushing throughout his entire body. Once he managed to remove the two articles of clothing, Patrick ripped them into shreds as best as he could, and tied them tight around his leg just above the wound; limiting the blood flow to his lower leg.

"Now that that's settled," Hawkins said, once he felt Patrick had patched up his knee enough. "Let me tell you how this is going to work. I have a few questions that need answering. You are going to answer them. Once you have, I'm going to put a bullet in your brain."

"How do you plan on justifying shooting me?" Patrick asked.

He may have had his plan, but Hawkins, undoubtedly, had one of his own. A man like Hawkins didn't just walk in to a situation like this without a strategic plan in place.

Hawkins did have a plan in place, and he unveiled it to Patrick with no problem.

He would tell everyone that he agreed to meet Patrick at the location Patrick had requested. Upon arrival, he would be accused of being the Long Island Surgeon, which, of course, would be the most insane allegation to everyone. They knew the tense history between Patrick and Hawkins, and they had seen the blowup in the locker room the day before. Hawkins would use that against Patrick to convince everyone of a grudge that got way out of hand.

Once accused, Hawkins would try to reason with Patrick, but his pleas would have fallen on deaf ears. Patrick would be incapable of being reasoned with. Eventually the altercation would have escalated far enough to where Hawkins felt he was in mortal danger, so after numerous attempts of getting Patrick to lower his weapon, he fired a round into Patrick's knee. Through all of the excruciating pain, Patrick would still make a desperate attempt to regain possession of his gun, which he had dropped when getting shot, to kill Hawkins. There would be no alternative left, but to deliver a fatal shot; killing Patrick Sullivan.

It was a well thought out plan, and it would work. They wouldn't question Hawkins too much about it. The history was there between the two, and with his reputation, not many would doubt the story.

"So, kid, tell me," Hawkins said; taking a seat comfortably on a crate. With Patrick wounded, he could let his guard down, and have a little fun. Thing was, Patrick was counting on that. "How did you figure me out?"

Patrick remained silent.

"You're only making it harder on yourself by not telling me what I want to know. You think it hurts having one knee cap blown off? Imagine what it might feel like if I shot you in the other. I would imagine it doesn't feel very good. If you continue this, I'm going to shoot you in the other leg."

"No," Patrick said. "If I tell you, then you know all you need to know, and then you kill me."

Hawkins let out a disappointed sigh at this answer, and started to get up.

"I really didn't want to have to do this, kid."

"I won't tell you what you *need* to know," Patrick cut in before Hawkins could inflict the damage he intended. "But I will tell you something you *want* to know."

Hawkins stopped from getting up, thought momentarily, and then sat back down. His gun remained pointed at Patrick's good knee.

"There is nothing else that I want to know from you, other than what I have asked for."

Even then, Patrick knew Hawkins was lying. He would've shot the gun already if he wasn't intrigued. The truth was, there was something else he was interested in knowing. He had asked Patrick about it during their scuffle in the locker room. Only then, Patrick was too infuriated to answer it—not that he would've, anyway. Now, he was willing to share his story, and enlighten Hawkins. He needed to buy himself some more time, and he needed to hold on to that last piece of information Hawkins desired. This would keep him occupied for the time being.

So Patrick mustered up all the energy he could to speak, and told Hawkins exactly what happened almost a year ago between him and Wallace 'Baby Tooth' Freewaters.

CHAPTER 35

When Patrick Sullivan and Baby Tooth first met, the infamous New York City drug dealer's face had been just like everyone else's; whole and without flaw. Before he could pulverize Wallace Freewaters' face on a Bronx street corner, there had been a whole sequence of events that drove Patrick to the event that would inevitably change his life forever.

Henry Meyers had been a friend of Patrick's throughout his entire tenure on the NYPD. They linked up on the first day of the academy, and had looked out for each other ever since. So when Henry got a promotion to detective in Narcotics, Patrick was ecstatic for his friend. He didn't know it then, while he was congratulating his friend, but it would be Henry and a tidbit of information that had managed to escape Patrick over the years that would lead him and Baby Tooth into each other's lives.

The Police Department is like a brotherhood in many ways. Cops look out for one another every way that they can. However, it was also a job, and, like all jobs, people want to get ahead, and do right by them and their families. One night, while the guys had just gotten off duty, and were out for some drinks and food, Patrick was approached by his friend. Henry had a few questions regarding a drug bust a few years back that had gone terribly wrong. One that involved Patrick shooting a pregnant woman named Vivian Chambers. He had no interest in the woman Patrick had to gun down in self-defense. She was just a small spec in a much larger picture to Henry Meyers. What he was more interested in was the details of the actual bust, and what had gone wrong with it. Patrick recalled it the best he could, and told Henry what he knew, which wasn't much; nothing he couldn't have gotten from the file on that particular bust. Still, Henry wanted to hear it from someone who had been there, and being him and Patrick were good buddies, he thought he'd ask his pal for a favor.

"Why are you so interested in that particular bust, anyways?" Patrick asked. He was asking just to be friendly more than he was out of curiosity. He hadn't thought about that day, or Vivian Chambers in a very long time, and he liked to keep it that way.

Henry was familiarizing himself with a case he had been thrown into. Narcotics, along with the FBI, had been working for years to try and bring down Wallace 'Baby Tooth' Freewaters. The drugs they were trying to gain possession of on that day had belonged to Baby Tooth. It was a storage hideout for his gang.

For whatever reason, that piece of information set something off in Patrick. Feelings that he hadn't felt in years began to resurface. They were feelings of guilt over Vivian Chambers, and her death. He could see her face after the bullet had entered her belly. He could see the sadness in her eyes. It wasn't anguish because she was dying, but that her unborn child was going to die, as well.

Patrick could feel himself becoming overwhelmed by emotions. He excused himself early, and left the bar. Instead of heading straight home, he wandered around the streets of Manhattan for an hour; thinking. He was feeling those old familiar—unwanted—feelings, but they were also different this time. Back then, before Claire had saved his life in more than one way, whenever he thought of gunning down that pregnant woman, he would blame himself. No matter what other way he tried to look at it, he was responsible for that woman's death.

That was then.

Now, Patrick Sullivan had someone else to blame for what happened. That man was Wallace Freewaters.

Patrick had pulled the trigger of the gun that killed Vivian Chambers, and he would always feel a sting of guilt about it, but that was part of the job. It was Baby Tooth who was to blame for her demise. Baby Tooth, even if he did not introduce her to that lifestyle, allowed Vivian Chambers to be part of it. He didn't care about her, or anyone who worked for him. All he cared about was his product, moving it, and making his money. Vivian Chambers was just another means of doing so. Who cares if she was a young women; throwing her entire future away? He sure didn't! Did he know her personally? Did he know she was pregnant? Did he even know she was dead? Patrick guessed not. He didn't know Baby Tooth (not yet), but he already knew that someone like Wallace Freewaters didn't give two shits or piss about anyone doing his dirty work.

Over the next few days, all Patrick could think about was Vivian Chambers, and how Baby Tooth was responsible for her ending. He became obsessed with this heartless individual, who, only days ago, he didn't even know existed. Even though he tried, he refused to let it go.

Something had to be done.

It had, once before, driven him to the point where he had barely gotten out, and although circumstances of his obsession on the matter were different now, he wouldn't let it eat away at him again. Not after he worked so hard the first time to overcome it. There was only one thing

THE REPLACEMENT

Patrick felt he needed to do to squash this overwhelming feeling.

He needed to confront Baby Tooth face-to-face.

The idea of that was completely absurd. For starters, he knew nothing about Baby Tooth, like where would he find him. That part was easy to get around if he talked to the right people. The real problem was getting close to Baby Tooth. This man was New York City's most powerful drug dealer. It wasn't like anyone, especially an Irish, white boy cop, could just walk up to him, and engage him in a conversation. His entourage was, without a doubt, going to be huge, and they were going to be dangerous.

Still, despite all the obvious warnings to why he should just let the subject rest, and stay away from Baby Tooth, Patrick decided he was going to look this man in the face, and let him know what he was responsible for.

Just as Henry Meyers had used him to try to gain information, Patrick returned the favor. It was really easy, actually. He just invited Henry out for dinner and drinks, and picked his brain as the alcohol loosened his friend up. He made it seem as if he was interested in how Henry's new position was going, and Henry, who was just excited about someone asking him about his new job, was eager to give out any details of Wallace Freewaters that Patrick inquired about.

In only a few hours, Patrick learned a great deal about the type of operation Baby Tooth ran, like how much drugs he actually pushes, how large his gang is, and, most importantly, where he usually hangs out and does his business.

Patrick had everything he needed; the information, and he even had a plan. He just needed to do it.

It's one thing to say you're going to confront a man who could potentially shoot you in the face, and would likely get away with it, but it is a completely different ballgame when it comes to actually doing it. You can plan all you want, but actually marching up to him, and speaking your mind… that took real guts.

One frigid city night in late January, Patrick found those guts, and went to the club Baby Tooth most often frequented at. Something in him just snapped. He had had enough of the conflict within his head, and he was ready to confront this uncaring monster of a man.

He walked up to the door of the club, completely ignoring the massive line of people waiting to get in, and was immediately denied entry. Even showing proof that he was a cop got him nothing but a crude snicker from the bouncer. He was merely told to shove it, and go somewhere else.

Patrick did agree to go somewhere else. He agreed he'd go somewhere quiet, and call in an anonymous tip to the NYPD that Wallace Freewaters, New York's biggest drug dealer, was in that club; doing business with the clientele. This remark got a stony death stare, which Patrick returned. He was daring the bouncer to call his bluff. It was never called. The bouncer folded. He moved the red rope aside, and let Patrick enter.

The club was packed to the brim with humanity. The air was thick with humidity, and reeked of booze and marijuana. The music was unbearably loud. On any other night, Patrick would want nothing more than to turn around, and get the hell out of there, but not tonight. He scanned the area, and found the VIP section. He knew that's where Baby Tooth would be. He squeezed his way through the tight crowd, which was a task of epic proportion onto itself. When he reached the VIP section, he completely ignored that it was roped off. Patrick ducked under the rope, and made it up two steps before he was abruptly halted by a behemoth of a man.

"Where the fuck you think you going?" this man asked; in a voice about five octaves deeper than the late Michael Clarke Duncan's.

"I'm here to speak to Baby Tooth," Patrick yelled over the music, which wasn't as loud in this section of the bar.

"Go fuck yourself," was the response he received.

Unwilling to give up so easily, Patrick tried to tell this mountainous human being that he was looking for some drugs, and knew Baby Tooth was the guy to go to if you wanted to score the good stuff. This didn't work. Again, he was told to fuck off. Only this time, it was met with a vice grip that was this man's fist around Patrick's shirt, as he was about to be physically removed from the VIP section.

"Brick House!" a voice call out. "Put the white boy down for a second."

The man, who apparently went by the name Brick House, which was more than suiting to his gigantic frame, released Patrick from his grip.

"He says he's looking to score, boss," Brick House called back; not taking his eyes off Patrick.

"Let him up!" The voice was pompous and obnoxious. "Who am I to deny a man my product?"

Brick House moved aside, and Patrick was allowed to pass, but not before he was frisked first. It didn't take long for Brick House to find Patrick's piece.

"He's packing, boss," Brick House called back to Baby Tooth.

"Did you take it from him?" Baby Tooth asked. When Brick House said that he did, Baby Tooth told him to let Patrick pass.

Patrick was, rather forcefully, led—shoved—into the heart of the VIP section by Wallace Freewaters' muscle. It was then that Patrick Sullivan met Baby Tooth for the first time. He sat back with his feet kicked up; relaxing across a couch that ran across the railing of the VIP section that overlooked the club. This way, the patrons could see that Baby Tooth was there, and ready to do business. He wore one of his infamously expensive suits, and he had a girl—both, doped out of their faces—on each arm; half conscious.

Baby Tooth was a guy without a single care in the world. It was right then that Patrick was glad his gun was taken away by Brick House, because he would've put a single bullet right between the drug dealer's eyes. No question about it.

"You'll have to forgive Brick House over there. He doesn't think with his brains. He just likes to fuck shit up," Baby Tooth said to his new guest.

His demeanor was unchanging. He didn't get up—didn't even budge—when Patrick arrived. He was completely indifferent to this stranger's sudden presence, even after knowing he had come with a firearm.

"So why is it you are here?" He asked; wanting to get right to the point. Clearly, Patrick was interrupting his night.

"Well," Patrick said; trying to portray nervousness as well as he possibly could. "I was looking to score some drugs."

To this, Baby Tooth burst out laughing. One of the women that had been lying on his arm jolted up out of her semi-consciousness to the sound of his outburst of amusement. She looked around; not really aware of anything she was looking at, and then lowered her head back down where she dozed back off immediately.

"Don't waste my fucking time," Baby Tooth said. "You ain't here for no drugs, nigga. That's for sure. I've been doing this shit long enough to know the type of white boys who are looking to score. You," He looked Patrick up and down; clearly amused by his appearance. "Are not one of them."

He slid up from where he was seated. Both girls collapsed onto the couch without even waking. He walked over to Patrick, and stared down at him; that smug look of amusement still on his face.

"Let's take a walk out back."

"I'd rather not," Patrick responded. He was beginning to think he was biting into something more than he could chew. He thought he had a pretty solid idea of what going out back meant, and he wanted nothing to do with it.

"I wasn't asking," Baby Tooth said very matter-of-factly. He motioned his head, and before Patrick knew it, Brick House had his vice grip clutch around Patrick's arm; leading him along.

Patrick was led out back to a sectioned off portion of the alleyway behind the bar. Here, VIP guests could hang out when the weather permitted, and enjoy a smoke (or a line) without a single bother. Right now, it was shut down and deserted. It was the heart of winter in New York City, and no one wanted to be hanging outside in the cold. They would have to do their lines in the bathroom, like everyone else that night.

Patrick was shoved through the door leading outside by Brick House. The force sent him stumbling forward, but he didn't fall flat on his face. He managed to keep his footing, and the dignity of not looking like an ass in front of these criminals. When he turned around, Baby Tooth was standing there; inches from his face.

"I'm going to ask this again," Baby Tooth said. There was no more patience in his voice. He was telling Patrick this was his last chance. "Why is it that you are here?"

Patrick still hesitated.

But why?

He had come there with the sole intention of confronting Baby Tooth. To let the cocky drug dealer know he had ruined so many lives with his illegal business. Yet, he couldn't seem to get the words out of his mouth. They were there; on the tip of his tongue, but they wouldn't slide off of it into the cold winter air for Baby Tooth to hear.

He took a deep breath, and mustered up the courage he needed to speak; not because of his desire to get the heavy burden of Vivian Chambers off his chest, but because he was actually becoming afraid of what might happen to him if Baby Tooth's patience actually did run out.

So Patrick found his nerves, and let it all spill out. He told Baby Tooth about the drug bust gone wrong, and how he was put in to the position where he was forced to shoot and kill Vivian Chambers. He told him how heavy the burden of killing that woman was; especially once he had learned she had been pregnant with child. He even went as far as to say how the guilt of it all consumed him to the point where he almost threw himself off a Brooklyn apartment building rooftop.

He said everything, and as he did, he felt that guilt he managed to suppress for so long beginning to rise off of him. He was passing it to someone else. The person who actually deserved to feel that crushing weight. The person whose fault this whole thing had been.

Only, when he was done, Baby Tooth didn't give a shit that Vivian Chambers was dead.

"Why the fuck are you wasting my valuable time by telling me this shit?" Baby Tooth asked once Patrick was finished saying what he needed to say.

"Because, I wanted you to know that what you do—the life you choose to involve yourself in—has an effect on other people's lives, and sometimes that effect is permanent. Vivian Chambers is the perfect example of that."

Baby Tooth, more than anything, seemed annoyed by what Patrick had to say.

"Let me get this straight... You shoot some bitch, and it's somehow my fault?"

"She was a member of your gang. You let her into that lifestyle. It was because of you that she was in that building on that day, and because she was there, she was shot and killed."

"She got shot, because the bitch was dumb enough to open fire on a mother fucking cop." Baby Tooth had heard what Patrick had to say, and now he had his own opinions on the subject to share. "That bitch—what was her name; Vivian?—she chose to do drugs, and hang out in that unsavory environment long before she came onboard my operation. Yeah; maybe if she grew up in a different house on a different street in a different state with different parents, things might have turned out different for her. You can say that about any mother fucker who wasn't dealt the perfect hand in life. She wasn't some perfect angel that I tricked and lured into my world, like some pervert with a van; offering her candy while holding his dick in his hand. She was probably getting high as a mother fucker since before she had titties, and once she got older, she decided she wanted to make some money. So she came to me. I didn't do shit to influence her decisions."

That was not the response Patrick was hoping to get. Did he just assume that because he felt an enormous amount of guilt for Vivian Chambers' death that Baby Tooth would too? Of course, he did. Why else would he be taking the chance in calling out New York City's top drug dealer?

But Baby Tooth didn't care.

In fact, his logic made perfect sense. Vivian Chambers wasn't a drug addict because of Baby Tooth. She was already a user, and the truth be told; she was more than likely the one who sought him out when she decided she wanted to get in to the drug dealing game.

Still, there were always two sides to every argument, and Patrick still believed strongly in his. He was determined to make Baby Tooth see that point of view before all was said and done.

"You may not have introduced her to it, but she could've gone the opposite way. She could have gotten out, and gotten help. She could have cleaned up, but, because people like you exist in this world—drug dealers—she went in the wrong direction. You didn't lure her in directly, but you might as well have."

Baby Tooth heard Patrick's words, and he may have even had a rebuttal, but if he did, sharing it wasn't worth his time. As far as Baby Tooth was concerned; the matter was dropped. He had said what he needed to say, and he was not interested in any counter arguments. He decided it was time to change the topic.

"What's your name?" He asked.

Patrick's insides froze up. He did not want his name brought into this. It was the absolute last thing he wanted. He had been so careful to not make any mention of it, and he had hoped the matter wouldn't come up. It did, though, and he needed to squash it fast. He could've given a fake name, and hoped Baby Tooth would believe him or just didn't truly care enough to push the matter, but, for reasons unbeknownst to Patrick, that wasn't his first instinct. Instead, he told Baby Tooth that his name wasn't important. This was not the response Wallace Freewaters was hoping for, because with one look, Brick House's wrecking ball sized fist was being planted into the small of Patrick's back.

A bolt of pain shot up Patrick's spine. His whole body went numb, his knees gave way, and he collapsed on the cold ground. He was unable to bring himself to move. That was until he felt Brick House's hand in his jean pocket; reaching for his wallet. He then made an attempt to struggle, but it was to no avail. Brick House held him down with ease as he removed the wallet from Patrick's back pocket, and tossed it to his boss.

"Let me give you some advice…" Baby Tooth flipped open Patrick's wallet, and examined his ID; reading the name printed on the piece of plastic. "Patrick Sullivan. If you're going to have a face-to-face with a gangster drug dealer, leave your wallet at home. You'd be shocked by what a nigga could learn about you just by your wallet."

Patrick couldn't believe how stupid he had been. Of course, it made perfect sense to leave his wallet at home. The thought hadn't even dawned on him once while plotting out his big plan to confront Baby Tooth.

"Let's see;" Baby Tooth said; going through the contents of the wallet. "I now know your name, and exactly where you live. That is definitely very important information. I also know you're a cop—well, I already knew that much, because you were stupid enough to bring your service pistol with you—and, look at that!"

Patrick saw Baby Tooth pull the picture out of his wallet, and made an attempt, without even thinking, to attack him. His attempt, however, was thwarted when Brick House's boot came crashing down into his spine; sending him back down to the pavement.

"Calm down there, Patty Boy," Baby Tooth said; not bothering to look up from the picture. "Don't like when other guys have their filthy eyes on your wife?" He pulled out a second picture in Patrick's wallet. "You have a son, too. Very cute. Looks nothing like your ugly ass."

He put the pictures back, and closed Patrick's wallet. He tossed the wallet down on the ground, approached Patrick, and knelt down in front of him.

"That really is a pretty wife you have there, Patty Boy. Let me be blunt; I'd like to climb on top of that."

He grinned, and, for the first time, Patrick saw that baby tooth that gave Wallace Freewaters his infamous nickname. Just like it would in his dreams for the next year, it taunted him, and Patrick wanted nothing more than to knock it out of Baby Tooth's face with his fist.

"Maybe since I know where you live, I'll go, and pay the Missus a visit. What do you think, Brick House?"

"I think it sounds like a great idea, boss."

Patrick felt his stomach twist and turn, then clench up tight. What had he done? His whole family was now in danger. All because he had to be selfish, and confront Baby Tooth.

And what did that get him?

Absolutely nothing.

Baby Tooth didn't give a damn about Vivian Chamber, her unborn child, or either of their deaths. He, without a doubt, grieved more for the drugs that had been lost in the fire that day than he did for the death of another human being.

"I don't think Patty Boy over here agrees with you. In fact, I'd bet all my money on that he thinks it is a terrible idea. Am I wrong, officer?"

Patrick remained silent.

"Of course I'm not wrong. No white boy likes the idea of some nigga fucking his wife; especially when that nigga is ten times more a man than he'll ever be. She might not like it at first—she'd feel wrong doing that to her loving and devoted husband—but it wouldn't take long before she warmed up to me. Next thing you know, she's begging for you to give it to her from behind, and let me tell you something, Patty Boy; I never say no when a bitch is begging to get it from the back. I'm always eager to please."

THE REPLACEMENT

Patrick had been too nervous to eat anything before his meeting with Wallace Freewaters. Now, he felt warm bile crawling up his esophagus into the back of his throat, but he refused to vomit. He was scared—more for his family than anything else—but he refused to let Baby Tooth or Brick House see how petrified he really was.

"But then your son might walk in from all the screaming your wife would be doing; thinking his mommy was being hurt," Baby Tooth continued; drawing out this painfully descriptive image. "And that would be so awkward. He wouldn't know who this strange man was, and what he was doing to his mommy! Don't worry though, Patty Boy, I'd be courteous enough to let her take a break so she could assure him it was okay, and she wasn't being hurt by that man. I'm not a cruel man. I don't like to see children cry. I promise you, though; once your son was back to sleep, she'd be right there again, in bed, on all four paws; begging Baby Tooth to finish off what he started."

Wallace Freewaters wasn't finished just yet. As if the image he was drawing out for Patrick wasn't sickening enough, what he said next was just to add insult to injury.

"You know; maybe I do know this Vivian bitch, after all. Come to think about it, I might. It is so very hard for a lady, especially a druggy whore, like the one you shot down, to resist Baby Tooth. Maybe I fucked her. Maybe that baby you killed when you shot her was mine. That could be very possible." He paused, as if he was heavily contemplating that possibility. "In that case, I should really be thanking you, Patty Boy. You helped me dodge that bullet by putting a bullet in that bitch's belly."

As Baby Tooth laughed at his own joke, Patrick made a move to attack him. That last remark had sent him over the edge. To not care about Vivian Chamber's death was one thing, but to make a mockery of it was something else entirely. He wasn't about to let Baby Tooth get away with being so disrespectful

Unfortunately, like he had already proven that night, Brick House not only had maddeningly absurd strength, but cat-like quick reflexes. Before Patrick could act, Brick House reacted; wrapping his arms tightly around Patrick. Baby Tooth took this opportunity to take a single cheap shot, and he made it count. He landed a jab right to Patrick's stomach. The wind left Patrick, and he fell to the ground the moment Brick House released him.

"I'm going to draw this out for you, so you better be listening real good, you got me?" Baby Tooth said; all sarcasm and joking were void of his tone. This was business. "I could kill you right here, and no one would even come at me for it. I could go after your family. I don't rape bitches, nor do I hurt children, but there are people— some poor ass, struggling niggas—in my gang who aren't as morally sound as I am. They'll fuck your wife, and pop your son just to get in my good graces. Luckily for you, I'm not going to do any of that. You or your family aren't worth my mother fucking time. You've already wasted enough of it here tonight. I get why you came down here, and I'll admit; it took some serious fucking balls to do it. I'll give you that much, but I'm also going to tell you straight to your pathetic face; I don't give a shit about Vivian Chambers, and the fact that she's dead. I certainly don't care how her death has impacted your life. She's not worth my fucking time, and she shouldn't be worth yours. Think about your own wellbeing, and think about your family before you come, and do something so selfishly stupid. Is some drugged up black bitch worth your family's safety? I don't think so, and you shouldn't either."

As far as Baby Tooth was concerned, the meeting was over. He turned away from Patrick, and headed back inside; out of the cold. Before he allowed the door to close shut behind him, he left Patrick with a few more words of advice.

"Before you leave, Brick House is going to have a little fun with you—don't worry; he won't be too rough with you—but consider this your warning. If I ever see your white ass again, or hear the name Vivian Chambers from your dumb fucking mouth, I won't be so kind and forgiving, and it's your family who is going to suffer first, then you. Think about that long and hard as Brick House is fucking you up a bit, Patty Boy."

With those words, the meeting was adjourned. Baby Tooth vanished back into the night club.

Patrick then felt what could only be a telephone pole come crashing down across his back. It was Brick House's arm delivering the first of many blows Baby Tooth had promised him.

When he woke the next morning, Claire was standing over him; asking him why he had slept on the couch. When he made the attempt to pull himself into sitting position, his entire body screamed out in agony. He ached all over. It felt like he had been in a car accident. No, a more accurate description would've been that it felt as if he had gotten into the car accident, had been ejected through the windshield, and was thrown full force into the unforgiving wall of a (brick) house.

Patrick decided to tell Claire he had drank more than he had wanted to while out with the guys the night before, and just passed out on the couch when he got in late. A hang over would also explain the obvious aching pain he was currently experiencing. Claire didn't question him. Why would she? Patrick had never lied to her before. All she did was tell him to lie in bed, where it was far more comfortable, and rest while she and Connor went to the park.

As he lowered himself down into the comforts of his mattress, Patrick felt a twinge of guilt for lying to Claire. They had always been so honest with each other throughout their entire relationship, but he had to this time. He couldn't tell his wife he had gotten in so late, because he was confronting a drug lord about a woman he had shot, and killed years ago. He couldn't tell her that he was in excruciating pain, because some behemoth of a man, whose name, as far as Patrick knew, was Brick House, had beaten down on him for a half hour before unceremoniously dumping him on the sidewalk outside of a New York City night club. The lie was the easier route, and it was also the safest. Claire didn't need to know about Baby Tooth. That issue was crushed. It was over and done. If it wasn't, Baby Tooth had promised dyer repercussions.

But it wasn't done.

It should have been, but it wasn't. As Patrick laid there in bed; attempting to recuperate from his thrashing, his mind kept going back and forth between the image of Vivian Chambers dying right in front of him, and the thought of how little Baby Tooth cared about her demise.

As these thoughts flooded his head, Patrick's anger kept ballooning; expanding within the confines of himself. He was reaching his breaking point, and, at any moment now, he felt he was going to lose control, and snap.

Sure, Baby Tooth may have been right on some points; it wasn't his fault that Vivian Chambers grew up with the wrong crowd, and got involved in the less savory aspects of life, but he wasn't entirely blame-free; as he claimed to be. His hands were still dirty; stained with the blood of Vivian Chambers and her unborn child. On top of all that, Baby Tooth had made threats against Patrick, and, more importantly, his family. That was just more coal being thrown into the furnace of Patrick Sullivan's rage.

Still, despite all this, he still should've put it all to rest, like Baby Tooth advised, but he couldn't. So he started to plan for his next face-to-face confrontation with Wallace Freewaters. Only now, Patrick knew the next time it wouldn't be as verbal as it had been the night before.

Throughout his entire tenure with the NYPD, Patrick Sullivan only needed to use one of his sick days, and that was for an extreme case of food poisoning. In the week following his first meeting with Wallace Freewaters, he had called out every day; claiming he had the flu, and just couldn't shake it. Claire had no idea her husband was doing this. As far as she knew, he was at work; doing his duty of protecting, and keeping safe the streets of New York City. The lies were now piling up.

In reality, Patrick was doing reconnaissance work on Baby Tooth. He spent that week learning Baby Tooth's movements. He needed to know what hangouts the drug dealer frequented at—hopefully, finding one that wasn't too high profile, like a nightclub. He needed to learn how many people Baby Tooth surrounded himself with at any given moment during the day. Most importantly, Patrick needed to find an opening for an opportunity. He needed Baby Tooth alone and vulnerable.

After days of keeping a safe distance; making sure he remained invisible while doing his recon, it seemed as if that single moment of solitude would never come. Baby Tooth was constantly surrounded by protection. Patrick wasn't the only person who wanted to cause serious harm to Wallace Freewaters. Brick House, amongst others, were there at all times to make sure no harm ever came to their boss.

Then, as the week wound down, and he was nearing the cusp of completely abandoning all hope of scoring himself a few minutes alone with Baby Tooth, Patrick spotted Brick House and three other guys leaving Baby Tooth's apartment building in the middle of the day. Only two hours prior, he had seen those exact men enter into the building with their boss. Now they were leaving, and Baby Tooth wasn't with them, which could only mean he was alone up in his apartment.

Or so Patrick had hoped.

The opportunity he had hoped for had finally presented itself. Baby Tooth was up there; by himself in his apartment. Only Patrick had not the slightest clue which apartment that was. He didn't even know which floor to start his search on. It wasn't like he could just start knocking on every door throughout the building until he found the one Wallace Freewaters resided at. For starters, an obviously middle class white guy knocking on random doors in an apartment building in the middle of one of New York's poorest areas might raise some suspicions amongst the residences. Patrick couldn't afford to have Baby Tooth tipped off in any way. The element of surprise was the key to his plan.

Also, even if Patrick knew which apartment unit was Baby Tooth's, the chances of the front door being conveniently unlocked for him to just mosey on in were highly unlikely. Baby Tooth may have felt comfortable enough to not have his muscle around him while he was at home, but there was no way he was dumb enough to not lock and deadbolt the front door.

All those obstacles were washed away twenty minutes after Brick House and the others had left the building.

Patrick couldn't believe his eyes. His imagination was, undoubtedly, playing tricks on him; manifesting what he so badly wanted to see. It couldn't be real. It was impossible.

Baby Tooth was walking out of his apartment building, and he was alone.

THE REPLACEMENT

Everything Patrick had hoped for had fallen perfectly into place. He had Baby Tooth exactly where he wanted him; alone and vulnerable. Looking back on it, and now knowing what the aftermath would be, he wished things had gone differently. Maybe he wished he had walked away moments before Baby Tooth came out of his apartment; when he first felt the urge to give up. Maybe he wished Baby Tooth had never come out of that building. Looking back, and dwelling over that year that followed, Patrick wished just one tiny thing had gone differently, but at that moment, the stars had aligned, and the wheels were now in motion.

Patrick Sullivan let obsession and anger carry him.

He clicked off the safety of his gun, and began to follow Wallace Freewaters.

For the first few hundred feet, he kept a very safe distance, as to not to be made, but when it became apparent Baby Tooth was oblivious to the fact he was being followed, Patrick hastened his pace, and closed the gap between the two of them. Even as he drew nearer, he could feel the burden of Vivian Chambers lifting off his shoulders, where it weighed heavily for so long. Soon it would all be over. Soon Baby Tooth would take the ultimate responsibility for being so callous with a bullet to the back of his head.

Patrick drew his firearm, but when it came time to raise it, and fire the deadly shot; he froze.

Just as he was about to end the life of Wallace Freewaters, Patrick thought about how this all began… with a gunshot. It was a fatal bullet wound to Vivian Chambers which served as the catalyst for all this. Yes, Baby Tooth had played an integral part in all of it, but it was still Patrick who had taken a human life, and he was about to do it again. Only this time, it would be in cold blood. He could rationalize Vivian Chambers, and boil it down to self-defense, but if he did this, there would be no other way he could see it other than revenge.

Patrick Sullivan could not bear the burden of taking yet another life; even the likes of Wallace 'Baby Tooth' Freewaters. He would not raise his gun, and pull the trigger.

Still, it wasn't enough to fully quell his anger. Sometimes fury builds up too much momentum that no conscience is strong enough to stop it fully.

He pulled the gun from the waist of his pants, and gripped it by its barrel, instead of its handle. He closed the small gap between the two, and called out Baby Tooth's name.

When Wallace Freewaters turned around; acknowledging the voice that had beckoned him, Patrick briefly wondered if he even recognized the young man standing behind him. Did he even have an idea of what was about to come?

Patrick never bothered to find out. Instead of putting a bullet through the skull, and into the soft brain of Wallace Freewaters, Patrick buried the butt of his gun in Baby Tooth's cranium.

Upon the first blow of metal and skull, Patrick felt the impact of thick skull cracking shoot up his arm like vibrations through a tuning fork. He immediately felt sick, and thought he would vomit, but it wasn't enough to stop him.

Baby Tooth collapsed to the ground; defenseless, and Patrick was bearing down on him once again; landing another blow with his gun. This time it was Baby Tooth's temple shattering under the weight of impact. There was a third and fourth blow; Patrick knew that much, but after that, he lost count.

People around him were screaming, but he could not hear them. Abhorrence encapsulated him, and all he knew was causing damage to Baby Tooth; making him pay for, and regret being the heartless drug lord he was.

At some point during his attack, someone must have been wise enough to call the police, because one moment Patrick was landing blows into the skull and face of Baby Tooth, and the next he was getting pulled off him by a police officer.

As he was being yanked away from the man he was bludgeoning, Patrick began to yell to whoever was pulling at him that he was a cop. He wasn't exactly sure what he would accomplish by doing this. It wasn't like they would let him go, and continue doing what he was doing.

However, whatever the reason he had for informing the police officer restraining him, and every other person standing nearby, that he was a cop, it kept Patrick out of cuffs, and a formal arrest.

Instead, he was tossed into the back of a squad car, and the door was slammed shut behind him.

As he began to come out of his haze of hatred in the backseat of the car, Patrick heard more sirens approaching; both, police and ambulance. He looked down at the man lying face down on the sidewalk in a puddle of his own blood and broken teeth (none of which was a baby tooth).

Had Patrick killed him?

He had stopped himself just moments ago from shooting Baby Tooth in order to prevent himself from taking another human life, and now he might have done it, anyways. He didn't care, though. He was glad. He was relieved. He wasn't thinking about whether or not Baby Tooth would live to see another day.

Patrick Sullivan just wondered if now, as he fought for his life—if he wasn't already dead—Baby Tooth felt any guilt or remorse for the role he had played in Vivian Chambers' demise.

CHAPTER 36

"Here's what I don't get," Hawkins said once Patrick was through telling his tale of how he bashed in Baby's Tooth's face on a city street corner "How the hell did you manage to stay out of prison after you beat somebody to death?"

Throughout his story, Patrick had managed to compose himself enough to speak coherently, instead of through gritted teeth, and heavy moans of agony, but the truth was his knee was still roaring with pain as excruciating as the moment the bullet blew apart his kneecap He was beginning to feel lightheaded and dizzy. There was a good chance he was going to pass out from the pain, not to mention the heavy amount of blood he had lost.

Patrick realized he needed to speed things along to the ending stages of his plan before he lost consciousness, but there was still one more piece of information he needed from Hawkins. He couldn't just switch the topic of conversation while he was still in the middle of another. Hawkins would catch on, and know something was up. Patrick needed to remain calm, and let it all play out.

"I was never actually arrested for anything," Patrick said; applying pressure to his knee in an attempt to slow down the blood loss. "I think that had a lot to do with the fact I wasn't the one who had killed Baby Tooth."

Baby Tooth had survived Patrick's assault. Doctors had managed to stabilize him, and save his life at the hospital, but the amount of brain damage the pistol whipping had inflicted was unclear. The doctors weren't certain if Baby Tooth would ever regain consciousness.

Those questions would never be answered. Two days after his lashing, Baby Tooth was murdered in his hospital bed by one of the men who had, only days before, called him boss.

Unbeknownst to anyone other than an elite few, there were moves being made within Baby Tooth's gang to take out the drug lord. Some felt Wallace Freewaters had too much power, and received too much credit for the drugs being trafficked throughout New York City. Most importantly, they felt Baby Tooth was making too much money. They thought if they took control of the gang by removing Baby Tooth entirely, they could share power equally. Thus bringing them in more money than they had been making with the current regime.

This would inevitably lead to the downfall of Baby Tooth's once flourishing illegal business, because egos sometimes can't be controlled, and the new bosses did not see eye-to-eye on some matters—namely, money—causing unamendable rifts.

What was once New York City's largest drug trafficking gang was broken down, and sectioned off; making them much easier targets to be picked apart and dismantled by the NYPD.

"They had grand plans to kill him," Patrick told Hawkins. "They just didn't have an opportunity yet. I, apparently, gave them one. In the end, we helped each other out; I gave them what they needed, and they kept my ass out of prison."

The details of the pistol whipping were never fully released by the NYPD, so the general public were unaware of the fact that it had been a police officer who had done the deed. There were some eye-witness reports that it had been a cop who assaulted Baby Tooth with a deadly weapon—likely those who heard Patrick yelling that he was a cop as he was being pulled off of Baby Tooth—but those were confirmed by the NYPD as absolutely false.

When Baby Tooth was murdered by his own men two days after his attack, the NYPD found their scapegoat, and quickly turned the story as the first attack being a failed attempt to take Baby Tooth's life, and the attack in the hospital were his men finishing what they had started.

"The FBI wanted my head, regardless." Patrick continued. "They had been building a case against Baby Tooth for years, and, just like that, I ruined everything. All their valuable time and money poured into taking him down was a huge waste. They didn't give a shit about the NYPD's reputation to the public. They wanted to burn my ass to the ground."

Luckily for Patrick, the NYPD was adamant about Baby Tooth's former gang taking the fall for his attack and demise over one of their own. They remained steadfast—not for Patrick's sake, but their own—and eventually managed to convince the FBI to let the fabrication stay as it was.

Still, just because he was dodging the bullet, and avoiding an arrest, trial, conviction, and jail time, it didn't mean there wouldn't be serious repercussions for Patrick's actions.

"They demanded my resignation from the force, and it wasn't a decision I could fight. The alternative was I end up in jail for assault in the first degree. So in the end, I got lucky."

"Did you though?" Hawkins asked Patrick. "Do you really consider yourself lucky, kid? Sure, you avoided jail time, but look at where you are right now because of all that. You have a gaping hole in your leg where your kneecap used to be, and you're minutes away from getting your brains blown out. I wouldn't really consider any of that as being lucky. No matter what road you chose, in the end, you lose everything. And for what? What was the payoff? You almost went to jail, but instead you put your family in extreme financial peril, because of your obsession with Wallace Freewaters. Now, you're about to leave your wife a widow at the age of thirty-one and your toddler son fatherless, all because, again, you just couldn't let it go. You couldn't let sleeping dogs lie. Everything went according to plan... Gary Kaste took the fall, like he was supposed to, and the case was closed. You had to go, and change the plans. Now look at you!"

"It doesn't matter. It wasn't the truth. You killed all those people... you! Not Gary Kaste. You did it! You're the Long Island Surgeon. You played everyone, including your longtime partner and friend, for complete fools. I just couldn't let you walk away."

"Well I hope it was worth it, kid. I really do."

"What I don't get," Patrick said; taking what he felt was a safe opening to change the subject. "Is how did you get Gary Kaste's semen to plant on the children."

A smug grin stretched across Hawkins' face. He was admiring his own brilliance.

"That one stumping ya, kid? Even I have to admit; if I hadn't been the one who came up with it, I probably wouldn't have even been able to figure it out." Hawkins took a moment to himself; debating whether or not he wanted to tell Patrick his big secret. "I'll tell you what... I'll tell you what you want to know, but you have to tell me how you figured me out."

"You tell me first, then you'll learn everything you want to know."

"Do I need to remind you that you're not exactly in the position to be calling the shots, kid?" Hawkins pointed his gun at Patrick's knee.

"I'm not saying anything until you tell me what I want to know. You can shoot me in the other leg—go ahead—but you still won't get a single God damn word out of me. You can torture me with whatever sick method you concoct with that disturbed mind of yours. Yeah, it will hurt beyond words, and I'll scream, and I'll want you to stop; you might even get me to beg for it to end, but the one thing you won't get out of me is what you want to hear.

"There is not a single thing you can do to me that will get me to spill that information. You'll be left with no choice, but to kill me, and then your answer dies with me. You'll never know how I figured out that you were a fucking disgrace to the human race. You'll spend the rest of your miserable existence wondering how, and you will never ever know. So if I was you, I'd put your ego aside, quit playing big shot, and tell me what I want to know."

"This is exactly why I wanted you as my replacement, kid. You know what you want, and you know what needs to be done to get it. Most importantly, though, you're willing to do whatever it takes; no matter what the cost. Sadly for you, the cost for all this is going to be your life."

"Then let me to go out with peace of mind."

Hawkins thought it over for a few moments. He then lowered his weapon, and leaned in towards Patrick. He spoke in a hushed tone; as if there had been someone nearby who might have overheard the brilliant secret he was about to let Patrick in on.

"You'd be surprised what a desperate hooker is willing to do for an extra few hundred bucks."

And there, Patrick had his answer.

Hawkins sat back up; relaxed, as if they were two friends simply shooting the shit, and boastfully explained his brilliant plan to frame Gary Kaste for the horrific crimes he had committed.

First, he found a hooker. That part was easy enough—Hawkins knew all the spots on, both, Long Island and Manhattan where prostitutes conducted their business. Once found, the young lady would take the trip upstate. There, she would position herself at the rundown dive bar that Gary Kaste often frequented at, and would wait for him to arrive to drink away the demons of his pathetic life. Part one of the job, in which she was getting paid handsomely for, was to come on to Gary Kaste once he had a few in him. She was to make him believe she was interested in him, and then, after sharing a few more drinks together, lure him back to a local motel.

This would be the easy part. Hawkins joked that he feared Kaste might get so excited over the fact a female was actually coming onto him, he would bust his nut right there in the bar; thus ruining the plan.

What came next would be the hard, and certainly the strangest, part of the plan. It was what would earn the young prostitute a hefty cash bonus once completed.

Once she got Gary Kaste back to the motel, she had strict instructions from Hawkins not to engage him in sexual intercourse. Oral sex was also a no-no. Hawkins had instructed the young lady, as he put it so eloquently while walking Patrick through his plan, that she could only get Kaste off using her hands.

"Essentially, an easy night's work for the hooker," Hawkins joked. "And you know Kaste wasn't going to argue. The sick bastard was going to take whatever he could get. In fact, I'm willing to bet he was glad he didn't have to fuck her. He probably had his eyes closed the entire time, and imagined it was a seven year old boy tugging at his dick, instead of that woman. That's what probably got him off."

Whether Hawkins was right or not, the plan worked. Gary Kaste took whatever the hooker offered him with zero argument.

But the plan wasn't complete just yet.

Once finished, the hooker was instructed get as much of Kaste's ejaculate onto her hand as possible, and then excuse herself to the bathroom to 'clean up'. Once in the bathroom, she would deposit the semen from her hand into a vile that Hawkins had supplied her with. She would meet Hawkins later that night to deliver the sample, and collect her payment.

"It's too bad she'll never get to use the money she worked so hard to earn," Hawkins told Patrick.

And just like that, Patrick thought. *Another victim added to his list.*

Of course she would have to die. She was an extreme liability.

Sure, Hawkins' money had bought her silence along with her services, but she would see the news or read the papers. She would see Kaste's face plastered everywhere once word got out that the Long Island Surgeon had been identified and killed. She would also see the detective who shot him down. She would hear about the dead kids, and the semen samples left behind at the scene. She would put two and two together. She may not have been able to figure out Hawkins as the real Long Island Surgeon, but she would definitely figure out that Gary Kaste had been framed.

Still, that didn't mean she would go to the police. After all, it wasn't her business to get involved with, or maybe she just wouldn't care enough to bring to the attention of the police. That was until it worked in her benefit.

Who was to say that one night she wouldn't find herself arrested for hooking or drug possession, or whatever reason she might end up in the custody of the police for?

She could easily use that information about the detective hiring her to collect the semen of the man that everyone thought was the Long Island Surgeon to help get herself out of trouble. Hawkins definitely couldn't risk that. She was a loose end, just as Julianne Frankles surviving her attack was, that needed to be taken care of.

Of course, Hawkins viewed it simply as collateral damage in his quest to groom the perfect replacement.

In reality, it was him covering his own ass.

"Okay, kid." The expression on Hawkins' face turned somber, and the tone of his voice became solemn. The gun he held was now, once again, pointed at Patrick. "We did things your way, and you got to hear the story about the pretty hooker and the pathetic sex offender, but now it's time for you hold up your end of the bargain. Now, spill the beans."

Patrick didn't need to tell Hawkins a single thing. He had bought himself all the time he needed, but he wanted Hawkins to know exactly how he had bested him at what Hawkins thought he was perfect at.

"Those ridiculously overpriced shirts you're constantly wearing…" Patrick gestured at the shirt Hawkins currently had on. "When we got to the hospital after you murdered Julianne Frankles, you were wearing a different shirt than you had been before we left. At the time, I figured you had just changed into fresh clothing when you stopped off at home. What really happened was you forgot to take your shirt off when you slaughtered that poor girl and the five innocent people who stood between the two of you. A pricey shirt like that wouldn't have fit with the rest of the clothing we found in that shed outside of Gary Kaste's trailer home, so you needed to dispose of it. What you failed to do after you thought you destroyed all the evidence was check the tee-shirt you wore for any fibers. A loose thread from your shirt got caught on it. The moment I saw it, I knew it came from the shirt you were wearing that night."

"Thread," Hawkins snickered. He was certainly amused by the whole thing. "A piece of fucking thread. I'll give it to you, kid... I knew you were good, but damn; that's impressive"

"It wasn't just the thread..."

Like the color from a person's face when they suddenly find themselves sick and about to upchuck, all the humor drained from Hawkins' face. It was replaced with a look of shock and disbelief. Patrick felt a twinge of pleasure course through his body at the site of that look.

He let his words linger there for a moment in the still cold night. Jonathan Hawkins—the Long Island Surgeon—a man who was infamous for his attention to the fine details, had made, not only one, but *two* mistakes. It was obvious he was thunderstruck by that notion. Patrick knew, as he waited out that silence to finally decide to speak again, Hawkins was racking his brain over what else he could have possibly done wrong. The silence must have been driving him crazy. Despite the severe pain emanating from his destroyed kneecap, Patrick savored that moment.

"Don't beat yourself up too much over it," Patrick finally said, once he decided it was time to move along. "Anyone else would've paid no mind to it—I'm not even sure you would've thought it of any real importance, in any other case—but for me, it was the clincher."

"Care to share your brilliant find then, kid? After all, you seem so proud of yourself."

Patrick only smiled, in response.

Hawkins knew Patrick was playing with him. Taunting him. He swallowed deep; forcing his anger back down inside of him. Undoubtedly, he wanted to empty the contents of his gun into Patrick's chest, but he wouldn't.

Not just yet. Not before he learned what his second mistake had been.

"You spilled your coffee on yourself."

The look that Jonathan Hawkins now bore was the one of realization.

Ever since Thanksgiving, and their stop at 7-11 on the way to Evangeline Carpenter's apartment, Patrick could smell the rich aroma of hazelnut coming from Hawkins' cup of coffee every time he had one.

As Christmas neared, Hawkins traded up his hazelnut flavored creamer for a pungent, more festive peppermint flavored one. This switch was right around the time the fragile relationship between the two began to deteriorate. Every time Patrick smelled that overwhelming scent of peppermint, whether coming from a cup of coffee or from some other source, he associated it with Hawkins, and he associated Hawkins with rage and hatred.

So when Patrick brought the shirt up to his nose, and smelled the faint scent of coffee mixed with peppermint, he knew for sure Hawkins was the man they had been chasing for over a month.

"You must have been nervous," Patrick continued. "With everything potentially falling apart right in front of your eyes, you needed that cup of coffee to calm your nerves, and you needed to load it up with that creamer crap you always put in your coffee. Then you went, and spilled it on yourself. You had no time to go home and change. Anyway, what's the point? Who's going to take notice of a coffee stain on a shirt, and think anything of it? Well, I did."

"And because of it," Hawkins interrupted to finish Patrick's thought. "You were able to figure out the great mystery of the true identity of the Long Island Surgeon. Only now, it cost you your life."

"And now you know you aren't as perfect as you or anyone else thinks. On top of being completely psychotic, you're as clumsy and careless as any other piece of garbage murderer you've chased throughout your career."

The next thing Patrick felt was Hawkins knuckles connecting dead in the temple. Everything went momentarily blinding white, and when it faded, Patrick was laying on the floor.

"Get up," Hawkins instructed. His gun pointed at Patrick.

Patrick, with his head now throbbing, obeyed.

"You got lucky, kid," Hawkins clarified. "Plain, run-of-the-mill luck. You found nothing substantial that could hold up in a court of law. Had you pursued that route, you would have jack shit to tie me to those murders. If you didn't hate me so much, you would have dismissed both those things, just like anyone else would have. That doesn't make you a good detective. Like I said… it makes you lucky. And right now, your luck has completely run out."

He stepped towards Patrick, so that he was at point blank range.

"Hope it was worth it, kid. Any last words?"

Patrick remained silent.

"So be it, then. It doesn't matter what you have to say. The only thing you're going to be remembered for is a guy who cracked, and got himself killed. Hope Claire's proud of you, regardless."

I hope so, too, Patrick thought, then closed his eyes, and waited.

The next thing he heard, for the second time on that cold Christmas morning, was the sound of a gunshot.

Only this time, it would be a fatal shot.

CHAPTER 37

In the split second it takes for a bullet to be fired from a gun, travel from point A to point B, tear through flesh and muscle, pierce and destroy vital organs, and finally lodge itself in either bone or a nearby wall, Detective Patrick Sullivan's entire plan replayed before him.

It had gone down exactly as planned, and without flaw.

He knew the first thing Hawkins would do after blowing off his replacement's kneecap was disarm him. He also knew he would search Patrick for a wire. Even before arriving, Hawkins, undoubtedly, knew that whatever evidence—if there was any at all—linking him to the Long Island Surgeon murders wouldn't be enough to book him, let alone hold up in court to convict him. What Patrick needed was a confession, and he needed a recording of it. Patrick, liking to think he was one step ahead of Hawkins, now, was smart enough to not wire himself up for a taped confession.

Patrick, however, had high hopes that he had managed to rile up Hawkins enough so that the veteran cop would fail to do a search for any additional weapons. If he had remembered, he would have found a revolver .38 strapped to Patrick's calf.

As he slowly fed Hawkins all the information he desperately desired, Patrick used his obliterated kneecap as an excuse to have a constant grip on his leg. While keeping Hawkins distracted, Patrick was able to unholster the revolver, and slowly slide it down his leg.

Although the punch to the face wasn't part of the grand plan, it provided Patrick with the opening he needed. As he slowly got back to his knees, he slid the gun from his pants; making sure he angled himself perfectly, so that his right arm was kept slightly behind him, and out of Hawkins' site.

Hawkins planned to execute Patrick at point blank range, so aim wasn't much of a concern. All that was left to do was for Patrick to lift his arm, and fire.

And that's exactly what he did.

He didn't remember the exact act of pulling the trigger, but he heard the sound, and felt the kickback of the gun being fired, followed by the crashing sound.

Hawkins had gone down.

Patrick didn't react; at least not yet. He waited there, eyes still closed, for a few moments. A few precious moments where he allowed the sensation of peace to roll over, and engulf him. He had done what he had come there to do; what needed to be done. Before he would open his eyes and return to reality, he was going to enjoy the feeling of a few seconds of serenity.

Once the moment had passed, Patrick opened his eyes.

Detective Jonathan Hawkins laid sprawled in the mess of broken crates he had crashed down into after being shot at point blank range. He was pushing down on his stomach, where the bullet had entered; trying hopelessly to stop the bleeding, but there would be no stopping it, and he was well aware of that. A crimson geyser poured from his wound; covering his hands and torso with blood. Patrick knew—as Hawkins surely did—that it wouldn't be long.

Unable to stand, Patrick pulled himself across the floor to where Hawkins lied; dying. He felt lightheaded. He knew he was losing a lot of blood, and he was losing it quickly. What he needed was a hospital, and he needed it sooner than later, but not yet.

He swept Hawkins' gun away as a precautionary measure. Hawkins wouldn't try to take Patrick with him to the other side. It was over, and Hawkins knew that.

"You have the whole thing recorded…" Hawkins started to say. He coughed, and what came up was a cupful of blood. Still, he tried to speak through his dying. "Don't you?"

"I do."

On one of the quiet days preceding the morning that five children the Long Island Surgeon had strangled to death were discovered in a Kindergarten classroom, Patrick had his iPhone upgraded to the most recent model. It was to be an early Christmas gift from Claire. When he got into his car following his new purchase, he tossed his older model phone into the glove compartment. He opted out of trading in his last phone for a reasonable credit just in case the newer model went down, and he needed a backup while his phone was getting fixed.

Only he had forgot about it, and it stayed in his glove compartment. This turned out to be a blessing in disguise. The phone, despite being a little slow, worked perfectly. There was not a single thing wrong with it. So Patrick charged the phone to full battery, and brought it with him. When Hawkins arrived, he hid the phone, but not before opening up the voice memo application, and hitting record. He didn't need to wear the wire he knew Hawkins would search for. He was going to get the whole thing recorded, anyway.

Hawkins was impressed by this. Even when dying, the man had an appreciation for good police work.

When he tried to speak, all that came out was a painful groan followed by some more blood. So they sat in silence, instead. Just waiting. Patrick wondered in that moment if Hawkins regretted what he did, or if he still believed he did it for the greater good. He would never know. Even if Hawkins would own up to it in his final moments, he was in no condition to do so.

Patrick noticed, after about a minute, Hawkins staring off; fixating on something. He followed his gaze to outside one of the huge hangar windows.

There, stood a tall street lamp right, and in the light of the lamp, Patrick saw snow falling. Huge flakes of rapid snowfall were falling to the earth. He had no doubt that in a few hours Long Island would be covered in a blanket of snow.

"Merry Christmas, Patrick," Hawkins managed to get out; using all the energy he had left in him.

"Merry Christmas, Ace."

Those were the last words the two ever spoke to each other while both of them were alive.

It didn't take long after that.

Patrick waited; staring out the window at the beautiful snowfall. He was also battling with his consciousness. He knew he should call for help, but he needed to wait for it to be over. He couldn't risk Hawkins being alive when they got there. Hawkins didn't deserve life, and Patrick was going to make sure he got exactly what he deserved.

His breathing was rapid at first as he fought to stay alive, despite the fact he was bleeding out. The body's natural defense against appending death is to survive, but eventually, like Hawkins, his body accepted defeated.

His breathing slowed. His breaths were short and shallow, and Patrick could hear each and every one of them pounding in his ear like a timer counting down until there was no more.

Then there was just silence.

THE REPLACEMENT

Jonathan Hawkins; the greatest homicide detective any police department had ever seen... the Long Island Surgeon; the most monstrous serial killer the world had ever seen... was dead.

Part III

One Year Later

CHAPTER 38

A lot can happen in a single year.

Some of us might meet, start dating and fall in love, while others grow apart and break up. Some might get engaged, plan their dream wedding and get married, while some might realize there's nothing left to fight for and get divorced. We welcome new additions to our families, and we say our final goodbyes to some. Some of us might graduate high school or college. Some of us might get that dream job or that big promotion with the hefty raise. Some of us discover our passions, and others realize their dreams. There's an endless list of things that can happen to a person over the course of a single calendar year, but none of those things meant anything to Patrick Sullivan.

The only thing Patrick Sullivan knew were ghosts.

He drove westbound along the winding single lane of Northern Boulevard, also known as Route 25A. The temperatures that morning were frigate, and Patrick doubted it would get much warmer as the day progressed. Mother Nature had seemed to be making up for lost time from the freakishly warm weather the year before, as it was only Christmas Eve, and Long Island had already seen four major snow storms. Patrick hated the cold—he couldn't find love in many things these days—because it would bother his surgically repaired knee.

The doctor's had managed to save Patrick's leg after he had suffered a gunshot wound to the knee. He had lost a lot of blood, and if he had not been found when he was, his leg would have been a lost cause. In fact, any longer, and Patrick Sullivan would have bled out and died.

He was found by Adam Burton, who heard that second gunshot that night, and rushed to the aid of his childhood friend; hoping he'd finally be able to play the part of hero that had alluded him his entire life. When Adam arrived at the old airplane hangar, he couldn't believe his eyes.

Two men lay there, one was a man he known his entire life, and the other was a middle aged male he had never met before. Both men were covered in blood. The front of the stranger's shirt was saturated in blood. All the color had been drained from his skin, and his eyes had an empty stare to them. He was dead. Patrick also lacked any color and, at first, Adam thought he was dead as well, but he noticed Patrick's chest slowly rising and falling as he drew breath, and exhaled it. He was alive, but he wouldn't be for much longer if Adam didn't act. He got out his cell phone, and dialed 911. Adam Burton was the reason why Patrick Sullivan's life was saved. He would be able to go to his grave knowing that, at least once in his life, he was able to be the hero he always dreamed of being.

However, it would be Detective Patrick Sullivan who would go down as the real hero of this story. He was transported to the Nassau County Medical Center, where surgeons stopped the bleeding, stabilized him, and saved his leg and life. He was in dire need of blood, and it was Carl Murphy, who had type O blood (the universal donor), who stepped forward to save his new partner's life. As for his old partner and longtime friend, Jonathan Hawkins was pronounced Dead on Arrival.

What exactly had happened that night, no one knew. Patrick remained unconscious for nearly forty-eight hours, so until he woke up, everyone from his colleagues to his family to the media could only speculate what had transpired that Christmas morning between him and Jonathan Hawkins. No matter what theories were formulated, the general feeling shared amongst everyone was shock.

Only they had no idea how shocked they'd really be, in the end.

When Patrick finally woke up, the first person he saw when he opened his eyes was Claire. She was crying, and hadn't left his side for days, but she was still the most beautiful thing he'd ever seen. With all the ugliness that would soon come rushing back, he was grateful that it was her face he had seen when he finally came back to reality. She took his hands, and kissed his face and his lips; staining him with her tears of joy and relief. She told him she loved him, and he tried to tell her he loved her too, but he could barely speak. She told him not to talk, and she would be right back; she was going to get a nurse and a doctor.

A few minutes later, Claire returned with Patrick's doctor, a nurse and two men dressed in suits. Patrick, who was already remembering what had happened, and why he was waking up in a hospital, knew immediately who these men were. They were from the Nassau County Police Department. They worked for Internal Affairs.

The doctor examined Patrick, and tried to explain to him what they had done to his knee, and what would need to be done in the near future—he would need a knee replacement and months of serious physical therapy—but he was so groggy, he barely heard what the doctor was saying.

He was told he needed to rest up so he could get his strength back, but that didn't stop Internal Affairs from attempting to question him. He was awake, so to them, he had enough strength to be questioned. They were wrong, soon after the agents started questioning Patrick, he passed out, but not before he could tell them about the recording device he had planted in the hangar.

When they found that, they would find all their answers.

The crime scene had been searched that snowy morning when the bodies of two Nassau County Police Homicide detectives had been found—one dead, one barely holding on—but no recording device was found. During their second scan of the airplane hangar, it was torn apart from top to bottom.

This time, they found Patrick's old phone. It was Carl Murphy who listened to the recording before turning it over to Internal Affairs. It was Carl Murphy whose heart was broken when he learned the truth about that night, and the truth about his deceased friend.

The recording of the final moments of Jonathan Hawkins' life provided Internal Affairs with everything they needed (more than they wanted) to know. They looked past a few details, like Patrick going rogue and confronting Hawkins on his own without any backup, and the fact that they had a recording of Patrick saying he had no intentions of turning Jonathan Hawkins over to the police, and every intention of killing him. As far as they were concerned, Patrick's name was cleared of any suspicion, and they would allow him to be the hero he deserved to be.

After all, they now had far larger problems on their hands... like having to explain to the public that the murderous serial killer that had been haunting Long Island was one of the very men working the case.

Patrick drove down Route 25A; trying not to think of the events of one year ago, and what had followed, but that was as useless as trying to hold your breath until you were

THE REPLACEMENT

no longer breathing. Eventually, no matter how stubborn you were, you were going to breathe.

As much as he wanted to shut those memories out, they were the only thing on his mind. They hadn't left him alone for a single day the entire year. Why would today be any different?

As the single lane became two, Patrick checked his rear view to see if there were any cars approaching in the adjacent lane, so that he could get over to make a left onto Route 106. What he saw was not an approaching car, but a familiar disfigured face sitting comfortably in his backseat.

"I'll tell ya something, Patty Boy," Baby Tooth said with that usual obnoxious grin painted on his face. "I really give you credit for still continuing to contribute as an active member of society. If I were you, I'd be sitting at home being one lazy-ass nigga; just watching my big ass television, or some shit like that."

Upon his release from the hospital following his knee replacement surgery, Patrick Sullivan walked away, for the second and final time in his life, from law enforcement. He didn't have much of a choice in the matter. Even if he had any desire to stay, which he didn't, the Nassau County Police Department didn't want him. He may have been bestowed with every honor the Department had to offer for bringing down the Long Island Surgeon—the department referred to Jonathan Hawkins as the Long Island Surgeon rather than by his name as much as possible in a failing attempt to distance themselves from dead detective-gone-killer—but at the end of the day, Patrick was just another link between Jonathan Hawkins and the Nassau County Police Department. They needed to clean up the huge mess Hawkins had left in his wake, and like the name of the man who tarnished their good name, the department preferred if Patrick disappeared, as well.

Of course, they never flat out said this, and they offered Patrick a high paying desk job—because of his surgery, he would never be cleared to work in the field again—in hopes of tucking him away under mountains of paperwork, but it was pretty clear that their true ambitions were to get him out the door as quickly and quietly as possible.

Their hopes had been realized when Patrick happily opted to resign from the department, rather than stay on in any capacity, but not before accepting a sizeable payout from Nassau County. They offered him a full pension for only two months of work, and compensation for being injured on the job.

This deal wasn't free, though—as if bringing down a psychopath wasn't enough to warrant security for Patrick and his family's future. In exchange, Patrick promised his silence on the matter of the Long Island Surgeon killings.

Even before his release from the hospital, offers were pouring in from various media outlets for Patrick's story. Newspapers, radio show, magazine, publishing companies… they all wanted to be the first to release a detailed story of Patrick Sullivan's heroics. He could have made himself a pretty penny off his story, but the truth was he had no desire to tell and retell the tale of Jonathan Hawkins. He relived it enough in his own mind. So agreeing to the deal was no issue. He just road off quietly into the sunset with his family and his ghosts.

"I have to keep myself distracted somehow," Patrick responded to the dead drug dealer sitting in his backseat. "Not that it does me any good. No matter where I am or what I'm doing, you're right there, by my side!"

His anger was beginning to build up inside him, and he knew that, eventually, it would reach its boiling point, but he didn't care. Not like he used to.

THE REPLACEMENT

These days, Patrick Sullivan wasn't much concerned with controlling his emotions. Taming and trying to domesticate his rage never did anything for him before.

"Well I do enjoy these scenic morning rides home every day," Baby Tooth said. A few months after his retirement; Patrick took an overnight security job at a lab on the North Shore. "But c'mon... why do I always got to ride in the back, like some reversed Driving Miss Daisy shit?"

"Because," a voice from the passenger seat said. "You now take a back seat to me."

Patrick looked over at the passenger side of the car, and sitting there, riding shotgun, as he did every single day, was Detective Jonathan Hawkins, better known to the public as the Long Island Surgeon.

"How's it going, kid?" Hawkins turned his attention to the man who was meant to once replace him in the homicide unit of the Nassau County Police Department. "I would imagine not well. It's been a rough year, I'll give you that, but today must be especially hard on you. It's been one whole year since you and I had our final showdown."

"And you haven't left me alone since," Patrick snapped back.

"That's your own doing, kid. I'm dead. My Earthly remains burnt up to dust, and tossed to the wind or in the trash... who knows. I'm here every day, because of you. You should have known I'd be here. If you couldn't shake this amateur," He nodded his head towards Baby Tooth lounging about in the back seat. "How did you ever expect to escape me?"

Hawkins had a point. Patrick was never one to just let go. Starting with Vivian Chambers, he always walked with the ghosts of his past by his side. He once thought Baby Tooth had ruined his life, but Wallace Freewaters didn't hold a candle to Jonathan Hawkins.

"Please, just leave me alone," Patrick pleaded. "I killed you! Why won't you just go away?"

"Damn, son," Baby Tooth chimed in, which wasn't helping Patrick calm down. "And I thought I messed him up good. This nigga's got you all sorts of fucked up in the head."

"He just didn't have what it took," Hawkins responded. "He let his emotions get the best of him, and because of that, he's right where he is today. A shit show of a mess."

"I caught you!" Patrick snapped back. The furor that had been marinating inside of him was now making its way up his throat. It wouldn't be long before his fury was fully released. "You thought you got away, but I figured you out and I exposed you, and I killed you. You thought you were untouchable, but now you are dead!"

"And look at all the good that got you! You're a mess. You are barely hanging on. Even right now... the conversation has only started, and you're ready to bury a bullet in my head."

Patrick jerked the wheel suddenly, and bought the vehicle off the road onto the shoulder. He then slammed on the brakes so hard that if he had not been strapped in, he would've definitely gone through the windshield head first.

I should've unbuckled myself first, Patrick thought as the car came to an instant halt. *At least then, I'd be thrown from this freaking car, and then all this would be over. At the least, I wouldn't have to deal with these two.*

"Oh, shit!" Baby Tooth exclaimed. Not helping to subdue Patrick's temper. "You gone crazy, mother fucker!"

I went crazy long before this. Patrick placed his head down on the steering wheel, and attempted to get his breathing, which was currently deep and heavy from anxiety, under control.

"Why can't you just leave me alone?" He asked the two of them; almost pleading. "I don't deserve this... I don't."

"Let's just take a moment to get ourselves under control," Hawkins said; sensing Patrick was on the brink of snapping. "Let's change the subject, shall we? Have you heard from Carl?"

Carl Murphy had visited Patrick from time to time during his stay in the hospital—he was one of first people, along with Claire, who Patrick saw when he woke up from his knee replacement surgery—but Patrick knew Carl was keeping his distance, and he knew exactly why.

Carl was grieving. Patrick couldn't hold this against him, either. Carl Murphy wasn't mourning the monster that took all those innocent lives, but for the man that monster had consumed. Jonathan Hawkins was once a man who everyone loved and respected. That was the man Carl Murphy worked with for the majority of his career, and that was the man he chose to remember.

In some ways, Patrick blamed himself for all those innocent lives being snuffed out before their time. The whole time he had been working side by side with the perpetrator, and was completely unaware. He couldn't begin to imagine how that guilt was weighing on Carl. He and Hawkins were more than just colleagues. They were friends, and his friend had slipped into the darkest of places, and Carl had no idea.

Maybe Carl thought that if he had been more aware, maybe he could have saved Hawkins. Maybe he thought there were signs he had missed. Patrick could only speculate, but he knew guilt weighed down heavily on the shoulders of Carl Murphy.

Not long after Patrick's resignation from the police department, Carl Murphy voluntarily stepped down from the force. Two weeks later, his house was up on the market, and he was moving to Washington D.C. to take a job with the FBI.

"No, I haven't," Patrick told Hawkins; lying.

Granted he hadn't heard a word from Carl since he moved—Patrick was obviously too much of a reminder of what had happened, and Carl Murphy didn't need reminders when he was doing just fine remembering all on his own—but he did send the Sullivan's a Christmas card two weeks earlier. It was a simple as simple could be. No personalized message for his former one-case partner, or his family. He even wrote *To Friends,* instead of *To Patrick, Claire and Connor.*

Patrick was shocked they got the card at all, but he figured Carl thought it was something he needed to do. Patrick had discovered Johnathan Hawkins' dark secret, and almost died to bring him down. The card was a formality more than it was sentimental.

"Too bad," Hawkins said; probably knowing Patrick was lying. "I miss Carl."

"Then why don't you go visit him, and leave me the fuck alone?!" Patrick screamed; lifting his head from the steering wheel, so that he could punch it. He wondered in that moment if Carl was haunted the way Patrick was. Undoubtedly, the guilt weighed down on Carl Murphy, but he didn't think the man was haunted by the ghosts of his past.

No, that privilege was reserved solely for Patrick Sullivan.

"Patty Boy, you need to calm down," Baby Tooth chimed in. "All this anxiety can't be good for your health. Maybe you need to do some breathing exercises, or some Zen shit like that."

"You know what… why don't you go with him?" Making reference to the suggestion Hawkins go off, and haunt Carl. "That way I can just get a moment's peace from the two of you!"

"Kid, you and I both know that if you want me or the backseat driver over there to leave you be, you're the only one who can do that. You're the only one who could send us away"

"Don't send us away, Patty Boy," Baby Tooth pleaded. "I really love these car rides. I just get sad, because Vivian never joins us for them."

Vivian Chambers was the last person Patrick needed on these morning drives.

"Just leave me alone." Patrick was almost begging now.

He couldn't take this for the rest of his life. He was barely holding onto his sanity when it was just Baby Tooth showing up in his dreams. There was no way he was going to stay sane with the both of them constantly breathing down his neck.

Inevitably, Patrick was going to end up in an institution, or worse.

"Wish we could, kid. Unfortunately, we are here, because you want us here."

"I DON'T!" Patrick snapped back.

"Yet here we are," Hawkins pointed out. "Every morning, taking the same car ride. You think I let cases get to me like this? I thought you were better than that, kid"

"You're kidding me, right?" Patrick couldn't believe what he was hearing. "You of all people shouldn't have a right to talk about letting the job get to you. You're only responsible for the deaths of sixteen people, and in your delusional head, it was all in the name of the job."

"I kept my sanity, though."

"That's debatable," Patrick scoffed.

He couldn't believe he was getting lectured by Jonathan Hawkins. The man was almost a year in his grave, as the saying goes—Jonathan Hawkins was actually cremated—

and he was still trying to convince Patrick he was the model human being to look up to.

"My conscious is clear."

"That's because you're dead."

"That doesn't really matter, does it?

"No! It doesn't," Patrick snapped back. His anger was holding on by a thread. In life, Hawkins knew how to push all of Patrick's buttons. Now, even in death, he continued that tradition; taunting him every step of the way through life. "All that matters is you leaving me alone. I don't deserve this."

Patrick was right; he didn't deserve this at all. He could even argue he didn't deserve Baby Tooth's constant company—Lord knows, Baby Tooth deserved exactly what he got—but, under zero circumstances, did he deserve to be haunted by Jonathan Hawkins. He stopped a vicious serial killer in his tracks. He put a bullet in him, and ended his existence. He refused to give up when everyone else considered the matter of the Long Island Surgeon case closed. He was a hero, and he wasn't reaping the benefits.

No, instead, he was haunted by his past every day of his life.

"You know what," Baby Tooth said; adding zero to the conversation. "I'm really beginning to feel like I'm unwanted. If it wasn't for me pushing your ass in the right direction, and keeping you going, you never would've caught this sick mother fucker. Yet you still don't want me around. That shit stings, Patty Boy."

"Wanted or not," Hawkins answered on behalf of Patrick. "We have become, and we will remain a permanent fixture in your life."

"No," Patrick stubbornly argued. He refused to believe there was no hope to rid himself of these phantoms.

THE REPLACEMENT

"Kid, lie to yourself all you want, but you know we are here because of you, and only you."

"You're here because you have ruined my life, and you insist on continuing to ruin my life. I wish I had never joined the Nassau County Police Department, I wish I had never pistol whipped Baby Tooth, I wish I had never shot Vivian Chambers. I wish none of this happened, because this isn't worth it. I tried to do right, and this is what I get."

"How sweet life's rewards can be."

Patrick would never know if Hawkins planned on saying anything after that. As far as he was concerned, he had reached his breaking point. The conversation was over. He allowed the flood gates to open, and he welcomed his rage with open arms.

Patrick reached for the pistol he kept strapped to the side of his seat (Revolver .38; the very same gun he used to end Jonathan Hawkins' life a year ago), took hold of it, aimed it at Hawkins, and squeezed the trigger. He then aimed it into the back seat, and fired a round into the skull of Wallace Freewaters.

There was the exploding sound of window glass shattering, and then there was silence.

Patrick sat in the driver's seat of his car on Northern Boulevard on a freezing cold Christmas Eve morning with his eyes closed tight. He would give himself a few moments to get composed, and then he would open his eyes.

He knew that when he opened his eyes again, and allowed the world back in, the two men who constantly haunted him would be gone. He also wouldn't be in his car; driving home from work. He would be in his bed, because that's where he always was after these meetings. In his bed.

Patrick Sullivan gave himself a few moments, and then he finally opened his eyes.

JASON PELLEGRINI

He was sitting in his car; the freezing cold winter wind was blasting through his exploded passenger side window, and rearview windshield.

CHAPTER 39

He took the Long Island Railroad to Jamaica Station. There, he transferred, and took the train a few stops to Atlantic Terminal, and from there, he walked. It wasn't a long walk, but it was an unnecessary one, none the less; especially in the cold weather. Still, he needed to walk. He needed to consider the repercussions of what he was thinking about doing.

He had left his car at a mechanic/body shop owned by Mitchel Henderson, formerly Officer Mitchel Henderson of the Nassau County Police Department. Like Patrick Sullivan and Carl Murphy, Mitch Henderson no longer had any desire to remain an officer of the law when he learned the man responsible for taking his young son's life was one of the very men he had worked with, side-by-side, for so long.

Hawkins had held Mitch down that morning, as he grieved uncontrollably for his little boy. Hawkins had promised they'd bring down the son of a bitch disgusting enough to take the life of a child. Meanwhile, all along, it was Hawkins who had squeezed the delicate throat of Luke Henderson until he was no longer alive.

Mitchel Henderson called it quits, and left law enforcement in his past, even before Patrick officially resigned. He opened up a mechanic/body shop with his brother and close friend, so that he would be able to provide for his family.

It wouldn't be the first time Patrick showed up to Mitch Henderson's shop with busted out windows. At first, he blamed it on kids in his neighborhood, but after the third time, he doubted Mitch believed him. Mitch never questioned him, though. Patrick was the man who exposed, and single handedly took on the beast responsible for taking his son's life. Whatever the truth was about Patrick's missing windows, Mitch didn't care. He was happy to do the repairs at cost.

The door to the roof had been unlocked, as it had been all those years before. He made a few laps around it, aimlessly, to gather his courage. He couldn't even bring himself to look over the ledge, so forget about actually stepping up on it. It was different this time than the last. Sure, the guilt of shooting and killing a pregnant woman in the line of duty because she was firing at you seemed like a walk in the park compared to what he had gone through over the last two years, but he had other factors to take into consideration now.

Namely, his family.

He couldn't leave them behind. He loved them both, uncontrollably. The love for his family was boundless, but he couldn't keep going on like this. Not with ghosts riding his coattails for the rest of his life.

Even at the realization that he would never see Connor grow up, or never again kiss Claire's soft lips, Patrick Sullivan still walked over to the ledge he once stood upon. It was the thought of endless car rides with Jonathan Hawkins and Wallace 'Baby Tooth' Freewaters that pushed him towards that ledge, but it was Claire and Connor pulling him back towards life.

Patrick Sullivan was a man torn between living and dying.

He reached into his back pocket, and removed his wallet. He pulled out a single photo from the money slot. He just stared at it; trying to find a reason to let himself be pulled rather than pushed.

The photo was of Patrick, Claire and Connor from the fall right before he started with Nassau County. They had gone pumpkin picking as a family. Patrick remembered that day perfectly. He had made it his mission to find the most obnoxiously oversized pumpkin in the patch, and he had succeeded. Claire thought he was ridiculous for wanting to actually take it home, but he insisted. It was his conquest. So he posed with his prized possession next to his wife, who at this point, found the whole thing humorous. She held Connor, who had his own Connor-sized pumpkin in his hands, as they asked a nice elderly couple to take the family photo for them. The photo served as a nice reminder that Patrick Sullivan was able to have a happy life.

He slid the photo carefully back into his wallet, and pulled out a folded up business card that had been stowed away for almost a year now. He unfolded it, and stared at the front. It was your regular run-of-the-mill business card—name, occupation, phone number. He flipped it over, and read the handwritten message on the back, as he had done a multiple times over the course of the last year.

If you ever need help.
Just someone to talk to.
Please, don't hesitate to call.

He flipped the card back over, and stared at the phone number printed on it. He never once called it, but he knew it by heart.

He shifted his gaze from the business card to the street below him, and then back to the card. One was living, while the other was dying. One was pushing, while the other pulling.

He returned the card to its spot, and put the wallet back in his pants pocket. He took his phone out, punched in seven digits, and hit SEND. When the voice came on the other end, he explained that he needed help. The person on the other end asked where he was, and he gave them his location. He was given strict orders not to move, and that they would be there as soon as they could. Patrick gave a simple *Okay*, and terminated the call.

That had been an hour ago.

He had been sitting against the ledge of the building when he heard the ascending footsteps climbing the stairwell leading to the roof.

"Patrick," she called, even before she got to the roof. "Are you up here?"

He tried to speak up and tell her he was there, but no words broke the barrier of his teeth.

Seconds later, Claire emerged from the roof entrance. She didn't need to scan the rooftop for her husband. She knew exactly where he'd be. It was the exact spot he was seven years ago when they first met.

And here they were again.

"Patrick, baby, what are you doing here?" Claire asked.

She was carefully choosing her words. She was scared; that was obvious. Maybe she feared Patrick would leap to his death right there in front of her eyes if she said the wrong thing, or spoke in the incorrect tone. She was treating her husband like he was a bomb. One that could go off at any time without warning.

THE REPLACEMENT

That's what he had become to his wife: a ticking time bomb. He had already been unraveling when they met, but she chose to look past it towards the better man. Now, because of numerous traumatizing life events, it had become abundantly clear that her husband's counter was reaching zero.

On a frigid winter morning in Brooklyn, New York, Patrick Sullivan's life was coming to a dramatic climax, and Claire knew she was the only one who could pull him back from the brink. Guilt consumed him, knowing his wife was feeling such a heavy burden of responsibility. No one should ever feel like another's person's life is in their hands, but Claire had saved him once. They both knew she was the only one who could do it again.

"Baby…" She inched towards Patrick slowly. The bomb was opened up, and all she had to do was cut the right wire to disarm it. She just had to make sure she didn't severe the wrong one. If she did, it was over. "Talk to me. Tell me why you're here."

Patrick wanted to speak. He wanted to tell her he was here, because he wanted it all to be done with. He didn't want to have to live with the ghosts that now followed him, not only when he was sleeping, but now when he was awake. He wanted to tell her that it was all too much. He even wanted to tell her that, in the darkest corners of his thoughts, he had wished she had never had come up to that rooftop for a smoke the night they met. If she hadn't, he would've jumped, and there would have never been a Wallace Freewaters or Jonathan Hawkins to ruin his life.

Life had become too hard to live, and Patrick wished he could just tell his wife these things, but he couldn't articulate. He was too far gone.

He felt Claire's arms wrap around him, and start to pull him up. He didn't resist her. He just did as she wanted without putting up a fight. He felt her hands go to his cheeks, but he couldn't feel her touch. It was like he was shot up with Novocain. He heard she was speaking to him, but her words were muffled. For all it mattered, the two of them could've been having this conversation under water. Things just were not registering for Patrick.

The last shred of hope made its way through that thick fog of despair when Claire took his face, and made him look her in the eyes. Those beautiful blue eyes. They could be seductive when they wanted to be, and they could be dangerous when they needed. Right now, they were desperate. They were begging Patrick Sullivan to just hang on. They pleaded with him to dig down as deep as he could, and find the man Claire loved, because he was strong, and he could overcome.

Patrick collapsed into his wife's arms, and started to cry.

She said no words to console him. She didn't try to wipe away his tear, and tell him it would be alright. She just hugged him, ran her fingers through his hair, and let him cry. She knew he needed it.

He finally pulled away from her, and looked her in her face. Tears streamed down his face, and her eyes now were becoming glassy with tears of her own.

"I'm sorry," Patrick said through heavy sniffles. "I'm so sorry, Claire."

"Oh, baby…" Claire took him, and kissed his wet, salty lips. "You don't ever have to be sorry. Not once."

He did feel sorry, though. He should have been stronger for the both of them. Instead, he relied on Claire, who had walked into her classroom one morning, and saw five dead children, to help pick up the pieces of his shattered life. It had been part of Patrick's job to see dead people, but it was never part of Claire's. She was supposed to further the life of children; not see their ends.

Yet here she was; trying to hold onto what was left of her husband. Claire was the strong one. She the one who trudged through the mess, and came out the other end okay. Patrick owed it to her, as her husband, to not give up. She never gave up on herself, she never gave up on her family, and it was clear she was not about to give up on her husband. So what gave him the right to even consider calling it quits?

"Thank you," he said, and began to cry again. Claire simply hugged him again, and let him weep.

His hands moved down her back, and around to her stomach. Through her thick winter jacket, Patrick could feel the swell of her belly. He knew it was all in his imagination at that point, but he swore, right then, he could feel the life growing inside of Claire.

I have to keep fighting, Patrick thought, and he felt the spot where his second child was growing, and developing. *I have to for them.*

If he couldn't do it for himself, then he had to do it for his family. He needed them, yes, but they needed him more. Demons can be defeated, and ghosts can be vanquished, but if he truly gave up, he would never have his family again. He would fight the good fight. He wouldn't let Baby Tooth or Jonathan Hawkins get the last blow. Whatever they threw at him, Patrick Sullivan would fight back, and he would overcome. He would do it for his family, because they were his light at the end of the tunnel.

"Let's go home," Claire finally said when his crying had tapered back to mere sniffles.

Patrick kissed his wife on the lips. He felt a surge rush through him, like kissing Claire brought new life into him, and for the first time in a good long while, he felt hope.

"Let's go home," he repeated.

Patrick pulled out his wallet, and, once again, removed the folded up business card.

"What's that?" Claire asked.

He unfolded it, and read the name printed on it one last time.

DR. JENNIFER HADLEY P.H.D.

Jennifer Hadley had visited Patrick in the hospital a few days after he woke up. He didn't say much. She did most of the talking. She thanked him for all the obvious reasons. He had given her closure, and sometimes closure can be the greatest gift a person can receive. She gave him the card, thanked him again, and left. They hadn't spoken since.

"It's nothing important," Patrick answered, and it wasn't. He had stared at that card, time and time again, debating whether he should call Jennifer Hadley, and ask her for help. In the end, he turned to Claire, because she was the only one who could save him. There was no one else.

He folded the card back up and flicked it off the rooftop.

"I love you, Patrick Sullivan. Through it all, I love you."

"I love you, too."

She kissed him one last time, took him by the hand, and they left that rooftop to live their lives to the best of their abilities.

Ghosts be damned.

EPILOGUE

And they lived happily ever after…

That's such a pleasant concept for stories. Leaving us all thinking that when a story winds down, all is right in the world, and our hero rides off into the sunset; his life perfect as can be. According to the standard in which people expect stories to conclude, Patrick Sullivan should have walked away from the rooftop hand-in-hand with Claire, and everything that followed should've been alright.

But that's not real life.

Ghosts, demons, and monsters are relentless entities. Especially the ones that live within us. They will not let up, and they will not give in. Not until they break our spirits. They don't respect the fight to overcome them, and they do not waver in their approach. They will always claw their way back in an attempt to wrap those claws around us to bring us down.

Patrick Sullivan was no exception.

Yes, he walked from that rooftop feeling that he was in a battle he could possibly win, but he knew it was far from over. Jonathan Hawkins had never given in that easily; not in life, and certainly not after his death. Patrick would need to find some method to keep his ghosts at bay.

Unfortunately for Patrick and everyone close to him, he found what he was looking for in the wrong place.

Later that evening, Patrick and his beautiful family, which in a few months would have one more addition to it, celebrated Christmas Eve at his in-laws.

His father-in-law's tune had changed in regards to his opinion of Patrick. Now that he was a hero in the eyes of the nation (despite his attempts to just fade away), Patrick was the perfect fit for his daughter.

Patrick never called him out on this. Best to let sleeping dogs lie, he figured.

After the exchange of presents—Connor was now running around the living room with his new toy truck; making a *VROOM, VROOM* sound—as dessert was being put out, Patrick felt a burley arm wrap around him. He looked over to see who had felt the need embrace him, and saw his father-in-law.

"How's it going, Patrick?" Ted Johnston asked. His words were beginning to slur.

"Going good, Ted," Patrick answered; as formal as can be. "How's it going with you?"

"Can't complain. Merry Christmas!" He took another sip of his drink, and gave his son-in-law an obnoxious pat on the back.

"Merry Christmas, Ted."

"Listen... how's your mother holding up, since your father's... you know... passing?"

Patrick's father had passed away a few months earlier in his sleep.

"She's getting by. She's spending Christmas with my sisters and their families."

"That's good to hear. She's a lovely woman, and you let her know she's always welcome to join us whenever she has nothing to do for a holiday."

"I'm sure she would love to hear that."

Ted Johnston polished off whiskey on the rocks, looked at his empty glass, and told Patrick it was time to refill.

Patrick felt relieved that he was excusing himself. Despite his drastic change in attitude, Patrick still tried to avoid the man as much as possible.

"Come join me for a drink, Patrick."

"That's kind of you, Ted, but I'll pass."

Patrick's last drink was the night at O'Reilly's Pub with his new colleagues, and he really had no desire to have one right then; especially with his father-in-law.

Still, Ted Johnston insisted; claiming they never truly celebrated Patrick's heroics with a drink. Before he could object again; Patrick was being guided towards the liquor cabinet.

Ted poured him the same drink he was having, and toasted to Patrick. Patrick lifted his glass, and drank. It burned going down, and he could feel it spreading in his stomach. He knew it would be minutes before it went to his head.

"One more!" Ted insisted.

Patrick's first instinct was to decline the offer, but then decided against it.

Why the hell not?! He thought, as he held out his glass, and let his father-in-law fill it up. Claire couldn't drink on a count of being pregnant, and Patrick deserved to let loose after the all the crap he had gone through.

So he had his second drink, and then a third, and by the time they were ready to head home, Patrick was good and drunk off liquor. Claire found this humorous; as she did every time Patrick drank, and Connor repeatedly called his daddy silly.

It was a good ending to the night. Patrick felt what might have been happiness as he went to sleep. He had no thoughts of Jonathan Hawkins or Baby Tooth as he drifted off. It was a good sign of things to come.

But sometimes we can be deceived by things that, on the surface, look promising.

Sometimes hope is just misery in disguise.

He didn't dream that night of Hawkins or Baby Tooth. If he did, he didn't remember it; just like a dream he had a little over a year ago about a circus that featured an elderly couple ripping their skin from one another.

Later that day, his in-laws came over for Christmas dinner, and Patrick, again, enjoyed an alcoholic beverage with his father-in-law.

It wouldn't be long before he finally was able to understand his own father.

You see, it turns out, the best way to rid yourself of ghosts is not to bury them, but to drown them.

ACKNOWLEDGMENTS

Every good story has its cast of supporting characters to help bring it to life. In the story of *Jason Pellegrini Writes the Replacement*, the supporting characters were just as indispensable to the story as the main character, who in this case would be me. They deserve their names praised. This wouldn't be possible without them.

Michael Sonbert – If it wasn't for him publishing his own novels (*The Neverenders* and *We Are Oblivion*: CHECK THEM OUT!), I probably would've never gotten the motivation to try and get my ideas down on paper.

My Family – Who always pushed me to embrace my creative side, one way or another. Whether music, drawing, or writing, they never treated me like I was wasting my time on chasing after my dreams.

Erin – At the time of this writing, you've been part of this journey for the shortest duration of time, but you've made the biggest impact on it. Before we met, this project was hanging on by a thread, and almost never saw its ending. You came along and relit a fire under my ass that had gone out a while ago. You read my book when it was a garbage first draft, and you read it again when it was acceptable for people to see. I've said this to you before, and I'll say it here: You're the Claire to my Patrick.

Kevin Schnurr – You served as my editor, because I trust no one else to dissect my novel, and tell me my strengths and weaknesses as a storyteller and writer. You were brutally honest, and you served as a huge motivation to keep on chugging along when you kept coming back, and asking for more. I'm glad you found yourself a new kidney, because I, selfishly, need you around to tell me when my stories suck so that I can fix them up!

Jennifer Schwartz – While reading this book, you found a hefty amount of silly typos that I missed while editing and re-editing. You were an enormous help with the fine tuning in the presentation of this story.

Paul Horak – You let me bounce my ideas off you, and you always gave me an honest opinion of them. You gave me a perspective on my material that I couldn't see for myself. We have clashing styles of writing, not to mention completely opposite styles of storytelling, but having that opposing opinion can be all the difference in creating something great

Patrick Berlinquette – When I first started writing, you were there with advice, being someone who had been in that position before, and you imparted your knowledge and upon me, which was a tremendous help for a newbie. You also told me to read *On Writing* by Stephen King, which is the best advice any new writer could receive.

Lisa Bianco – For starters, she hired me at my current place of employment, and if it wasn't for all that time spent in a room by myself with nothing but my thoughts, my stories wouldn't be anywhere near what they end up becoming. She also got me on the right path when it came to researching *Pancuronium Bromide*; the paralytic drug the Long Island Surgeon used on his victims. I would never have even known where to start when it came to finding this drug, and if she didn't take the time to help me, I'd still be stuck writing the chapter where they first see the coroner.

Justine Brando and Sarah Mondello – Just like Joe Lanza and the police aspect of this story, you two helped me with all the medical mumbo-jumbo that made my story feel that much more real.

*Whether you loved, liked, or hated this novel, please,
voice your opinion of it.
Leave a review of* The Replacement *on Amazon.com and
Goodreads.com!*

*Become a fan of, Like, or Follow Jason Pellegrini on
these social media platforms:*

Goodreads
https://www.goodreads.com/JPellegrini

Facebook
https://www.facebook.com/jasonpellegrinibooks

Twitter
@JPellegrini1983

*And remember, word of mouth is still the most powerful
form of promotion in the world.
If you liked this novel, let people know and suggest it to
your family and friends!*

CPSIA information can be obtained
at www.ICGtesting.com
Printed in the USA
BVHW042151260423
663136BV00003B/122